The extemporaneous Existence of Nadine Tallemann

A Bildungsroman

Ursula W. Schneider

iUniverse, Inc.
New York Bloomington

The extemporaneous Existence of Nadine Tallemann

A Bildungsroman

iUniverse books may be ordered through booksellers or by contacting:

iUniverse
1663 Liberty Drive
Bloomington, IN 47403
www.iuniverse.com
1-800-Authors (1-800-288-4677)

ISBN: 978-1-4401-3859-1 (pbk)
ISBN: 978-1-4401-3857-7 (cloth)
ISBN: 978-1-4401-3858-4 (ebk)

Printed in the United States of America

iUniverse rev. date: 9/4/2009

For Kurt-Mihran and Gigi, for Lynn and Jeff

Contents

List of Characters

of

The extemporaneous Existence of Nadine Tallemann

1. Nadine Tallemann, the nineteen-year-old protagonist
2. Heinrich and Monika Tallemann, Nadine's parents
3. Anna and Otto Nußbaum, Nadine's maternal grandparents
4. Gertrude and Adolf Tallemann, Nadine's paternal grandparents
5. Julie and James Johnson, English couple in Groombridge
6. Lipsey, aged 5 and Peter, aged 3, the two children of Julie and James Johnson
7. Rudolph and Melanie Hibson, Julie Johnson's parents
8. Beatrice, seventy-seven year-old-cook of Melanie Hibson
9. Bertram, childhood friend of Heinrich Tallemann
10. Christian, Nadine's beau in Mannheim, Germany
11. Jean Kaiser, Christian's slightly older rival in Mannheim, Germany
12. Arthur Wellington, Nadine's beau in Brighton
13. Andrew Gibson, Nadine's beau in Hastings
14. Mrs. Gibson, Andrew's mother
15. James G. Spencer, Nadine's beau in London
16. Ray Sheldon, Spencer's roommate in London
17. Janet, a Yorkshire student in Harrogate
18. Dexter Paxton, Nadine's second beau in London
19. Arnold Illingrose, Nadine's beau in Harrogate
20. Isolde Illingrose, Arnold's mother
21. Nameless custom's officer in Dover
22. Nameless police office in Groombridge
23. Hanna Herbert, Nadine's German girl friend whom she visits in Paris
24. François, Nadine's beau in Versailles
25. Denis, Hanna's beau in Versailles
26. Nameless Moroccans in Paris
27. Three, nameless taxi drivers in London

28. Helen and Bruce McDonald, married couple with children, friends of the Johnsons
29. Cathy Woodbridge, girlfriend of Arnold Illingrose
30. Sidney, a black American soldier in Ludwigsburg, Germany
31. Mr. Heidlauf, music teacher at the gymnasium in Mannheim, Germany
32. Mrs. Adelheid König, neighbor in Feudenheim, Germany
33. Three American officers, friends of Adelheid König in Feudenheim, Germany
34. Fred Brandt, child molester in Ludwigsburg, Germany
35. Mrs. Christel Stein, math teacher at the gymnasium in Mannheim
36. Ms. Löwenhaupt, Latin teacher at the gymnasium in Mannheim
37. Mrs. Diane Smith, wife of an American Army colonel in Ludwigsburg, Germany
38. *Betschwestern*, Anna Nußbaum's lady friends at a Baptist church in Mannheim
39. Mrs. Filsinger, rich peasant woman in Unterschmitten, Germany
40. Hans, son of Mrs. Filsinger
41. Liese and Rosemarie, two classmates of Nadine at a one-room village schoolhouse
42. Bertha, the daily help of Julie Johnson in Groombridge
43. Nan & Jason Gardiner, friends of Julie's and James Johnson
44. Sally Hibson, Julie Johnson's unmarried sister

February 22, 1996, October 16, 2008, March 28, 2008, Nov. 6, 2008

I

Unterschmitten

Crossing the English Channel had a somniferous effect on the young girl. She had been born in Germany at the leading edge of the Second World War and lived through its entire atrocity. She remembered only too well the heavy bombers of the Royal Air Force, which had relentlessly crossed the sky above her. With their guns sticking out of turrets at the nose and tail of the fuselage and the hip, if not belly of the heavy, four-propellered plane, the noisy, slowly moving aircraft looked like oversized hedgehogs with wings. The mostly young and, when viewed from the ground, always totally invisible English airmen, who operated the B-24s or B-29s, had come across the blue-gray water bracelet that now, as then, glowed between the chalky cliffs of Dover and Ostende. Night after night the pregnant planes had zigzagged through a dark sky. Later the steadily flying monsters, now reinforced by the US Air Force, had come during the day too. And all of the planes caused death and destruction. Not just factories or important railway junctions, the military target, were demolished, but also endless city blocks went up in flames, killing the civilian population by the hundred thousands during a single night. Firestorms had been deliberately set in Hamburg and Dresden. But in addition to these two big cities, there were also several smaller ones like Pforzheim, the well over seven hundred year old town, noted for its jewelry and watch-making industry. It was located not far from Nadine's hometown that suffered the same unspeakably savage fate by which helpless people were scorched, boiled and baked to death by the thousands. The burning of witches during the Middle Ages were relatively small events in comparison.

Until recently, the immeasurable and black depth of the sky had been reserved for birds and the white sails of ships. Only once, way back and just for a fleeting moment, there had been Icarus, the disobedient *homme oiseau*. But WWII changed all of that.

For the little girl the bombers had been birds as well, huge and evil ones. They were like those grotesque, amorphous shapes that haunt the minds of mad people and flutter through the nightmares of sane men and women. For Nadine the raptors were voracious griffins, closely related to dinosaurs, whose metal wings had emerged from the thin pages held by grandmother's nine pudgy fingers. Her tenth finger, the second-to-last one on her left hand, the *ring finger*, could not hold anything. Its tendons had accidentally been severed when she was still an adolescent and her finger had remained permanently bent. At fifty-seven, grandmother looked as if she were in her seventies. Her hair was completely white and although once thick and long, it had started to thin out in certain spots. She had never cut her tresses. Instead, at the nape of her neck, she wore them bundled together in a large knot that resembled a songbird's carefully constructed nest. Grandmother had a bad heart, was short and so obese that she breathed hard each time she climbed a few steps or walked at a fast pace. A quiet and highly religious woman, she had been in the habit of reading fairy tales to her granddaughter while she gently fed her spinach. The five-year-old child abhorred the dark-green, slimy puree, which the elderly woman had cooked and carefully placed on a thick white china plate in front of her. But Nadine did not touch the vegetable. Rather her fingers traced the black corrosive lines that had formed on the white waxy tablecloth. It could not be washed or replaced and the remains of spilled food had to be wiped off with a damp cloth. The little girl was not able to swallow the steaming legume. Sometimes she would stare at its ugly greenness without touching it for an hour that grew into an eternity or until grandmother finally took pity on her and allowed the child to get off her chair. But occasionally Nadine was tricked into opening her mouth by the soothing voice of grandmother. On "*Oma's*" gray-pink and fleshy tongue that was embedded between steadily decaying, yellowish teeth lived Red Riding Hood and Sindbad, the sailor. The little girl was transfixed by their stories. She could never hear enough of them and for their sake she learned to read early. Reading, she soon understood, was the key to a magic kingdom; it was the escape from an unbearable reality into which she had been born.

Inside the bellies of the bombers that flew low across the steep, red German rooftops, waited death. It was neatly divided into massive containers, which were piled up next to each other. Extermination slumbered side by side in shiny, elongated, iron-skinned eggs ready to burst open at impact. The child, and even more the teenager later in retrospect, could not imagine that a man, someone similar to her father, was able to pull a switch knowing that he would inflict a horrid death on children, their mothers and grandmothers. Small as she was, she knew that no god, loving or angry, could save her from this human atrocity. Yet, constantly encouraged by grandmother, each night she folded her hands, bent her head full of unruly curls and prayed feverishly for peace and victory.

"The Lord is on our side," Oma would explain. Nadine, looking up from her white, propped-up pillow, saw that her full lips, which added a youthful touch to her face, trembled. Apparently there was a German god and then there were the other deities, which the enemy worshipped. There could not be just one god, Nadine thought. It did not make sense that friend and foe implored the same idol for victory and peace. How could the same god decide who would live and who would die? And what kind of an idol was he anyway to allow such unrelenting horror?

During most of her prayers the child shut her eyes tightly and hoped that she would look like one of the pious, black-dressed, old ladies, who during two nights a week sat next to her in a small, stuffy, austere room that belonged to a Baptist church in Mannheim. They were lamblike women, ancient and strange smelling females in crumpled skirts, who lived like saints and would die soon in any event. Their clothes exhaled the sharp, unpleasant odor of moth powder. The feathers and dried flowers on their small, black hats, which still perched smartly and often slightly on the side of their heads, were half eaten by mice and other vermin. The child watching them, thought:

'Perhaps the angel of death is not so terrible when you are old. But I am little and scarred.' And a new wave of fear shook her. She gave Oma a quick look. The tired woman remained sitting next to her in the dark bedroom, darkened even further by black blinds which each window of the big city had been required to install. The blinds were supposed to mislead the roaring bombers above their heads. But they never did. Nadine, somewhat reassured by grandmother's closeness, squeezed her hands more tightly together and tried even harder to concentrate on the evening prayer, which she had long ago learned by heart.

Night after night, and toward the end of the war during the day too, grandmother and child, awakened by the screeching sirens of a *Fliegeralarm* (air-raid warning), fled to the cellar of their building. Sometimes they barely made it before the bombs were dropped. In the humid, subterranean, dirty rooms where coal and potatoes were stored, grandmother and child clung to each other and prayed while they listened in paralyzing fear as the bombs were plucked out of the sky one by one. Sitting hunched over in the corner of an overcrowded, sparsely lit, murkily smelling shelter and clutching Oma's hand, Nadine heard the bombs falling and waited for their gruesome detonation. She knew the bombs were being pulled down by each red roof and by each chimney that spat out - like a *clochard* clearing his throat - the waste of factories lining both shores of the *Rhein* and *Ruhr*, the two busy rivers between Mannheim and Düsseldorf. Day after day, the little girl and her grandmother experienced the annihilation of people and the still smoking *Trümmerhaufen* (heaps of rubble) they discovered the next day when they went in search of milk and bread. The rubble had turned familiar streets into an unknown, threatening wasteland. As far as they could see, there was nothing but still smoldering stones and burning wood among which sometimes stood a portion of a ghostly looking wall that on the day before had belonged to a big apartment building. There was never any relief. The sheer monotony of this unending terror drove everyone crazy. Which had been the intention of their enemies.

To the child war was a constant, deadly threat. It was like an earth-quake or a hurricane man had no control over. She felt it was her personal misfortune that she had been born at the rim of a volcano. There was nothing she could do about it. She knew that even before she had reluctantly left her mother's womb, she had been imprisoned on top of a mountain whose razor-sharp walls were so steep that only the most experienced climbers could descend them. Children were not taught the art of climbing. No one had time for them. The few men, who had learned how to get off the mountain, laughed at her or pushed her back rather roughly when she had expectantly approached them with a beating heart. She had smiled at the uniformed men, mostly still boys barely out of their teens, and had hoped that her pretty, strong teeth - grandmother had taught her to brush with baking soda - would camouflage her fear. At the age of four or five she did not understand that she was a prisoner. There were no visible walls. She had not been forced out of her house at gunpoint and ordered to stand in line at the rear end of a German army truck. And she had not clung to a small suitcase, waiting to be thrust inside the large vehicle where whimpering women, children and frail, old men huddled together. But for an instant, forever burned into her memory, she saw that their faces had turned to stone and that their eyes had become two dark pools of water surrounded by violets. And she knew, although no one had told her, that violets could not grow in concentration camps. They would die there. One evening she had asked Oma about these unfortunate people who were so mistreated. But grandmother, instead of answering her, only silently pulled her away and, not letting go of her hand, the two of them had quickly crossed the street. Anna was in a hurry to get away from a group of gun-carrying German soldiers with their young, confused-looking faces that guarded the Jews and two middle-aged, hard-featured men in long black leather coats, wearing soft fedoras, who had just arrested them and forced the unfortunate group into the truck. She was afraid of these men and didn't want anything to do with them.

Monika Tallemann, the mother of Nadine, had not married her Jewish fiancé but a German instead. Fate had spared the child from the camps and the unspeakable horrors that took place there, that occurred at every hour as those in command watched and did nothing. Or in the worst cases, the officers in charge even reinforced the daily atrocities. But crimes were not only committed in Germany and the countries Hitler had conquered during his *Blitzkriege*. Crimes, though in lesser numbers, occurred overseas as well, as happened with one big ship full of frightened fugitives that for days had docked in New York's harbor. At all hours the thin, alarmed faces of young Jewish women, children and old men could be seen staring through portholes. Silently, they pleaded for their lives. But no permission to unload was given. And the vessel, which was filled to the brim with human cargo, was forced to steam back to Germany, back to starvation, torture and certain death. The world, Nadine learned early, too early, was a nightmarish place to live in. Only the very rich, or the unusually talented, the writers, scientists and playwrights who stood in the limelight, were able to survive.

* * *

Now the sea with its gray, choppy waves that turned into shiny silver slices each time the sun struck them, seemed so friendly. It bore no grudge toward man, toward the vainglorious Lilliputians, who had invaded it with their U-boats, their ashen-hued destroyers and their aircraft carriers. Men at war kept their minds occupied with those clever, mechanical toys. In one long breath, these deadly playthings had provoked man's pride and his fear of extinction.

* * *

Nadine Tallemann stared empty-eyed at the surface of the sea that weaved uninterruptedly its pale net below her as she bent over the ship's railing. She was neither sad nor glad to leave Germany for a prolonged sojourn in England. Her heart beat its monotonous rhythm to which she was accustomed. It was a steady, healthy thrum not unlike the ticking of a well-made watch designed and executed with care. It was supposed to last forever or at least until she had wrinkled, loosely hanging skin, a stooped back and thighs so malformed that she would no longer dare to show them in a swimsuit. As a child, while she walked next to her meek grandmother whose back was hidden under a hill of fat, she had unconsciously measured herself many times against ugliness. She remembered, or she thought she did, that even as a little girl, she had shuddered at the idea of her body turning into a pile of frail bones, ready to break at the touch of a stick. Yet she had also heard the faint chiming coming from Monika Tallemann's small glass hutch where transparent china cups and saucers were so tightly stacked upon each other that a footstep in their immediate vicinity began to vibrate them. Even approaching middle age, her mother had remained slim and desirable. Only her face showed her age. As it always showed everything: her joy, her rage, her health or the lack of it. But her body with its round breasts and slender, masculine thighs still competed with most women half her age.

Just once had Nadine's heart hurt. She had barely been five years old when she suddenly, in the middle of the night, felt sharp chest pains that came and went and soon left her convinced that she would not survive them. Earlier during the day, grandmother had taken her for their daily late afternoon walk in Mannheim. The city then still stood up fairly well to the frequent bombing attacks from RAF planes. Mannheim was still recognizable. It was about two years before the city and its twin, Ludwigshafen, across the Rhein, would be totally destroyed. Former homes, Anna Nußbaum's, her grandmother, among them, would then look like a mouthful of rotten teeth, and smelling worse.

Slowly, hand in hand, granddaughter and grandmother had moved through one of the city's lovely, perfectly straight boulevards. In the middle of its course was a wide promenade that was lined on both sides with tall, old oaks. In the summer, when the trees were in full bloom, their crests touched each other and formed a delightful arch. Shady and cool, a walk beneath these trees had a calming effect on shattered nerves. For a little while even grandmother forgot how harsh life was during World War Two and stopped complaining. This was already the second war she tried to survive. During the First World War she had become an orphan when she was about eight years old, small for her age and skinny. Anna was forced to work hard for the farmer's family that had taken her in. Being awakened at 5:00 am, summer and winter alike when it was still pitch-dark, she had to milk two brown-furred, fat cows and clean their stalls. Her fingers were hardly strong enough to force milk through the four leathery teats of a bovine and the shovel, which she needed to remove the soft, splashy, black cow manure, was so heavy that within minutes she broke into a thick sweat. When she first started this work, which was not meant for a child, the insides of her hands became quickly covered with blisters for which the white bandages, which the farmer's wife wrapped around her fingers, were not adequate. For weeks she cried from pain and exhaustion and thought that she would surely die from these Herculean labors. Her only friend was a female cat, a tiger-striped, nameless creature that visited her punctually every morning. Always hungry and pregnant three times a year, the feline would beg for milk, rubbing her big-eared, velvety head against Anna's knees as she milked the two mooing, hay-munching cows.

Next to the long broad road in Mannheim where Nadine and her grandmother strolled, were large, well-trimmed shrubbery and enormous iron-wrought fences. They were hiding and protecting the elaborate villas of a handful of industrialists, whose factories provided income for a large portion of Mannheim's citizens.

The banks of the Neckar defined the midpoint of Anna and Nadine's outing. Long before they reached the slow, greenish-gray glowing current of the river, Nadine would get restless. As soon as she saw the glistening surface of the water, she slipped her hand out of grandmother's soft one and started to run ahead of her. Naughtily, she ignored Anna's voice where admonitions mixed with pleas and a short plaintive cry. The child knew the elderly, overweight woman could not follow her and for a little while enjoyed her freedom. She was as reckless and eager to explore the unknown as a puppy let off its leash.

The weak eyes of Anna followed her granddaughter anxiously while she ran under a row of majestic chestnut trees. Here too, the mul-tilayered, green-leafed crowns formed a splendid dome. Then Anna watched apprehensively as the child rushed down a long flight of stone steps. Two centuries ago the flight of stairs, now in need of repair, had been hewn into a grass-covered, high dam. The deep wide wings of the embankment, which most of the year overflowed with tall grass, pro-tected lawns, roads, meadows and homes from sudden spring floods of which the quietly coursing Neckar was quite capable.

Her cheeks flushing and her heart pumping, Nadine had spotted a flock of sheep that grazed in the pink-blue light of a fading summer evening. When she reached the animals, she was unafraid of a black, longhaired dog whose fur was so matted with dust and dirt that the palm of her hand carried the canine's odor long after he had moved out of sight. With a half caressing, half impatient gesture Nadine pushed the barking mongrel aside. Then still running, she caught and clung to the dense, fatty, woolen coat of a sheep that moved in front of her. Next to her stumbled a lamb. The ewe was terrified of the child's clutching fingers and her shrill, happy cries. With gurgles of laughter Nadine held on to the mother sheep and kept seizing one of its ears. Bleating loudly with fear, the animal tried to get away on its thin legs. But the child clutched its back and was dragged along across grass hammocks and small stones. The frustrated dog whose half lusty, half angry barks caused havoc among the rest of the flock kept chasing the adult sheep, her small offspring and Nadine.

Each time the little girl tried to pick-up the terrified white lamb that ran on wobbly legs next to its mother, the mutt's muzzle interfered with her grabbing hand. Although she was able to avoid the dog's teeth and, suddenly letting go of the mother animal, as she ran at full speed among the undulating backs of the sheep, she was unable to pick-up the tiny lamb that ducked in and out between its mother's protective belly and kicking legs.

Meantime, Anna Nußbaum had sluggishly, afraid of slipping and falling, descended the long row of rough high stone steps.

"The child simply doesn't listen. She will cause my death one of these days," she muttered morosely to herself. Midway down the dam, her heart started to hurt. Pressing her hand to her large bosom, she stopped and watched Nadine's head bobbing up and down among the rough current of the stampeding sheep. To her worried eye it looked as if the small girl were swimming in a stormy sea.

Finally, the shepherd had climbed down the short ladder, which was attached to his tiny, wooden hut that rested unevenly on two large wheels. He carried his handkerchief-sized home with him, moving up and down along both shores of the river where his sheep grazed from sunrise to sunset. The tall, thin man caught up with Nadine, angrily looking at her as he raised his long wooden staff. Only now, under the shepherd's immediate threat, did she reluctantly emerge from the crying sheep. Their odor, so different from her own and the dog's, had intoxicated her. The panicky movements and frightened bleats of the animals, with their bodies, which looked so fat and inviting in their thick layers of wool, and their large eyes in their lengthy skulls, had awakened the instinct of a hunter in the child. She was beside herself with an unknown joy in which she indulged whole-heartedly and completely unaware of her actions or the pain she had caused her grandmother.

The old, shabbily dressed shepherd stared at the small intruder, but never said a word. He did not need to. His eyes, so black that his irises were not discernable, spoke for him. So did his muddy leather boots whose points were directed threateningly toward the little girl. She knew that one more step would deliver her into the angry hands of the guardian of the sheep. So Nadine, also not saying anything, quickly turned around and went back to Anna. Breathless, the old woman had almost caught up with the child. The child saw right away that she was as annoyed as the shepherd.

"You are so bad," she scolded Nadine as soon as they were close enough to each other. "You deserve a good spanking."

Yet although these words were spoken harshly enough, the child knew her grandmother just threatened her with corporal punishment. She did not whip her. Only Nadine's father did. But he was far away – at the Russian front – and she didn't need to fear him.

During the night following her wild run, the child had slept badly and toward the very early morning hours she had awakened in her grandmother's wide bed. At first not knowing where she was, she recognized the four brown, wooden posts of the bed that she loved. The simply carved pillars were like four protective gatehouses of a large English mansion and its surrounding park. Within the periphery of the posts she felt safe from any prowler, real or imagined. Only when the bombs fell, did the bed quickly lose its charm.

Nadine had been tossing about, given her grandmother little rest, until the child finally, driven by distress, had sat up in bed.

"I don't feel well," she declared in a whiny voice and shook Anna's arm, pulling at the cotton sleeve of her nightgown. It was the hour when the night still hovers close to the ground and throws its dark shadows across garden fences, pavements and gutters. A small creature, a cat or a stray dog, then becomes almost invisible among the shades of walls, although it might be just a few feet away. The animal's presence – keenly felt – is reinforced by its odor. And its contours, hardly seen but strongly imagined, turn into something larger than life.

A sharp chest pain had made Nadine sit up. Cramps forced her to listen to her heart that beat madly as if, even in her sleep, she were still chasing sheep. Anna Nußbaum had slept lightly next to her grand-daughter. Her sleep was so fragile that Nadine often wondered how her own snoring did not wake her up. Anna had heard the child cry and, with a moan, she had pulled herself up until she leaned against the headboard of the bed.

"What's the matter, honey?" She asked softly before she enfolded Nadine in her plump, short arms where her sweet smelling skin soon started to sooth the child. The little girl, who was convinced that death was close by, felt calmer long before her grandmother's voice, now partly whispering and partly humming like a bird, started to appease her fear.

During the day, Anna Nußbaum wore her white, long hair pulled away severely from her face, gathering the coils in a knot, which she fastened low on the nape of her neck where it looked like a generously powdered doughnut. But now her hair hung straight and loosely, like a short ermine cape, across her shoulders and mingled with the child's curly hair that was cut off at the height of her earlobes. Grandmother's open hair made her look younger. Flowing freely about her face, it seemed to remove some of the sharp, deep winkles around her eyes and her full-lipped mouth looked even softer and more sensuous than it usually did.

For a long time, woman and child leaned against each other as they watched a slow dawn climb through the top of the gauze curtains of the window.

"Am I going to die, Oma?" the child asked apprehensively as she felt another sharp stab at her chest.

"I don't think so," Anna replied.

"But if you do, you'll go straight to heaven and meet Jesus, sur-rounded by his angels, in person," she added very seriously.

Together with her physical suffering, the child's fear of death van-ished slowly. Grandmother's solicitude and her story about floating, golden angels with whom Nadine might soon play, had chased her terror away.

* * *

Two months after the incident with the sheep, Anna Nußbaum, upset and ailing and with her heart that was either beating too quickly or too slowly, was evacuated from Mannheim and transferred to the tiny village of Unterschmitten located near Nidda, north of Frankfurt. In a great hurry she had to leave her three-room city apartment, which she and her husband had occupied for thirty-five years.

Otto Nußbaum, the child's maternal grandfather, was a highly trained and astute mechanic who was well liked by his customers and made a fairly good living. He could have earned much more money had he wanted to, but his love and ambition were spent on an invention. In his spare time he worked on a neat little machine he called *"my perpetuum mobile"*. His hobby was surrounded by a deep secrecy that was made even more impenetrable by grandmother's sullen silence about it. She was jealous of her husband's endeavor, which took up every free moment of his time and left her mostly to her own devices.

"I am good enough to wash his dirty clothes and cook for him when he is home, but I'm not good enough to keep him company," Anna complained occasionally. Mostly to herself. She was in the habit of talking to herself. Nadine, playing in the living room, often heard her holding soliloquies that could last for hours while she was working in the kitchen.

Grandfather was of medium height and squarely built. His bodily strength became immediately apparent as one looked at him. His wide shoulders and well-muscled arms spoke for him. That was a good thing because he rarely said anything at all. He was mild-mannered, but kept to himself. An incessant worker, he spent his leisure time in a small shed that jutted out into a rectangular, gray-cemented city courtyard. The sun was hardly able to penetrate the dark, narrow enclosure. Most of the day deep shadows that fell from the backside of four large, somber and ugly apartment buildings, more like tall army barracks than private homes, covered the yard. Its tenants were mainly working class people. Most of them did not search to make friends with each other. "*Chaqu'un pour soi,*" could have been their motto.

Even with his granddaughter, Otto Nußbaum was taciturn. But he always held her tenderly when she, usually after lunch as he rested for a few minutes, climbed on his lap. And he smiled when she patted his round head and touched his soft, brown hair that he wore in a Bismark crew-cut. Its color did not fade until the day he died. The little girl was far closer to her maternal grandfather than to her father, who during his long absence in Russia had turned into a vague and foreboding being.

Otto was not yet seventy years old when he was diagnosed with advanced cancer of the stomach. It was a cruel death that kept him in agony for weeks. The child had seen his terrible pain on her mother's blood-drained face after she came back from his bedside where she had kept vigil many days. Nadine cried bitterly at his funeral. She missed her grandfather for a long time. She longed for his mute kindness, his patient tenderness, which no one else was able to give her. Grandmother, at best, let the child snuggle up to her at night when the two of them shared Anna's large bed.

"Get off, child. I have no time to play," she would say to Nadine when she tried to sit on her knees.

"You are a big girl now. Go and finish knitting your sock," she would admonish her granddaughter, as with a deep sigh she got up from her chair and started to wash dishes.

While Otto was still alive, the only occasion when he had ever grown impatient with his granddaughter was during lunchtime. He was used to listening to the news. And when his concentration was cut short by the child's incessant chatter, he grumbled:

"Keep quiet and eat. You can ask me all you want later." Nadine looked at him with her large, hazel eyes, and then glanced at her plate and fork, which she was learning to hold properly in her left hand. Hurt and bored, she uttered not a word until they had finished their meal. It seemed to take forever. But then finally came a few glorious moments when she was allowed to get grandfather's full attention as Oma, pretending not to listen, stored away the remains of their *Mittagessen*.

* * *

As the war went on, the nightly fleet of Allied bombers grew steadily larger and deadlier. By now the British planes had destroyed most of Mannheim and, across the Rhine, its twin city, Ludwigshafen where the huge BASF, a chemical monstrosity, was located. Ceaseless destruction and mortal fear had pressed Anna Nußbaum to move. She was also afraid that another tenant might beat her to the little house her husband had been able to secure for her in Unterschmitten before she would be able to reach the village. Looking back at her flight, Anna felt she was uprooted so hurriedly that some of her leaves, the flat, round ones that keep the water lily from drowning, were permanently damaged.

Carrying only one suitcase and Hansel, the fluffy canary whose cage she covered each night with a white cotton cloth because otherwise he could not fall asleep, she caught a crowded train. She traveled north of Mannheim, past Frankfurt where she changed the city train for a small, local one to Nidda, "ein *Bummelzug* (slow train) that stopped at each apple tree", as Anna, used to fast trains, described it disdainfully to her granddaughter. Rattling indolently through pretty countryside, the train took her to her destination, a sleepy little town with no industry, called Nidda.

The houses of Nidda and its simple Protestant church sat, as if long ago caught by a clever paint brush, among clusters of trees, bushes and wild flowers, honeysuckle, hyacinth and the small, golden glistening buttercups that bloomed from early spring until the first days of frost. A few short, asphalted roads, which crisscrossed the town, were kept immaculately clean. Nidda was named after the river that could be seen from almost every street corner. It was a shallow stream, wide but often only about three feet deep and in some parts the water would barely cover its bed. Many of its large, smooth stones and small boulders then sat highly visible in the middle of the water. Occasionally, even a discarded, old boot slowly floated along before it got stuck in the sandy bottom. But after the river had meandered out of town, it suddenly became deep and afforded geese and ducks plenty of space to swim and feed. As beautiful as swans, the big white geese drifted upon the now fast running current. Their strong, reddish-brown feet could be clearly seen as they paddled next to one of the lusciously overgrown banks. During summer its grass was high and where the watercourse took a curve, the dam, overgrown with cockscomb and blue cornflowers, bent gracefully across the edge of both shores. While the hot weather lasted, it seemed as if the marguerites, the tiny, purple forget-me-nots and the yellow stars of the dandelion whose leaves were not only eaten by rabbits but by Nadine and her grandmother as well, spread forever between river and horizon.

Having lived most of her adult life in a city, it took Anna over a year to become used to tiny Unterschmitten, located next to the town of Nidda, and its barely seven hundred inhabitants. In spite of her husband's skill at mending even the oldest farming equipment, among them the fiercely looking threshing-machines that spat out mountains of chaff, Anna was never fully accepted within the tight circle that the farmers and their wives had narrowly drawn around themselves. From generation to generation the peasants were born and bred in the confined space of their village from which they hardly ever ventured forth. They did not welcome strangers in their midst. To the rough-handed, bony farmers' wives Anna was a soft-looking, city-bred woman who spoke to herself. That was reason enough to dislike her. Standing on their big, broad feet that clung to the ground, the peasants stared long and hard at her whenever she crossed their path. As soon as the village women spotted Anna in the early morning or late evening, there was open contempt, if not hostility, on their brown, wrinkled faces that were beaten by wind and rain and burnt by the sun. Her obesity, her different diction and her face that was covered by a fair, smooth skin, made her stand out as a mistrusted alien. None of the prudish farmers and their wives, who were barely able to read and write, knew that Anna, as a child and young teenager, had lived in a place similar to Unterschmitten. But even if they had known, it would have hardly made a difference to their animosity.

It did not help either that Anna lived in the only stone house, which the village owned. The other buildings, big farmhouses to which barns and stables were attached, were constructed from wood, dry tree branches and wattle-reinforced mud.

Each sunrise and sunset Anna set out from her house across an old short stone bridge that spanned the Nidda, and went along the only dirt road of the village. The dusty pathway that came up to each simple stoop of the farmhouses was laboriously swept on Saturday afternoons.

It was a woman's job. When the skinny, long-skirted, always gossiping peasants had finished their task, there was not a trace of the oxen pulled wagons left or any manure from the cattle that had been using the road all week long.

By the time Anna reached the end of the village, she was breathing heavily and had to slow down. Trying to ignore her handicap, she moved for a moment both hands to her heavy bosom. Then, with an ashen face and slightly tottering, she turned right and crossed several sturdy, wide wooden boards that had been put over an icy mountain stream. Here she passed a sawmill that had been put up in a shed without walls and was barely covered by a waterproof roof. From morning till night the screeching of the mill could be heard a mile away.

There was never a day when Anna's narrow blue eyes and her once high cheekbones, now covered by layers of fat, went unnoticed. Her dress, as simple as those of the farmers' wives but of a different cut, was commented upon and the way she moved was criticized.

"She waddles like a fat goose," one of the old peasant women, her face partly hidden under a black kerchief said quite loudly one day. Nadine's grandmother heard it and was deeply offended.

Twice her daily walk led Anna from her house to her garden were she grew large, yellow tomatoes, potatoes and beans. Toward the end of summer the beans had climbed so high that she needed a tall ladder to reach the green, sickle-moon shaped vegetable that hung in bundles at the tops of the stalks. At one end of the big fenced-in garden, Otto had built a chicken coop for his wife. In the morning Anna let the poultry out of their smelly confinement where, during the long night, they had been secure from foxes and weasels. Often toward sunset, one or two of the large, brown-feathered chickens that had not returned with the rest of the flock, had to be chased back into their pen, it was a job at which Nadine quickly became good.

"Are they all inside?" Anna would call out to her granddaughter as she watered the last bed of cabbages.

"Better count them again," she added watching the little girl stand at the door of the chicken house, her face serious with concentration. In spite of their possessive, sharp-beaked behavior when Nadine tried to pull the large, brownish tinted eggs out from under them, and their fierce squawking and flapping of wings, she was fond of the fowls. But she kept her distance from the big rooster, who proudly strutted around his hens. Yet although she was afraid of him she thought that he was very handsome with his black plumage, which sparkled in iridescent colors whenever the sun struck his thick, long feathers that curved gracefully down his broad back.

* * *

During the first year of her evacuation, Anna missed Mannheim terribly. She longed for her tidy apartment, the territory whose odors and sights had become like the shell of a tortoise to her. Inside its moist darkness, where flesh connects with bones and skin, she had felt safe. Daily she had sat down three times at her kitchen table, which was covered by a white oilcloth that was held down with four brass brackets. Morning, noon and night she had piled simple food upon the table. There had been bread, vegetables, salads, potatoes and sometimes meat. Before starting to eat, she always gave thanks to an invisible visitor. Anna, as she tried to explain to her granddaughter, was convinced that the mysterious stranger, whose presence she felt during every mealtime, dwelled not only among the heavens but stood also next to her. So close was he that he felt as if he were embedded among her heart muscle. Nadine closely watched grandmother's behavior. But try as she might, she was never able to see this spirit to whom the corpulent woman paid homage. Yet Nadine knew that grandmother's pious thoughts allowed her to fall asleep while she still sat at the kitchen table.

Satisfied by a modest, well prepared repast that appeased her stomach, the tired, white-haired woman, who washed her husband's heavily soiled clothes by hand, closed her eyes and like a babe was instantly caught in a web of dreams. Weightless, she floated among imagined and semi-sensed shadows that continued to move behind her closed eyelids. The child could never understand how, for one minute, grandmother was able to speak in a lively, chatty manner and the next moment, as her head fell forward and was caught by her fleshy arms, she would be fast asleep while her unfinished sentence, often spiced with an admonition, still hung in the air. So heavy was the noontime stillness that the buzzing of a fly, a bulky, black housefly who was determined to descend upon the leftovers on the rims of their dinner plates, became audible.

Almost more than her apartment, Anna Nußbaum missed the Baptist church to which she had belonged for so many years. On Wednesday and Saturday evenings, she had felt at home among its intimate prayer group that consisted mainly of elderly ladies. The child, at first driven by what seemed to be an ever present curiosity, soon started to dread the weekly assemblage of this circle of devout women. She hated it when she had to sit still for what seemed to be several eternities piled on top of one another like the unused, additional prayer books on which she kept her eyes fixated. Near the front of the simple hall, the somber, black-bound books were kept on a table under a crucifix. Their silent, but highly visible presence dominated one corner of the room. Apart from the books and crucifix it contained nothing except the bare wooden benches on which the female congregation sat, erect, serious and silent, not once being able to lean back. As she listened to an interminable mumbling of withered lips and stared rudely at old, wrinkled faces, Nadine was consumed by black boredom. She could only swing her legs, which were too short to reach the floor, and were partly hidden under the hard seat on which she crouched. But sooner or later Anna Nußbaum noticed her rocking. Usually indulgent toward her granddaughter, she was afraid to lose face among her *Betschwestern* (literally "sisters who pray together"), as Monika Tallemann called contemptuously the members of her mother's religious affiliation, Anna, annoyed by her granddaughter's gymnastics, would reprimand her in a hushed, angry voice.

"Sit still, child! And behave yourself! Who do you think you are? A monkey?"

Contrary to the stories of the Old and New Testament whose beauty, covered with archaic glitter, often held the child spellbound, prayers were nothing but a monotonous singsong to her. From the fairy tales of the bible her immature soul absorbed some of its ancient wisdom. She stood in awe in front of the black book's many layers of dead generations that, together with their outlandish names, had been pressed into its thin pages. And she understood the human miracle that had been able to turn blood, bones, skin and muscles into sparkling words. But prayers, which had refined and distilled passions and then had contorted them until they were nothing but plain, pale words bored the child immensely. Frustrated she watched as the once poetic richness of spirited thoughts was turned into a ritual that had lost its magic. Prayers were unable to alleviate her fear. They were harmless herb teas that lulled restless sufferers to sleep. Yet their primness was powerless to interrupt the terrible flow of bombers that now had begun to darken the sky even in the middle of the day.

* * *

During her three years of exile in Unterschmitten, Anna Nußbaum sighed many times a day. Her moans could be heard already in the early morning when she had to walk down the steep flight of high, hardwood steps of her house and cross a cobblestone courtyard. Out of breath, she put her large enamel bucket under the water faucet attached to the wall of the farmhouse across from which she lived. As in many buildings of the village, hers had no running water. Her kitchen had only a square white sink into which she poured the dirty dish and bath water. And emptied the suds of her laundry tub.

On Fridays, grandmother and child took their weekly baths in the large, oval shaped zinc container that was also used to wash their dirty linen. On those days, Anna Nußbaum's workload doubled and to the child her groans became almost visible, turning into tiny, furiously battling men, so frequently did she hear them. The amount of water that needed to be carried upstairs then was increased at least four times. Seeing grandmother's red, perspiring face, Nadine without being told, got hold of two small beach buckets. Climbing down the stairs, she filled them with water and then swung the red pails on both arms as she ran ahead of grandmother. Being in a hurry, she often spilled nearly half their content while she ascended the steep, somber steps of the house and, upstairs quickly taking a left turn, ran through a parlor that led to the kitchen. It was the last room of their abode and one of its two windows faced the enormous, five-story high barn, Nadine's favorite, forbidden playground.

"Can't you be more careful," the exhausted woman, wet with perspiration that ran down her back and between her breasts, panted as she came up slowly behind Nadine.

Anna Nußbaum, who week after week hardly spoke to anyone except to the child and her frequently absent husband, had started to seriously talk to herself. There were days when she kept up her unintelligible muttering for several hours. Her full, generous lips, which she had passed on to her daughter, lips that became Nadine's measuring cup for female beauty, were in perpetual motion as if she had been chewing gum. While she faced her imperceptible adversary, her eyes, buried in deep, fleshy wrinkles, narrowed and widened in unrelenting aggravation. But only every so often, a word spoken with great conviction became suddenly understandable. It always startled the child who played close to her. At those moments Nadine became apprehensive of her grandmother. She loved her but she hardly recognized her mean spirited countenance in which her eyes, sparkling in blue, had become shrunken slits.

Before a year was over, Anna Nußbaum's infrequent, social intercourse with the other villagers had turned the once friendly, meek woman into an acrimonious creature whose mood turned sullen at the slightest provocation.

The transplanted, ailing woman with her bad heart, which would kill her within a few years, had no allies and no protection. There was no one she could trust except her husband who was often away from home. Unterschmitten was not the only hamlet with broken threshing machines and Otto Nußbaum was frequently called to other regions of the county to repair the huge equipment. Especially in the summer, some of his labor required him to stay away from home for several days in a row. During his absence Anna Nußbaum had to fight her battles silently. Outwardly, she continued for a long time to be rather placid, sometimes even pleasant. This was particularly the case during the days when she needed something from the tiny village store, whose uneven wooden floor was daily scrubbed.

She liked its melodious doorbell as she stepped inside the shop that never failed to remind her of an oversized but fragile dollhouse. Standing still for a moment, she pulled down the sleeves of her dress and inhaled deeply the strong aroma that floated through the room. The odor, which issued from various dried spices that were stored on thick glass shelves, always pleasantly filled her nostrils and made her feel hungry. As if under a spell, she walked slowly from the entrance of the store to its other end where the counter was located. Looking with delight to her left and right she passed the few neatly encased shelves that lined three sides of the shop. Most of its meager, almost worthless articles were covered by dust. But they were daintily displayed and reminded her of toys rather than articles for adults. Among the layout and partly hidden by it, like a forgotten relic, the owner of the store stood motionless. An old, ugly woman with a wart on her nose and a swarthy skin, she was almost bald. The sparse hair left on her head was knotted together on top of her forehead where it looked like a rotting onion. The brown-pinkish skin of her skull was visible almost everywhere. It was loathsome. But perhaps the most spectacular aspect of her physiognomy was a *Kropf* (goiter). As large as a tennis ball, it grew immediately under the right side of her chin where it stuck out, prominently, ever-present and disgustingly, even when the poor woman wore a dress with a high collar. No shawl was large enough to permanently hide her awful outgrowth, which stemmed from a lack of iodine in the water. In many German villages women walked around all their lives, carrying a disfiguring goiter. Strangely, goiters did not seem to affect men. At least Nadine had never seen a male handicapped by this affliction.

Like the other village urchins, Nadine was afraid of Mrs. Filsinger who owned the only store of the village and several of its farms. Emaciated and quick on her feet, she was the wealthiest woman of the hamlet. Her husband had fallen ill and suddenly died several years ago. She had only one son who never married and now helped her with her many chores. The peasants, and especially their children, feared the harsh manners and withered repulsiveness of the widow. She rarely left her house, which was located opposite Anna Nußbaum's dwelling. But whenever Mrs. Filsinger did venture forth, children, as soon as they saw her, ran away screaming and howling. Some of the older boys would follow her from a distance, heckling her and even throwing pebbles at her back. No child ever entered the store of the widow without its mother or an aunt. Often a little girl or boy held on to its mother's dress and hid half of its face among its long folds. Only one child's eye ventured a fearful look at Mrs. Filsinger's ugliness from which any traces of youth had so utterly vanished.

Calm on the exterior, Anna Nußbaum had begun to rage inwardly. Her highly developed religious sense did not permit her to use profanities. Yet her endless tirades did not prevent her from calling anyone stupid or impertinent. It was usually those pejorative adjectives she unexpectedly brought forth in a highly pitched, wrathful voice. Many times her silent speeches started out by saying to herself semi-loudly:

"Oh, this Mrs. Filsinger is..." at which point her talk would continue to run river-like underground for a considerable length of time. The child had learned to watch grandmother's lips move and tried to read them as if she were a deaf-mute. This way, she was able to brace herself for the inevitable, sudden eruption that occurred within several minutes and found its culmination in a shouted "outrageous!" or "this stupid, mean woman!"

There were days when Anna Nußbaum repeated the same speech five or six times in a row as if she had been a lawyer preparing for a difficult defense. As time passed, the child was no longer able to play calmly with her doll or try to decipher a story when she was in the same room with her grandmother. Nadine was too busy watching the sick woman and at night she no longer enjoyed sharing grandmother's ample bed. She had changed so much since she no longer lived in the city. Her snoring had intensified and when she did not breathe hard, she talked in her sleep and threw her heavy body about. Several times an arm or a hand of hers had fallen hard on the child's face who then woke up with a scream.

Since Anna Nußbaum did not get along with the peasants, Nadine did not play with their offspring either. The one-room schoolhouse she had started to attend at five was built on a hill. The children, each carrying a satchel, reached it by climbing a winding, narrow dirt path lined on both sides with neatly kept farm buildings. The school was surrounded by a large, luscious looking, untidy garden. Among a row of old apple trees, the schoolmaster kept his beehive. Nadine thought he looked funny when she watched him one day collecting honey. A huge hat that had a strong, gray net hanging down his neck and across his face, rendering his eyes and mouth almost unrecognizable, was supposed to protect him from the stings of ill-humored bees. He wore gloves whose leather ends went half way up his elbows, which were enclosed in thick cotton sleeves. His feet were covered by muddy rubber boots over which he had tightly drawn his pants and bound with string. Yet in spite of his elaborate armor, he still every so often let out a yelp when one of the offended insects stung him.

The child liked the white painted school structure. The village had no church. The farmers, proud of their intellectual achievement, had embellished the schoolhouse, which sat on a hill looking down on the hamlet, as a castle might have done, with a belfry. But Nadine had heard the mournful sound of its single bell only once at the death of an old peasant. A priest had been hastily summoned from a neighboring village and the coffin was carried from the living room of the farmhouse, where the body was laid out during the night, straight to the cemetery. A group of five or six grieving women and a small boy had surrounded the grave that was decorated with a single wreath of half-wilted flowers.

But once inside the small school, she either was bored or became frightened. This occurred each time the schoolmaster's patience had reached its limit and he would suddenly hit the knuckles that were closest to his ruler. The boys, except for a few stealthy looks, showed no interest in Nadine. And the girls, her fellow first graders with whom she shared a short front row of seats, also mostly kept their distance. On the way to and from school, they stared at the little stranger from an unknown city who lived with a babbling old woman. Sometimes one of the little girls, who still stuck her thumb in her mouth, would quietly stand in the middle of the dusty, unpaved road before she started to step from one foot to the other as she intensely watched Nadine with her large, round eyes. Yet no sound ever issued from her lips. Only eyes spoke.

Occasionally, a girl who was considerably older than Nadine plucked up enough courage to approach her. She was one of several pupils who sat way back where the last benches of the schoolhouse for the tallest students had been installed. This meant that the girl was fourteen years old and ready to graduate. Her parents needed her to work full time in the fields, the kitchen and stables where, at the age of ten, she had learned to milk the cows. It had been a hard job for those small hands that needed a lot of strength to squeeze the bovine's tough nipples.

The light-skinned young girl, who had dared to speak with Nadine, had pretty pink cheeks that flushed a dark red as she shyly walked toward the child. She was pushed by a curiosity that proved to be stronger than the xenophobia that had been early nurtured by her parents. Nadine, as she saw the girl approach, became spot-bound and was unable to move a hand or a foot. While she waited, she wriggled her toes in her wooden clogs and pulled at her short frock, which she had outgrown. Consumed by loneliness, she wanted to please the peasant girl.

Nadine soon discovered that Liese, her new friend, had never watched a movie. Nadine, delighted to suddenly have an attentive listener, told her all she remembered about fairytale and adult films, as well as newsreels she had seen in Mannheim all of which the young girl knew at best from hearsay.

"You mean they show you how the tanks move, planes fly and soldiers are killed?" Liese wondered incredulously while her mouth remained open in astonishment.

"Tell me more," she asked Nadine and, standing close, eagerly pushed her arm with an open palm.

At first, it had been difficult for the two girls to communicate because the dialect of Unterschmitten, which belonged to a different province than Mannheim, pronounced most words in an unknown manner, putting emphasis on the wrong syllables and eliminated entire endings or contorted them in a new, hilariously sounding way.

"Why do you speak so funnily?" Liese had asked her one day.

"I don't know," Nadine replied and blushed. She did not like it when she could not answer any of Liese's questions. But she quickly learned to understand and speak her new friend's tongue. As time went on, she was flattered when she got the attention of yet another girl who had also reached pubescence and therefore was much closer to the coveted world of adults. From the child's point of view, it was a world in which freedom reigned unrestrictedly and where she would no longer be subjected to a teacher's ruler or her father's hard spanking hand.

But Nadine's friendship with the teenage girls did not last. As soon as Liese and Rosemarie discovered Nadine could neither tap dance nor sing like the movie stars she had described in such vivid colors, they lost interest in her. Sadly, the child fell back playing her solitary games in which she pretended to move more gracefully than Anna Pavlova.

* * *

Nadine's father, a tall man with an angular body and a hairline that had begun to rapidly recede from his round, fair forehead, making it look larger and higher, had shown her a photograph of the great danc-er's interpretation of Tchaikovsky's *Dying Swan*. Heinrich Tallemann had been home on a short furlough from the Russian front and talked mostly of the dreaded, seemingly limitless fighting line Hitler had created between Germany and Russia. As he spoke, a venomous no-man's land where death reigned supremely in form of tanks, planes, anti-aircraft guns and fast running or half-hidden men in soiled, torn, bloody uniforms, rose in front of his family's eyes. Nadine soon became alarmed and tried to divert her father's attention.

"What did the ballerina look like?" she wanted to know. Then she listened in rapture as he described in brief, vivid remarks the dancer's exquisitely shaped head and her lithe, thin body that dominated the stage.

"When she folds her legs beneath her and crouching, waves her long, white arms while she curves her wrists and elongated fingers and when she bows her head until it touches her knee, there is nothing more beautiful in the world." Heinrich Tallemann looked at his small daughter's face. Her eyes seemed twice as large as usual as she smiled at him.

"Can I be a dancer too when I grew up?" she wanted to know and her tongue went quickly in a half circle across her upper lip.

"I don't know," her father said. "Let's hope this war ends soon so that you can take lessons. Then we'll see." Nadine's face fell.

"Oh, this stupid war! It will never be over. I hate it. I want to be a ballerina." And she stamped her foot on the floor.

After Heinrich Tallemann was ordered to return to Kiev, the child searched everywhere for Pavlova's dark hair, which had been so skillfully adorned with white feathers. Nadine was sure that she would see the dancer emerge as soon as a swan on a city pond - one of the few that had not yet been destroyed - curved his snake-like, elegant neck.

* * *

The Russian prima ballerina was still on Nadine's mind when her mother had first brought her to Unterschmitten where she started to live with her grandmother.

"What a lucky child you are! Here you will finally be safe from the bombs," Monika Tallemann said before she gave her daughter a quick hug, turned around and went back to Nidda where she tried to catch a slowly moving train back to Mannheim. From the bedroom window that faced the only street of the village, Nadine followed her slender silhouette. She wore open-toed, old but still pretty shoes and her high heels struck resolutely the ground.

"I wish you would not have to leave," Nadine said under her breath as she watched her mother walk away, her blond hair bobbing up and down with each step she took. Leaning out of the window, the child stretched her short, undeveloped body forward and waved, but her mother did not turn around.

From the same bedroom where Nadine had watched her mother disappear, Oma and the child would listen twice a week to the town crier. Unterschmitten was far too small to have a newspaper, or a radio station, so a peasant, who had been elevated to the position of a town crier, would appear on Mondays and Wednesdays to inform the hamlet of local news. It was late afternoon, after most farmers had returned from their fields, when the town crier showed up, swinging a large bell in one hand and a sheet of paper in the other. After he had vigorously shaken his bell, several farmers would gather around him while others, like Nadine and Anna, could been seen standing at open windows facing the crier. When he thought that enough people had gathered, he would start his announcements. He read loud and well and after about seven or ten minutes, the middle-aged man walked off to his next stop where he, self-consciously, yet clearly enjoying his importance, repeated his performance. There were five such gathering places distributed throughout the hamlet. One of the news spots was below Anna's bedroom.

On the day Nadine's mother had left Unterschmitten again, the child slowly went back from her observation post in the bedroom to the kitchen where Oma was preparing lunch. Moving, she scratched her head in great frustration. Her scalp had been itching all morning and she was wearing a kerchief bound tightly around her forehead that for once did not show a single curl of hers.

"Don't touch your head, honey. It will only make it worse. Let the stuff soak in," Anna Nußbaum said. "I am going to wash your hair this afternoon and rinse it with gasoline. That will help to get rid of the lice." The elderly woman smiled encouragingly at her granddaughter.

But worse than the vermin that took more than one gasoline treatment to eliminate, was the *"Krätze"*, a severe, highly contagious skin disease that soldiers and prisoners from Poland, Yugoslavia and Russia had brought back with them. Microscopic lacerations broke out all over the body and without making the patient so ill that he could not work, the relentless itch was almost unbearable. The skin at the root of each finger was especially sensitive and Nadine could not sit still for half a minute without rubbing her hands until they started to bleed. Grandmother, patient and solicitous, eventually cured her by spreading every night a tar ointment all over her body and then wrapping her in a sheet so the black, viscous grease would not soil the bed too badly.

* * *

In Unterschmitten the child tried right away to make friends with the geese that, snow-white and splendid, swam aloof and serene on the Nidda's transparent, leisurely moving surface. The shallow river, which here and there had created deep beds where the current increased fast and furiously and proved dangerous to anyone who couldn't swim, was just a step or two away from grandmother's house. Yet the big geese, like Anna Pavlova, were always out of reach. The moment the elusive birds saw the child approach, they hurriedly moved toward the middle of the river where she couldn't follow. Left behind, she looked at them plaintively and called out to them again and again. Yet despite her tender cries, the regal looking geese kept their distance. Silently, they sat on the glittering water and ignored her.

But Nadine did not give up easily. For half an hour at a time she remained standing precariously close to the river's edge, at a place where the waters were deep. Her feet were barely held by the grass clusters that grew abundantly along both banks. Looking at the flock of birds, she forgot where she was and longed for their languid, seemingly weightless bodies. More than anything else she wanted to touch their white-feathered, beautiful shape. Yet in spite of her soft calls she stubbornly kept up, the geese never swam toward her.

The next day when Nadine had forgotten the birds, she spotted them on a narrow, hardly visible footpath. The trail led from the village into wide, soft meadows and the wafting, golden-brown fields that surrounded it. Mostly hidden by the rye that stood high, the little girl felt as if she were walking on the bottom of a riverbed. She was thrilled with her new surrounding and pretended to be Andersen's mermaid looking for her prince. Unseen by the geese, she watched them from close by and was amazed at their change. Out of the water they no longer floated but now they shuffled awkwardly on the ground instead. As they shifted their heavy bodies from one large-webbed, reddish foot to another, they looked as if they were intoxicated and would not be able to keep their balance. Their clumsy, land-bound movements took away most of their beauty. And in no way did they any longer resemble the great Russian dancer.

* * *

Having no one of her own age to play with, the little girl became more and more dependent upon casual contacts with adult farmers. In the early evening at milking time, she sometimes suddenly appeared at a stable and offered her help. She usually went to the stalls that belonged to Mrs. Filsinger. The barn and stables were located next to her grandmother's house, whose first floor was used as a storage place for farming tools. Only the second floor, with its dark, steep steps leading upward, remained for living quarters. There was just enough space for a narrow sitting room, a bedroom and a spacious kitchen whose cast iron stove had to be fed with wood.

The child reached the stables by walking past a wooden outhouse that was shared by at least two, often three families. Its green painted door had a hand-carved heart installed at the height of a man's head, standing up. Like a small sun, the heart hung high above Nadine's face as she sat on the putrid, coarse throne. It was the only source of light. When it became dark, it was necessary to bring a flashlight. For the night, Anna Nußbaum kept an enamel chamber pot under their shared bed. It had been much used and some of its varnish had come off so that large, black spots had burst forth on its white, polished surface. Round and big, it was placed next to several pounds of apples that were also kept on the wooden floor under the bed. During the night, the fruits' delicious aroma eliminated part of the acid smell of urine.

To get to the barn and stables Nadine also had to pass a large, square dunghill. It was built deeply into a concrete basin and covered up to its stone rim with dark brown urine upon which cow dung and straw were piled highly. Since the privy was located next to the dunghill, cow manure mixed with human excrement. During spring and fall, a large amount of this smelly concoction was pumped into an oblong shaped, steel wagon. Then a team of sad-eyed oxen, their tails swishing back and forth to ward off flies, carried the smelly mixture on rough roads to beyond the village where it was used to fertilize the fields.

In the mornings, Anna Nußbaum emptied their chamber pot by opening one of her kitchen windows and pouring its content on the large pile of manure that was located below it. Mrs. Filsinger, whose bedroom faced the river, threw her and her son's waste into the gently flowing, shallow water. Only the geese, if they got splashed, complained.

Anna Nußbaum's house, like several others of the hamlet, belonged to Mrs. Filsinger who lived across from the gray, rectangular cobblestoned courtyard that had been built in between the two structures. Each time Nadine ran into her, she looked intently at her face, the cherry-sized wart on the side of her nose and her goiter. The child was disgusted yet fascinated by her ugliness. The old woman's constantly frowned forehead and her scowl reinforced the perpetually belligerent expression of her face. Nadine had never seen her smile. At night, after she had said her prayers, she forgot about Mrs. Filsinger. And the next day when she met her again, she was struck anew by her repulsive features.

"She looks just like a witch," Nadine complained several times to Anna Nußbaum.

"I know, sweetie. But don't stare at her all the time. That's not nice," grandmother said and patted the child's head reassuringly. Not being able to get used to Mrs. Filsinger's unsightly appearance, Nadine feared her.

It was Hans, the old woman's thirty year old, unmarried son whom the small girl encountered almost every time she left or entered her grandmother's house. The stable he worked in was attached to a five-story high barn. Its towering floors were stacked with bundles of hay and straw even at the end of winter when most farm buildings of the village had become bare looking. The cattle of the poorest farmers started to starve then. And at feeding time Nadine heard their pitiful cries when she passed one of their mews.

Even after Mrs. Filsinger had become a widow, she remained Otto Nußbaum's best customer. He rented one of her sheds for his repair work. The enormous shack was located at the periphery of the hamlet where meadow after green meadow gently sloped toward the horizon. In June, when the grass had grown tall, it was mowed by hand, stacked to dry and taken back to the barns. Everywhere was the delicious scent of drying grass. The heavy, noisy bombers, as they passed across the sky where, for a moment, a wing seemed to throw a shadow darkening the sun, no longer frightened Nadine. She knew the planes took their deadly loads to larger cities. But for a moment she could no longer smell the grass whose odor she loved passionately.

Between the pastures were well-tended fields where wheat and rye were growing. Before it was cut during the hot days of July and August, the corn bowed in the breeze. It looked like a sea of liquid gold. And Nadine, as she passed the fields on almost invisible footpaths, kept searching for mermaids.

Grandfather's work place was a wooden, open door structure whose proportions were those of a medium-sized cathedral. It was built to accommodate the enormous threshing machines. At harvest time, their incessant droning mixed from dawn to dusk with the screeching of the sawmill.

* * *

Quite often during the afternoon Nadine sat in her grandmother's parlor. She thought that its purple-pinkish, velvet-covered sofa was one of the most attractive pieces of furniture that she had ever seen and she was only allowed to sit on it after Oma had admonished her again and again to be very careful not to soil anything. But in spite of the sofa's purple beauty, which Nadine so greatly admired, there always came a time when her book started to become boring and she craved companionship. In the kitchen grandmother was talking to herself, summoning her imaginary friends and foes. She had completely forgotten the child's presence in the next room, and Nadine, rather than trying to speak with her which she had attempted in the past, only to be grouchily told to stay where she was, decided not to go into the kitchen. Instead she got off the couch, tiptoed to the far end of the room where another door led to the staircase. Reluctantly, she went downstairs where she crossed part of the courtyard and then slipped through a small door that had been cut into the barn's two large gates. Its thin, high boards rattled and quivered each time they were opened to let a tractor or the two-story high hay wagon slowly pass through them. The child was always awe inspired when she watched two straining oxen, their nostrils dripping with mucus, make a last effort to pull the oversized vehicle through the gate. The brownish-gray hide of the docile bullocks was soaked with large patches of perspiration. Working under a scorching sun, the animals, long past their prime, had hauled the overloaded wagon from a field far beyond the village. Now a deep gasp came from their throats at regular intervals. And both bovines rolled their eyes in mute despair.

The barn was the child's playground. She used it almost every day. Once inside, she looked quickly to her left and right to make sure that no one was watching her. Then she threw off her wooden clogs and covered them carefully with a small bundle of straw that lay at the foot of a ladder. She did not want anyone to find her. Least of all grandmother when she called her at suppertime.

Barefoot and agile as a cat, Nadine climbed up the widely spaced, sturdy steps. The ladder was securely attached to each of the five spacious levels of the barn. She greedily breathed in the scent of hay that wafted through the large, airy building. Especially on a humid or rainy day when the odor of fresh hay and straw was particularly strong, Nadine became a little dizzy with an unexplainable, concrete, brief sensation of happiness that seemed mostly connected to the intoxicating effect which the aroma had on her. It was as if suddenly and only for an instant a huge hand had brushed aside all fear.

Sometimes, when she could not hear anybody, she jumped several feet from one floor to another one that was situated below her. Here a big pile of hay caught her fall and buried her in its sweet smell. After her game she had to make sure that she got rid of the small pieces of dry grass that stuck to her hair and clothes because grandmother would spot them and then severely scold her. Oma did not want her granddaughter to play in the barn. Once, stepping unexpectedly through the ungainly, slightly vibrating door of the shed, Anna Nußbaum had watched Nadine leap from a sixteen-foot high beam and with a small shriek disappear under a mountain of hay. For a moment, as the old lady stared in disbelief into the air through which the little girl had dropped like a stone, her heart had stopped beating and she pressed both hands over it to relieve its fierce pain.

"You must never do this again," Anna had hissed at her granddaughter in a hoarse whisper when she finally reappeared from the stack of hay, smiling, red-faced and obviously unharmed.

"Children have a special angel," Nadine overheard Anna Nußbaum saying to her husband in a soft tender voice when she reported their grandchild's latest sport. And the little girl continued in secret to hurdle herself from barn floor to barn floor. She had discovered a short-lived, intensely exhilarating release from gravity.

On the fifth and last floor of the barn, far removed from any potential intrusion of an adult, Nadine had erected her castle. Her secret palace stood between the roof and one of the walls of the building. Wind, sun, and rain had free access through parts of the wall that had mostly been built from twigs and loam. In a few spots the elements had eaten entire sections of the fragile structure. The holes were never repaired. Hans usually had more urgent things to take care of. He rarely climbed up to the fifth floor of the barn where only a small amount of straw, hay and grain were stored.

When Nadine stuck her head through the wall's remaining, intricately twisted branches and the dirt that was caked onto them, she looked upon the Nidda flowing way below her. The river was her moat. Her *château* was a temporary abode constructed from nothing but a fluffy mountain of chaff, leftovers from the days of threshing wheat. But to get to it she had to balance across a strong beam, a permanent fixture of the barn that rested freely in the air with no support on either side of it so that each time the child crossed it, she was looking straight down five floors below her. To get from one side of the long, free floating wooden shaft to the other was far more dangerous than her high, reckless jumps onto a hill of hay. Fortunately, Anna Nußbaum was completely oblivious to her granddaughter's perilous trapeze act, which she performed unprotected over a floor that was three times higher than the rooftop of the small, overcrowded house next to this granary in which Nadine lived with her grandparents.

For days the little girl had toiled with great zest at her stronghold, a labor of love that was inspired by her imagination. With her hands and feet she had formed a passageway that wound in a cylinder shape from the ground to its lofty top. The one-room abode was about eight feet tall; but it was not bigger than the size of grandmother's large kitchen stove. To reach the great hall, in which she resided in lonely splendor, she moved on a spiral staircase softened with stolen hay that steadily ascended higher and higher around its own axis. Seen from a distance, like the top of the barn's ladder, the ingenious dwelling resembled the shell of a common, brownish-red garden snail.

Hidden away and for once feeling secure, she often remained for a long time in her fortress and played with her doll, which she called Amalia. She spoke to her as if she had been alive. Nadine was the queen and Amalia a rich, young princess who was brought up strictly. Only the best tutors the country could offer educated her. There was no king. He was far away at war.

When the child grew tired of being a mother, she started to serve coffee in tiny cups and saucers she had carefully shaped from mud. Before carrying her sculptured treasures up the barn's vertical ladder, she had hidden them in a deserted corner of a small vegetable garden where the sun needed to dry them.

During her soirées, which she gave once a week, no one but she and Amalia could see and hear her invisible guests. The ladies, who came to visit, were dressed in expensive, handmade robes that rustled seductively when they dismounted from their carriages by stretching one, barely visible foot delicately in front of them, as they angled for the ground below them. Nadine also enjoyed listening to the men's sabers clicking discreetly against their thighs when they handed their horses to a waiting stable boy. Smiling, the elegant women and men walked toward their hostess. Some of the gentlemen started to bow and to swing their large, feather adorned hats long before they reached her. The ladies inclined their heads gracefully and curtsied. They did not remove their hats, which perched daintily on top of elaborate curls, often helped by hairpieces. For an hour each morning a personal maid had worked at the hairdo and its complex embellishment, which adorned each noble woman's head. As they approached Nadine, they artfully set, almost like a ballet dancer, one satin slipper in front of the other. Their hands raised imperceptibly the front part of their floor length blue and white silk dresses. Nadine, turned queen, watched in delight as their full, wide skirts, with an embroidered bodice encasing a tiny waist, whipped up and down with each step the countesses took.

Her visitors were quite unusual. They were far smaller than the child was and the youngest among them was about two hundred years old. Mostly French, the exquisitely dressed men and women entertained the Prussian aristocracy of Frederick the Great in Potsdam. Among them were such keen spirits as Maupertuis, the mathematician and La Mettrie, the philosopher of materialism. And, of course, there was Voltaire, the king's favorite.

Nadine had chosen the site of *Sans Souci* carefully by building it at the farthest end of the broad, wooden beam. Like herself, her company always had to cross this narrow, dangerous bridge. Being so small her noble visitors had a wider space. But it was still a perilous traversing. The little girl watched as the elegant men and women tried not to pay attention to their palpitating hearts as soon as they became aware that there was nothing but air between the beam and the cobble-stoned barn floor twenty meters below. Just one wrong step and they would have fallen to their death. But luckily, although most of her callers had come from as far as Paris and the treacherous, horizontal beam was located at the end of their long tedious journey, none of them ever came to any harm. Nor did the child.

The *Alte Fritz*, as Frederick was called unceremoniously, had invited most of her guests to join him at his famous midnight suppers. During one of his frequent absences when he fought the Silesians, the Austrians, the Saxons, the Russians and the French, with only the English as his allies, Nadine, miraculously fully grown, took over. Her luxurious, gray dress, made of the finest material and worked into its stylish shape by several seamstresses, was cut in a large, low square at the neck and, as it was the custom, emphasized her waist. The lower halves of its semi-long sleeves were embedded in costly Venetian lace. Slowly moving forward, she nodded graciously at Voltaire. Her father, who loved not only Pavlova but also French literature, had spoken several times of the *philosophe*. She knew him quite well. At least by sight. During a moment of leisure, so rare in her father's life, he had shown her a black and white photo of Houdon's sculpture of the old Voltaire.

"I have seen his marble sculpture at the Hermitage in Leningrad," Heinrich Tallemann had told his daughter one day. Small as she was, she had never forgotten it.

* * *

Often deeply involved in her games, Nadine did not want to listen to her grandmother, who called her at dinnertime. At first standing at the barn's door, which she had opened just a crack, Anna Nußbaum cried out in a soft, lamenting voice:

"Where are you? Your supper is getting cold. Come upstairs and wash your hands."

But when Nadine did not answer grandmother, there was an increasing threat in her tone:

"I know you are in there, you little brat. Come this instant! Don't pretend you cannot hear me."

For a while Anna Nußbaum, who did not like to enter the barn, stood still at its thin door, which started to tremble at the slightest touch. Then her foot knocked impatiently against it, sending the door into a wide swing, as she clapped her hands calling out once more to her granddaughter. Yet Nadine, naughty and upset by the unwelcome interruption, did not answer. High above her grandmother and hidden beyond the beam she did not move until she heard her receding footsteps.

Instead of following Anna Nußbaum's summons, Nadine was more intrigued by the smell of warm milk that had started to float up to her airy seat. Not being able to see Hans, she knew he was spraying the rich white fluid from the cow's udder into an aluminum bucket. Disobediently, she decided to pay the farmer, who worked in the cowshed, a quick visit before she went home to eat her evening meal.

* * *

When she walked through the stable's door, she saw the young peasant leaning his head against the bovine's belly for better support as he sat somewhat haphazardly on his three-legged milking stool. Hans Filsinger was lean and quite tall. His watery blue eyes were red rimmed from an inflammation he could not get rid of. He had his mother's ugly curved nose and straggly hair. He often patted it down with a nervous gesture while he stared vacant-eyed into a corner of the shed. Hans was the only farmer who occasionally smiled at the child. It did not take long for her to like him. She needed an ally. His friendliness distinguished him from the other villagers whose face muscles never moved while their eyes scrutinized the child. Except for Hans, the rest of the inhabitants of Unterschmitten considered her a stranger and treated her in an almost undisguised hostile manner. Their unkindness forced Nadine's smile from her face as if it had been a badly fitted mask. On some days the open aversion of the xenophobic peasants was so strong that it would upset her stomach. Her mouth then filled with an undigested vapor and made her feel as if she were chewing cotton balls soaked in acid.

Occasionally, when Nadine appeared at the door of the low-ceilinged warm and always pleasantly smelling stable, Hans interrupted the steady flow of milk that poured forth from his hands. He would then slowly turn around and look at her open-mouthed and with an imbecilic expression on his face that always puzzled Nadine.

His fingers had grown strong from performing the same movement over and over again for what seemed, when measured against the quietness and the immobility of the stall, an interminable length of time. As if his hands had been part of a machine, they pulled and squeezed the thick-skinned nipples of the cow he was milking. Once in a while the tame, attractive beast moved her head and looked at Hans. Nadine had never seen such long, thick eyelashes before. Nor such large, beautiful eyes. Sometimes, the cow gave a low cry and flicked the flies off her haunches with the bushy, leathery tip of her tail. An earthy, agreeable smell rose from the fresh straw under the animal's hooves.

As Nadine watched silently, the bucket filled with warm, foaming milk. The scent frequently attracted a short-bodied, yellow-eyed cat. Deftly, as an acrobat, she emerged from a pile of hay and rubbed her high back against the bucket and boots of Hans. Standing almost on the tips of her toes, she pitifully begged for a few drops of milk. Each time she cried, she revealed a tiny, rough, pink tongue and gleaming white canine teeth. If Hans was in a bad mood, he just squirted the cat by aiming one of the cow's udders at her. Baring his teeth in an ugly, idiotic grin, it looked as if he were holding the end of a water hose.

'How stupid he looks', Nadine thought as she watched him disgustedly, keeping her distance.

But the farmer, knowing the value of a good mouser, would often spray some milk into a small dish, which the child had quickly fetched from a corner of the shed. The purring of the cat, as she lapped the still foaming liquid, could then be heard even outside the stalls. Its happy sound announced to the world at large that it was dinnertime. It made the child suddenly feel hungry and saying good-bye to the farmer, she ran home.

* * *

One August afternoon while it had been drizzling for several hours, grandmother and child had grown more and more restless with each other. It was laundry day. During this, her most laborious task of the week, Anna Nußbaum talked to herself longer and in a more animated manner than on other days. And although the child had several times tried to interrupt the incessant mumbling of her grandmother, the exhausted woman paid no attention to her.

As she bent over a zinc-laminated washtub, her rolled-up sleeves exposed the mottled arms of ruthless, old age. She wore a heavy, gray, patterned cotton apron over her dress, which stretched tightly across her bulging stomach. Under her long black skirt her stocky legs were bare and her feet stuck in her husband's felt slippers that were way too big for her and worn down at their heels. Standing, with dark patches of perspiration clustered at the opening of her blouse and on her back, she worked steadily hour after hour over her tub, which she had placed on two kitchen chairs before she filled it with hot water. The water had been heated on the big wood stove where she kept a blazing fire going. Her hands, all red and swollen from the hot, soapy water, washed one after another of her husband's dark work shirts and pants, smeared with black grease. As Nadine watched, grandmother rubbed the cloth vigorously up and down a stretch of heavy metal that was folded like an accordion and attached to a wooden board. The steaming trough stood in the middle of the kitchen next to the table. Within a short while the room had filled with a pungent, unpleasant odor. Every so often lifting one dripping forearm Anna wiped her sweaty, bloated face.

Not being able to get her grandmother's attention, the small girl went into the parlor where she sat for some time on her adored purple sofa. As so often before, she admired again its sumptuous, highly polished wooden frame, which ran along the edge of the settee. In its middle the wood was carved into two chubby-faced *angioletti*. Painted in gold, their short, protruding wings formed a tiny roof for those who sat under them. Nadine loved these miniature carvings with a passion. And she was hurt when her mother during one of her infrequent visits to Unterschmitten, had called them *kitsch*.

"Those figures look like the angels of death you'll find in a cemetery," Monika Tallemann said to her daughter and grimaced. She had grown-up with the purple settee and despised it.

But for Nadine the sofa was some kind of a living creature. She talked to it and loved to pat its velvet-covered seat. When her fingers moved against the grain, its prickly sensation excited her. As if they were an army of ants, the synaptic nerve endings of her fingertips seemed to totally absorb the soft cloth that rubbed against her skin and sent her off dreaming. She then forgot that she was supposed to sit still on grandmother's best piece of furniture and, starting to swing her legs back and forth, she bounced up and down on the fuchsia couch until tiny clouds of dust filled the air.

"What are you doing?" grandmother's voice startled her through the open kitchen door.

"Nothing, I am just playing," Nadine called back as she nervously waved both hands through the air, trying to get rid of the dust.

"Behave yourself and start knitting your sock," Anna Nußbaum grumbled in a hoarse, angry voice.

Grandmother did not believe in idleness. In her eyes even reading was part of this *dolce fa niente*, which led a person on a straight path to eternal hellfire. Each time she saw the little girl with a book in her hand, she scolded her and told her to take up the four short, metal needles she used for knitting socks, an art which Anna had painstakingly taught her granddaughter during long evening hours.

Nadine listened anxiously to grandmother's heavy, shuffling step as she went to the stove where she got more hot water to pour into the tub. While the water splashed on the soiled clothes the child, sitting very still, was gobbled up by her grandmother's pitiful moaning.

After a while there were only the sounds of vigorous rubbing of clothes as the old woman continued to press each item up and down the washing board. A few minutes passed before Nadine heard once more grandmother's muttering through the kitchen door. As the child remained motionless, the old woman's words reached a sudden peak before several sounds ejaculated in a burst of loud, furious exclamations. Then Nadine knew that Anna Nußbaum fought again her solitary battles with her enemies, which, as so often before, she had conjured up in her mind.

Noiselessly, Nadine slipped off the sofa and stole out of the living room's other door that led to the bedroom located in front of the house and the fume-filled passageway. She climbed down the cumbersome steps and tried to squeeze through the front door. It was still not easy for her to reach its highly placed, bulky door handle; but after a brief jump she was able to hang onto the iron wrought shaft and pull it down.

Outdoors, the fine rain had finally stopped. The rays of the setting sun painted large patches of pink on the sky. It looked lovely and peaceful. In an instant the child forgot the hardships of her grandmother. She was glad to escape the small house where most of the day the humidity had enclosed the heat in tiny, transparent bubbles that sat on windows and mirrors. Periodically, they would burst open like blisters.

"Look, the windows are crying," Nadine laughed when she had first noticed the running globules. But grandmother never raised her head from her large washing pot.

Once outside the entrance door, the little girl took a right and walked straight to Mrs. Filsinger's stable where her son, as usual at this hour, milked the cows.

The farmer was working in a short-sleeved shirt and shorts. As soon as the child had come through the stable door, she had called out to him. Then she saw him. He had his back turned to her and sat wide-kneed on his milking stool. She walked carefully around the head of her favorite cow whose big, alluring eyes looked calmly at her. The child was sure that the pretty bovine recognized her as a friend and as always the cow's jaws, which were moving in a slow, steady rhythm, fascinated her.

Then, as she faced the farmer, she saw that his penis was coming through one of his cut-off trouser legs. Yet he beamed as usual at her and appeared to be totally unaware that his genitals were exposed.

The small girl took his attitude as a clue and stared at his face where his features were set in a stony grin. The rims of the peasant's eyes seemed even more red than usual. It was as if tiny particles of dirt were irritating them and forced him to blink incessantly. Half reassured, although without noticing it at first, her stomach muscles had started to contract and her hands felt unusually cold and clammy, Nadine thought that Hans had simply forgotten to button up his short pants after he had relieved himself.

As usual, the farmer began to chat in a low voice with Nadine. In crude, simple sentences he commented on the endless rain and the bad mood his mother was in.

"She is plagued with rheumatism. The Lord makes her suffer when the weather changes." Hans was speaking softly. The child watched his mouth whose lips pouted, widened and contracted with each vowel. His words came forth evenly. They dropped off his tongue like dribbles from a hastily abandoned honeycomb. Not once did the timber of his voice change and the corners of his mouth were bent upward in a perpetual beam.

Nadine remained totally mute and immobile. She avoided at all cost looking below his waist. After a short while, she became conscious how taut the tendons of her legs were. Without realizing it, simply obeying healthy instincts, she had readied herself to jump forward at the slightest motion of the farmer and to disappear behind a bundle of straw like the amber-eyed cat.

Yet when Hans made his sudden move – as if he were pulling his car off from a highway into a small, hidden road – the child was unprepared.

"Would you like to touch it?", he asked and, fully aroused, he stared excitedly at his organ that was huge, blood-swollen and stiff.

Now his voice no longer sang but was harsh and his red glowing eyes were set on her maliciously. The child shook her head violently from left to right while blood rushed to her head and she felt the familiar, acid vapor rising from her small belly.

Then, fearing not to be able to dodge him by going forward, she stepped slowly backwards until she felt the wall of the stable touch her shoulders. For an instant she was reassured by its customary grainy firmness and clung to it with her back, rubbing against it as if she were able to make a hole and vanish into it. Then all of a sudden, she was distracted by of a pair of swallows swooping low above her head. They had built their nest in a corner between the highest part of the wall and ceiling of the cowshed. The graceful birds were busily flying back and forth, feeding their young. Each time one of the parents, having caught a fat fly and coming to rest on the rim of the nest, four black triangles appeared, their borders outlined with yellow. She heard tiny, needle-sharp chirps but did not see anything of the fledglings except their huge, open beaks.

"It feels so nice", Hans continued to press the child, as if he had not noticed her intense refusal and fugitive turn. He was half mad with desire and wanted more than anything for the child to touch him.

"You must not be afraid..." With those words, he quickly reached for Nadine's hand and half with a jerk half carefully he guided it toward his penis. For a moment, pressing his big fist over her hand, he succeeded to close her reluctant fingers around his slimy flesh. Garishly white, with an ugly red mouth, it felt and looked to the child like a horrible, huge worm.

The child screamed, yanked her hand out of the farmer's fingers and ran out of his reach. Sprinting through the barn, she heard his raucous laughter behind her. Yet on his face appeared fear, regret and self-loathing.

"I hate you, you pig," Nadine shouted as she turned halfway around and saw that Hans did not follow her. The sky above her occluded with all sorts of bizarre, threatening shapes, not just clouds.

* * *

With crimson cheeks, her heart pounding from her run through the courtyard and from climbing the steep flight of steps, the child entered the kitchen. Here she found Anna Nußbaum still standing over her laundry rubbing away at her husband's grimy work suits. More than before, the kitchen was penetrated with a strong, sour smelling odor that rose from the soaking clothes in the trough. The windows, although they were partly open, were covered with a watery veil. Large drops of condensation were visible through the white lace curtains.

Anna's face was as flaming red as Nadine's. But her scarlet skin was mixed with a sickly pallor that broke in patches through the purple of her nose and chin. Her cheeks were so puffy that her eyes had become two cracks. She resembled the yellow-eyed cat when she crouched in the sunlight that proved too strong for her. One by one, large drops of perspiration kept falling off her forehead and the wrinkled flesh above her upper lip.

Then Nadine saw that her grandmother had hardly touched her meal, which was still on the table. Normally Anna did not leave a morsel of food on her place and often she had wiped off the last speck of vegetable with a piece of bread. But today, she was too oppressed to eat.

When she heard the footsteps of her granddaughter, she turned around, pushed her hand against her aching back and said in an raw, high-pitched voice:

"Where have you been? I called you a long time ago!"

"I helped Hans milking the cows", the child answered in a hardly audible voice. Feeling guilty and utterly ashamed, she kept her head low and her eyes avoided those of Anna's.

"I am not hungry", the child whispered and tried to leave the kitchen. But her grandmother came straight toward her and pulled her roughly by the arm. Then she forced the child to sit down at the table.

"I want you to eat everything on your plate!" Anna, who knew her granddaughter hated spinach, ordered her in a galling voice. Fearfully, the little girl looked at the heap of dark green vegetable that was piled high in front of her. She felt her throat tighten as if someone had tried to close it with shoelaces.

When she looked up pleadingly, she saw nothing but a fraction of her grandmother's blue eyes. They were half concealed between her eyebrows and the fat that bulged on top of her glowing cheekbones. Her usual gentleness was no longer present and Nadine knew that one more word of protest would result in a sounding slap on her face.

Slowly, half chokingly, she started to force down a few forks full of spinach. Watching her grandmother's bent back, she looked repeatedly at Hansel, the canary who hopped up and down the bars of his cage. Every so often, he peeped and emitted spiky, short trills while he coquettishly tilted his head. Yet his black eye seemed to challenge her to do battle.

In the winter, at suppertime, when all windows were closed, Anna had sometimes opened Hansel's cage. After a few minutes, the tiny bird had usually come swooping down upon the table where he soon started to peck at some food. A few times, he had even sat at the rim of a glass of milk, dipping his diminutive beak into it. But today, the child knew, grandmother would not let Hansel out of his cage. She was being punished for not having come on time to supper. Yet she longed for Hansel to be close to her so that - with her right forefinger - she could gently stroke his minute, fragile body.

But the canary remained in his cage. Behind his bars, he kept hopping back and forth in short leaps. Every so often he, like a trapeze artist, flew down from his horizontal perch while he, as if trying to get Nadine's attention, burst into little, piercing cries. He was in no mood to sing. He just shook himself and then blew up his fluffy feathers until he looked like a golden tennis ball. In Mannheim, during the frequent air raids, Hansel had been their constant companion. Anna Nußbaum would grab the handle of his cage and, holding on to her grandchild with her other hand, the three of them fled to a shelter. Each night grandmother would get the canary's abode ready to be rushed off by carefully emptying the minute porcelain bathtub that was part of the cage's furnishings and where, several times a day, Hansel loved to splash vigorously. Like Anna and Nadine, the adorable, captive songbird survived the bombs.

Grandmother, with her back turned to the child, continued talking to herself and rubbing at her dirty clothes. Still gulping down her food out of fear, the child started very quietly to cry and was less and less able to swallow. Then, when she had finally almost finished her pile of spinach, her stomach suddenly contracted in one brief strong muscle spasm and brought forth its entire content.

II

Dover Groombridge Brighton Hastings

As the rickety, heaving vessel approached the cliffs of Dover, their evocative shape rose languidly at the far end of the horizon. Nadine could not yet hear the aggressive screeches of sea gulls that lived at the bottom of the high rocks. But for a moment, as she bent her head backward and shaded her eyes against the sun, she observed one of the wide-winged birds that had come far out into the sea and circled gracefully above the ship. Sea gulls were a novelty for her.

Leaning against the ship's rail, she watched the grayish-white bluffs move up and down in rhythm with the ship's rattling engines. Enveloped in mist, their hazy, roundish humps looked to her like gates that divided space between two horizontal lines: the sky and sea. Seen from the dancing deck of the boat, the white escarpments did not seem real. Standing dreamily in the breeze the young girl did not consider for a moment what a welcome sight these chalky cliffs must have been to young British Air Force pilots who made it back to England after they had dropped their bombs over Germany.

During her two hour crossing from Ostende to Dover, she had gotten used to the uninterrupted stretch of water that lay about her in, what she perceived to be, a strangely solid form. The way the sea moved and glittered in the sun reminded her of a ripened cornfield swaying in the wind.

The steep gray rocks, as they slowly became more visible, had no substance for her. As far as she knew, there was nothing in her past that evoked an echo of them. Nadine's father had often told her that his ancestors had come from France. Those of Mother's were from Russia. None of her forefathers had come from England. The white cliffs and the sea that spread in front of them were more like painted matter, the haystacks of Monet perhaps, rather than rock and water.

But then she realized that she didn't want the cliffs to be real. She was afraid of their newness and their otherness from the far more sea-deprived German coastlines. Only once had she been taken to the *Nordsee*. Her skin had turned blue, as she had faced the cold, onrushing, high breakers. She was born and raised in the south and did not know the northeast or northwest of her country where the oceans were.

Too long had the cliffs of Dover stood as a symbolic gate to a new world. Now, as she was about to pass that threshold, she hesitated. She looked back upon the German cities she knew. In spite of their post-war, transparent façades of glass and steel, which western Germany had so hastily erected, in almost total disregard of their former, now forever destroyed beauty she felt that those towns still represented to a large degree Sodom and Gomorrah. And for a brief moment she wished she could turn herself into a pillar of salt. With a masochistic impulse she wanted to repeat the destiny of Lot's unfortunate wife, the woman who is only known under her husband's name. Just as the young girl was aware that she was only recognized under her father's name.

'I have no identity of my own. Who am I?' She often demanded to know when she stared in the mirror. But unlike the queen's talking looking glass in the fairy tale, her own mirror remained silent.

The customs officer at Dover had gone thoroughly through the contents of Nadine's luggage. With stern, non-seeing eyes that purposely looked through her, he had caused complete havoc among her clothes and shoes. After he had finished his search, Nadine had to struggle to put her belongings in order again so that she could close her suitcase. During his hostile endeavor, the middle-aged official had mumbled something about her having to register as a foreigner as soon as she reached her destination.

His face was square, almost box-like and closed up as if someone had shut its lid. Ill at ease, Nadine had not understood the words he spoke hastily, as if he couldn't wait to get rid of her, and in an accent with which she was not familiar. His uncouth command had little to do with Emily Brontë's English or the one of Wordsworth, Coleridge, Byron and Scott to whose words she had been introduced at school. Irritated as the customs agent seemed to be with her, the young girl was afraid to ask him to repeat his orders.

When Nadine thought the inspection of her few belongings was finally over and wanted to move on, the officer waved her back. Towering over her, he impatiently signaled with his hand, as the lines in his face grew sharper to open the small, black leather jewelry box her father had given her for her eighteenth birthday. Nadine had filled it to the brim with jewelry. Most of its content, divided into two velvet-lined sections, consisted of inexpensive fashion items, which she had collected over several years. She was particularly fond of a pair of long, pendant pearl earrings that flew back and forth when she made a quick turn on the dance floor. The earrings, more than her evening dresses that were either flaming red, a poisonous green, or yellow like a lemon in its most ripe stage, made her feel beautiful. So did make-up.

As Nadine looked at her earrings, the grim and unhealthily reddish face of the custom's officer mercifully receded into the background. Behind the official's large, yellowish ears, which looked as if made from wax and stood away from his head like the handles of a soup cup and behind his scrawny neck, where the tight collar of his uniform had left a raw, itchy mark, rose a familiar image.

* * *

During her imperceptible move forward from childhood, when she had not doubted that she was simply a part of her parents, to adolescence when she craved to break away from *home*, she suddenly had a thousand questions about this large, vague, circular-shaped concept called identity. But she soon discovered that she did not understand anything about herself or the environment in which she lived. Yet the instant she tried to see herself objectively, she saw that it was a hopeless task. Her reflections only confirmed one thing: She was plagued by an ever present and apparently insurmountable sense of insecurity. Yet it took several years before she understood that her lack of confidence had also enclosed her in a suffocating circle of narcissism from which she did not know how to escape.

At fourteen, when for the first time the *Little Mermaid* was allowed to rise to the surface of the sea, she started a habit, which she kept up for a long time. The moment she woke up in the morning she took a look in the mirror. Her self-examination was her first conscious act of the day. It was more urgent than going to the bathroom. She used a full-length mirror that had been inserted into the door of a large armoire made from cherry wood. The roomy wardrobe had belonged to her grandmother, Anna Nußbaum, who had died two years ago.

Her reflection in the mirror reassured the teenager that she had not disappeared during the night. She feared the dark and felt imprisoned by it. In her dreams, most of them quite vivid, she possessed neither a face nor a body. While she dreamed, she only recognized herself when others treated her as the person she was supposed to be during the day. Her identity depended solely on her parents, teachers and friends. She was whatever others wanted her to be. By calling her name, they gave form to a skin-encased, flowing substance imprisoned in her body that was supposedly her. She did not even have a voice as some apparitions do. And her name was nothing but a cloak that closed around her otherwise ghostlike appearance. But if the skeletal shadows and shades she saw while she slept, had not identified her by calling her name, she would not have been able to materialize. Yet it was only her first name that counted. The family name, Tallemann, was her father's and she did not want it.

In the morning, when she looked in the mirror and recognized herself, she shuddered. Under her skin - that of a pretty, young girl - a skin, dry and fine-pored and smooth to the touch, she felt old and worn.

There had been several awful mornings, particularly those when a fine drizzle forced clouds down as low as the steep-gabled red roofs that loomed everywhere across the city. A fine mist then clung to chimneys, antennae and gutters like the tail of a rat. Above the roofs of buildings, fog and rain had built a second top that covered the sky like a smooth coat of gray paint. During those bleak days, she felt as if she had lived a thousand years. Years that had been unbearably monotonous and resembled each other like endlessly multiplying twins. Unending and boring days at school and work had dragged her along the ground as if she had never fully emerged from it. Rainy mornings made her bend over the earth and forced her to caress the evergreens that lusciously grew around her grandparents' large, square tombstone. Their names that were inscribed on the upper part of the smooth stone had left space for the succeeding generation to be buried here, too. It was called a family grave and was expensive to sustain so it could compete with other elaborate, flower- and shrubbery enhanced tombs, which surrounded it in large numbers. For the young girl these laboriously cared for burial plots were just another ludicrous, time-consuming German custom, mostly driven by guilt for *Unterlassungssünden* (sins of omission) committed while the dead had been still alive. She hated those conventions and swore that no one would ever find her grave.

"We are next," Monika Tallemann, Nadine's mother, had said just after her own mother had died. As she looked at her daughter, her face was gray and there was a dark hollow under her wide, prominent cheekbones. It added an eerie beauty to her features. But there were no tears in her light green, oddly slanted looking eyes. Only once, when her mother was asleep, had Nadine seen her cry. Unlike most other women the young girl knew, Monika Tallemann did not readily show her emotions. She was a practical, quick-thinking woman, who worked hard during the day and in the evening wanted to enjoy life. Her psychological make-up was the opposite of Nadine's father, who believed only in the value of work. Pleasure was a sin from which he daily purged himself. Taking the typical macho attitude of unquestionable male superiority, he considered his ethical outlook superior to his wife's and tried hard to impose his point of view on each family member, especially his offspring. The result was a constant battle of words between husband and wife with Nadine in the middle. Monika Tallemann was not a woman who could be easily pushed aside. She had learned to stand her ground and fight. During the war Monika had shouldered the responsibility of most men or women and after the miraculous return of her husband, she was not about to give up rights that she had earned the hard way.

On many winter days, sunless and perpetually gray, the young girl had been jealous of the earth that covered her grandparent's skeletons. At those moments, in spite of her disdain for tombs, she longed to be enclosed in the stillness of the graveyard. Utterly depressed, she then wanted nothing more than to hold on to the leafless branches of a small birch tree that grew out of the spacious tomb.

Waking up, she was cold in her room whose windows had been left wide open all night. Her father believed in fresh air during his daughter's sleep and did not allow her to close her windows.

"Put on another blanket," he said when she complained. "You have no idea what real cold is. Now, during the war, when I was in Russia..." As he tried to get his daughter's attention, his features expanded into a curious assembly of weariness and expectancy. But she no longer listened to him. She had heard his story so many times before. Pitying him did not make her feel warmer at night.

Being chilly and suffering from lack of sleep, she was often ill tempered in the morning. Her rotten mood made her feel ugly, unwanted and stupid. Dejectedly, she stared at her cheekbones, a gift from her mother, and thought once more that they were protruding too far from the rest of her face including her nose, which was short and straight. But she felt that her zygomatic bones made her features look too broad.

'Somewhere there must be some Mongolian blood flowing in my veins, not just Russian,' she reflected. Those classmates, who did not like her, called her "moon-face".Had these girls – there were no boys at the gymnasium that she attended – known that the raven-haired princesses in the *Arabian Nights*, who walked forever in rose-studded palace gardens, were always compared with the beauty of a full moon, they would not have given her that name. Besides, her father had told her that her wide molar bones would always keep her look younger.

"Later, when you need it and providing that you stay slim", he had joked. But this parental consolation did not help her now when she thought she looked repulsive and craved a perfectly oval shaped face. Elizabeth Taylor as Cleopatra was her ideal. Yet however much she felt internally like an ancient drone, something prevented her from externally seeing herself as an old woman. Her mirror protested too much. The wardrobe returned a picture of blooming youth.

Yet even as she grew more mature, in the morning she always felt her mouth was too small and her hazel eyes had the wrong color. Her eyebrows were hopeless. Their brownish hair grew in the wrong places like above the bridge of her nose where they gave her face a sullen, manly look, such as she would later admire in Frida Karla's self-portraits. But for now a masculine expression was to be avoided in a man's world, which was dominated by an all-feminine, huge-bosomed ideal. To achieve the required appearance, she pulled out the offensive hair, reducing her eyebrows to a razorblade-thin line that made her eyes resemble those of an owl, one of these small, round-bodied, adorable saw-whet creatures that seemed to fear human beings somewhat less than other birds. On days when she didn't want to look like an owl, she filled her brows in heavily with a charcoal pencil, which changed her appearance dramatically. To add to her suddenly sinister look, she pulled her hair over her forehead in asymmetrical, dark strands that contrasted sharply with the white of her forehead. Her hair and black eyebrows gave her a Mephistophelean profile. Day after day, she did everything possible to hide her natural prettiness, including her peach colored, smooth skin that was the envy of most of her classmates. To achieve this feat she would meticulously cover her cheekbones with white powder. That way not a hint of their rosy hue, the glow of health and youth she disliked, was visible. No heroine whom she admired had pink cheekbones. Theirs was always a deathly pallor, emphasized by long, flowing, dark hair and equally long, well-fitting, décolleté negligees. Her adored protagonists reclined in luxurious, occasionally exotic looking chairs, like those of Cleopatra, which were furnished with lion heads. Or if such a *femme fatale* were cast in more modern times, she would often decorously drape herself across an expensive, brilliantly white bedspread, a luring *Dame sans merci*.

Once every two weeks when her father reluctantly gave her permission to spend a few evening hours with her friends, Nadine mixed the rouge for her lips strongly with a white zinc paste that eliminated almost all of the red. And in a film she had watched Desirée, Napoleon's first fiancée, stuff handkerchiefs in her bosom that were apple-sized and small nippled. Nadine thought that this had been a smart idea and quickly imitated the young French girl from Marseille. In this manner the front of her torso came closer to resemble the required oversized eggplant shaped breasts, which were so much in fashion. But she had also noticed what eventually happened to those coveted feminine attributes. After their first bloom, their weight, helped by gravity, pulled the big female assets irresistibly toward the navel, unless they were severely restrained by tightly fitting undergarments that left their owners breathless and severely limited their participation in most sports. But many men, she was told by an older, more experienced and friendly neighbor, never quite outgrew their first moments of unconscious infancy when mother had been nothing but a big breast. Relentlessly, they tried to cling to it all their lives.

On those rare evenings when Nadine had secured her father's permission to go to a dance, he often stopped her at the front door, horrified when she confronted him looking like a vampire.

"No daughter of mine is leaving my house in such an *Aufmachung* (get-up)," he said sternly and sent her back to her room to remove her *impossible mask*, as he put it. So Nadine often left home without make-up. But before she reached her destination, she put it on somewhere on the road, where a telephone booth or the semi-dark, deserted entrance of a building would have to do.

At the hospital in Mannheim where the young girl studied to be a *Kinderschwester* (nurse for children), none of the white-uniform wearing staff was allowed to wear any make-up either while on duty. At six o'clock in the morning, when Nadine started her laborious routine in the children's ward of the large hospital that stretched along the shores of the Neckar and beyond, sometimes a trace of lipstick was left on her mouth from the night before. And though she would vigorously rub her lips with tissue and moisturizer, she could never completely remove the rouge. The morning soon came when she was called into the office of the head nurse. Here, standing up and facing her superior who sat belligerently behind a desk as if it were a barrier from which to shoot at the enemy, the young girl was reprimanded for having reported for duty while wearing *maquillage*. The middle-aged, prim and ugly superior, whose gray hair was pulled back severely and mostly hidden under her starched uniform hat, looked sternly at her. Over-sized and stony-faced, she was waiting to hear Nadine's guilt-ridden whisper: "I'm sorry".

"Well, see to it that it does not happen again, will you," the heavy-joweled woman said. And before the young girl was able to hastily make her exit, she blushed once more under her head nurse's last severe look.

But these restrictions made Nadine more than ever "hide her face under a garish disguise", as her father called her make-up disdainfully. Concealed in his criticism was a concern for her rebellious nature, which irritated him endlessly. Yet, like with most teenagers, insurrection against parental, scholastic and any authoritarian discipline was a necessity for her. It seemed that only by objecting to her parents' and teacher's authority, she got glimpses of herself. They were, of course, mostly distorted ones. But she started to see herself a little.

'Even a negative identity is better than none,' she would argue with herself. Looking in the wardrobe's mirror, she sometimes seemed to see a vague shadow; it was the hardly discernable outline of another face, or rather a profile that she barely recognized. She was not sure at all if she were able to accept her dark sides. Self-knowledge, she discovered, was a slow, painful and sometimes intensely humiliating process. She soon realized that if she had silently submitted to those more powerful than her, she would have been less frequently punished. Yet no rational reflection was able to change her dissident behavior.

* * *

While a young adult, Nadine saw her father as a large, big-boned figure whose apparently unlimited authority had terrified her as a child. She now easily came up to his shoulders. But the emotional distance between them, which had, she believed, mainly been caused by his absence of many years at the Russian front, had not allowed developing any warmth or closeness between them. Father and child approached each other cautiously; they sniffed at each other like two wolves. It was a relationship in which the younger, female beast was forced to constantly display signs of submission. And as if they had been real wild animals, father and daughter did not hug or joke with each other. There was often an awkward silence between them that easily grew into a fearful and hostile one.

When she was eighteen, Nadine's father permitted her twice a month, usually on a Saturday night, to attend a social event. Of course, she had to adhere to an early curfew. But she was so happy to escape parental supervision for at least a few hours that she would have promised anything. While she went to a dance with her friends in Mannheim, she became a different person from the one she was obliged to be during the day.

On such an evening, alone in her room, it became her dressing room. Here, as she had selected a *Streichquartett* (string quartet) flawlessly performed by the *Stuttgarter Kammermusik*, she prepared herself for her outing. The music was not her choice but was the only type her father allowed her to listen to in "his house and on his radio", as he had put it categorically. Slowly, as if entranced by some magic and in blatant defiance of her father's wishes, she started to color her face. Working in front of the mirror, she changed into someone else. In stark contrast to the civilized tone painting that issued from the radio, make-up and glass seemed to connect her with Sioux tribal rituals, as they readied themselves for war, or with African tribes who practiced witchcraft. Yet the more she emphasized her feminine aspects, the less she felt like a woman. She did not see herself as a man either. Then who was she?

Eventually, after she had spent at least an hour to get dressed, then, having somehow escaped her father's inspection, had taken a bus from the suburbs where she lived with her parents, she arrived at the *Rosengarten*.

When she was very young there had been no need for public transportation. Her father's house, spacious and five stories high, stood in the best area of Mannheim, the *Planken*, a short boulevard flanked with banks, professional buildings, department stores, townhouses and an entire array of cafés. But during the last year of World War II her parents' home, together with most other structures of Mannheim, had been reduced to a pile of rubble. It took at least ten years after the war and the bleak years of the *Wirtschaftswunder* before small restaurants and ice-cream parlors would extend their facilities on the *Planken* again. And before each summer tables, chairs, food and a crowd of well-dressed *Stammkunden* (patrons) once more created a colorful display as they spilled onto meticulously kept pavements protected by huge, red and white striped parasols and well-tended, expensive, potted trees. But when the townhouse of Nadine's grandparents was rebuilt, the property had changed owners. The house no longer belonged to her family. Had the sale not taken place, her life and the one of her parents would have been quite different. There would have been money. A considerable amount of it.

The *Rosengarten* was a large *Art Nouveau* building made from reddish sandstone and embellished with elaborately carved pillars and statues. The structure was situated in the center of town, not far from her parents' former home. In front of the *Rosengarten*, as if it were one of the princely palaces of which Europe boasts so frequently, was a spectacular display of fountains. A circular park with wide, lusciously green lawns, multiple flowerbeds and wrought-iron arcades, covered with thick, evergreen shrubbery, enclosed the multiple watery extravaganzas. The interior of the *Rosengarten* contained several graceful, enormous, perfectly lit halls, which were used for professional conferences and festive events, such as those in which Nadine tried to participate as often as possible.

But as she entered this coveted place, her heart jumping with irrepressible joy, the young girl, overcome by shyness and complexes, often felt as if nature had left her behind in her rush to climb the evolutionary ladder. Of course, seen from a distance, she was just another pretty, energetic, female teenager among many who danced to their heart's content, preferably with boys of their choice. No alcohol was ever served at these popular events, which were appropriately called "*Coca-Cola Balls*". Smoking, too, was frowned upon. As the adolescents turned and twisted around their own axes, mostly just holding on to each other with their fingertips, they released pent-up tensions and anxieties that they had involuntarily collected during a long week of work and study. Under the admiring glancing of boys, the girls tapped their feet in high-heeled, uncomfortable, fashionable shoes and seductively twirled their skirts. Several, multi-colored petticoats often reinforced their garments, and as they pirouetted from one foot to the other, they daringly exposed a well-shaped leg. Together, the young students, clerks and apprentices danced themselves free of a daily, tedious routine. On the invisible wings of a Mambo, Rumba, Cha-cha or an occasional Foxtrot and under the glittering lights of big chandeliers, they entered wide-eyed a world of dreams and wishful thinking. It was a short-lived world, which they needed and cherished.

During brief pauses when the big band stopped playing, some dancers withdrew from the dance floor to get a soft drink. Afterwards, holding an open soda can in their hand, they ran up the wide, low steps to the "*Empore*", as everyone called it, a spacious gallery with many stacked rows of upholstered, permanent folding chairs that surrounded the ballroom along three walls. Mostly standing or leaning against a chair, the teenagers, hardly any older than twenty, gossiped, smiled shyly and looked down on the huge, highly polished parquet that spread below them. Here, the unreachable chandeliers haughtily mirrored themselves on the floor's emptiness like several full moons above a dark pond.

No one would have guessed that some of these graceful girls, these "*jeunes filles en fleur*", who moved lightly, laughing open-mouthed in the arms of their partners, were serious plotters and thinkers, the promising hope of another generation. Watching the adolescents giggle and scream, one did not suspect that for hours on end they discussed the arts and literature and tried hard to find a few simple solutions in a world that was utterly confusing to them. For some of the least fortunate boys and girls, this world that had been created by their parents and grandparents was nothing but a hostile and unbearable environment. Most of the bright young people were only able to express their desires in negative terms: They knew what they did not want to be. Nadine was one of them. She rejected the identity she was offered: a young student nurse from a middle-class German background, who had not yet found her self, but kept drifting on a current of air.

Almost every morning when she scrutinized herself in the mirror, her reflection showed but a fair face. It was an empty beauty, she thought, like a robbed tomb in the Valley of Kings, where only a small vase with her father's name inscribed upon its jagged rim, had been left behind, dropped or rejected by hastily retreating thieves.

As soon as she tried to separate herself from her father, she lost her human shape. She then could only see herself as some exotic, greenish plant that sprouted a profusion of gray-white flowers. She recognized nothing except strange-looking blossoms, which neither resembled roses nor orchids. They were more like cabbages that grew best near water or actually in water. Their odor too, which she was unable to recognize, must have been unpleasant because it often attracted the type of men she was least interested in. They were the middle-aged, round-waisted and married ones. These men were heavy with the vapor of their inflated egos and their moral convictions seemed to her nothing more than slippery, sharp-edged stones thrown upon forgotten childhood dreams. She hated their patriarchal, practical attitudes and the common sense they braggingly displayed as if they had found the answers to life's great riddles.

And then there were the boys. When they got close to her, she watched them with growing discomfort and poked fun at their sugary-sweet, odious whispers coming from partly hidden lips, encircled by a first, barely growing mustache and beard. Their often softly spoken and awkward words, which sprang from their mouths as if out of control, quickly revealed an immature mind that was harassed day and night with sexual needs. She reacted to these often relentless exigencies from boys and some of the slightly older young men with a stomach that was forced into producing an overload of acid. Its bitter taste rose to her throat in burning, nauseous gulps. Under these unfavorable circumstances, her heart remained unoccupied. She only became aware of its muscles and valves when she ran fast or tried to follow her father down an icy ski slope.

During most days, filled with work and studies, she felt spot-bound like a water lily and, being desperate to find an adequate role model, she identified herself more and more with her dead, maternal grandmother. Her father was at best her competitor who still outpaced her swimming and skiing. Even at eighteen she was not able to see him as a friend. And she had not yet learned how to defend herself against intruding strangers. She had barely begun to weed her water-garden rigorously and without fail once a week. If a frog or a small, slippery, bigheaded toad decided to sit on one of her half submerged, large, round leaves, she didn't know how to chase the aquatic trespassers away.

* * *

Nadine understood well why her father did not like her to use make-up and preferred her face in its natural, youthful look. He was not concerned about aesthetics - beauty in its multiple forms and colors that meant so much to her, was far less important for him. Instead, his was the age-old fear of fathers who wanted their daughters to take on the trite colors of the tribal members among whom they lived. Not to be different from any of the ultra conservative burghers in dress and speech was the expected goal. It was an unwritten law, which was imperceptibly communicated and reinforced by century-old rituals. Young people about to become fully responsible participants in the German middle class were carefully measured against these beliefs.

Subtlety was the foremost command in the logbook of Nadine's father. It was synonymous with elegance and beauty. His ideals demanded a plain, long-skirted dress and did not allow rouge or mascara on a fresh face. And only if the young girl did not reveal any bare limbs was she permitted to quietly mix among a larger group of adults. When Nadine was first exposed to these formal customs, she felt as if she had become invisible and had suddenly lost the use of her legs. Dressed in a long-sleeved dress, she offered a tray of hors d'oeuvres to her parents' guests, men and women, who consistently disregarded her, busily chatting among themselves. At those social gatherings she felt as if she had turned into some kind of oversized fish or a snake that slithered from person to person, voiceless and mindless.

The objective was, according to her father, to perfectly mimic the behavior of mature men and women of her class and to become gradually accepted by them, to melt into the caldron like wine stirred into water. Fresh blood was, of course, constantly needed for the group to survive. But the young girls and boys, who were initiated, usually during a spring night when the moon was full and hung like an eye in a starless sky, did not know this. Their elders, jealous of their positions, deliberately kept the young people in the dark.

Approval by the caste, by neighbors and by impalpable but powerful authorities, was considered superior to the single citizen's talents and needs. The individual was the outsider who risked drowning. His survival in the high seas was only protected if he swam within the pod into which he was born.

* * *

Nadine's father was a tall and, in spite of his balding head, still attractive citizen of Mannheim with no visible distinctions except that he had miraculously endured the horrors of World War Two. As a German soldier in Russia, he had studied this complex language and, defying severe German army rules, had become friends with an educated, middle-class family in Kiev. Reading was one of his greatest pleasures and, after a glass of wine or two, he loved to entertain dinner guests with well-told stories. Back in Germany after the war, he tried to rule his small household with an iron fist. And if it had not been for his wife's constant interference, home might have been heaven. As it was, living room, kitchen and bedrooms became a battleground for the marital couple. The neighbors often benefited from their shouting matches, especially during the summer when windows stood ajar. But outside the house and being the brother of a well-known physician and the son of a wealthy merchant, doors were still open to him.

His protestant father, Adolf Tallemann, had married Gertrude, a Catholic, who was far younger and a head taller than her husband. His small, fine-boned size did not prevent him from mercilessly tyrannizing his wife. Suffering from old age and *Arterienverkalkung* (arteriosclerosis), he lost his temper easily. And when he was enraged, he did not hesitate to hobble around the grand piano in the middle of the living room and brandish his walking stick, the steady companion of his later years, at Gertrude. Once Nadine had watched her grandmother as she hastily gathered her long skirts and ran with a shriek before her staff-swinging husband. That scene in one of the rooms stuffed with books and furniture had made an indelible impression on the small child. It was the main cause why she disliked her paternal grandfather. After witnessing his chase, each time he tried to gather her up in his arms for a big hug and a kiss, she screamed and struggled to escape his embrace.

Still stately when Nadine knew her as a child, her paternal grandmother had turned into a recluse and became utterly withdrawn even to close family members. Although Gertrude had tried, she had never been able to cross the chasm that separated her Protestant husband from her own Catholic background in which she was raised. Religion, taken seriously by both partners, was the main reason for their marital unhappiness.

In her youth, Gertrude had been known for her beauty and when she was nineteen years old, she had even been crowned as Miss *Germania*. But a disastrous marriage had made her seek refuge in the Church's lap. By the time Nadine was old enough to appreciate Gertrude she had become a devout Catholic and always dressed in ankle-length, black gowns or skirts that concealed most of her slim, tall figure. Outside her home at the *Planken* she was never seen without a large, fashionable hat - also black. Standing or sitting she kept her torso perfectly straight. With her slender waistline and her full hair under her wide rimmed hats, she looked appealing and elegant even when she was elderly. Before she stepped outside her house, Nadine next to her, was fascinated as Gertrude stood in front of the heavy hall mirror where she would lift her hands, often clothed in fingerless gloves, and pull a semi-transparent veil across her face. The little girl loved her mysterious look and she greedily inhaled the faint odor of perfume that exuded from hat and veil when grandmother lifted her off the floor and kissed her.

Her most vivid memories were certain afternoons when she had sat next to Gertrude in one of the high-ceilinged, spacious but somber and over-laden rooms of the town-house while grandmother read stories of saints and martyrs to her. Those myths greatly differed from the fairy tales in cheap paperbacks that Anna Nußbaum had read to her granddaughter with such patience and love. Gertrude's books belonged to an expensive, leather-bound collection whose enormous pages felt smooth like silk. In contrast to the fairy tales of Anna, which rarely had any pictures, Gertrude's books did. The mostly black and white illustrations depicted attractive, half-nude young men and women in contorted, painful positions. The sensuous and raptured expression of their delicate faces was kept in balance by a mystifying, forlorn look from large eyes.

"Not even Raphael could have painted them any better", Gertrude Tallemann had once whispered, hoarse with an unfamiliar agitation, as she bent her head next to the child's over the pages in front of them.

There was one handsome saint Nadine liked particularly well. He wore nothing but a loincloth. His exquisite chest and muscled arms were pierced with arrows. His head was bent gracefully backwards and his eyes were half closed. But strangely he did not seem in agony from the horrible pain he must have suffered. Instead, he appeared to be in ecstasy. The female martyrs were equally enticing. There was especially one young woman Nadine liked. Her soft back and perfectly rounded buttocks were completely revealed and she, too, seemed to enjoy the terrible flogging she was subjected to. The attractive victim had a beatific smile on her half-turned face and her lips were full and luscious; partly open, they revealed milk-white teeth and the tip of a rosy tongue. Like her grandmother, Nadine loved to look at these drawings. They excited her in an inexplicable way, a way that made her feel lascivious and ashamed at the same time, and without understanding why.

* * *

Monika Tallemann, Nadine's mother, seldom agreed with her husband's points of view. There had been times, especially right after the war, when marital fights broke out almost daily. The family was starving, rooms were barely heated during the long, cold winter, tempers were short and Monika was not submissive as Gertrude, her mother-in-law, was. But Monika preferred a halfway peaceful household to a stormy and tearful one and making an effort, she would attempt again and again to keep her emotions under control.

When she listened to her husband's lecturing voice, she usually stood in the shadow of his large frame. Out of the slightly slanted corners of her eyes, she watched him with apparent indifference. But her calmness was hard won and it had taken a long time to reach its current perfection. Her patience contained only a small amount of acquiescence, the fraction her husband, even after many quarrels, still insisted upon.

In an unconscious way, Nadine's mother was surer of herself than her husband whose sense of self-judgment had been highly developed. Adolf Tallemann, Nadine's paternal grandfather, had several times severely beaten his son for slight infractions. The sometimes irrationally and always sadistically administered punishment not only hurt the boy physically, but it did also considerable damage to his psyche. As a result, when he was grown-up and married, Heinrich Tallemann's high morals were often expressed in painful accusations, which pertained to his own inadequacies and even more to those of others. Being a businessman like his father but far less successful, he had the mind of a scholar. Most of his life he longed to live among books rather than people. Books were kinder. And he could remove himself from his library, but not, or only barely, from the men and women among whom he lived. Even before World War II, which had added additional harm to his psyche and body, he had been inadequately equipped against a reality that daily stepped upon him. He felt like Kafka's beetle and saw himself in imminent danger from a crushing foot.

"Each day is a battle" was his favorite motto. But although her father was tall, wide-shouldered and had the long, muscled legs of a runner, Nadine, after she had reached her teens, rarely saw him as a warrior figure. He complained too much. Heroes were supposed to suffer in silence. Achilles and Hector only shouted when they killed their opponents and they crossed the Acheron, their closed eyelids weighed down with a gold coin, without uttering a sound. Yet her father lamented every day:

"What an awful world we live in. I can't stand it any longer. When will we ever have enough to eat again?" were some of the statements and questions he threw into the air like small, heavy balls, which no one was able to catch.

Heinrich Tallemann was the product of two world wars. During World War One he had almost starved as a child. He had grown up in Mannheim, close to the French border where hundreds of thousands of young German and French soldiers had dug the trenches in which they lived like wild dogs. Officers and their men on either side had little food and no facilities to sleep, to clean themselves or to defecate. Tired when they woke up in the morning, they froze in the winter and in the summer fleas, lice, worms and other vermin ate them alive. Then came the worst. As soon as these German and French military men, or rather those strong, intelligent, talented and idealistic boys, often the best either country had to offer, left their dugouts for an attack, they were killed by the dozen within a few minutes. This inhuman and totally senseless suffering on both sides of the border occurred in the name of each respective fatherland. Yet the epitome of such disastrous madness was that both fighting parties prayed to the same god for victory. Yet how, I ask you, was this God of War to decide "who were the bad guys?" and "who were the good ones?" How could he? He was, after all, as human as the rest of mankind, as it is so ably recorded by endless mountains of black-bound books that testify to the existence of the man from Nazareth. Yet the heads of both nations accused each other to be the evil ones and while the young warriors were sick in their hearts, not just their bodies, they continued to follow orders and went on to commit their idiotic and horrid murders. For four long years a living recruit miraculously replaced any dead soldier.

At school Bertram, Heinrich's best friend, was the son of a well-to-do baker. Each morning, the small, frail looking Jewish boy shared his roll of bread with his friend. It was the only food Heinrich had until dinnertime, which often consisted of a watery soup made edible with a few pieces of onion. The boy, tall and lanky, was constantly hungry as he grew up. If Bertram did not make it to school, Heinrich starved. On his way home after class, he went through trashcans and stood for a long time outside the shop of Bertram's father. Heinrich did not dare to go inside and ask for a piece of bread. He had done it once. But the baker had mentioned his charitable act quite innocently to the boy's father and Heinrich had been cruelly beaten.

"I'll teach you to beg from a Jew," Adolf Tallemann had screamed as he thrashed his small son with a heavy leather belt.

By the time the First World War was over, Heinrich was nine years old, severely malnourished and his lungs had suffered.

In the beginning of the Second World War, Heinrich was twenty-nine years old and he was, though married and father of a child, soon enlisted. Unbelievably, he survived four years of Russia, including Stalingrad. Bashfully trying to hide his tears because they were considered unmanly, he had to leave his friends in Kiev, a starving, middle-class and well-educated family of four. The parents and two daughters in their early twenties had soon started to trust the decent, young German soldier. In spite of the threat of ultimate disciplinary measure for fraternizing with the enemy, Heinrich had often shared his soldier's ration with the four Ukrainians. They had also quickly understood that he took his family responsibilities seriously and helped him to send some of the food he was able to barter home to his wife and daughter.

Just before he was ordered to Stalingrad, Heinrich traded his Leika camera for a medium sized pig. It was slaughtered, cut up and salted. Then the meat was wrapped in many small parcels and over a period of six weeks, to avoid attracting attention of the authorities, his Ukrainian friends forwarded the packages to Monika and Nadine in Germany. Heinrich and his friends in Kiev ate some of the pork but the main share was sent to the soldier's daughter and wife.

As a member of one of the intelligence divisions at the Russian front, Heinrich belonged to the staff of General Haudegen who was in charge of twenty thousand soldiers. At the end of World War Two the haphazard coincidence that he knew Morse code and was part of a general's intimate circle saved his life. The day before the Russian army took over the general's headquarters, he had deciphered a code about their immediate and final attack. That night Heinrich stole a German army truck and, at the risk of his life (a deserter was shot on the spot) urged anyone close to him to jump on it. Eight soldiers and officers, including two young Russian women, came with Heinrich. The small group drove westwards as fast as they could. Being taken prisoner by the Russians meant almost always certain death. If not executed within a short time, German prisoners-of-war were usually deliberately starved in Russian camps. The Russians themselves had very little to eat and passionately hated the Germans, who had killed so many of their people. There were few German prisoners who survived. They had mostly succeeded in staying alive by practicing cannibalism. Even under the worst conditions these young soldiers desperately clung to life; they learned to cut up their dead comrades and eat them before their flesh became frozen or started to rot.

On their long, hazardous flight through Russia, Heinrich and his crew had no papers. This meant that they had to circumnavigate German posts as much as possible. Not being able to identify them-selves, they would have been taken prisoners and shot as deserters. But Heinrich, and the rest of the group of fugitives of whom he was in control, needed food, gas and even had to replace two flat tires for their truck. The team many times defied danger by stealing a tire and gasoline and by driving through German control points without stopping as machine guns were fired at them. At night Heinrich and his companions slept anywhere, often in the terribly cold truck. If they were lucky, they found an abandoned barn or school. After a few days on the run, the refugees in their tattered uniforms started to stink. They had eaten the few loafs of *Kommisbrot* (a dark, firm bread made from rye especially for the German army) and tins of beans, which they had been able to stuff into their *Tornister* (field pack). One of the soldiers even carried a *Tornistersprechfunkgerät* (walkie-talkie) with him, which didn't prove to be of any help. After they had finished their meager provisions, they never knew from where their next meal would come. If they passed a field of beets that had not been completely harvested, they stopped the truck and hastily dug the hard ground with their fingers. Bending as far down as they could, they crept along the black earth and looked anxiously around them as they pushed a few forgotten vegetables into their coat pockets. But they seldom had such luck. It was early spring and anything edible had long been put into Russian cellars or sold to the German army.

The six men and two women were constantly hungry and lightheaded from lack of food. At night they did not have enough blankets to cover themselves. Although they tried to take advantage of each other's body heat by lying as closely together as they could, they were always cold. The truck was hardly any warmer than if they had slept outdoors. But at least they stayed dry from the snow and the long lasting rains that came in March and turned roads into mud beds, making driving almost impossible.

Ljudmila and Sonja, the two Russian women who had escaped with Heinrich, had worked as interpreters for General Haudegen. If they had remained behind, their own people would have hanged them as collaborators. Ljudmila, blond with slender legs, an evocative smile and not yet twenty-five years old, was killed during a shoot-out with German soldiers. Sonja, dark-haired and with a ready smile, survived and at the end of March 1945 she, with the rest of the crew, became a prisoner of the Americans. She was eventually released and returned to Russia. But Heinrich lost track of her whereabouts. When he was unable to get in touch with her, he feared that she was sent to one of Stalin's gulags as penalty for her incredible courage.

"Stalin has murdered far more people than Hitler," Heinrich told his family several times.

The war had ended in May 1945 with the total surrender of Germany. Seven months later Heinrich was released from prison camp and came home. It was Christmas. He was very thin, had lost most of his hair and had a permanently malfunctioning digestive system. His brother, a specialist for stomach and intestines, could not cure him. Monika, Heinrich's wife, was as emaciated as her husband and looked brittle to the point of breaking. But beneath her weak exterior she was determined to relinquish as little as possible of the power she had gained during Heinrich's absence, when she had been forced to become head of their household.

Since Heinrich had seen his father rule his marriage with an iron fist and knew no other model, this meant constant domestic battle between Nadine's parents. It lasted twice as long as the two world wars put together and left both combatants emotionally and morally drained.

Nadine, who was in danger of being crushed between her fighting parents, felt like a duckling on which a huge horse hoof was about to descend. With wings too short and stubby to be of use, she fled screeching under nearby bushes. There she sat for hours and looked at the world, which seemed to consist of little else than oversized, heavy hooves that trampled anything smaller than themselves.

* * *

As a child, Nadine had made up her mind that marriage was not for her. Then, as a young girl during her prolonged stay in England, she was surprised to see for the first time that two married people were able to live with each other peacefully. Even more perplexing was the fact that the English couple at whose home she stayed was still in love with each other, although they had been together for several years and were raising two children, named Elizabeth and Peter. Julie and

James Johnson's wedlock was the first good union between a man and a woman Nadine had ever experienced.

* * *

After the burly and sullen Custom's officer at Dover was finally satisfied that Nadine's papers and belongings were in order, she had taken the train to London. It was late afternoon before she got there. As the train approached the big city with its ponderous name, the young girl could not believe the unending lines of houses, office buildings, shops, factories, bridges, parks and palaces that sprawled outside her window. Mannheim, a 17th century town in which she was raised, had been built according to a carefully laid out plan. Yet London, so much older than Mannheim, seemed to be composed of nothing but a confusion of straggling buildings that had sprung up and grown out of the ground like organic matter. The city, as it unendingly whisked past her, was neither square nor round, long or broad. It was so huge that Mannheim could have easily fit into it several times.

'I can't wait to get a closer look of it,' Nadine thought and smiled to herself.

Neither one of the two children whom she was supposed to look after were at Victoria Station from where James Johnson, their middle-aged father, picked up the German au pair. He quickly told her that he had to go back for a while to the Foreign Office where he worked:

"But I'll drop you off at the Basil Street Hotel for tea. I think you will like the place. And Harrods, the department store, is down the road. I'll fetch you again in an hour."

Before she could thank him, the big man had left her standing in the lobby. The young girl stared after him as his broad back, above which his reddish-brown hair was cut in military fashion, disappeared among the crowd.

"There is no way that I'm going to move from here," Nadine whispered to herself as the waiter put some biscuits, butter and jam in front of her. Intimidated by her novel, elegant surrounding, she did not say a word to the attendant, but her eyes admiringly followed the graceful sweep of his arm as he bent down and poured her some tea. After the waiter left her low table, she took a look at the antique furnishings around her. Then carefully, afraid to break something because her knees were dangerously close to the short-legged tabletop, she leaned back in her velvet armchair. Her roving eye quickly caught peach colored walls that underlined dark mahogany tables and strategically placed cupboards where several flower arrangements had been skillfully aligned. Way above her head crystal chandeliers shed a soft light from the ceiling. And among a dozen hushed voices she distinctly heard faint piano music. The air was filled with the aroma of hot tea, the odor of fruitcakes and, far less pleasant, thick cigarette smoke.

'I can live forever with this,' Nadine thought and feeling pampered, she clutched the one-pound note James Johnson had kindly given her before he left. She threw off her shoes and wriggling her toes, enjoyed touching the thick carpet with her stockinged foot. When he returned to pick her up, she was more than half asleep and wore a happy expression on her face.

"Wake-up, Sleeping Beauty," the Englishman laughed and shook her lightly by the arm. "We have to get back to the station to catch our train."

Once again he picked up her heavy suitcase and Nadine, shouldering her hand luggage, followed him in a daze.

'This man is going to be all right,' she thought as she yawned, politely holding a hand in front of her mouth as her parents had taught her.

Lipsey, aged five, and three-year-old Peter were long in bed after Nadine and James arrived at the tiny village of Groombridge. Located just north of Tunbridge Wells, their ride had taken about an hour as the train steadily went south from London. It was nearly nine o'clock at night before they got to the Johnson's home. Surrounded by wide, well-trimmed lawns, the outlines of the house, though only half visible among tall ash trees and a few beeches, looked lovely even in the dark.

In the comfortable living room, where a large, chintz-patterned couch, a love seat and two matching chairs were arranged in a semi-circle around the fireplace, Julie Johnson had waited for her husband's return. She was impatient to finally meet the young German girl with whom she had corresponded during the past several weeks.

Nadine never forgot the first look Julie gave her as she walked through the front door of the house. Standing in her small foyer where she kissed James and bade Nadine welcome, Julie, for a fraction of a second, simply stared at the young girl. Nadine was sure that she saw, in the Englishwoman's pale-green eyes, astonishment mingle with a sense of jealous apprehensiveness. Julie's look was not merely composed of curiosity. In her forties, tall and dressed in a sweater and full tweed skirt that cleverly emphasized her waist, Julie sized up the German girl. Nadine, in turn, could not help studying her employer's wide mouth, whose edges had started to descend at their farthest corners. Her lips were dabbed with rouge and she had used powder under her eyes to partly conceal the dark rings beneath them. Later Nadine came to like those black, semi circles because they added depth to her face. While the two women scrutinized each other, Julie's mouth opened a little. But she didn't say a word; there was just a slight gasp as if she suddenly needed more air.

'I hope she is not the jealous type,' Nadine thought uneasily and gave the Englishwoman a reassuring smile.

Julie not only observed Nadine's figure closely as she helped her to take off her thick winter coat that had concealed her body, but her look tried to get under the skin of the young girl. It seemed as if the Englishwoman were searching for the secret of her own lost youth. Nadine felt that Julie wanted to know now, this instant, what was in store for her during the following months when the young girl would sleep just a few feet away from her children's bedroom and the master bedroom where Julie and James shared night after night their queen-sized bed.

As the evening came quickly to a close, Julie attempted to hide her suspense under several warm smiles and a stream of words spoken in Oxford English. Yet her impeccable manners did not deceive Nadine. Contrary to the Customs officer at Dover, Nadine understood her well enough although her English was inadequate and she was now very tired from her long trip. She also quickly noticed that for every word James spoke, Julie used ten.

"That's why my wife speaks so much better French than I," James explained, teasing Julie. He had watched the two women as they circled tensely around each other, hiding their anxiety under meaningless words. Kind-hearted as he was, he tried several times to make them feel more relaxed.

* * *

Having spent many years at boarding school, one of the best not only of England, but also of France, Julie Johnson spoke French fluently. Her cooking, too, influenced by her having lived abroad for years, was superior to most English kitchens. Julie and her sister, Sally, were raised in Harrogate where Julie's father, after marrying a wealthy woman, had made a fortune in Leed's steel industry. By her late twenties, and with World War Two still raging, Julie had become an officer in the English Navy. Being assigned to destroyers that accompanied merchant ships, her duties had taken her as far as Hong Kong. James and Julie had met after the war. The couple had married late and moved to East Africa where James had been sent on a three years tour as the First Secretary of the British Embassy in Nairobi. Both of their children were born in Kenya.

James, the son of a general and educated in Eton and Cambridge, was a highly trained professional who took his duties in the diplomatic service seriously. He spoke Swahili, worked hard and was well liked among his peers. He got along better than most of his British colleagues with the native Africans, whether they were Kikuyu, Maasai, Somali or Nandi. Each of these tribes had their own language but Swahili was the *lingua franca* among them. And a large portion of the Africans spoke at least some English. When in 1952 the Kikuyus – who had lived in the *White Highlands* long before European settlers regarded this fertile land as their own – began to take their territory back and Mau Mau terrorized the highlands, there were rumors that James had friends even among these violent warriors. Contrary to other Europeans and Americans, Julie and James' home at the outskirts of Nairobi was never raided.

Large-faced, James's white skin was unevenly streaked with red spots and tiny veins around his nose, chin and forehead. He was a big-boned man and without being fat, his body, deprived of any type of sport except for short walks in a bowler hat and black umbrella on

London's streets, had become heavy. It clung to a chair as if it were made for it. By contrast his wife, in spite of having given birth to two children, had worked hard to keep her figure. Where James spooned up ice cream and cookies, Julie watched her diet, played tennis, swam and took long walks whenever possible. As a result, Julie's body, with her long, firm legs was in better shape than those of quite a few young girls and James, in his quiet, unobtrusive way, was very proud of his wife. It was clear that he was still in love with her. And she with him.

Nadine, who had almost immediately become fond of James, never heard him utter an unnecessary word except when he became engrossed in a special subject. He loved history, especially English history and was a loyal monarchist. Given a chance, he elaborated on Henry VIII, Elizabeth I, Queen Victoria and the British Empire in a witty and informative way that had quickly won Nadine's heart.

Being used to a talkative father, she at first thought that James did not like her because he hardly spoke to her. Only later when he freshened up his German by tutoring her in English, did he reveal his vast reading knowledge, a knowledge that Julie was lacking. Nadine admired his calm intelligence and his behavior that did not discriminate against her. Right from the start, James treated her as an attractive, yet a-sexual and intelligent member of his household. He always behaved correctly toward the pretty girl. Even in the early morning when the house was still quiet and there were just the two of them while Julie slept a little longer and Nadine was on kitchen duty preparing breakfast before James caught his train to London, did he ever make the slightest advances toward her. And Nadine was very grateful for his respect. She knew what it was like to be molested by an employer.

Occasionally, just before James left the house to drive to the train station, Julie appeared in a faded dressing gown at the kitchen door. Standing on tiptoe with the frilly lace hem of her night frock showing under the raised robe, she lifted her pale face up to her husband and kissed him good-by. But she never displayed her affection without a hasty, soul-searching stare at the young German girl as if by simply looking at the au pair she could tell if she had behaved properly. Inwardly, Nadine smiled at Julie's possessiveness.

'Well, that's the price she has to pay for loving her husband,' Nadine reasoned with herself. Being considered a rival evoked at best her sense of humor. She was flattered by it, yet at the same time she was also annoyed.

'She ought to know me better than this,' she angrily reflected before she marched out of the kitchen, leaving Julie and James for a moment longer in each other's arms. Without looking around, she had the strong feeling that Julie would release her husband's neck the moment she was out of sight.

The young girl quickly walked down the hall toward the staircase. Then going upstairs, she took two steps at a time as she headed toward Peter and Lipsey's bedroom, where she helped the children getting dressed.

Although James was a decent and caring person, Nadine did not even consider whether she found him physically appealing. To her he was strictly a father figure. Like an avalanche on a steep, snowy mountaintop, he hung unreachable and threatening above her. Had he showed any amorous intentions, she would have been terrified. As once in the past, she would not have known how to escape the silent masses of snow she watched separating from the mountain and crushing into the valley below, taking her with them. Adultery, from early on, had been painted in the darkest of colors by her father. Innately inclined toward jealously, he did not trust his wife's charms. Again and again he had made sure that Monika Tallemann understood his belief in absolute marital fidelity. She did understand indeed. And annoyed by his possessiveness, she had several times challenged him by quickly mumbling: "you are worse than any sultan", as her eyes flashed greenish-blue with anger.

Yet in spite of James' impeccable behavior, Nadine preferred Julie's company to that of her husband's. For the young girl, women (even big, matronly mother figures) were neither awe inspiring nor threatening. Contrary to men, women spoke the same language all over the world. Julie, who hardly managed a word of German, which she had briefly studied at boarding school, understood Nadine far better than James, although he was well versed in her native tongue. At night, alone and in bed after their bath and after James had used the same water in which his wife had just scrubbed herself because water and electricity were still, after so many years since the war had ended, expensive and not easily accessible, Julie, if she was in the mood, translated some of Nadine's feelings and thoughts to her husband.

The bridge that had once connected Nadine with her father's psyche, hung in threads over an uncrossable abyss, but it still existed between her mother and herself. Julie and Nadine benefited from this maternal/ filial bond. In spite of their age difference and the initial shock Julie experienced over Nadine's unexpected, attractive exterior upon their meeting, the two women became friends within a matter of days. They needed each other. Julie and James did not know many people. By choice, they kept mostly to themselves.

"We had to entertain a great deal while we lived in East Africa," Julie explained. "But whenever we stay in England, and before James is send abroad again for another assignment, I want to enjoy my family as much as I can," she added with a large smile, a smile that almost closed her green shadowed eyes.

* * *

Living an hour south of London and being surrounded by a countryside that sometimes reminded Nadine of one of Corot's bucolic landscapes, the Johnson's met with their friends and acquaintances only during rare cocktail parties. When these festive events did occur, usually once in the spring and fall, the family prepared feverishly at least two days ahead of time for the occasion.

The parties were well organized and then set-up like a play in which each participant had a specific, more or less glamorous, role. Nadine's part was to look as pretty as possible and talk briefly in her still faulty and rather heavily accented English to the guests as she walked, unsure of herself and in a black skirt that was too tight, through the crowded living room. Her only consolation in the midst of a sea of strange faces was the familiar furniture of the room: its chintz sofa, love seat and chairs that were grouped even more picturesquely than usual in front of the fireplace. Julie, if she found the time for it, would come to Nadine's rescue and introduce her to their guests. They, especially middle-aged, happily intoxicated husbands, often graciously replied with:

"Finally we have a chance to meet you; Julie has told us so much about you." Nadine also received compliments from women. Yet the next day she could no longer remember the pleasant words two particular women, on whom she had focused her attention, had issued. But she vividly recalled the outfits of the two ladies. Chatting with each other and carefully holding their cocktail glasses, they had been standing in a corner of the room from where they had eyed her curiously most of the evening. One woman was a vision in red. Her lipstick and long, varnished nails were coordinated with the color of her dress. And when she moved, which she obviously enjoyed doing, her full, round buttocks were provocatively propelled from left to right, while, for a split second at mid-point they quivered as if trying to keep a perfect balance before they reversed their direction and now trembled from right to left. Nadine noticed that most men's eyes, as if they had turned into magnets, were drawn discretely and irresistibly to the woman's elongated back the moment she took two or three steps.

As soon as Nadine, embarrassed and with her face feeling uncomfortably hot, started to speak with their guests, Julie unobtrusively withdrew to the kitchen to make sure that their laboriously manufactured canapés did not run out. Whenever either woman returned to the kitchen after they had carried their heavy silver trays through the teeming first floor of the house, she would tell the hired chef how much everyone enjoyed the hors d'oeuvres. Under an impressive white hat, the shy, young man would proudly, and a little intimidated by the praise, nod his head.

"What an agreeable face the young man has," Julie commented, as her voice no longer sounded as even as in the beginning of the evening. Wine did not agree with her. She quickly became nauseated from it. And the next morning she would suffer from a severe hangover. It was one of the few times when she showed a darker side. Slumped over her dressing table where she attempted to put on make-up with shaky fingers, she would disregard Nadine's attempts to be friendly. Instead, her voice sharply edged, she ordered the young girl to take the kids for an early walk:

"And take your time. I need a nap; my head hurts terribly," she roughly explained to the astonished young girl, who was hurt by Julie's brusque behavior. She had never seen Julie rest during the day before.

While the cocktail party had still been in full swing, James was acting as a bartender. Alcohol had no ill effect on him. On the morning after a rare social event he was as nice as ever.

A little after eight o'clock, and after their guests had dispersed, Julie and Nadine had been left with the unpleasant task of cleaning up. They put the rest of the food away and soon dishes, glasses, cutlery and ashtrays were stacked up high in the kitchen sink. In the morning, Bertha, the daily help, a fat, jolly village woman, who came three times a week and with whom Nadine got along splendidly, would put the house back in order. For now Nadine just superficially straightened out chairs and wiped off tabletops. Her mind was blurry from too many names and faces, which she tried to sort out. And from the wine she had consumed. Now, too late, she regretted that she had not exercised more control. She didn't like the feeling of floating in the middle of things and her stomach hurt from too much food. She decided that cocktail parties were not her cup of tea.

* * *

Julie and James' closest friends lived as far away as the southern coast of Spain. They had their homes on the continent, as Julie was fond of calling the rest of Europe. Several of these old friends occasionally came for short over-night visits. But apart from those guests, the Johnson's did not have many acquaintances. And they did not mingle with the local people of Groombridge, small shop owners, farmers and domestic help.

It was early June when Nan and Jason Gardiner, a couple whom the Johnsons had known in East Africa, spent a few days with them. Only a little while ago the apple blossoms had been in full bloom, wearing their splendid bridal frocks. They had now turned out a multitude of small, new, thin leaves, so shiny that they looked as if someone had put varnish on them and the meadows had become yellow with the last, fading daffodils. The occasion of Jason and Nan's visit was a ladies' garden party at Buckingham Palace. One morning the gold-bordered invitation had arrived in Groombridge encased in a stiff, square, slightly perfumed envelope on which Julie's name and address were embossed with beautiful dark letters. Julie had met Elizabeth II a few years ago at a similar event, and as a teenager she had attended the same boarding school as one of the queen's cousins. According to an age-old royal etiquette, these two incidents gave Julie permission to introduce another woman to the wealthy monarch.

On several warm afternoons before the big event Julie and Nan went upstairs to the guest bedroom, the place they had chosen to familiarize themselves with some of the formal rules required at court.

On one of these occasions Nadine was allowed to follow her employer and her guest to the upper floor. Earlier during the day she had opened the windows of the room, which had one of the best views of the house permitting to look at Julie's rose garden. An elderly peasant had worked long hours on the symmetrically installed, carefully tended rows where the first yellow buds were slowly unfolding and adding a touch of gold to the green foliage. When the wind blew from the right direction, their faint, delicious scent wafted through the entire house. Nadine could never get enough of the flowers' intoxicating odor. Today, too, as she leaned for a moment against an angled window frame, she inhaled the fragrant air with great pleasure. Afterwards, she turned around and watched the two English women who had started to practice their prescribed curtsies.

Julie, who was familiar with the procedure, impersonated the role of the queen. Nan played herself, namely one of many women who were going to be introduced to the young ruler. Again and again she had to stretch out her right arm fairly far forward while, at the same time, she was asked to bend her head and to subtly describe a half circle with her right foot while her left knee, also bent, supported her entire bodily frame. Nadine tried to take Nan's earnest and labored attempts seriously but several times she had to bite her tongue so she wouldn't laugh out loud at the comic figure in front of her. Contrary to Julie's slender and supple body, Nan had put on a considerable amount of weight. Her waist had disappeared and her stomach, even when she took a big breath and tried to pull herself up straight, protruded in a conspicuous manner. Big-breasted, her legs, as they extended under her broad, fat-upholstered hips, seemed far too short. The poor woman looked more like a beer barrel than a ballet dancer whose skills she desperately needed to accomplish the complex curtsy.

Sighing and breaking into a mocking grimace, Nan would try to bend her left knee down far enough so that she would be, as required, below the queen's shoulder. But being a little taller than Julie this was hard to do. Also, in addition to her strenuous effort to complete the ritual, Nan had to smile dreamily. As she did, Julie, the queen, shook hands with her and graciously smiled back at the woman paying homage to her. After half an hour of practice, a thick film of perspiration covered Nan's forehead, the sides of her nose and long dark streaks of sweat ran down her back. She was also completely breathless.

"Oh my dear, I didn't think it would involve such hard work," Nan made a noble attempt to shrug off the tedious exercise that had exhausted her.

"I still seem to confuse my right foot with my left one," she laughed sheepishly. But after Julie had finally released her from bowing and curtsying, her voice was hoarse from the unaccustomed physical and mental effort she had undergone.

"You will do just fine and enjoy meeting the queen. You know that her skin alone is worthwhile being seen from close up. It is a wonder to behold," Julie said admiringly as she commented upon one of the best-known attributes of Elizabeth II.

"Even when you stand next to her, her face is absolutely flawless. And what a thin waist she has!" Julie, as she turned toward a chest of drawers where she started to look for something, continued to sing the young queen's praises:

"I'll never forget those days during World War Two, when she was still an adolescent and drove an ambulance. Then later, in spite of the terrible destruction London suffered because of the relentless German bombings, neither she nor her family ever left the capital for a safer place."

Julie's green eyes were wide open and started to moisten as she recalled the courage of the royal family during the war. Their mingling with the surviving inhabitants in those parts of London that had been hit the worst during an air raid had made Elizabeth II very popular among her subjects.

Julie and Nan were sitting down on one of the beds. As they spoke with each other, Julie clearly saw in her mind's eye Nan standing in the garden of Buckingham Palace. She was one of dozens of well-dressed ladies, all mute and nervous to be introduced to their royal ruler. The women stood patiently in a long waiting line at whose beginning the queen was receiving them. Seen from a distance the ladies, dressed in the required pink and yellow, looked like a hedge of multi-colored roses.

The courtly ritual had to be executed in high heels and in a calf-length evening gown of a pastel color as if to match nature in her summer splendor. Julie's elaborate wide-skirted garment was yellow. It was cut low and showed to its greatest advantage her enticing bosom. The dress made her waist look small and its skirt was so full that it did not allow her to sit comfortably in a chair. It was, of course, rather expensive. But James, who wanted his wife to look her best, never breathed a word that they could ill afford it.

Before the garden party Julie and Nan had gone twice to London to search for the right outfit. The first two dresses, which they had purchased at Bond Street, were not to their liking when they tried them on at home again. Taking once more the train to the big city, the garments were promptly returned and exchanged for more suitable ones. Matching gloves, shoes and handbags had to be gotten as well. And a hat. A big, wide-rimmed one.

Two days before the great event Julie and Nan prayed that it would not rain. If the weather did not cooperate, the party, always held in the open, would be canceled. When the big afternoon finally arrived with clouds and winds but no rain, Julie looked pale in spite of her make-up. Nadine, after she had seen the two women off, stayed in Groombridge.

Had it not been for Lipsey and Peter who demanded her attention, she would have felt like Cinderella left behind after her two older stepsisters had gone to the ball. She certainly had been quite sad as she helped getting Julie and Nan prepare for their final departure to the city. During the last minute, before the two women climbed into a waiting car that would take them to the village station, Nadine took a photo in the garden. It later showed Julie harmoniously merging with the flowerbeds beside her. Her outfit was a perfect mimesis of her surrounding. Shaded by her large hat, which seemed to be part of the landscape, she looked like a huge rose with a human face. Whistler, who as Nadine had been taught, had first broken the iron rule that a background must be of a different color than the figure placed in front of it, would have appreciated Julie's picture. But Peter and Lipsey called it disrespectfully: "Searching for mummy among the bushes..."

Nadine did not see the two women again until the next morning. After the garden party, the curtsey and the queenly handshake, they were staying in town for dinner with their husbands and afterwards a play at one of London's great old theaters.

* * *

Julie and Nadine shared household tasks in the old, rambling and charming house in Groombridge where the oak floor of the bathroom of the master bedroom sloped so dramatically that the far end of the room was almost a foot lower than the one at its opposite side near the door. In the evening, before Nadine gave Lipsey and Peter their bath, the children enjoyed sliding "downhill" in this room where a large window faced the garden.

"Are you sure that such floor will not fall off?" Nadine had asked James one day in her erroneous English. He saw the concern on the young girl's wide-eyed face and laughed:

"This house has been built over four hundred years ago. Its floor, sagging or not, will outlast your and certainly my lifetime." James looked at her kindly while his brown eyes sparkled with mischief. Being less tired than usual, he felt like hugging the lovely girl – nothing but a paternal hug he thought. He liked the German girl who took such good care of his and Julie's offspring.

From that evening on Nadine enjoyed running "downhill" with the children on the grotesquely uneven and extensive bathroom floor as she got her charges ready for their evening bath.

Bertha, the big gregarious peasant woman, who came without fail three times a week to the house cleaned the bathroom the next morning and took care of the rest of the heavy work. At 11:00 am, when she indulged in her break over a cup of tea in the kitchen, she loved to gossip. But she expressed herself in a local dialect, which Nadine for the longest time had trouble understanding. Bertha, who at first had eyed "the German foreigner" suspiciously and, as the former and quite recent enemy, had not spoken to her at all, soon started to call Nadine "my love", or simply "love", an endearment whose meaning Julie had to explain to her. Before long Nadine became very fond of Bertha's loud, hearty laugh, her friendly smile and even her heavy footstep. There was never any doubt that the two women liked each other and that, in spite of their language problem, they had quickly formed a close bond.

Julie was in charge of the kitchen. She guarded jealously that part of the house against Nadine's timid offers to help with her cooking. With a quick smile and an agile shrug of her shoulder, Julie kept the secret of cheese soufflés and steak and kidney pies to herself. Nadine was only allowed to fry fish for James's breakfast at dawn. Their unaccustomed smell so early in the day nauseated her. She felt strongly that fish in the morning was a barbarous custom. With her stomach in her throat she watched James in perpetual amazement as he ate with great gusto the mackerel or sprat, which she had prepared for him. Chewing slowly as if the fish were a delicate morsel, James left a clean plate before he got off for a long day's work in London.

"Fish is one of the healthiest foods that one can eat. You would learn to like it if you tried," he every so often attempted to entice her to taste a small sprat. But the young girl disgustedly shook her head.

"Never! Never! Fish is for you, not me," she occasionally would burst out laughing, with her joyful voice echoing through the house and bringing Julie downstairs to the kitchen door.

* * *

Nadine loved looking after the children and soon treated them as if they had been her own. She dressed and bathed them, threw their clothes into the washing machine, ironed Lipsey's thin cotton blouses and took the kids for their daily walks. At six o'clock in the evening she gave them their tea, let them play for a while and then, chasing them upstairs to their bath and later to their bedroom, where she read them their bedtime stories. After she exhausted Winnie-the-Pooh, Flopsey, Mopsey and Peter Cottontail and wanted to read them other fairy-tales, she encountered Julie's resistance. She did not approve of little girls in red hats and their grandmothers being eaten by wolves. Nor did she like young, rosy-cheeked and ebony-haired ladies with evil stepmothers who had them bite into poisonous apples and afterwards watch them displayed in transparent glass coffins. Most other Grimm's tales were unacceptable as well.

"I do not want my children to have nightmares," Julie explained as her green eyes scraped across Nadine's face. The young girl had been raised without such tender sensitivity for a child's pliable psyche and, at first, was amazed at Julie's concern. But she understood the motherly plea and every night obediently hunted for harmless stories.

In the beginning of Nadine's sojourn in England the children had shown a natural animosity toward the strange young girl. On the morning after her arrival in Groombridge, Lipsey, the five-year-old, fine-boned girl, bending her head and taking a step backward, refused to shake hands with her and Peter had immediately declared open warfare.

The three-year-old boy was sturdy like his father and he had also inherited his soft, hazel eyes, eyes that his mother was fond of calling "naughty eyes". His chocolate-colored eyes dramatically contrasted with his bright blond hair and together with a mouthful of milky-white teeth he was a very handsome child. His maternal gift was a no-nonsense attitude, which, from early on, made him stand up to his older sister. As he watched his sibling being introduced to Nadine, he clung to the railing on top of the staircase that led to the second floor. When his mother tried to coax him downstairs, he stamped repeatedly his short, stubby legs on the floor and shook his head violently back and forth. Getting quickly red in the face, he screamed:

"I don't like her! I'll chop off her head and put her in the dustbin!"

It was his favorite battle cry, which he issued at regular intervals whenever he got upset with Nadine, and during the first few days he got angry at almost any moment. He kept up this fierce resistance for what seemed forever and threw his most fearsome temper tantrums at bedtime or when the young girl tried to put him on his potty after his nap in the afternoon, which always made him cranky. During the first month Julie often had to intervene on his and Nadine's behalf as they tried to get used to each other. Both of them took their fights seriously and emerged several times from them hot-faced and starring at each other with wild, confused eyes. Peter tried to be brave and confronting Nadine with his cheeks on fire, he would kick at her shins with all the strength of a healthy, small boy, lustily yelling his war yelp:

"I hate you, I hate you! Go away! Don't touch me! I'll chop off your head!" During his worst assaults he was often only half dressed. His short shirt exposed his little round bottom without his being in the least aware of his nakedness. As he stood in the middle of the spacious bedroom, which he shared with his sister, he looked funny and adorable in his anger.

If his kicks, usually after Nadine had with considerable difficulty put on his socks and stout walking shoes, missed her legs, she laughed. But if she was not quick enough, her screams mingled with his while she hopped on one leg around the room, holding up the one that had been attacked and would soon show blue-black telltale signs. It took a while before peace, mostly with the help of Julie, who quickly appeared on the scene, was established again.

But then came the day when Peter, who was around the young girl for more hours than he was to his mother, got attached to Nadine. He clung to her first thing in the mornings and at night he didn't want her to leave his bedside until he was fast asleep. He also begged to be carried by her during their hour-long walks, which they took every afternoon, no matter what the weather was like. During those outings when Nadine was not held up by some chores that she had to perform in the house, she felt particularly to close to both children. Soon the three of them had become an inseparable unity.

"Lift me up!" Peter requested when his chubby legs got tired and he could no longer keep up with his sister and Nadine. She then carried him until her back ached. His short, pudgy arms clung to her neck and his legs tried to encircle her waist. She put both of her arms behind her and supported his plump buttocks. Or she would bend over a little so that her hands were able to hold on to his soft-skinned thighs that were spread around her. She had come to love the affectionate boy. After each ten steps they took on deserted country roads or on some small, half-hidden trail, a dusty *viòttola* that led through meadow upon lusciously growing meadow, she called him "my darling", until she realized how jealous his sister had become when she used these words.

At the age of five Lipsey was already too big to be carried. But Nadine tried to compensate for her feelings of neglect by tenderly holding her hand.

"You are the prettiest and most clever little girl I have ever known," the young girl would say and bending down, she gave her a hug.

"Sing us a song," Lipsey usually commanded before they continued their walk through another field. The southern English countryside was stunningly beautiful. Frequent spring rains had turned the landscape into a scale of vivid greens. And by June the weather had become drier and a flora of wild flowers had grown taller than the children. They loved to play hide and seek among the high grass and patches of yellow sunlight that seemed to be everywhere. The earth undulated gently as they moved along on almost invisible footpaths. Except for a narrow road on which a car seldom traveled, there was nothing but green hedges and groups of poplar trees, interrupted by oaks and silver maples that lined the horizon. Occasionally, they encountered a fenced-in piece of grassland. At one end of it, a few black and white cows leisurely grazed along the ground. Their heads hung close over the grass and their long, fleshy tongues rolled around large bushels as they devoured it in one enormous gulp. The fat beasts, saliva dripping in long strings from their jaws, would calmly look at the children and the young girl.

"Cows have no table manners," Lipsey observed and made Nadine laugh.

* * *

Several months later, after Nadine had come back from a trip to Paris, where she had delayed her excursion by one crucial day, the only member of the household who was openly pleased to see her was Peter.

Once more, as she entered the house, he stood on top of the stairs that led to the second floor, but now he shouted with delight as soon as he heard her voice. Then, without waiting for her, he started to descend so fast on his stumpy legs that he would have fallen, had Nadine not rushed toward him and caught him in her arms. Burying her face in his soft, little neck, the young girl cried with joy and relief and did not care that her mascara became a black streak on Peter's silky skin. Repeatedly, she dug her mouth into his cheeks and small, pink ears that made him laugh and was reluctant to let him go.

After a stormy outbreak on Julie's part, the rest of Nadine's English household gave her the silent treatment. It included Lipsey, who was fond of her but sided with her mother.

Nadine had sent a telegram from Paris, where she had visited Hanna Herbert, an old school friend, to let Julie and James know that she would arrive twenty-four hours later than planned. Normally, Nadine's lateness would not have mattered much. But the Johnson's had planned to drive to Cornwall the day after her return from France. And Julie was angry that the family's travels had to be delayed on account of Nadine.

"Who does she think she is to keep four people waiting?" Julie raved after she received Nadine's cable. "We have rented a cottage as of tomorrow, not the day after!" She added, her forehead turning into a row of vertical and horizontal wrinkles.

"It is not such a big thing and the girl has had her first glimpse of Paris," James had tried to calm down his wife. But, of course, he achieved just the opposite.

"You are a fine one to side with our unreliable, irresponsible au pair," Julie threw at her husband, her eyes blazing with exacerbation. "You might as well just take Nadine and the children and I will stay home," she screamed and then started to cry.

On the morning after Nadine's late return from France, which had held up the family's travel plans, a gloomy mood, mainly upheld by Julie, penetrated the house. Even before everyone had climbed into the family's car for their long drive to Cornwall, Julie had let the young girl know that she did not like having her schedule changed. Then, sitting in front of the vehicle next to her husband, her irascible voice had reverberated through the cramped car while James thought it best to remain silent and the children huddled closely to Nadine. Julie's anger started to stretch and pull hard at the mauve ribbon that had been woven during many days and weeks of intimacy between the two women.

* * *

Fortunately, two days later, helped by a sunny and windy beach in Cornwall, Julie and Nadine were friends again. As if nothing had happened, they picked-up their daily routine and endless talks that sometimes continued late into the evening. The velvet cord between them had not broken in spite of Julie's fierce assertion of being the stronger of the two.

Before their trip to Cornwall in July, there had been days in the spring, especially those during which Julie's husband worked late in London, when the lonely Englishwoman had knocked at Nadine's bedroom door after they had both retired for the night. With an unfinished thought on her mind, Julie stood in the doorframe of the darkened room. Nadine, already in bed where she had been reading, faced her silhouette as it was outlined against the light of the hallway, which had gently shaped her figure into a shadowy, ethereal form. In her oval face her eyes and mouth swam vaguely like dark leaves on a pond. Through the open window wafted a fragrant night breeze. No tree branch moved and the birds had fallen asleep. Horizon and sky had vanished. Calmly the two women continued their conversation where they had left off an hour ago. Nadine had propped her pillow against the headboard and her face was hidden by the night as she listened to Julie's softly flowing words, which came straight from the heart. The two women could barely see each other, but their voices effortlessly wound themselves around their sparsely visible bodies held by the dark. Although they never touched each other, they were as intimate as lovers. An hour later, Julie left as quietly as she had come. She did not close the door behind her and for a few moments Nadine's eyes followed her as her thin shape moved silently down the dimly lit hallway. They were closer than sisters.

* * *

Soon after her arrival in England, Nadine had collected a large arsenal of perfectly pronounced English words. She had no trouble understanding their meaning but their spelling remained a mystery to her. The dictionary was of little use. Unlike German and French words that were spelled according to a strict code of pronunciation, which once learned, could be applied to unknown expressions, the verbal announcement of English nouns, verbs and adjectives often differed sharply from their spelling. There were simply too many of them. Even those words that were written the same way but phonetically sounded so different, were so numerous that Nadine often gave up a seemingly hopeless struggle. Julie was indifferent to Nadine's intellectual endeavors. Language interested her only on the most superficial level, as a tool of communication. James tried to come to her rescue in the linguistic jungle upon which she tried to impose some order. He enjoyed Nadine's good mind. Yet he was so engrossed in his work that it was not often when he found the time to assist her.

Perhaps her environment handicapped her specific scholastic efforts, but not a day went by when Nadine didn't learn something from Julie's vast experience in life. There was particularly one area, which the two women would endlessly talk about: The realm of men and their nature, juxtaposed to the role of women. This vast field, in which either one of them quickly got lost, especially Nadine, was of great interest to them. Both of them believed in feminism, feminism in its purest, simplest form: a protest against masculine dominance. Julie, as well as Nadine, had become feminists before they knew what this term meant. The Englishwoman, raised in a wealthy household in Harrogate, Yorkshire, where her father had owned a steel mill in

Leeds, had become a British Navy officer while she was almost still in her teens. She had been integrated into a system in which men on board of her vessel were not just her superiors, but also her equals and even her subordinates. Rank came before sex. At least on a superficial level, with many sailors looking alike because they shared the same uniform. And Nadine's mother had become an independent woman during World War Two, too. Not by choice but by need. The men, who had operated factories, held managerial positions in large companies, driven trucks, buses, trains and streetcars were "at the front". By sheer necessity their wives, fiancées, sisters and grown daughters had to take over their jobs. At first intimidated by their unusual tasks, the women soon learned that men's work was not as difficult as their fathers, brothers and husbands had often claimed. With their new tasks the women gained a new sense of freedom, new insights and they demanded the recognition of females being equal to males.

Feminism was not a new concept. Over two thousand years ago Spartan women had ruled their country while their men fought wars. And there had always been formidable queens, who had no trouble seeing themselves as equals to men, starting perhaps in the 16th century with the well-educated Queen Elizabeth I, who had been preceded by the unfortunate, short-lived reign of Mary I. Later, in the 18th century, only one male, Prussia's king, Frederick the Great, was as influential as the rulers of the rest of Europe. Frederick's biggest rival was powerful Catherine II in Russia, quickly followed by Maria Theresa, who sat on the throne of Hungary and Bohemia and last not least came Madame de Pompadour, better known as Jeanne Antoinette Poisson before she became the lover of Louis XV of France. Through means considered ignoble, if not worse, by her contemporaries, the astute woman had gained more or less openly control of the big kingdom. But all of this was mostly feminism on the highest level. Now, after World War Two, many women, not just the aristocracy, wanted equality. Yet society was not in favor of women. Men had been in control for centuries. They were not inclined to give up their rights or share them with females, who, for so long, had been mostly their servants. Women soon understood that rights were never given. They had to be taken.

James worked long hours and sometimes did not get back from London until shortly before midnight. Julie was not pleased with her husband's endless devotion to work and showed it. The only reason for an infrequent quarrel between husband and wife was over time spent, or rather not spent with the family. Julie, who was far more practical than James, felt that her husband was a dreamer and too methodical and that his work could have been done in half the time he devoted to it. When she was in a bad mood, she accused him of being unable to delegate some of the more menial parts of his labor to his assistants. James knew himself. And for once he did not listen to his wife. Or rather he could not change his compulsive work habits, which made Julie lose her temper. He committed his worst offense when, in addition to catching a late train from London during the week, he would bring work home on weekends. Saturdays and Sundays were reserved for the family. Those were the rules. And Julie expected her husband to follow them. So when on Friday evenings Julie saw that her husband's attaché case bulged more than usual, she got furious and quickly banished him to the attic.

"You didn't bring home any of your nasty papers again?" Julie wanted to know with a rasping voice while her eyes spat fire. Her husband hung his head guiltily and did not say anything. And although he had on the first floor of the house a nice study, he was not allowed to work in it on weekends. With a sigh, but otherwise not uttering a sound, he climbed up the steps to a cold, dusty, overcrowded, perpetually semi-dark attic to work there. During the day he would hardly emerge from his imposed exile except for meals, silently consumed in the dining room, and a brief trip to the bathroom. Sitting under a bare light bulb, which he put on and off by pulling on an attached string, he wrote his reports. During the day, when the young girl went to the second floor and looked up to the opening of the junk room above her, she often saw his large body squeezed into a small chair that wobbled precariously the moment he tried to change his position. As his figure partly protruded from the open trap door of the lumber-room, she was reminded of an oversized doll, which a child had stuffed into a box that was far too small for it.

In this marital battle Nadine was unable to decide whose side she was on. She could not help but admire James' patience, his unwillingness to fight and his good will. Especially when she thought that under similar circumstances her father would have exploded and created an ugly scene. It never occurred to her that James might just be a henpecked husband. She was not used to submissive men. Instead, she sympathized with Julie who had looked forward all week long to her husband's presence in the house during the weekend.

* * *

Julie's anger lasted until Sunday afternoon. It was then when she left the children with James and asked Nadine to come with her on a long, brisk walk.

"I would have preferred James' company, but you'll have to do," she had teased Nadine as the two women went off together. Blond, of medium height and slender, Julie was always conscious of her figure. Now, as she walked energetically next to Nadine, she wore comfortable shoes and, even though it was summer, a long-sleeved cardigan. Nadine was dressed more lightly, particularly in this warm weather. She had put on a thin cotton shirt and skirt and slipped into sandals, which she liked to kick off at the slightest excuse. She was sensitive to heat and, if not careful, suffered from sunstrokes.

In the beginning of her summer afternoon walks with the children, Nadine had, on several occasions, taken off her shoes and walked barefoot. Lipsey and Peter had quickly imitated her. Heinrich Tallemann had impressed upon his daughter that walking barefoot on grassy ground was healthy. Yet once more the young girl was in for a surprise and had to revise her value system. Although she had rebelled against most of her father's ideas, she still assumed naively that they were accepted on a universal level. When Julie did not share Nadine's enthusiasm about bare feet, she thought at first Julie was joking. But Nadine quickly learned that having lived in the tropics, the Englishwoman had become disease conscious and took bare feet seriously. She also did not appreciate her children being seen by the village people without shoes. The peasants did not connect shoeless feet with health, but with poverty.

When Julie and Nadine went for a rare walk together, they would keep along the edges of the lovely, narrow, hilly country roads laced with thick, impenetrable hedges and old chestnut trees, birches and an occasional white pine or shingle oak that add such charm to the landscape of Southern England. But when Nadine took the children on their daily exercise, the three of them strolled often across pathless meadows and fields and once, having climbed over a fence, barely escaped an unfriendly bull that had seemed harmless at a distance. Fortunately neither Julie nor James ever discovered those adventures. Before long Nadine fell thoroughly in love with the English countryside, which set her heart free.

* * *

Next to the Johnson's property in Groombridge was the large, enclosed estate of a wealthy Englishman. He was almost never at home. A bachelor, he spent his winters in St. Moritz and his summers in Cannes or Monte Carlo. While away, the invisible landlord left his mansion and its several acres of land in the hands of three adept gardeners and a housekeeper.

Their never-present neighbor kept a herd of white, tame deer on his grounds. The graceful animals were the first ones of their kind Nadine had ever seen and they exerted a great attraction over her and the children. Every day, the three of them clung to the high fence and observed the deer, as they grazed not far from them under stately chestnut trees and scarlet oaks. One sunny afternoon, the small hoofed animals had retreated to a different part of the park where they could not be spotted by the children or the young girl. Looking at the disappointed faces of her small charges, Nadine quickly suggested playing *"let's search for the white deer"*. She had hardly finished speaking, when she and the children started to run along the enormous fence until they were out of breath. When they still could not find the dear, Lipsey started to cry and wanted to go home. "We will never find the silly, old deer," she wailed and pressed her head on Nadine's hip.

"Oh, yes we will," the young girl said and gently patted the child's head. As she bent down to Lipsey and kissed her on her smoothly shaped skull, a pleasant scent rose from the child's fine hair and tickled her nose. While they slowly returned to the house, she kept her arm around Lipsey's frail shoulders. For once, she ignored Peter's wailing as he trailed along her other side and begged for attention. He was jealous of his small sister and wanted to be carried.

Inspired by castle gardens in France and England, the owner of the park had constructed an oval shaped, dark pond on his huge grounds. On either end of it were two delicately carved Chinese bridges that led across shallow arms of water. At one shore of the dreamy, still water, stepping stones, half hidden by the sweeping branches of weeping willows, invited one to use them.

Although the iron fence surrounding the estate was high and several miles long in circumference, its horizontal bars were spaced widely enough to let a child or slim adult climb through. Nadine had little trouble persuading Peter and Lipsey to squeeze through the barrier together with her and to explore the forbidden territory to their hearts' content.

On a rather cool but light and dry autumn afternoon the three of them had once more climbed through the fence and had slowly approached the small lake. When they got to it without being seen by one of the gardeners, Nadine used for the first, and as it turned out, the last time the stepping-stones. At certain spots delicate patches of chartreuse and rose surrounded the semicircle of the big, square stones that were solidly anchored at the shallow end of the water. And here and there the ivory of dogwood interrupted in several places the recently trimmed lawn that swept down to the edge of the deserted pond. Paradise could not have offered a more enticing slice of nature.

As usual, Nadine, bursting with energy and with her mass of hair windblown, walked in front, followed closely by Lipsey with Peter making up the rear. For Nadine the short watery distance between the smooth stones was just a small leap from one white rock to the next. But for Peter with his short, plump legs it was a different matter. He was the slowest of the three and even then he had a hard time keeping up with his sister and Nadine.

"Don't run so fast," he would complain as he hopped from stone to stone as quickly as he could.

Yet the two girls hardly heard him. They enjoyed themselves too much as they jumped and skipped from stone to slippery stone, hypnotized by the water that lay without a ripple at their feet. A cool sun painted silver circles on the lake's almost black surface. Everything was very quiet and none of the caretakers could be seen. There was only the vague rustling of leaves as the small, exquisite deer grazed not too far from them under several magnificent swamp white oaks.

Peter had not wanted to stay behind while Nadine and his fragile-boned sister whose skin was so white and thin that most of her blue veins were visible on her bare arms and legs, laughed and bounced through the air. For a while the little boy did well. Yet his legs, although strong, were not long enough for one particular leap and he suddenly fell into the cold water. Behind her, Nadine heard a scream followed by a big splash. As she spun around, she could barely see Peter's blond hair emerging from the lake. With a few lurches she reached him, pulled him by his arms and lifted him out of the water. With closed eyes, he shrieked and clung tightly to her, spitting and coughing water. While Nadine held him against her breasts and stomach, she started to run toward the fence.

"Hurry up, Lipsey," she yelled at the little girl who followed upon her heels. Squeezing through the enclosure was easy; but half-way home Nadine got out of breath and had to put Peter, whose weight seemed to have increased ten-fold, down. He was shivering, his lips had turned blue and Nadine was terrified he might catch pneumonia. She picked him up again and walked as fast as she could toward the house. As they got to the front door, she was praying that Julie would not be home. Not seeing her car, Nadine raced silently through the house with Peter still dripping over the floor and various rugs. Lipsey stumbled after them. She did not say a word and was breathing hard too.

Upstairs, in the children's bedroom, the young girl quickly pulled off Peter's wet clothes and rubbed him down until his skin started to glow. As she got him dry and dressed him again, she tickled and hugged him until he giggled and thought it was all a big game. Soon Peter's face was rosy again and Nadine kissed his cheeks and the tip of his tiny nose several times. She was greatly relieved that nothing had happened to him. Lipsey became involved as well in this new sport of undressing and dressing, and within a short time the three of them were once more out of breath. When Julie returned from Tunbridge Wells where she had been shopping, she heard their laughter and wanted to know why everybody was so happy. Nadine quickly put her finger on her mouth and looked at the children beseechingly. Before Julie had finished climbing the staircase, Lipsey said:

"We are just playing, mummy."

Neither Lipsey nor Peter ever spoke of the accident and to the enormous relief of Nadine, the little boy did not even catch a cold. She had sworn the children to secrecy, an old trick she herself had succumbed to several times during her childhood. But then came the day when Lipsey rather innocently, and without mentioning the stepping stone incident, talked about their adventurous climbs through the neighbor's fence. Julie was flabbergasted and she sternly reprimanded Nadine:

"How could you do something like that and teach the children the invasion of other people's property? I thought you had more sense than that! How would you have explained your presence if you had you met one of the gardeners? Don't you have any regard for things that do not belong to you? You cannot just climb fences! They are there for a purpose! I don't believe you actually did such a foolish thing."

Julie went on for several minutes with flashing eyes and waving a towel she had picked up near the hot stove where she was broiling broccoli for dinner. She repeated herself over and over again. It was always a sign of how upset she was. Nadine turned her face and kept it averted. Standing in the middle of the kitchen, she remained silent like a fish, but hung her head guiltily and was glad Julie did not know the worst of their exploit. In her justified rage, the Englishwoman reminded the young girl of her father. Red-faced and shouting he had often enough lost his temper over his daughter's disobedience.

From that day on Nadine no longer dared excursions into their neighbor's solitary park. Passing it daily, it lay there in its lone splendor. The young girl and the children had only fleeting glances of the white deer as they nibbled daintily at the grass while they kept their distance from the forbidden fence. Their delicate heads were bent between their thin legs and it was impossible to see their enormous dark eyes whose velvety depth had attracted Nadine and the children.

* * *

On that Sunday afternoon when James had once more been banished to the attic and his wife told him unceremoniously to keep an eye on the children, Julie and Nadine had gone off by themselves. In low-heeled sport shoes, sneakers were still unheard of, they moved swiftly through the landscape on familiar narrow and slightly hilly roads that were bordered by hedges or by low, crumbling stonewalls and occasionally by entire groups of beeches and ash trees. Breathing deeply, they forgot about time and kept on talking for what must have been well over an hour. They were so engrossed in their conversation that neither one of them had paid attention to where they were going. Suddenly, the two women found themselves in a ravine into which the road had led them imperceptibly. They had never been here before and did not recall how they had gotten there. Looking up in surprise, they found themselves surrounded by steep, high piles of rocks whose tops were covered with pines and copper beeches. As they followed the small, private, asphalted street, it started to curve and lead upward. The farther they went, the more the walls of the pass closed in on them. Within a short while the grass and bushes on both sides of their winding path disappeared, leaving only boulders and unruly growing shrubbery that seemed to form a barrier from which it would have been hard to escape. A setting sun that glowed scarlet before them, as it drowned in the sky, created deep shadows around them. It was early evening but it felt much later. As Julie and Nadine slowly and for once silently went on, the sun completely receded behind the treetops that grew in dark profusion on the summit of the ravine. Not a sound, except for invisible birds and crickets, could be heard. Both women were almost painfully conscious that they were alone in this remote landscape. There was no sign of any human habitation.

For quite a while neither one of them had felt much like speaking. But they kept on walking, pushed by a curiosity that was stronger than an unexplainable feeling of apprehension, if not fear, which had gripped them in an almost physical form. Side by side they marched on without uttering a word. Yet out of the corner of their eyes, they would every so often glance at each other's profile, making sure that they kept very close. Their footsteps made no sounds. And the child in them longed to hold hands to alleviate their nervousness that increased with each stride they took. But they didn't go that far.

Then, seemingly out of nowhere, a mansion emerged from behind the pines. It was large and the shutters of its many windows were closed hard like the stony eyelids of a person who had died. A splendid, red tiled roof leaned against a bluish horizon with nothing beyond it. They had reached the top of the hill. For a moment Nadine and Julie's eyes tried to cling to a focal point. But the land, which spread before them, looked as if the world had suddenly become flat again with an abyss lurking where the crust of the earth was breaking off abruptly. Shrubbery, which bore traces that it had once been carefully shaped into round and oval forms, extended their branches everywhere in wild, offensive disorder. And hedges that closed off one part of the extensive grounds had begun to look like impenetrable undergrowth. It was as still as a churchyard. No odor arouse from the abandoned flowerbeds that spread in front of the big house. Both women realized that no one lived in this place.

When only a large lawn, which needed desperately to be taken care of, separated them from the main, vaulted entrance, which had been built to accommodate a carriage, the two women even stopped their occasional whispers. Then, without needing to look at each other, they turned around together as if they were obeying an inaudible command and walked quickly back to the road from where they had come. A shiver ran down the young girl's neck. Unable to perspire because of malfunctioning sweat glands, she felt her hands had got clammy and for a moment she had difficulty breathing.

After the enormous, abandoned home had once more disappeared behind the old fir trees as if it had been swallowed by the ravine, Julie said, matter-of-factly, but still sotto voce:

"I have heard that the place is haunted."

"You don't mean it," Nadine said and was not sure if she should laugh or cry.

"Yes I do. I remember now hearing about it some time ago. Village gossip has it that this great house belonged to a wealthy man who had made his money in the shipping trade. But greed made him turn to crime. He would load the vessels, which he heavily insured, with worthless merchandise. Then he made sure that the ships sank at high sea. Yet after a few years, he paid for his crime. The peasants claim that the drowned sailors came to harass him in his lovely home on the hill where he lived by himself. Even Bertha, our daily help, told me that night after night, the ghosts howled throughout the mansion. Of course, I didn't believe her. But now, seeing this mansion, I'm sorry I laughed at the woman. She also told me that except for an old, deaf gardener who had been with the family throughout his life, all the other servants fled. They were too frightened by nightly ghosts to remain in spite of unusually high pay. Rumor has it that the owner became mad before he suddenly died and that he left no heirs. The estate has been abandoned for a long time. Nobody wants to buy it although one can have it for a song." Julie looked at Nadine and, her hand trembling a little, she brushed a strand of hair behind her ears.

The young girl did not believe in apparitions. She considered them figments of the imagination and she was convinced that, at best, spirits appeared in dreams or in the minds of insane people. With the innocent eagerness of youth that has to put into words almost every thought passing through one's head, she defended her opinion against those who challenged it. Yet neither she nor Julie ever went back to see the ship owner's abandoned house again. For a while, they constantly talked about it. And for some time the eeriness that had surrounded the strange estate captivated their leisure moments. At those instants, bizarre and intimidating sensations spilled forth from Nadine's memory banks as if a drawer were no longer shut tightly.

* * *

Nadine worked six days a week. She loved her job. The one thing she didn't like was having to get up at 6:00 am to cook James' breakfast. Being still mostly a late blooming teenager she loved to stay up at night and sleep late in the morning. But it was only on weekends when she was allowed to stay an hour longer in bed. At 7:00 am Lipsey and Peter were wide-awake, wanted to get dressed and have their cereal.

One day a week, usually a Wednesday or Thursday, was the young girl's day off. She used her freedom to explore places she had so far only heard of such as Brighton, Eastbourne, Margate, Ramsgate or Hastings. She would have liked to visit every seaport of Southern England. But after her first day trip to London, it was this city that kept her under its spell. Its unceasing allure drew her forth from Groombridge like a groundhog on a bright spring day.

Yet before Nadine explored London, she went to Brighton. It was on a late, cool summer morning when the air was brisk and the promise of sunshine penetrated even the darkest corners of the pleasant old house. The night before Nadine left, Julie, with maternal concern, had explained how the trains worked, what the young girl should see and eat and then wished her a good trip. In the morning Nadine slept a little longer, savoring every minute she did not have to get up, while light dreams spun her into a sensuous cocoon. After she finally pushed off her blanket and sat at the edge of her bed, she yawned voluptuously and looked at her outstretched legs and feet whose toes, which seemed as long as fingers, she wriggled. She felt great and was looking forward to her excursion. Then, before she dressed in one of her more expensive, bright outfits, she threw her raincoat over her nightgown and marched down the hall to take a bath. She felt as if she not only owned the slowly awakening house but half of England as well. Fractions of Christian's face, her childhood sweetheart whom she had left back in Germany, floated through her mind. There was particularly his mouth, his full lips and part of his nose, which haunted her this morning. For a moment or two she seemed to feel the tingling sensation of her hand when it was held in his large palm. Their hands fitted so well. Letting the warm water run into the tub, she enjoyed his long fingers that squeezed hers gently as, not too long ago, they had walked through some of Mannheim's crowded streets.

"You are the prettiest girl in the city," Christian would say when he noticed the curious glances of passers-by, men and women alike. The two of them were slowly marching across the *Planken*, Mannheim's

short, colorful Champs Élysées. And, happy in his possessive owner-
ship, he pressed her hand a little harder.

"You are not so bad looking either," she teased him as she brushed
her head against his wide shoulders. His head, even when she wore
high heels, always loomed way above her own, although at 5' 7" she
was not considered short.

Nadine took time putting on make-up, which Julie approved of as
little as Heinrich Tallemann had.

"You really look far prettier without all that color on your face,"
Julie had said once or twice before she realized that Nadine did not
believe her.

Through her closed door Nadine heard Lipsey and Peter running up
and down the stairs while Julie told them to keep their voices down.

"You are going to wake-up Nadine. It is her day off. Be quiet, you
two!" The young girl smiled and put on her only pair of high-heeled
shoes. During a last minute impulse she had wisely stuffed her walking shoes into her large linen bag. In it she also carried a camera, her
make-up pouch, a slim book of German poetry and a sandwich that
she had made the night before. Her allowance was small and most of it
she would have to spend on train-fare today.

It was ten o'clock when she closed the creaky garden gate behind
her and set hastily forth on the narrow, dusty village road. She was late
and had to run for her train. What Julie had neglected to mention,
or what Nadine did not pay attention to was how, or rather when, to
return to the tiny village of Groombridge. Julie had forgotten to warn
her not to miss the last train out of Brighton.

Lurching forward, Nadine walked as fast as she could on
Groombridge's still empty main-street that led to the train station.
Getting out of breath, she glanced with sparkling eyes at some cottages,
a small store and several farm houses to her right and left. She was
happy to explore the world beyond the vicinity of the village. While
still close to the house she had, without turning her head, the distinct
feeling that Julie watched her as she stood behind the white curtains of
her bedroom. Yet Julie's sisterly solicitude did not prevent Nadine from
making several mistakes. The worst was that in the evening she missed
the last train back to Groombridge. Feeling greatly embarrassed, she

had to call Julie and let her know that she would have to spend the night at Brighton's train station (she had no money for a hotel room) and arrive only with the first train in the morning.

Nadine saw Brighton just once. But she never forgot the day she spent there. Months later, as she looked back on this first excursion on her own in a foreign country in whose language she got entangled like a young spider in its first net, she realized something: England with its southern seaports and London that kept her captive each time she set a foot on its soot encroached pavements was becoming part of the patch work that eventually, so she hoped, would turn into the soft, multicolored quilt of her life. England metamorphosed into an important slice of her psychic landscape. It became almost as important as Germany.

Occasionally this quilt would become heavy with rain and fog and stiff from snow, which could quickly turn to ice. Her patchwork then changed into a horse's blanket that scratched her and threatened to suffocate her rather than keep her warm. But one day she realized that she was deeply in love with the old, sophisticated island whose invisible borders stretched as far as India and Africa. It was an uneasy love because she thought that her affection for England meant a betrayal of Germany. Several times, as she took Lipsey and Peter on their extended, daily walks, she would reflect about this until one afternoon she plucked up enough courage to speak to Julie about her predicament.

"How can I love the English and not betray the Germans?" she asked Julie as she shook her curls and her large, brown eyes tried to keep focused on Julie's face. The Englishwoman smiled at the young girl:

"I thought you detested Germany. Didn't you tell me several times how much you condemn the horrors she committed during World War II?"

"That's true," Nadine admitted. "But I have also come to admire her beauty and courage," she added with an edge of defiance in her voice.

"Well, you see," Julie calmly added, "the way you love and hate Germany in one breath, in the same manner you are able to feel close to two countries at once. Having become fond of England does not mean that you are disloyal to Germany. Unlike a Western marriage where we favor monogamy, a person is able to love two countries at the same time."

Julie looked at Nadine. She knew the French, whose country she had visited many times, far better than the Germans. But this young girl of whom she had at first been a little jealous, became more and more a friend of hers. She enjoyed Nadine's openness, intelligence and her sometimes wild and absurd imagination. But most of all she loved her for the sake of her children who every day grew fonder of Nadine.

* * *

Her day in Brighton turned out to be almost cloudless. She had her first glimpse of the sea as she walked through one of the city's narrow and surprisingly hilly streets. At one point, as she stood still on top of a slope and looked down, the ocean seemed to be attached to the small road and its modest homes in yellow, white and red that stretched below her feet. It was as if the glistening surface of the water had turned into an oversized painting that someone had put up in a dead end street to create a special effect. But when the young girl slowly descended the hill and actually got to the first buildings of town near the ocean, the sea and its promenade along the wide, well-kept shore seemed to have considerably extended into the distance. It took her almost another hour to actually walk past one large beach hotel after another. Across a wide throughway the attractive accommodations faced the ocean in one line as if someone had tightened them up in an unending string of colorful beads. Nadine longingly glanced through the elaborate, rotating, brass-enhanced glass doors of the spacious hotels. She would have loved to enter one of them so she could admire its elegant lobby, but she was intimidated by a usually tall, bored looking, smartly uni-formed, potbellied, middle-aged doorman who was invariably posted at the entrance of the building.

Julie had briefly told Nadine that Brighton was an ancient settle-ment, which had evolved into a health resort during the 18th century, before George IV, while he was still Prince of Wales, turned it into a fashionable resort. Apparently the Prince Regent, after his first visit in 1783, often went to this sea town where he built the Royal Pavilion, an extensive palace of oriental splendor. But Julie didn't mention that this prince, who ruled England from 1820 to 1830, had quite a few flaws. Even as a young man of twenty he was already stout and a compulsive spender of cosmetic items, usually reserved for women, such as "... cold cream and almond paste, perfumed almond powder and scented bags, lavender water, rose, water, elder flower water, jasmine pomatum and orange pomatum,..."[1] From early on he had several mistresses, the actress Mary Robinson and Maria Fitzherbert, a lovely Catholic widow among them, before he married Caroline of Brunswick, his German cousin. It was a legal arrangement to get him out of debt. During his wedding night in 1795, he was severely intoxicated and "collapsed into the bedroom grate and remained there till dawn."[2] Eating and drinking unusually large amounts, he gained so much weight that he became the focal point of witty writers, sometimes with rather severe consequences. In 1812 Leigh Hunt, a poet, was condemned to spent two years in prison for having called the Prince Regent a 'fat Adonis of fifty'. Byron also poked fun at him in a short poem, but got away with it. Jane Austen was far more serious and ambitious enough to dedicate her novel, *Emma* to him. In 1822 when George IV went to Edinburgh, Walter Scott was flattered by his visit and welcomed him in person to his kingdom of Scotland. Even during the king's last weeks of life in the spring 1830, when he was an invalid who stayed in bed most of the day, his appetite was not diminished. On an early April morning his breakfast consisted of two pigeons and three beefsteaks. He consumed those together with "three parts of a Bottle of Mozelle, a Glass of Dry Champagne, two Glasses of Port & a Glass of Brandy!"[3]

Blinking into a bright sun that hung above the sea, Nadine walked along the oceanfront and then entered the West Pier and the Palace Pier. Seen from a distance both bulky constructions stretched like a narrow, dark, man-made peninsula on salt-eaten stilts into the gray-green water. At first too vain to take off her high heels, her feet eventually got so sore that she was glad she had taken a pair of flat shoes with her.

---

[1] Elizabeth Longford, *The Oxford Book of Royal Anecdotes*

[2] Ibid

[3] Elizabeth Longford, *The Oxford Book of Royal Anecdotes*

For a long time she leaned against the railings of the piers looking down at the swaying surface of the sea. Her eyes enjoyed following the gentle breakers that tirelessly overran the beach. She loved their unending, white-foamed dance and deeply inhaled the sea breeze, which blew into her face and mussed her hair. Walking out into the ocean on wet, slippery wooden boards, she pressed her nose against the windows of small shops that had been built on the piers. Their displayed content was out of reach for her tiny purse. And when she passed tables and chairs that were humid from the sea's spray, she watched thin, old men idly sitting in the sun, sipping tea and young mothers whose toddlers held on to their skirts and exposed knees with pudgy fingers. It was a happy scene.

Leaving the piers behind her like big, elongated vessels, solidly anchored at port, she passed the Dome where once the royal stables had been. Afterwards she stood for a while in front of the aquarium, which Julie had urged her to see. But when she studied the entrance prices, she decided that she rather wanted to save her money for a movie and a sweet treat for which she always craved. During World War Two and several years afterwards chocolate, bonbons, cookies and cakes had been an unknown luxury for most German children. When a friendly but unknown young American soldier had offered her her first stick of gum, she, not knowing what it was but liking its sweet taste, had slowly eaten it bit by bit. Nobody had told her that she had to chew a stick of gum.

Unhurriedly, since she did not have any plans, she let herself drift with the crowd again until she felt utterly caught by its sights, sounds and various smells. She loved the tangy odor of the sea that spread across the city and she relished looking at small private galleries, fountains, sculptures, cafés, pubs and bars all of which were covered in a buttery afternoon light. And she could not get enough of the unknown men, women and children, many of them seemingly day-trippers like herself, who moved around her in a steady rhythm, in a great dance. When she got hungry, she took out her sandwich and, continuing to walk, she devoured it. Then, ignoring Julie's well-meant advice to get hold of a salad or a soup, she bought some chocolates and she ate most of these, too, as she went on exploring Brighton.

In the late afternoon, she counted her money and when she realized that she still had enough, she bought a ticket for the just released film, *Guys and Dolls* whose main attraction was the young, highly seductive and distinctly macho Marlon Brando.

It had not been hard to choose one of the large, well-kept movie theaters. But she didn't know until she described the place to Julie that she had entered the Duke of York's Picture House, which had been in operation since September 1910. The theater was not crowded and with several unconscious sighs she settled herself on a luxuriously upholstered seat. And even if she had not already fallen in love with the gifted American actor's raspy, nasal and sensuous voice, this movie would have been the time and place for it.

As she listened to his dubbed voice vocalizing in his bravado style "Luck be a lady tonight," she thought again and again: 'How handsome and clever he is, and he can even sing.' She hated the end of the movie when the lights were switched on and she saw nothing but a big, gray screen on which black letters moved too fast to be read and where a moment ago Brando's beauty and talent had enthralled her for nearly two hours.

After the film was over, it was getting dark and not even thinking that she might miss her last train back to Groombridge, she looked for a place that offered dancing at night. She ate the rest of her Cadbury chocolates, not paying attention to her conscience, which told her with every delicious morsel that her gluttony was bad for her.

"You'll get fat," Julie had teased the young girl more than once when she had watched her putting a handful of black and red liquorices in her mouth and chomped down on them as if she were famished.

"Your teeth and liver will not appreciate this unaccustomed diet," the Englishwoman had added with a soft smile. But Nadine did not listen to her. She felt great with the sweet taste in her mouth and the sugar rush that followed it.

She found a public bathroom where she renewed her make-up and, although her feet still hurt, she put her high-heels back on. She would rather suffer than not adhere to an aesthetic concept in which vain young European women had believed for several centuries. Combing her hair as she looked into the mirror, she recalled that 17th century female Parisian aristocrats – who still embodied the most sophisticated dress code for her – would not have been caught dead in low-heeled shoes at one of Louis XIV command performances in Versailles. Why, even the sun king himself welcomed a heel on his delicate satin slippers. Dressed from curly wig to toe in silver and blue, his favorite colors, his high heels allowed him to show to their greatest advantage his elegantly shaped calves and ankles.

Louis XIV's authoritative image reminded Nadine of her father and as she left the quiet ladies room where she once more glanced at herself, she remembered that shoes with a high heel were in rebellious opposition to the puritanical concepts of Heinrich Tallemann. He had wished for his daughter to look prim and *anständig*. The part of her that faced the world and was exposed to the judgment of others was his constant worry. A look into his daughter's mind was usually too troublesome for him and he rarely wanted to know what she thought. This had been particularly the case when her performance at school was at stake. He wanted results and cared little how she achieved them. And she fared worse when she attempted to reveal her feelings to him. He did not know what to do with them. He was not able to handle his daughter's inner worlds. He did not do too well with his own sentiments. Sensing this, Nadine had almost no emotional affinity with her father's nature. When she was alone, she ridiculed and rejected his tradition-bound outlook on life and the power with which he enforced his beliefs upon her. She hated his dress code. For her to dress decently was synonymous with dressing dully. When it came to fashion, she preferred the flamboyant to the subtle. She adored high, thin-heeled shoes and at her most daring moments she would even put on black fishnet stockings, self-conscious that in her father's eyes those two items symbolized the ultimate depravity: a slippery descent into prostitution. Immature and searching impatiently for her identity, the easiest way to express her individuality was through lipstick, mascara, hairdos and clothes. She didn't need to say anything. She just had to wear a poisonous green or strident red dress as if she were carrying a flag into battle, a highly visible focal point for the enemy, to enrage her father. Too unsure of herself, she overrode his advice and, following her instincts, she expressed them through make-up, hairstyles and fashion. The more she looked like a low-class working girl or a harlot, the more she felt that her rebellion against parental restrictions was successful.

* * *

When the young girl first stepped into the blazingly lit dancehall in Brighton near the seashore to which she had returned, she didn't like it at all. Nor was she happy about the few young men and women who were assembled there. The hall was so big that it could have easily contained a thousand dancers. It was far too large for her taste and didn't have the graceful proportions of the *Rosengarten* in Mannheim to which she compared it. Chandeliers and soft table lights were absent and many couples didn't seem to have paid any attention to the way they had dressed for the occasion. Ill at ease, getting tired and completely deserted by any assertive spirit, Nadine looked about her as she leaned against a wall next to the entrance door, her route of escape. In the midst of about two hundred dance enthusiasts, she had never felt so lonely.

The distance between herself clinging on to the wall and the rest of the room was filled with seemingly uncouth strangers. Noticing by the way she was clothed that she was a newcomer, bystanders looked her up and down quite openly and none of the men displayed a trace of the gentleman-like behavior for which the English were known.

'How can they be so rude?' Nadine thought angrily and stared back at the small group of dancers close to her. For once being inconsistent in her sudden fear of the strange crowd surrounding her, she wished that she had worn one of the colorless dresses in which her father believed. All defiance of tradition had suddenly left her as she moved even closer to the protective wall so that she could touch it with her bare shoulders. The wall and the entrance door close to it were her only solace.

Trying to escape her own awkwardness, she fastened her eyes upon the opposite wall at the farthest end of the hall. There, the crowd had lost its hostile distinctiveness and the dancing men and women just seemed part of an ornamental play, or even a painting. She was mercifully removed from this tableau by the large space, which the floor, walls and ceiling created around her. After a while, shifting from one foot to the other, she drifted off into her own thoughts. It was then when the loud music took on more subtle tones and the floor in front of her filled more and more with a thousand dots of colors into which faces and bodies dissolved. Before long she felt as if part of her were suspended above the room. Suddenly quite at ease, she appeared to be looking down from the ceiling of the sparsely lighted hall with its dark, unpleasant corners. Floating upon cushions of air, she saw below herself her other self whom she had left leaning against the wall. And she was surprised how small and vulnerable she looked.

"As if I were made of glass", she mumbled, entranced. Then she noticed that some dancers beneath her stirred dreamlike and rather elegantly through the enormous room while others jumped about in staccato movements like puppets on a string. But none of them caused any sound.

'How funny they look,' she mused again, having lost her nervousness. Yet her self-imposed hypnotic state did not last long. As soon as the music stopped and she could no longer feel its rhythmic vibrations, which had helped her to escape, she found herself all at once down on earth again and having lost her lofty seat, she finally started to move through the huge, uninviting and half empty room.

"This place is big enough for elephants to dance in," she thought contemptuously. In Germany she was used to small intimate dance places. Nightclubs had to pay taxes on each foot of dance space, so their owners kept the dance floors as confined as possible.

She was too shy to talk with some of the young women, who, seeing that she was not one of them, eyed her with coldness. Feeling under a bad spell, Nadine wandered about aimlessly and soon got bored and uncomfortable. Whenever the music stopped, her high heels started to reverberate on the floor of the enormous, shapeless hall. Then, once more, the noise of her own shoes made her self-conscious. Unseeingly, she looked into many faces that had no meaning for her and she wished with all her heart that Christian were here, her German beau, who played the trumpet as no other man she knew was able to. He was her friend, the one who listened to even her most awkward remarks. He had been bitterly disappointed when she told him that she was going to England and for several weeks he had tried hard to change her mind. But he soon discovered that she became sharp and silent when he attempted to dissuade her from leaving Germany. And he, who was so much taller and stronger than she, was then afraid that she would hurt him.

On a rainy evening when they had said their tearful good-byes, he gave her the silver mouthpiece of his trumpet, his most priceless possession. Wrapped in their coats, they had stood close to each other in the gloomy train station of Mannheim, surrounded by suitcases, rushing strangers, blaring loudspeakers and train whistles. Mute and too intimidated to kiss in front of everyone, their eyes had clung to the other's face, trying to drink from it as if it had turned into a chalice filled with wine. With her hand in her coat pocket, she fingered his mouthpiece and knew it was his heart that had turned into a dead, phallic shape. She kept it, polishing it when the silver turned black, until the day she was killed.

* * *

Just as Nadine had decided to leave Brighton's unwelcoming dancehall, which she should have done to catch her last train for Groombridge, a medium-sized, slender man, who seemed somewhat older than the rest of the dancers, approached her. Later she thought that he must have been lured by the dreamy, soft expression of her face while she envisioned Christian. Lightly, almost frail, he stood in front of her and spoke in a low voice, the way one speaks to a sleepwalker who balances at the edge of a rooftop. The young girl looked at him with wide eyes but saw him only vaguely as if he were standing behind a transparent curtain. All she was painfully aware of was Christian who, as he receded into the background, started to disperse like flower pollen, which the wind carries away on invisible wings.

The stranger introduced himself as Arthur Wellington.

"No connections with *the Iron Duke*", he smiled quickly when he saw Nadine's inquisitive look. He had a rather ordinary, light-skinned face in which only his small, sensuous nose was attractive. His eyes were deep set and partly hidden behind glasses and bushy eyebrows that were out of place. He looked at her calmly and she imagined that his eyes held some mystery, some unknown depth that might be worth-while exploring. But in no way did he resemble Christian.

Arthur's speech was impeccable. So were his manners and, as she noticed only much later, his clothes. Carefully, even gently, as if Nadine had been made of glass, he led her to the dance floor whose gigantic proportions were "fit for a herd of elephants", she exclaimed as she followed the Englishman to the middle of the room. Yet now, as she moved next to her new admirer and quickly felt secure in his solicitous behavior, the hall seemed to have shrunk a little. The tune of Glen Miller's *Moonlight Serenade* fell pleasantly on their ears. As Nadine bent her head slightly toward the shoulder of the polite stranger, she closed her eyes and tried to imagine that Christian was holding her. But she soon gave up the idea. Arthur was smaller and frailer and did not have Christian's smile, his scent or his muscles. He did not smell, or move, like him. And when she impatiently opened her eyes, she was angry and disappointed that Arthur wasn't Christian at all. Like a toddler who, for an instant, confuses a stranger with a parent, she almost burst into tears.

After their dance Arthur invited the young girl for a drink. They walked to a partition of the ballroom and sat down at a small table – away from the now wildly playing band and the dancers who threw their arms and legs precariously into the air and against each other. Unhurriedly, the two strangers sized each other up and began to talk. Before Arthur said anything else he told Nadine that he was in his mid-thirties – which was ancient as far as she was concerned. But she couldn't help being impressed with his sincerity.

"Oh, so you are honest man," she burst out laughing and suddenly felt at ease in his company. "Like my father," she had almost added, but caught herself in time, not wanting to make the pleasant Englishman older than he was.

The next hour went by quickly. Arthur knew how to narrate a story, especially his own. And before long he told Nadine that he was an offi-cer in the British army and had traveled widely, including several trips to India. He had lived in New Delhi and Bombay and spoke calmly about the splendor and squalor of these two large oriental cities whose very names excited Nadine's imagination. Not handsome, Arthur was sensitive and considerate and not once said a wrong word to the young girl. Nadine listened more than she talked. This was usually a sign that she was interested in the person. Yet in the center of her curiosity where she felt safe, she was also quite intimidated by the newness of the situation. She smiled a little too often and as she played with the stem of the glass of wine in front of her, she stared silently at her long, pink nails, losing track of the conversation. Under the table, she whipped one of her heels and constantly crossed and uncrossed her legs. She was fidgety like a schoolgirl who was called into the principal's office.

When she listened to someone intensely, it was not so much as to an individual. Instead, the man or woman in front of her would often quickly turn into a symbol that stood for a class, a race, a moral value, or an aesthetic appeal. If after a first encounter with a stranger, someone had asked her what the person looked like or what clothes he or she had worn, she would have had a hard time explaining his exterior. Yet she knew with an uncanny certainty, which surprised herself, how that person had reacted during a crisis in his life and what his aspirations were. This was particularly so if she shared some of those characteristics with the outsider.

Arthur and Nadine did not dance again. They conversed for about an hour before she remembered that she had to get back to Groombridge. When she suddenly realized how late it was, Arthur called the waiter and gallantly offered to accompany her to the train station. Yet to Nadine's dismay, they discovered as soon as they got there that she had missed her last train from Brighton almost two hours ago.

"I am so stupid," she cried and looked at Arthur as if he were to blame for her carelessness.

"Julie will now worry that something has happened to me. How dumb can I be?" she reproached herself.

Arthur once more kindly came to her rescue. He suggested that he should telephone Julie and explain to her what happened.

"Thank you so much," Nadine accepted with great relief. She was afraid that Julie would be quite upset with her and even over the phone would make a scene. Yet with a stranger she was more likely to keep her temper.

After Arthur had spoken with Julie, he smiled at the young girl who had stood nearby and simply said:

"She seems to be awfully nice. Everything is fine."

Then he took the young girl back to town and offered to pay for a hotel room. But Nadine, not trusting her English enough, nor Arthur, to ensure that the room would just be for herself, refused. She had not a penny left and announced that she would spend the night in the waiting room of the train station:

"It will be quite fine. Place is dry and safe. I can read night and rest till morning," she tried to assure her new friend in her faulty English. But Arthur did not want to hear about that and in spite of having to report early for duty the next morning, he decided to drive her to Groombridge.

"It will be fun to enjoy your company a little longer," he said gallantly. Nadine, who saw that his mind was set, shrugged her shoulder and still feeling quite foolish got into his vehicle.

It was a two-hour car ride from Brighton to Groombridge. As they drove through the dark, narrow country roads of the Southern English landscape, where streetlights were an unknown entity, they spoke more about each other's hopes and dreams. By the time they reached Groombridge, Nadine felt almost completely at ease with the English officer. She started to trust him like someone she had known for a long time. Looking at his hands, which he kept on the steering wheel, Nadine noticed that they were beautiful. His slender fingers were covered with a thin, white skin that even in the dim light of the car clearly showed four bony knuckles on each hand.

When they finally stopped in front of Julie's home, Arthur got nothing for his trouble except a light hug and the quickly given promise that she would see him again. It was a pledge Nadine promptly broke although he called her several times from Brighton and Julie kept saying how pleasant and well educated he sounded:

"This man comes from a good family and he seems genuinely interested in you. You might want to take a second look at him."

But Nadine had started to go to London. Arthur soon slipped from her mind like a coin from a torn coat pocket. Not even his shadowy outline remained. Yet at certain moments when she walked by herself in the big city, or lay in bed at night and could not fall asleep, or when she felt alone in the midst of a loud, boring party, he once in a while unexpectedly stepped forward as if he had been a paper knight, which she had cut out and put into a forgotten book. His brief, spectral reappearances across a crowded room or in the middle of the street had a consoling effect on her that was combined with a vague sense of longing and loss. Floating in front of her inner eye, Arthur became a melody whose meaning she had once understood. He was one of the few men in her young life who, during a brief encounter, had helped her to understand herself a little better. And, perhaps more importantly, he had managed to eliminate some of her fears of the unknown male. Imperceptibly, his strange, ghostlike appearances helped her to change her negative concept – deeply engraved during childhood – of the male prototype. Although she never met him again, she did not forget his generosity, his articulated speech and behavior of an educated man and his ability to focus on someone outside of his own sphere, on someone so different from himself. Few people, as she was about to learn, were able to do that.

* * *

Two months after her adventure in Brighton and between her frequent trips to London, the young girl went once more back to the sea. But she did not go to Brighton, which was too far for the bike ride she decided to take. Instead, on yet another sunny, warm morning Nadine climbed on an old, black bicycle that Julie had lent her and went to Hastings, another one of the many seaports at the southeastern English coast. At least on the map Hastings had seemed closer to her starting point, namely Tunbridge Wells, the most adjacent town to Groombridge, than Brighton. Yet, as it turned out, Hastings was just as far as Brighton.

"Be careful, the handbrake is broken," Julie admonished Nadine when she waved good-bye to her. Nadine, as she started pedaling along the country road with her head turned backwards, returned Julie's kind gesture. On her back she carried a knapsack with sandwiches, the inevitable camera and a change of clothes in case she would run into one of the sudden English downpours.

Friends and family in Germany had warned her about the proverbial bad weather in England. But after she got there, she discovered that this was not true. After she had lived with the Johnsons for the first three months, she saw that the British Isles had at least as many sunny days as Germany. Besides she liked London's fog, which seemed to heighten her sense of smell and sound. The heavy mist added such mystery to a street corner and enhanced, sometimes to a frightening degree, the sudden appearance of passers-by. Sometimes, when she was in the big city just before sunset, she felt as if she were invited to participate in the great hunt with Mowgli and his brothers, the gray Indian wolves. On a miserable, foggy day in London she walked like someone on another star inhabited by aliens. The dense mist prevented her from distinguishing anyone who approached her until she met him or her almost nose to nose. At those occasions both parties often broke into a small, startled cry of surprise or a nervous, little laugh before they floated past each other and their outlines dissolved once more in the milky mist. For a while she listened to the sound of footsteps that receded into invisible streets and alleys. During these fleeting encounters she felt as if neither one of them actually existed. They were ghosts from different planets. And her sense of fear was overpowered by her sense of wonder and puzzled admiration. She had not yet heard of Jack the Ripper.

Pedaling hard on her bike, Nadine went straight south from Groombridge through Kent's dark-green, hilly, tree-rich landscape, which spread in its cultivated splendor around her. She took delight in every cow she watched as the bovine stood large-eyed on a long, narrow meadow, which was encircled by hedges. She had quickly passed Tunbridge Wells, Hartfield, Lamberhurst and even Crowborough. But then it took her much longer than she had anticipated before she entered East Sussex. She did not stop at the historic Hastings battleground because she had seen too many current ones. Eventually, well past Ninfield, she reached the port of Hastings. Her ride had taken several hours. It included a brief stop in the grass for lunch a few feet off the road and afterwards a short, leisurely stretch in the sun. Yet every muscle in her calves hurt when she finally began to push her bike along the seashore. She had made no plans. She was simply filled with the blind confidence of a young, inquisitive girl bursting with energy, sore leg muscles or not. And at a moment's notice she was ready for some eventful encounter.

For a while she stood still, again mesmerized by the sea that stretched endlessly at her feet. As before, she was drawn to its frothy breakers, which incessantly approached and withdrew from the sand like the heartbeat of a giant creature. And as always, she was enticed by the magic line far out where water and an evening sky seemed to melt in a mysterious embrace. It was getting too late for a swim in the ocean. She had to be content dragging her bike along the beach. Then she got hungry and searched for a small shop. There was none near the shore. Only screeching seagulls swooped down and searched for tiny crabs in the receding surf. But from a distance broken wafts of melodies were carried to her. She quickly recognized them as the old, familiar sounds of a carnival. Forgetting that she was tired and hungry, the child in her awoke and she excitedly followed the notes of music riding on the wind.

Soon she reached a few scattered houses at the outskirts of Hastings and started to walk down the middle of a crowded path that was flanked on both sides with shacks and merry-go-rounds. The noise was over-whelming. It came from red and silver flashing gondolas, which circled above her head and from small, gleaming cars on a fenced-in platform whose drivers tried eagerly to jostle each other out of the way. There were the incessant shouts from street vendors, performing Gypsies and a hundred idle strollers who laughed and called out to each other. The sweet odors of cotton candy, ice cream and pastries mingled with the pungent ones of sausages and meats. And, in between, floated the irre-sistible smell of freshly baked rolls. Nadine's stomach started to crave food in earnest. The music, alluring from far, had now become stri-dent. Every moment announcers who tried to snare spectators into their hastily erected shacks and tents now interrupted the antiquated songs. Loud-voiced carnival people in tattered clothes and unwashed faces would praise the charms of a bearded woman with the body of a snake, a huge, three-headed man, or small, naked headhunters from the jungle of the Amazon River, all fiercely painted from head to toe.

Relying more on her nose than eyes, Nadine found herself in front of a sausage stand and placed her order. When she did not receive a confirmation, and while being jostled from behind by other hungry customers, she looked up and was instantly caught by a pair of blue eyes and a smile that seemed to poke fun at her. Mouth and eyes belonged to a head of blond curls set between two wide shoulders. And although she knew she had never seen the tall, young man before, he looked familiar.

'I must have dreamed him up when I admired Praxiteles's *Hermes carrying Dionysus*,' she thought. Then she blushed as she remembered the Attic artist who had caught such explicitly perfect proportions in marble and light. To call the sausage vendor handsome would have been an understatement. Her legs felt suddenly rather heavy and she became conscious of her wind-tousled hair that clung to her hot face. Smiling impertinently, the sausage man repeated her order by imitating her accent.

Then he asked: "Where are you from?" Once more his eyes flashed over her face and body, as he tried to take in as much as possible of the girl in front of him.

"From a place you do not know."

Nadine's answer shot forth as if someone had pushed the button of an automat. Her cheekbones became scarlet and she felt humiliated and angry. The vendor shrugged his shoulders, turned around and filled more calls for sausages and sauerkraut. Yet the moment he was free, he returned to where the young girl stood looking at him. Like a small sun, his face shone quite a bit above her, made brilliant by white teeth and a glaring, boisterous smile. His eyes were set wide apart and luminous. Thick, dark lashes underlined his blue irises and brown brows formed symmetrical arches above his eyes, as if someone had penciled them in. And, as if this were possible, a light tan seemed to render his flawless skin even smoother.

While Nadine was completely taken aback by the young man's stunning beauty and showed it with every breath she took, the sausage man was not. But when he handed her a hot dog, he attempted to touch her hand. Nadine withdrew her fingers from him as if he had tried to burn her. An instant later the forward pushing crowd had swallowed her up.

"A dark-haired German and pretty too," the young vendor chuckled loud enough for Nadine to hear. Once more her face began to burn. Even her ears turned red. Unperturbed, the young man rang up another request for sausages.

No longer hungry, Nadine squeezed her food in her hand and, pushing her bike next to her, she wandered aimlessly about. She looked searchingly at the unfamiliar faces around her and became conscious that it was slowly getting dark. She shivered and thought she should put on her sweater. But she did not bother to take it out of her backpack. Holding on to the handlebar of her bicycle, she did not pay attention where she was going and no longer apologized if she ran into someone. After some time, as if pulled by a magnet, she found herself once more in front of the white and green sausage stand. Here immediately, another large, ironic smile, the smile of a battle-proven conqueror, greeted her. Then, before she could say anything, and before she had time to feel embarrassed or angry with herself, above the heads of hungry buyers came the words:

"I'll get off in an hour - can you wait that long?"

Nadine did not say anything but in spite of herself she nodded her head and once more her face flushed in a deep red. About an hour later she was back at the sausage stand.

The waiting had been terrible. She felt guilty of having let herself be picked-up by a stranger, handsome or not, like a streetwalker. Thrusting through the crowd, she could not understand why she defied every rule of her upbringing. She thought again and again of her father who would be terribly upset by her behavior. Then she realized that if she were to meet the sausage man, she would be getting home too late. The doors of Julie's house would be locked and the garden with its lovely rose beds and soft lawns would look dark and strange in the night. But it was all in vain. Even the recollection of Christian whose name she whispered several times, as if she were able to call forth his protection, did not help. On the contrary, there was a certain resemblance between Christian's tallness and the height of the sausage man that confused her even more. For a moment she wished desperately to be held by Christian's familiar arms and to put her head against his warm shoulder.

Yet not a trace of Christian was left as the young Englishman strode next to her while a faint sea breeze encircled both of them in a wide, limitless caress. There was nothing but air under Nadine's feet. Removed from any memory and suddenly freed from every worry and fear, she seemed to float a few inches above the solid ground. It was as if she had been reborn. She was sure that in her present state of mind she would have been able to walk on water. Her heart sang and for a moment, as she hovered in the air, she felt as if she had – snakelike – shed an old skin.

"I am Andrew Gibson. What's your name?"

The sausage man had hastily introduced himself before he took the clumsy, heavy bike out of Nadine's hands and started to push it. They walked along a small dirt road that ran parallel to the ocean. But Nadine no longer saw the sea's surface over which the sun, as it made ready to drown its glowing roundness, threw its last reddish rays. All she was conscious of were Andrew's forearms under whose tanned skin, a ribbon of muscles and tendons moved to a rhythm of their own. Every nerve ending of hers responded to their dance as if called upon by a voice, older and stronger than her own. Barely looking at him, she was keenly aware of the provocative undulation of his hips. And there were his lips, too. Every so often, those lips widened into a smile and then slowly relaxing, they became full and round again, ready to be eaten like a ripe fruit. If there had not been a certain cockiness about Andrew, which she intensely disliked, she would have completely lost her senses. It was bad enough as it was.

Trying to keep up with Andrew's long strides, which raised the sand around his feet, Nadine did not know where she was, or where she was going. If someone had asked her what she was doing, she would have said she was strolling in a garden with the seashore at one side and wooded hills at the other. This was Eden – if it ever existed.

Eden apparently had its voice too. Although they were the only walkers at the dry, dusty beach road where the shadows of the descending night grew longer, she was sure she heard whispers. They seemed to come from every dune, embellished with multiple yellow tassels of hard grass, which the two young people passed. At first being thoroughly distracted by Andrew's all-absorbing presence, she was unable to distinguish the words that surrounded her in ceaseless murmurs. When she finally did, she was appalled at the ludicrous but persistent meaning of the mumbling that pursued her.

'I must be going mad,' she thought and nervously looked at Andrew. But he continued to talk and smile at her as if nothing in particular were happening.

'Thank heaven, he does not seem to have any idea what is going through my mind,' she mused. Yet again and again she actually heard the same impossible, disturbingly weird words:

"He must not touch you below the waist."

Even in her lovesick delirium and while she seemed to ride high and bodiless next to Andrew, only pinned to the ground by the sheer force of his eyes, she finally understood that the strange whispers did not come from an exterior source but from her own head. With relief she realized that she simply had remembered the advice, which Julie had given her several times.

* * *

It had not been Nadine's parents who had explained to their daughter the moral codes of love or the secret of bees and birds. Instead, it was Julie, the gentle Englishwoman in her tweed skirts and flat brown shoes, which she wore almost every day, who had alleviated some of Nadine's sexual fears. Julie did not know anything about Nadine's childhood except for some almost inaudible sentences the girl had brought forth once in a while, or had – in an emotional outburst – spit up like small, flat, sharp-edged stones.

As she had talked to Julie, hastily and shamefully, Nadine's confessions had been made at random. They followed no logical structure. Her mind simply conjured forgotten images and patterns that did not make sense to her. But Julie had listened intently. Then one day the Englishwoman had talked about sexual behavior among adolescents according to the way she herself had been brought up. Slowly, Julie had put a certain amount of order into the chaotic worlds of Nadine that were at once colorful and repellent. Even Nadine's mother, to whom she was much closer than to her father, had not explained to her daughter the strange secret that hovered ghostlike but persistent around sex. When sex took concrete forms during a mother/daughter talk, it quickly turned into something Nadine perceived as unpleasant and even violent, something a woman submitted to and shared with animals.

When Monika Tallemann discovered that her daughter was becoming involved with Jean Kaiser, Christian's slightly older rival, she had said:

"If you get pregnant, your father will force you to marry your lover. No matter who it is."

Mother and daughter had stood in their living room in Mannheim, which was crowded with furniture that needed more space. The room belonged to a house that had been burned down during the war and rebuilt. It was far smaller than their old home and Monika Tallemann did not like it. While the two women talked, Monika had tried to look into her daughter's face. But Nadine kept her head bent low, hiding a guilt she could not name. The girl's back was half turned away from her mother and only when she twitched lightly with her shoulder, did Monika know that her daughter had heard her. She had said no more, for which Nadine was grateful, but she did not explain to her daughter how to protect herself from an unwanted pregnancy. Nothing concerning sex was ever approached in a meaningful manner. To a teenager like Nadine, it was one of the world's best-kept secrets. While she had to listen to endless parental lectures about almost everything under the sun, no words came forth about sex and if she shyly, driven by curiosity dared to approach the taboo topic, her questions were not encouraged. Or rather, both, her mother and father pretended that they didn't understand her desire to be informed about sex. It was easier to flee from the uncomfortable subject than to explain matters. But total obedience to parental commands, proper behavior inside and outside the house and the correct form of speech were preached almost every day. Especially by Heinrich Tallemann:

"I want my daughter to behave properly," he said sternly as he towered above her. What he meant was highly restricted sexual behavior. Yet he could not get the dreaded adjective across his lips and vainly hoped that Nadine would comprehend the meaning of his words. But she didn't. How could she? Sex was the ultimate and most feared terra incognita, a childhood country filled with disgusting ghosts who mercilessly clung to her.

Even for Monika Tallemann when she had her daughter to herself, an explanation about sex was too bothersome. Nadine thought, of course, that there was no protection when one made love. She took her mother's warning as a threat that punishment followed pleasure. As if there had been a lot of pleasure! For Nadine there had been quite a bit of pain, highly mixed emotions and soiled bed sheets. Sex, she decided, was at best like the heat of a fire during a cold night where she could only warm herself by almost touching the flames. If she faced the blaze, her back froze and if she turned around, she had to rub her nose and forehead to keep them warm. When she had been little, a man had held her hands against a hot stove. Her screams were his pleasure. The way her small body wriggled against his, trying to break away, gave him an orgasm.

During her adolescence Nadine's father had said nothing at all about sex. But when she became sixteen and on the rare evenings when she was allowed to go to a dance, he did not rest until she was home again. Awake, he lay next to his wife, sleepless at the thought that his daughter might indulge in sex. Monika Tallemann was not plagued by such fears. She soundly slept at her husband's side. Her breath came lightly and innocently like a child's. In the low glimmer of the night lamp Heinrich needed to read, her blond head was partly mirrored in the shiny, mahogany board of their bed. If Nadine went half an hour beyond the early curfew her father had imposed upon her he, after her return, made an ugly scene. Every sentence of his was filled with innuendos about her potential sexual misbehavior. Heinrich's verbal castigation against which she was defenseless could last for over an hour. Afterwards she was invariably grounded, confined to a house arrest, often lasting up to two weeks, which was an eternity for her age.

When Nadine became nineteen and Heinrich Tallemann under-stood that he could no longer keep his daughter in his ivory tower and she was on her way to England, his last words before she left were:

"Remember if you have too many dates, the children you look after will suffer and their parents are going to worry that you bring home diseases. Special diseases."

Her father still had not dared to say "sexual diseases". But in Nadine's mind, after she had listened to his warnings often enough and was aware of his fear beneath it, a kiss started to become synonymous with syphilis. Sex without marriage was something infinitely lascivious – not only physically, which was terrible enough – but mostly morally. Intercourse that was not sanctified by wedlock was a pact a young girl made with Mephistopheles. She was selling her soul. She became an outcast not just in this world but also in the next. A fate worse than death awaited her.

Nadine, having been part of her parents' painful marital example most of her life, quite early made up her mind that marriage was not for her. And she knew that she would always feel dirty when it came to sex. When she was five years old, her father's best friend had made sure of that. Ever since then even on a good day she had felt that she was destined to live between two chairs, between two worlds, ostracized by all good, god-fearing citizens. To minimize this bleak future, the mentioning of sex remained the biggest taboo among the three family members. Between father and daughter it was shunned with a religious fear. It was almost as if incest were beckoning in the background. Too narrowly bound within her own narcissistic circle, Nadine, while still living at home, was unable to see that her father, too, was a victim of obsolete sexual laws. The old commandments, delivered to him by his parents, had grown into his flesh like a ring that can no longer be removed from a finger, which had become too fat. Imprisoned, he could only pass on his point of view; but beyond the bars of his cell he was not able to see more than a fraction of his bleak environment.

It was Julie who taught Nadine that a kiss was innocent. It was a sign of affection carried forward from infancy. And with luck a kiss later in life developed into one of its most precious gifts. A kiss had multiple meanings. For Julie a kiss was something close to poetry, sensuous in its own right but confined to the upper bodily sphere of mouth and tongue. A kiss, she said, was a perfume offered to an individual in an intoxicating moment. Where the rest of the body was concerned, Julie shrugged her shoulders and laughed:

"As long as hands do not walk south across the borderline of the waist, no mortal sin is committed."

But even after the wise Englishwoman had enlightened Nadine, her tongue still walked cautiously among teeth, gums and the narrow, pink staircase that led toward the throat of a young man to whom she was drawn. And she remained fully alert during love play; like a rabbit she was always ready to jump and run.

* * *

Andrew did not live far from the grounds where the carnival had temporarily been set up. His house was a well-kept brick home, painted white and three stories high. He shared it with his widowed mother. Mrs. Gibson was almost as tall as her son, with even blonder hair, and she had the same dazzling smile. When Nadine met her in their large living room, she was dressed with care as if she expected guests or had just come back from visiting friends. Her tightly fitting, knee-length skirt and matching jacket emphasized her still youthful figure. Although in Nadine's eyes anyone over thirty-five was ancient, she thought that Mrs. Gibson was very attractive. For a moment she gave Andrew's mother an intense, wide-eyed stare, recognizing her as her fiercest rival. Then her eyes went back to her son's face. But while Nadine still felt scrutinized by Mrs. Gibson, she imagined, for no apparent reason, what Andrew might be like as a middle-aged man. And she saw that even with dozens of wrinkles around his eyes and with two deep vertical lines between his eyebrows and a chin line that no longer resembled chiseled marble, he would not lose his devastating looks. Her sausage man was a perfect. Even Apollo would have been jealous.

Mrs. Gibson's husband had been killed during the war and Andrew was her only child, home from college during a semester break. After the three had talked for some time – "now, tell me, my dear, where are you from and what are you doing here?" – Nadine was invited for dinner and then, as it was getting late, to stay overnight.

"You can't ride your bike back home in the dark. You'll only get hurt. You can sleep in the guest bedroom." Mrs. Gibson, who had apparently taken a liking to the young girl, broadly smiled at her.

"You are too kind, Mrs. Gibson. But I do not want to impose upon you." Nadine put forth in her best English as she blushed. She was all too aware that she used a trite form of politeness, which expressed the opposite of what she wanted to do: To spend more time with Andrew.

Mrs. Gibson seemed to be able to look through Nadine as if her heart had been made of glass. Yet she smiled again and said tactfully:

"Oh, don't be silly, my girl. I insist that you stay."

There was once more the inevitable phone call to Julie in Groombridge. And to Nadine's relief, Andrew's mother, pushed by curiosity, offered to undertake it.

"Mrs. Johnson sounds lovely, my dear, you are lucky to have found someone like her," Mrs. Gibson's face beamed with satisfaction when she came off the phone.

Nadine laughed and nodded her head in complete agreement. Later at night, after Andrew left the house for a short while, Mrs. Gibson came up to Nadine. She suddenly stood so close to her that Nadine was tempted to count each one of her eyelashes, all of which were thickly embedded in mascara:

"I don't quite know how to say this without hurting you", Mrs. Gibson started out.

"So I will be blunt. Andrew has a fiancée. It is the girl next door. They have grown up together and have known each other since they were that small." Her hand pointed to about three feet above the ground.

"I wanted you to know this because I like you and can see that you are greatly taken by my son. Quite a few women are, my dear. And not only young ones."

Mrs. Gibson produced another brilliant smile, which exposed most of her teeth and looked at Nadine with unabashed motherly pride. Her genes would survive her. Nadine was sure that she saw her hand-some son as some type of insurance for immortality, but only after she approved of the proper female of her choice. Andrew was her main weapon against Nadine's youth and against her glowing face, which Mrs. Gibson, in spite of her elegance and her worldliness, no longer possessed.

The two women once more stared at each other. But victory belonged to Mrs. Gibson. Down to earth and shrewd she had quickly detected how vulnerable the naïve girl was, and she was not someone who would give a rival any advantage. The girl next door was a familiar entity with which she had dealt most of her life. But the German girl was another matter. She had to be handled quickly and bluntly, as she had done more or less successfully with other unsuitable women, young and middle-aged, who had been competing for her son's love.

The room was so quiet that Nadine could hear Mrs. Gibson's breath. Then, so suddenly that the Englishwoman got startled, the young girl spun around and ran to a window that faced the ocean. Standing still, she saw nothing in the darkness. Only far out the faint light of a passing vessel blinked like a star.

"What a lovely view you must have during the day," Nadine, forcing her voice to be calm, said quietly. But she kept her back turned toward Andrew's mother, looking at the black sea. Tears she didn't want to be seen streaked down her face.

That was the end of Nadine's sausage man. Except when his mother had finally gone to bed, the living room soon started to become unbearably hot, so intense was their necking. The young girl knew that she would never see Andrew again and clung fiercely to him. Eventually matters became intolerable with their arms and legs entwined in such a way that from time to time neither one of them could distinguish any longer to whom their limbs belonged. Yet in spite of their desire, most of their clothes were still clinging to their bodies. Each time Andrew tried to raise Nadine's skirt above her knees, she heard the whispers again:

"No straying below the waist." And the stiffness between Andrew's legs suddenly became uncomfortable, if not threatening. With more strength than she thought she was capable of, she pushed Andrew's hands out of the way and sat up straight. He was apparently not accustomed to resistance and did not like the restraint Nadine put on him. His voice was hoarse when he sulkingly complained:

"Why don't you let me touch you? You might like it, you know." Even in the almost completely dark room, Nadine felt that he was smiling sarcastically.

"You don't know anything about me," she said. "And don't confuse me with your girlfriend," she added angrily. She felt the vibrations of his stomach as he chuckled:

"So you are jealous, my sweet one."

"No, I am not and I am not your sweetheart. So don't call me that," Nadine loudly retorted.

Neither one of them moved or spoke for a while. But they stayed close to each other and before long Andrew's hand once more caressed the girl's back. Through her thin blouse she felt his fingertips with their short nails move lightly up and down. Nadine's mouth became soft and they started to kiss again. Yet it was not like before.

In the subtleness of his voice and in his half murmured sounds that fondled her as much as his hands and lips, she now heard anger and a threat:

"If mother were not home, I would rape you."

Nadine had not learned the English word for "rape" yet but she knew it expressed a serious and distasteful meaning because shortly after he had hissed it, Andrew abruptly pushed himself off the couch and left her. He quickly walked out of the barely lit room. As she watched him with her heart thumping, his hardly visible silhouette moved through the open door. He vanished without leaving a trace. For a moment Nadine felt as if the sea and air were not what they were before. The water in which she had floated no longer carried her. She slowly started to sink. Had she not known how to hold her breath for a long time, she would have drowned. She wanted to drown.

It was impossible for her now to spend the night in Hastings. She quickly collected her shoes and cardigan and went back downstairs, hoping the front door would not be locked. It wasn't and she sneaked out quietly. Her bike was still leaning against the wall where Andrew had left it.

The ride back to Julie's house in Groombridge was a very long one. And how she remembered the road home was not clear to her. But she did. It was four o'clock in the morning before she reached the small village again. Emotionally and physically exhausted she fell into bed as if she would never get up again. She wanted to sleep forever.

The following day after breakfast and after Lipsey and Peter had been left in her charge, Nadine, still numb from lack of sleep, went into James' study and looked up the word "rape". When she deciphered its implication, she started to cry and then, as she grasped for a straw to get her through the day, she remembered, out of nowhere, the story of Daphne and Apollo. She soon watched as before her eyes, Daphne's outstretched arms changed into the black branches of a tree. And for the first time she thought that she understood Daphne's refusal to submit to Apollo, the luckless son of Zeus.

'Well, it was his fate to be turned down by the women he pursued,' Nadine thought heartlessly.

'Look at what happened to him and his haste to seduce Cassandra,' she kept up her mute monologue.

Yet she could not understand why Andrew wanted to rape her when he had just been with his fiancée, who lived next door. Was he that spoiled? Did he have so little will power to rein-in his testosterone urges? In her great sorrow she thought that Andrew's beautiful exterior was similar to a tree where just below the surface of the bark insects, caterpillars and maggots squirmed in an unending circle. And she began to cry again. She saw, perhaps for the first time clearly, that an attractive exterior was not necessarily synonymous with goodness. It was a hard lesson for her. Without being fully aware of it yet, beauty had made life bearable for her. She needed it to survive - although she began to understand that harmony and symmetry were part of the painted veil of which the philosopher/poet had spoken so eloquently.

III

London

The day before Nadine went to London, she excitedly announced to Julie, the words tumbling helter-skelter from her mouth, that tomorrow she would "drive the train to the city". Not bothering with any idiomatic expression, she had translated verbatim from German into English. Only when Julie laughed and said that she did not know Nadine was an engineer, did the young girl who suddenly saw herself sporting a mustache and a black-rimmed cap, realize her mistake.

Wearing a white apron over her dress, Julie stood in her large kitchen where a row of windows above the sink and stove provided ample light even during the shortening days of autumn. She was putting the finishing touches on a cheese soufflé, one of Nadine's favorite dishes.

"Next time you boil one, may I watch you?" Nadine asked Julie, unaware that she had used the wrong verb.

"You don't boil a soufflé, you bake it," the Englishwoman spontaneously corrected her.

"Thank you", the young girl smiled broadly as she looked Julie fully in the face. She was surprised at her own request. At home in Germany, she had avoided the kitchen whenever possible. Cooking was not an art in which she was interested. But Julie made no secret of how much she enjoyed preparing meals and since she had become Nadine's role model in almost every aspect of life, her enthusiasm was contagious. But before suppertime, which contrary to German custom was the big meal of the day, the kitchen usually became off limits for everyone.

"Don't pester me now, darling," she even told Peter when her small son was in urgent need of his mother.

"Go and ask Nadine," Julie said and with one elbow softly pushed her offspring toward the door before she wiped her fingers, covered with flour and butter, on a towel. Peter pouted, thrust a strand of hair off his forehead and with his big brown eyes looked accusingly at his adored mother whom he hated at this instant.

"You've got such naughty eyes," Julie said fondly and bent over the open oven door. For a moment Peter watched his mother's backside and then marched reluctantly out of the kitchen, his short, strong legs stamping the floor.

"Nadine, Nadine," he called out angrily and ran down the long hallway. As he passed a small, elegant mahogany table of which his mother was particularly fond, he gave it a hard kick before he continued his search for the young girl.

Nadine was not treated any differently from Peter when she, being puzzled by something, entered the kitchen just before their evening meal. Julie, flushed with cheerful, nervous excitement, would invariably tell her: "Let's wait until we sit at the table..."

The kitchen was the Englishwoman's kingdom and she defended it against any intruder. Only Bertha, the "daily help", who washed the dishes and cleaned the stove before she took out the ashes of the fireplaces in the living room and dining room, was allowed there at the crucial times. Julie's possessive behavior intrigued Nadine.

'There must be more fun to cooking than I assumed', she reflected as she went back upstairs to a pile of laundered children's clothes that needed ironing. Back in Mannheim, her mother had usually made it sound as if preparing a meal was but a burdensome duty and Nadine had taken up her attitude. Yet under Julie's tutelage, the young girl was slowly changing her mind. And not just about cooking.

* * *

Before Nadine started to explore London, she had pictured it as Charles Dickens's mid-nineteenth century city, including the terrifying Marshalsea prison that haunts many pages of *Little Dorrit*. For the young girl London had not just been an abstract, geographic spot on the map. Devouring Dickens when she was in her early teens, she had a good idea what the rat and flea-infested garrets of London were like, especially those described in *Oliver Twist*. Long before she was ever able to lay eyes on the great city, she had run up and down decrepit,

wooden staircases and together with Oliver had been hiding fearfully
in dark corners as both of their hearts beat so loudly that she was sure
their pursuers would hear them. When she had sat next to him in the
dark, bare dining hall of the orphanage, she had watched his blushing
face and blond curls as some of the other hungry, restlessly lingering
boys goaded Oliver into asking for more porridge. And only by a hair's
breath did she escape the same caning he got. But watching him, she
felt the cuts meted out by an excessively cruel arm as if they were falling on her own thighs and buttocks. And she hated the abusive man,
who was in control of several dozen small, thin, hungry orphans, who
wide-eyed were cowering over dirty, rough wooden tables.

"He is nothing more than a fully-grown, hairy animal with a low-
browed, apish head," she whispered. And she remained transfixed by
horror, listening to the terrible swishing sound of the cane descending
on Oliver's exposed bottom where thick, red welts started to rise. Her
fear outweighed pain.

Before the beating stopped, she woke up with a scream, half suf-
focated under the bedcovers she had pulled over her head. After this
type of a nightmare she forced herself to stay awake for as long as
possible. She was afraid that the same subhuman figure that had, just
before waking her up, aroused an unexplainable, not unpleasant feeling in her, would continue his torture as soon as she closed her eyes
again. The image of Oliver, being severely beaten, haunted her again
and again. Sometimes, when she dwelled upon the scene with her eyes
wide open, pain and humiliation, now only imagined, induced some
kind of excitement, which endlessly confused her and of which she
was, again without knowing why, immediately ashamed. Even after
she had become an adolescent and sexually mature, she did not dare
to speak with someone about those daydreams. She thought that there
was something very wrong with her and that it would be better to
sweep her dirty secrets and bothersome anxieties under the carpet.

Her image of London had also been reinforced by drawings and
engravings from Holbein and Van Dyck, the two foreign artists who
had been imported to England and whose copied work she had found
in her father's library. Long before she had set foot into the city, it
had become familiar to her by also studying the paintings of Hogarth

and Blake, and she greatly admired Gainsborough. His incomparable shades of blue rendered such beauty to the portrait of an ordinary 18th century boy of the upper classes. Later, as she became more interested in art books and started to go to museums, she added Turner's seascapes to Gainsborough's landscapes. And, of course, Francis Bacon fascinated her. His vivid pictures, on which he had left his mark of ghastly fantasy, mercilessly fed her mind.

Yet Nadine loved London best as the mysterious medieval city it once was. Her father had shown her rare illustrations of it. With no difficulty she saw herself walking through its twisted, narrow streets, which frightened her. On both sides of a dark, winding road, houses had been built so closely that their rooftops seemed to reach across the lane when, standing below, she looked up at them. Some of these old structures reminded her of large-coiffed housewives who stuck their heads together while they gossiped with each other in sharp whispers. Looking at her father's books, she learned that Saint Paul's Cathedral and Westminster Abbey had risen out of this immense confusion of densely clustered buildings. But that, she soon discovered, had not happened until after 1666 when London was burned down during the Great Fire, as it was called, a fire that lasted for five interminable, ghastly days and cost the lives of thousands.

Weeks before her departure from Germany, she had wanted to walk across London Bridge, one of the city's most famous landmarks. Somewhere she had read that until 1750 it was the only bridge that spanned the Thames. Not being able to fall quickly asleep at night ever since she knew that she would actually be allowed to go to England, she saw herself move slowly through the Tower of London with its ancient White Tower where poor Anne Boleyn and her brother – accused by Henry VIII of having an incestuous affair – were beheaded. She had often thought that Anne's husband had grown too quickly into a fat, over-dressed bully who burped unashamedly and fed his hunting dogs at table. But she liked the good taste Henry displayed in music and admired his audacity to defy the Catholic Church. Her father's books also taught her that this ambitious king had not wanted England's wealth going to Rome. Prejudiced by Protestantism, the faith in which she had been raised as a child, Nadine approved of Henry's decision to keep the English gold on the British Isles. But she couldn't accept the way he went about it. His brutal dismantling of monasteries was a shameful and disastrous act.

Yet it was Anne's daughter, the *Virgin Queen*, who occupied Nadine's mind the most – even more than Oliver Twist, her first English hero. No one had made London and England more powerful than Elizabeth I. Nadine was glad that the immense wealth and influence of the great city, on whose wooden stages the plays of Marlowe and Shakespeare were performed, reached their highest point under Elizabeth's long, difficult, clever rule. She liked the idea that it was a woman who established England's hegemony over Europe and made her ruler of the sea. Here was definitely someone with whom she secretly enjoyed to identify. The more she read about her, the more she adored the young, inexperienced, highly educated Elizabeth, cast aside by her father, as she had to live in constant fear for her life. World War Two had taught Nadine well what this fierce, never-ceasing *Angst* was all about.

Together with the First Elizabeth, she didn't like Mary Tudor, her half sister and one of her deadly rivals. Under Mary's short rule the Protestant Elizabeth survived the Tower mostly due to her wits. Only a little later she outlived a second imprisonment in Woodstock, a drafty palace to which Queen Mary had also confined her. In the winter the place was reportedly so damp that it was impossible to get the bed linen completely dry. When Mary finally allowed her much younger half sister to return to London, Elizabeth's youth helped her to gain the good will, if not the amorous pursuit of Philip II of Spain, Queen Mary's husband. After Mary, the only daughter of Catherine of Spain, had ascended the throne for her reign of five years, she reintroduced Catholicism and papal power to England. Deeply religious, she considered the followers of the Church of England, Elizabeth among them, as heretics. Consumed by piteous fanaticism she had almost three hundred dissenters racked and burned alive at the stake.

After the death of Mary Tudor at age forty-two and after the First Elizabeth had succeeded her and was in full command of England, Nadine never pictured the Virgin Queen other than in one of her heavy state dresses studded with gold encased jewels, pearls and small velvet bows. She admired the way her wasp waist extended into barrels of pearl embroidered skirts under which several small children, the ones she never had, could have played hide-and-seek. And with girlish curiosity Nadine wondered how long it had taken her ladies-in-waiting to put her reddish-blond hair, or was it already a wig, into a thousand ringlets, and then, also painstakingly, embellish them with pearls. Being intrigued, she would stare at the queen's overly sensitive skin that had the whiteness of a redhead and was transparent like bisque porcelain and apparently just as fragile. But she was not so sure about Elizabeth's face, especially her mouth. Quite small, it lay pouting under a prominent nose where it was somehow out of place. And she didn't know what to do with her green eyes, which, in their intelligent inquisitiveness, seemed naked without any eyelashes. Then, as she got hold of more paintings of the elderly queen, she was sure that this woman was no longer able to dream. Instead she saw her as a fighter. Her thin, almost invisible eyebrows seemed lost in the white space of her tremendous forehead. The skull underneath was intimidating in its visibility. It was the forehead of a man rather than a woman, the typical high brow of a middle-aged male who suffers from a receding hairline. Shakespeare had a forehead like that.

Yet like so many admirers of Elizabeth I, Nadine could not forgive her, although she understood her fear of betrayal, for keeping Mary, the tall Queen of Scots, imprisoned for eighteen years. That had been, she read as she sat spellbound in her parents' living room, in Sheffield Castle. And she was shocked to learn that after Mary was implicated in the Babington Plot, Elizabeth even had her beheaded. She was informed this had happened at Fotheringhay Castle on February 8, 1587. One late afternoon Nadine discovered Lady Antonia Fraser's imaginative and thoroughly researched biography, *Mary Queen of Scots.* Unable to put the book down, she shivered as she learned that it took two strokes to cut off Mary's head and that apparently a bloody butcher's axe, which was used for the slaughter of cattle, had been employed. The biography also contained a last gruesome, titillating, yet funny and now famous morsel: as the executioner lifted the queen's severed head up high for everyone in the great hall to see, it dropped to the floor. The masked man with his terrible bare arms did not realize that he had grasped a wig of auburn tresses, which the unfortunate Scottish queen had worn in her dreadful hour.

Living for a year on the British Isles, Nadine discovered that cutting off heads of queens and kings and lesser nobles was something English schoolbooks tried to rationalize. They did this with the help of narrowly trimmed points of views, opinions and explanations, the typical, elegant, yet rather subjective, if not downright deceitful, *"explications de texte"*. But Nadine still could not understand why the English, this highly civilized people, had indulged in such despicable practices but then were horrified when much later the French guillotined Mary Antoinette and Louis XVI. History, the recorded, formal, accumulative behavior of mankind, did not make any sense to her. It was filled with too much blood and gore.

At night, when she couldn't fall asleep and her inner worlds were as dark as the night outside her window, she reasoned that even children of pre-school age such as lovable, three-year-old Peter must have somehow gotten knowledge of these royal slaughters. How else could he have so often and with such obvious relish threatened to cut off Nadine's head when they had first met? Of course, she knew why the little boy had feared and hated her so much. It was clear to her that he saw her as an intruder who threatened to displace his mother, the very being his life depended upon.

"I'll chop off your head and throw it in the dustbin!" He had cried over and over again in the beginning of their encounter. Like a miniature soldier the blond child had defiantly placed himself in front of her. His fists poked into his sides, he stood up straight and stared at her with his delicate face that was red with rage and fear.

"Dustbin" was a puzzling word when it was flung at her with such fury, issued from a minute, rosy-lipped mouth filled with perfect milk teeth. She had to search for the noun in the dictionary and smiled when she found its synonym, "garbage can". But while she was hurt that insult was added to injury, she also had to laugh. She knew that the three-year-old boy was hardly able to imagine what she would look like with her head cut off and as it would, together with her bloody curls, torn skin and tendons, lie embedded among rotting salad leaves, potato peals and putrefying carrots, the usual content of dustbins.

* * *

As most tourists do when they first visit London, Nadine headed straight for Buckingham Palace. It was a cold day with snow already in the air and a thin, unending rain that kept the streets glistening and wet. She was glad that she had worn her blue, thick, almost ankle length winter coat. It was the warmest piece of clothing she owned and it was so big that it completely concealed her figure.

As soon as she stood, together with other sightseers, in front of the enormous, fenced in castle, she peered into the young, ruddy and expressionless faces of two palace guards, the queen's own loyal soldiers as they kept watch just outside the big, closed entrance gate. Their colorful uniforms, their immobility and their stern looks reminded her of the one-legged tin soldier in Andersen's fairy tale. Standing close, she stared at their busbies, the huge, black bearskin hats, which they wore with such pride. Then she watched in fascination as streaks of perspiration, mixed with raindrops, ran down cheekbones that apparently were, judging from their motionlessness, made from sandstone. Although she looked hard and long first at one and then at the other soldier, his companion during the long hours they stood together in front of the high, thick, iron wrought gates, she could not detect any of their facial muscles move. There was not even the slightest flicker of an eyelid. And behind closed mouths, kept firmly in place by the leather straps of their hats, no breath was noticeable either. Spot-bound, Nadine was, like so many before her, tempted to touch the face of one of the young sentries just to see if it were made of flesh and bones. Yet even when she moved closer to the queen's men, she decided that they looked more like carefully painted wooden statues than human beings.

'Perhaps they truly are after all descendants of Andersen's tin soldier,' she considered again. Then she realized that one of the young cadet's faces resembled a German recruit whom she had watched as a child. Straight-backed and with shouldered rifle, he had marched up and down in front of his tiny shed with its low, sharply pointed, green roof. He, too, had guarded a building. But it wasn't a palace. Instead it was a garrison, filled with many young conscripts, training to fight Hitler's war. And she remembered that there had been the same mixture of pride, discipline and youthful exhibitionism in the German's body language as that now displayed by the two English soldiers.

The German infantryman had protected one of the barracks of a small town whose king had been even fatter than Henry VIII. So ungainly was Ludwig that he could not ride a regular horse. Even with the help of two young noblemen, he was unable to get into the saddle. A strong, docile mare had to be trained to kneel down for him so he could mount her. That was over two hundred years ago. But his big Baroque castle survived two world wars and is now more elaborate than ever. It still stands in the midst of a wide park, shaded by old chestnut trees under which elaborate fountains spout and where lovely, formal gardens take up many acres of land. The king's golden bedroom continues to be located five hundred feet away from his queen's. She did not want to know who her husband's nightly female visitors were. Nor was she interested in his diurnal male guests, among them Napoleon, who looked like a midget next to Ludwig, his tall vassal.

* * *

As a child, the large German garrison in Ludwigsburg, which was located not far from Nadine's home, had intrigued her. She had often watched the constant flow of fast-driving army vehicles and motorcycles occupied by slender, smart looking, dark-green uniformed officers and their men.

On a fine summer day toward the end of World War Two, when she ran about barefooted because children's shoes were rationed, as everything else was, being kept for cold days, one of those cars had killed her playmate, a slightly retarded five-year-old boy. Blond and handsome, but with a more docile facial expression than Peter's, he had scampered across the street. The child had not seen the onrushing jeep, which could not stop on time. At the side of the road, close to the accident, she had seen her small friend being hit and she had clung to a dirty-white picket fence as if she were clinging to life. While deadly fear gripped her by the neck, she had watched the boy being thrown into the air. Suspended for split seconds, his arms dangled in the void like those of a bird with broken wings. Then came the heavy sickening thud on asphalt and she saw a blood stained face whose wide-open mouth had moved over to one ear. His one ghastly scream and the deadly silence afterwards woke her up during many nights. So did the deafening cries of the child's mother who had run to the scene of accident. One day, waking before dawn, she found her own vomit next to her face on the pillowcase. Screaming, she half choked from the acid, evil tasting bits that were still stuck in her throat. Like her dead playmate she had been barely five years old then.

* * *

As were so many foreigners on their first day in London, Nadine was overwhelmed by the city's scents, sights, thousands of blinking neon lights and uninterrupted noise. Not different from most visitors, she tried to see everything at once. From Buckingham Palace she went to Piccadilly. She took the two-level, red London bus whose winding staircase she ran up and down several times. Thrilled with her new toy, she smiled at no one in particular until the conductor, an old, thin man whose uniform no longer fitted him but hung loosely around his neck and shoulders, gave her a stern look.

By the time she got to Piccadilly and as crowded streets, commercial buildings, parks, mansions, squares, palaces, sculptures, galleries und white columned museums had rushed around her in an unending, confusing circle, it had started to get dark and she felt hungry. She looked into her change purse and when she saw that there were enough shillings and pennies to get a cup of tea and a cookie, she entered a sparely lit, cavernous coffee shop. Without waiting, she steered straight toward one of the place's high, transparent walls that was made entirely from thick glass and faced the center of Piccadilly.

The café was crowded and filled with thick smoke. There were voices speaking not just in English but also in French, German and Italian. And she heard languages whose words she could not decipher. The sound of a television was turned up at its highest volume. But after she looked about for a while, being intimidated by stares, some of which were real and others imagined, she found a small table with two empty chairs near the big window. She put her damp coat on one of the seats and at once started to watch the endlessly unwinding and rewinding ribbon of people that passed within half a foot from her seat. Behind the glass wall, she saw stranger upon stranger in a continued procession. Most of them walked by as if they had just come from some long forgotten country and tried to accommodate themselves in an unfamiliar place. Some of the men and women looked like ghosts. She was sure that at night, when no one was able to spot them, they had come out of the sea to where they would return as soon as the sun set. Others, with their old and young faces, floated past her like bubbles on the surface of a river. After a while, she felt as if she were looking down on water, leaning over the railing of a Brighton pier again that jutted out into the ocean. She was unable to distinguish any idiosyncratic traits on the faces of these strangers. She only saw many mouths open and close, fish-like, similar to the small, yellow and blue, exotic fish she had watched in an aquarium. A pink one had been lying dead on the bottom of the tank. The round holes issued words whose sounds, separated from her by a glass wall, she could not hear and if she had, she would have had difficulty understanding. Piccadilly did not speak Julie's English.

Lost in thought, Nadine looked above the now bodiless heads and the walking, empty, round, small fishbowls. And for the first time she noticed at the opposite side of the street the Brobdingnagian bosom of a blond movie star as it blinked in the incandescent light of ten thousand rhinestones. In tasteless silvery-red and green tints the monstrous breasts heaved as in a maternal-sexual gesture they appeared to embrace a thousand men at once.

While the young girl watched the gargantuan advertisement that was reflected high up against the night sky, she felt as if she had started to shrink and become invisible until she seemed to be completely hidden under a black cloth. Looking through two eye slits, she absorbed this utterly strange, confusing, fascinating cityscape. It was exhilarating and fear-inspiring at the same time. Light-headed, she had the weird feeling that she was gliding between layers of air, not above but below her. Aware of how stupid this sensation was, she felt as if she were pulled downward into regions to which she had not been before. It was frightening. But she also was conscious of a strong sense of curiosity and she was almost sure that she would not die in this unfamiliar environment, which had opened in front of her like the maw of a large, black cave. As her descent increased, so did her fear. But even when she seemed barely able to breathe and her head spun madly, she once more was convinced that this journey was not a deadly one. It reminded her of a roller coaster ride. However wildly one was twisted in one of the small cars and lurched forward at a terrific speed while bumping painfully into a heavy steel bar, which one's fingers held for dear life, one knew the ride would come to a stop and one would be able to get off.

Suddenly a voice pulled the heavy cloth from her face and she reappeared. With her head spinning, she emerged from the fish-rich river of unknown, mute faces, the walking, smooth fishbowls, which had so tightly enclosed her. Still confused, she realized that she sat on a chair and held a cup of tea in her hand.

"You must be German", a mature voice, which did not sound like Julie's either, said to her. Before she had time to reflect, she nodded and only then looked up.

"May I?" the voice said again. Then an arm pushed Nadine's coat aside and a male figure sat down on the other chair without waiting for her consent.

Blondish well-cut hair surrounded the face of the man. The tips of their long curls ended below the collar of a brown camelhair coat that looked new. The skin over the stranger's cheekbones had started to lose the terseness of youth and around his eyes fine wrinkles were visible even in the dim light of the coffee shop. His eyes, sharp and gray like a bird of prey, looked at her mockingly. But it was impossible to say whether the man poked fun at himself or at the girl.

Nadine, who possessed little self-confidence and was once more starting to feel overwhelmed by the vast number of people who seemed to suffocate her, instantly assumed that it was her he scoffed. It did not help the forlorn, bewildering mood, which had overcome her. Feeling oppressed and annoyed by his closeness, she looked at her intruder sullenly.

It had taken her only a second to decide that her uninvited guest was not her type. In spite of his stylish and expensive clothes, there was something shabby about his manners, accent and looks. She could tell that he was not of James or Julie's class. Julie and her husband, the only two English adults Nadine had started to get to know well, were her measuring stick by which she judged her new world. Being by instinct and inclination quite a snob, she tended to look down upon people who did not live up to Julie's brown tweed skirts and impeccable pronunciations. The aggressive city man, who still stared at her with a scrutinizing look as if trying to remember a familiar face, suddenly held a business card under her nose and said: "I'm Jim."

The card identified him as James G. Spencer, photographer, and it mentioned one of the city's better known, but not highly reputable, English fashion magazines. The next hour passed with Spencer telling the young girl about his work, the latest films he had watched as well as some of the major sightseeing spots of London. Certain words of his were unintelligible but she had no trouble following the gist of his stories. Then, to Nadine's dislike, he became unpleasantly personal:

"I noticed you walking past me in your low-heeled shoes and wide winter coat, which is hiding your figure. You could have been fat under that big tent of yours", he smiled at her and stared at her slim waist. Then, without a trace of embarrassment, he told her that he had followed her into the café.

'My God, this man is like a hunting dog who has picked up a fresh scent,' Nadine thought immediately.

Not saying anything but keeping her eyes on his face, she nodded her head once in a while as if she agreed with him.

'He is obviously in the habit of stalking women whose exterior appeals to him,' the young girl uncomfortably thought again. This realization did not increase her liking of him. The more he talked, the less Nadine wanted to be near him. She became upset when he leaned deeper back into his chair and it became obvious that he felt more and more at ease with her. He kept slowly exhaling the smoke of his cigarette above her head and only when he extinguished a cigarette and immediately lit another one, did he briefly cast a look around the room. With each puff he took, he sucked so vehemently at his cigarette that his lips were reduced to two thin lines.

Yet in spite of being nervous in Spencer's presence, it was as if a spell had been cast over the young girl. He seemed to be the only quiet pole in this strange new world that so relentlessly twirled about her.

'Piccadilly is nothing but an unfamiliar hodgepodge of sounds, sights and smells around which it turns incessantly,' she sighed inaudibly. She felt lost and homesick. But if someone had accused her of having such feelings, she would never have admitted them.

There was an air of paternal authority surrounding Spencer that kept her at his side.

'It is as if I were turned into a dog that follows his master's heel,' she mused again and felt disgusted with herself.

'I remember as a child I was untamed and strong-headed, but why am I now so passive and contemplative? I think it's because I have not been taught to make decisions. I was brought up to follow orders, not to give them. That attitude does not help me now, sitting opposite this slick man,' she continued to accuse herself. And she realized with dismay that in addition to her multiple insecurities she also lacked experience in handling big city people.

After a while Spencer, as his smile revealed a set of strong, uneven teeth, opened his wallet and took out a photograph. Watching her face, he handed it over to her. It was the picture of a pretty, young, blond girl without any unusual traits whose soft eyes looked a little forlornly at Nadine. When she remained silent, Spencer said triumphantly:

"That's why I was attracted to you and knew right away that you were German."

Nadine, who could not see any likeness between herself and the young woman on the photo, protested:

"But I do not resemble her at all". She wrinkled her forehead and was getting more annoyed, bored and nervous by the minute.

"I know", he agreed, "but she is from Germany, too".

Nadine gave him another quick look and wondered about his wit. She could not understand why he was so pleased with himself and so keen in getting to know German women.

'At least he appears to be good-natured,' Nadine tried to see the lighter side and sighed again. But she gave Spencer too much credit. What she perceived as amiable was a simplemindedness of spirit, which she encountered more and more among less complex beings. She also soon learned that once Spencer had discovered a goal worth pursuing, he set out to reach it. Bright, streetwise and practical, with almost no formal education, he relied on his persistence, his dogged perseverance. Several years older than Nadine and an optimist, who seemed fairly sure of himself, he was little concerned what another person might think of any of his endeavors.

After an hour had passed since the Londoner had set down at Nadine's table, she finally told him that it was getting late and she had to catch a train back to Groombridge. But he wanted to tell her about his German girl friend and paid little attention to her timid objection. Getting more excited as he spoke, he kept embroidering his story, putting himself in the best possible light.

He was talking fast now and with a Cockney accent, which the young girl started to have more and more trouble understanding. But she didn't say anything and Spencer was only too happy to tell her that the unknown young girl was madly in love with him and had no greater desire than to marry him. Only at the end of his long and inadequately presented story did he mention that the young woman had returned to Germany and the chances of ever seeing her again were slim.

Finally, Nadine got more and more anxious about her train. She had not forgotten her adventure in Brighton. Outside the window the night had long fully ascended and she knew it was getting late. But Spencer still did not stop talking. So she suddenly stood up, nodded to him and walked toward the exit of the coffee shop. The man, taken by surprise at her abrupt behavior, hastily paid the waitress – "no, no, keep the change" - and followed her.

But in spite of having taken a taxi to Victoria station, she, once more, missed her last train. And again, to Nadine's great embarrassment, Julie had to be called and matters needed to be explained.

This time Nadine felt utterly stupid and was near tears as she listened to Julie's half amused, half troubled voice:

"You and train schedules do not seem to get along too well together, is this not so?" she said and then, with motherly concern, added: "Do be careful. I'll see you early tomorrow morning."

The first train was at 6:00 am and Nadine wanted to stay in one of the large waiting rooms of the train station for the rest of the night. But like Arthur Wellington and Mrs. Gibson, Andrew's mother, her newly found and self-declared friend insisted that she should stay with him.

"You can trust me", Spencer said and smiled at her with his strong teeth. "I'm a decent fellow and I'll not hurt you."

'*Was meint er damit, daß er anständig sei und mir nicht weh tun würde?*' (What does he mean when he claims that he is decent and wouldn't hurt me?), she thought unconvinced. After she got tired, she reverted to thinking in German. But when they left the station, she was still at the Londoner's side – exhausted and hungry and weary of every step she took.

They had dinner at an inexpensive Italian restaurant where the Londoner drank almost a bottle of Chianti by himself and then told her that he shared a flat with a male friend. Nadine could spend the night in their common living room.

"You will be quite safe there", Spencer assured her again and tried to overcome her resistance. She didn't trust him and once more she protested, saying that she would rather go back to the train station. To spend the night at Victoria station was her only alternative because, as usual, she did not have enough money to stay at a hotel. Not even a cheap one. But Spencer would not hear of it. The two of them took another cab and went to his apartment.

The streets of London with their elaborately mounted gaslights and a confusing number of dark buildings, none of which she recognized, passed them by in hasty sequence. By now Nadine was too sleepy to pay any attention to where they went. But even during daytime she would not have known where they were going. Vaguely, she was once more aware that Mannheim, where she had mostly grown up, would have fit innumerable times into London. Her memory had never been fed this night's image before and her hippocampus, this primitive gray matter, which she shared with animals, had nothing to work with. She was fond of her "hippo", as she called it, because she had been taught that this part of the brain was responsible for constantly feeding her memory, a tool she needed to learn a new language.

Spencer's apartment was a typical bachelor's abode with dirty dishes in the kitchen sink, stained paper towels thrown all over the place and an overflowing garbage pail. On the wobbly, wooden dining table stood several beer glasses some of which were still half filled with their stale, dark brown liquid. Old cigarette smoke, unable to escape through the closed windows, clung to every corner. Spencer's roommate was nowhere in sight.

The living room was cold, long and narrow and resembled a train compartment. It contained a threadbare carpet over which a thousand feet seemed to trample every day. The ugly room was cluttered with chairs and several small tables that stood around seemingly without any purpose. The place looked like a storage chamber. Its wallpaper was full of oily spots and some parts of it had become loose and even torn at one end of the room. There were almost no lights. It was so dark that everything seemed to be bathed in black. A moveable washstand stood in one corner. Nadine would not have been surprised if a chamber pot had been hiding behind its crumbled and smudged plastic curtain. She took a deep breath, nervously brushed a curl out of her forehead and braced herself for the sight of a cockroach scurrying across the floor.

The room boasted a dusty, narrow faux fireplace whose concealed gas heater Spencer turned on right away. The air was chilly and Nadine watched the small blue flames not only in anticipation of warmth but also so that she did not have to look at her host. He had taken off his coat and moved about in his shirtsleeves that revealed rather broad, muscular but short arms. As he kept walking back and forth in the elongated, semi dark room, he clucked like a mother hen and drove Nadine half insane with his apologetic mannerism under which he tried to hide his embarrassment.

He had urged her to sit in the largest armchair and brought a blanket, which he carefully placed over her knees. But although he had asked her several times to take off her coat, she refused to do so, claiming she was cold. The thought that he might touch her so that she would feel his fingers through her thin dress, made her hands contract into fists. When she felt her long, varnished nails dig into the skin of her palm, she was glad.

'I intend to use them, if need be, and I know that they will leave fiery red streaks on his face, 'she thought filled with feistiness. Although she had not eaten much, their evening meal had given her back some of her energy. Spencer seemed to sense her fighting spirit and kept his distance. As she leaned back into her chair that was surprisingly comfortable, she kept watching him from semi-closed eyelids. After offering her something to drink, which she declined with an icily polite "no, thank you", he sat down opposite from her.

He had tried several times to engage her in a conversation, but she must have all of a sudden fallen asleep. When she woke with a start, she saw him looking intently at her. The gaslight faintly outlined the contours of his face in which his eyes were two deep, round shadows. She could not see his mouth and assumed he kept it closed. When she realized that he had not moved out of his chair, nor was he apparently about to, she dozed off again. They spent the entire night that way.

Her unwillingness to indulge in an amorous encounter, made her more desirable to him. They were sitting only a few inches from each other. While she slumbered, he had moved his chair closer to hers. But to Nadine's great relief, he never tried to touch her. Not even her hand. For a moment before she, white-faced from exhaustion, drifted off into sleep again, she had thought of Tristan's sword, which on dark nights had gleamed between himself and Isolde. Yet ashamed of her romantic conjecture and far from seeing Spencer in a rosy hue, she quickly discarded the idea.

"He certainly isn't a hero. And when it comes to Isolde, I am about as far away from being a princess as Cinderella was when she sat on her cinder box", Nadine mumbled, unable to keep her eyes open.

During the night Nadine woke up every so often and listened to the hissing of the gas flames. She kept looking at Spencer who had finally also fallen asleep. With both hands he held a blanket pulled up to his chin, which was beginning to form a double line. She liked him better that way: an inert, bleak mass, which rendered even his contours barely discernible. Across his facial feature a neon sign outside the bare window drew a pleasant pattern. It animated his face and added a softer dimension to it of which she had not been aware before. The faint light seemed to reveal a benevolent aspect of his character, and as she saw it play with his face and hair, she lost some of her earlier fears.

In the middle of the night, after she caught him again as he silently observed her, she asked him where his roommate was. He murmured something about an unscheduled business trip, which he had forgotten and then quickly changed the subject. Nadine did not believe that his friend existed. The flat was small even for just one person.

At five o'clock in the morning Spencer took Nadine back to the train station. The city was still asleep. A thick mist lay over the Thames as they crossed it. The air was moist and once, when she rolled down the window of the taxi, there was a breath of the sea in the air.

"Oh, Andrew," she whispered and saw the figure of the handsome sausage man emerge from the fog. And she moved even farther away from Spencer who sat silently next to her. Glancing at him, she noticed that his jawbone protruded slightly from his double chin.

As they slowed down to pass around a tight corner, a fat calico cat, sitting in a basement window, looked at them curiously. Then it yawned, fully exposing its sharp canine teeth. After the driver had pulled up in front of the large terminal, they had a cup of coffee and, at the insistence of Spencer, exchanged phone numbers. Shortly before Nadine boarded her train, they shook hands. Inside her empty compartment she had three seats to herself. She quickly removed her shoes and lay down. Listening to the reassuring, rhythmic clatter of the wheels, she promptly fell asleep and almost missed her stop at Groombridge.

* * *

The next few months Nadine spent her weekly day off in London. Spencer called her regularly and they arranged for a convenient hour and place to meet in the city. But Nadine was always late when she got to the appointed location. She misjudged the distance and took the wrong bus or subway. Or she got delayed in walking through Hyde Park where she stopped and admired a speaker who pleaded his cause as he stood self-consciously and with spread legs on a soapbox. A semicircle of curious idlers and office employees, who took their lunch in the open air while they listened to an often quite young man, surrounded one of the more popular orators.

* * *

Sometimes the young girl got held back in a large department store on Oxford Street where she could not get enough looking at different colorful displays. But she rarely was able to proceed past the vast first floor because here cosmetics and perfumes were promoted, her favorites. The salesgirls, lingering behind their illuminated glass cages like large, brilliantly feathered birds, would pleasantly surprise her. Most of them were hardly out of their teens and stunningly made up. Some of the pretty women had colored their eyelids with a flaming blue or gay green, their lips would shine in gorgeous reds and they wore dark brown or black, tight dresses that were the latest fashion. Their clothing, subtly provocative, emphasized their bodies in an alluring way. Nadine noticed particularly their elongated backs that often curved full and round under a skirt and ever so slightly would jiggle during their fast walks. Similar to certain African tribal women, the girls' necks, arms and fingers were embellished with pounds of jewelry. And one of them, as Nadine looked surreptitiously at her slender calf, had even fastened a thin bracelet to her ankle. Discreetly, it glittered under her nylon stocking. This was new to her.

'That's what the owner of a slave girl must have put on her,' she thought immediately. On some days the pearls, gold-plated wristbands and necklaces with their sparkling artificial stones some of the most attractive women wore, reminded her also of Egyptian queens laid out to be taken to their stately, secret burial grounds in the dry sands of the Sahara.

Daintily, the lovely sales girls tripped about in the highest of heels and they often behaved as self-consciously and as unapproachably as any film starlet.

Nadine was usually so intimidated by their stunning looks that she did not dare to approach them. Dazzled by the prolifically mounted, soft, flattering lights of the store and several enormous flower vases that were carefully arranged on heavy glass counters, she breathed deeply of the air, which was saturated with perfumes, powders and soaps.

But the longer she stood and stared at the saleswomen, the more she became aware of her own rather modest exterior. She could not afford to buy new clothes but wore her old ones, those she had taken with her from Germany. Sometimes she would put on a cheap dress, which she had made herself the night before she went to London. As an *au pair*, she only earned room and board. The semi-monthly allowance Julie gave her was so small that it was barely enough to pay for her train fare and some food bought at a cheap grocery store. She never had any money. But as a typical female, she would have loved to learn more about the various, luxuriously looking goods, which the salesgirls offered and with which they seemed so thoroughly familiar. From her side of the counter she did not realize that most of the vivacious girls, who completely ignored her as they busily talked among each other, were rather shy under their splendid plumage. And she couldn't see that these gorgeous creatures were frequently bored to death, especially when business was slow and the latest gossip of the day had been taken care of. Most of the young women would have been quite willing to chat with Nadine about anything in which she was interested, if only she had addressed them. Yet she never was able to muster enough courage to do so. She had to be content with her *"faire du lèche-vitrine"*. So she just kept staring and greedily absorbing the beauty about her. Occasionally one of the girls would notice her admiration and blushing under her make-up Nadine could see that she was half embarrassed, half flattered by it. Yet the saleswoman remained totally mute and unapproachable behind her sparkling glass counter.

One day, as Nadine hastily left Harrods with its thousand lights and thick, soft carpets to meet Spencer halfway across town, she suddenly saw a woman who must have been in her early thirties. The stranger had such magnificent proportions that Nadine followed her half way down a city block before she realized what she was doing. Not exactly small herself, Nadine had to raise her chin a little to be able to take in the woman's head fully, where long, thick, blond hair framed a pale, almost unhealthily white-powdered face. High cheekbones, striving to reach her brows and large eyes that sat widely apart, dominated her superb features. At their outer ends, near the temples, her eyes were slightly curved upward and emphasized their resemblance to those of a cat. Full lashes, generously helped by mascara and kohl, surrounded blue irises in an astonishing way. There was a thin nose that was too small and half lost among the eyes. But a luminous forehead rose nevertheless quite sharply from it. Above a slightly protruding chin she noticed lips whose sensuous curves were reinforced by a bright orange, which was a far cry from the accustomed dark red tint.

Spellbound, Nadine kept walking behind the woman who seemed to swing a long, purple cape in a deliberately slow movement. An ample yellow silk scarf was draped dramatically around her neck and shoulders. And above her breast a cluster of diamonds, real or synthetic, the young girl couldn't tell the difference, was fastened to her garment. The tall woman took such regular and measured steps that Nadine looked at her feet to see if she wore, like Salammbô, a golden chain between her ankles to control her pace. When she saw that she did not, the vision of Christina, queen of Sweden, quickly replaced the one of the Carthaginian princess, as a raucous-voiced Greta Garbo had portrayed the royal Swede so expertly on the silver screen. The Londoner's studied beauty, perfected in a big city, had an intoxicating effect on Nadine. She was not used to such a high degree of sophistication in women.

As the young girl tried to overtake the stranger for a second look, she was jostled by several people who hurried in an uninterrupted stream, toward her. An elderly, sloppily dressed woman with a burning cigarette stuck at the corner of her mouth, let her know in no uncertain terms that she moved against the current.

"Watch your step, Miss! Don't you got eyes in your head?" And, underlining her coarse words, she pushed Nadine aside with her elbow.

'Londoners are rude', the young girl thought absentmindedly and being pressed by more important matters, she scrambled along. Then she came to an abrupt stop. The beautiful woman had turned to the right and disappeared behind two large, brass-framed glass doors that were tended by a heavy-set, blue uniform wearing, gold-buttoned doorman. So quickly had she gone that Nadine still inhaled her perfume after the doors had been closed. Like a lost puppy, she sniffed the air and then slowly, her head hanging and suddenly feeling depressed, she turned around. Still confused, she searched for an entrance to the London tube, which she had learned to ride.

* * *

After a glance at such regal symmetry and grace her meeting with Spencer, whose paunchy waist disturbed her more with each successive encounter, was a letdown. Even in Paris, where a friend of her father had briefly taken her to a private show of Christian Dior, she had not met with such a lovely face as the one of the female stranger from London. The thin Parisian models were enticing, but when they started to show elaborate, deeply cut evening gowns, it became clear that they had no bosoms. Their coveted riches had vanished under a heap of protruding bones.

"This is necessary," her middle-aged escort had explained. "Otherwise the beauty of these young women would detract from the clothes they wear. The girls by themselves, as ravishing as they are, mean little. Their only purpose is to sell dresses. They are nothing but walking coat-hangers."

It was one of those enlightening statements, which Nadine hated because they destroyed her illusions. For her, beauty was more than skin deep and the idea that aesthetics were subservient to money was utterly repelling.

The same friend had also told her about a Nina Ricci fashion show, which he had attended at the French embassy on Manhattan's Park Avenue. But although he vividly outlined the building's elegant hall-way, which was immersed in white with flowers in huge, white pots that lined each step of the broad, gently curved staircase of the embassy and though he praised the exquisiteness of the young models, also all dressed in white, nowhere in his lively description could Nadine detect a resemblance to the tall woman from London.

Nadine's first encounter with an English beauty in her utter sophistication had left an indelible impression on her. And just as she compared James and Julie Johnson's impeccable manners with those of other

English men and women whom she met, the Londoner now became the paragon against which she measured feminine flawlessness.

The unknown English woman's charms had camouflaged to perfection illness and death. Not for an instant did Nadine see the skull under her immaculate skin. For her, this woman would never die. Nor was she capable of imagining her eating, sleeping or making love. As time passed, this woman, whom Nadine had pursued like an amorous lover, became less and less real. Trying to recall her face and body, she realized that the stranger had turned into a rainbow. One could see it but not touch it. One could walk through it, like through Danaë's golden shower, but then one could not see it.

* * *

That day, not long after Nadine had encountered female flawlessness, she met Spencer. During her half an hour subway trip she had been totally unaware of her surrounding. The people to whom she stood or sat next in the crowded car and whose breath she breathed, whose clothes she inadvertently touched and whose shoulders, arms and hands pushed her as passengers got on or off at various stations, did not exist. They were only as real as the figures in an advertisement that was pasted along the narrow space above the hard seats and ceiling of the cars. As her train rushed through the blind bowels of London and she looked around her, she only saw the vanished woman. Staring into dozens of eyes without seeing the faces that belonged to them, she finally decided – and there was an enormous consolation in this thought, mixed with pride and self-flattery – that she must have seen an incarnation of one of her ideals.

"Perhaps even," she whispered, "as absurd as it might seem, I could have met with a mirror image of an obscure corner of myself."

Standing up among other straphangers and being squeezed on both sides by London's tube riders, her imagination ran away with her and she thought that if she had she been born four hundred years earlier, she might have been struck by a similar vision after confronting a young woman who resembled a particularly artistic rendition of Mary, the mother of the man from Nazareth. In spite of her maternal grandmother's endeavor during Nadine's childhood, the young girl was not religiously motivated. But she had slowly, and seemingly without any exterior help, developed a liking for Mary, the only female god in the complex set-up of Christian myth where patriarchy had become the ruling force, mercilessly stripping women of their rights.

And she remembered again that during an Easter vacation on a brief trip to Rome not too long ago, she had stood quite a while in front of Michelangelo's Mary. His sculpture of a seductive young mother holding a just crucified Christ on her lap had been placed in an obscure corner of the Vatican. Nadine would have walked past it, had she not almost run into one of Mary's wide spread knees on which the magnificent, nude, lifeless body of her son was resting.

Like most admirers of High Renaissance art, Nadine preferred Michelangelo's male sculptures to his female renditions. Especially his superb Adam intrigued her as he holds hands with his bearded god while the two of them float forever on the ceiling of the Sistine Chapel. And she thought that his young David in Florence was exquisite. Yet long before she knew that Michelangelo was a homosexual, she had felt that most of his women were treated as leftovers from a mythological male rib that somehow had grown a bosom or shamefacedly tried to hide their castrated sex under a raised thigh. Then, as she had remained awe struck in the Dome of St. Peter and admired Mary, Nadine had to admit that here the great artist had finally paid homage to a woman's beauty. And she liked the way the Virgin held her dead son like a lover who clings to her beloved.

"How young she is to be the mother of a fully grown son," Nadine had commented to herself as she cast a last look at the sculpture, which undeservedly had been placed in a shadowy nook of the great church. It took years before Mary and her offspring were rescued from oblivion and put into full view of the Cathedral.

* * *

No matter how late Nadine was for her date with Spencer, he was always waiting for her. Calm and obviously happy to see her, he smiled long before she had crossed the wide stretch of pavement teeming with people that separated them. If he was frustrated about her delays, he never showed it. Sometimes he reminded her of one of the guardsmen in front of Buckingham Palace who had been trained so carefully in the art of waiting. At first Nadine had thought that her unknown German predecessor, whom she only knew from the photo Spencer had shown her, had also been late when she met him and had trained him to become patient. But when she brought up the subject, he assured her that his former girlfriend had always been on time.

The thing that puzzled Nadine even more was that it did not matter what she did or said to him. Nothing changed Spencer's tolerant behavior. His seemingly unlimited indulgence in which she had begun to wrap herself as if it had been an expensive shawl she wanted to have but could not afford, appeared to be his nature.

Like a child she knew no limits when she was with him. With a strong penchant toward narcissism she was almost always self-centered when they were together. She would talk about things in which she was interested and dragged him to places she wanted to see. Although Spencer did not care about museums, Nadine took him several times to the National Gallery, which she preferred to similar institutions. Each week she wanted to see something else. So during the fall and most of winter they went to see the Houses of Parliament, Downing Street, Westminster Abbey, and Big Ben. And she was disappointed when they couldn't climb up its enormous tower. They even went to Windsor Castle and Stonehenge. Also, once in a while when she was in the mood for alcohol, for which she didn't care much, she persuaded him to have a drink with her at the Ritz. Nothing seemed to be too expensive or time-consuming for him.

One day, when Spencer suggested that they should see the London Zoo, a place which he liked to visit, Nadine quickly and with no regard for his feelings told him that all zoos were not only alike but also an abomination:

"Don't you see that these poor animals are forever deprived of their freedom?" she asked querulously.

"It is like putting you or me in solitary confinement in a dungeon," she added indignantly and looked at him with blazing eyes.

"I think you exaggerate a little," Spencer made a half-hearted protest.

"Oh no! Have you ever seen a tiger walk endlessly back and forth in a cage not bigger than a shoe box and his eyes never letting go of yours," she retorted, quickly angered by his opposition.

"Take it easy," the Londoner tried to calm her down.

"We'll visit the Tower again, if you prefer that," he laughed a little forcefully. His irony, as she stepped in front of him, escaped her. She held her head high, shook her curls so that they flew around in wild disorder and was happy to have apparently won another battle. With Spencer she always felt an irresistible urge to be "in the driver's seat", as Julie called it.

Whenever she perceived a trace of masochistic behavior in the Londoner, she treated it with the full insolence of a young, thoughtless girl. In her ignorance she perceived his submissive attitude as contemptible and as a reversal of the classic roles men and women were supposed to play. Her memory, so easily deceived, did not reveal to her a scene in which her father had given in to her mother during one of their frequent arguments. In typical male manner her father felt the constant need to subjugate his wife. He knew it was his right, a right that had been supported by law throughout the centuries. A husband, who agreed with his wife's sometimes-superior judgments, risked being seen as henpecked. A gentle feminine aspect in a man toward a woman was misread.

Nadine often despised Spencer exactly for the wrong reason. But instinctively she relished in his patience, his willingness to please and his soft smile that made him likeable. For a few instants it gave her control over a situation, which she did not desire, yet was unwilling and too lazy to change. Every time she met Spencer, she was drawn deeper into a relationship, which she was no longer able to enjoy but did not know how to break up gracefully.

From time to time she would semi-audibly argue with herself: "Nadine, *dieses Techtelmechtel wird dich teuer zu stehen kommen.* (You are the one who is going to get hurt in this affair.) And I don't want that. *Ich kann ihm nicht länger trauen, also mach' Schluss!* (I can't trust him any more, so get out of here!) You, my girl, don't know what he'll do when he gets really angry."

She was only too aware how helplessly Spencer had fallen in love with her and knew that, if nothing else, he would be badly injured in his vanity if she were the one to end their weekly meetings. But she never made that decision. As so often in her short life, fate, or whatever else she wanted to call it, took matters in hand.

Their one-sided romance continued for a few cold winter months without any perceptible change, except, as Nadine became more frustrated with Spencer, his feelings for her deepened. Wanting to sleep with her had slowly become an obsession with him. He lost his interest in the other women, about whose conquests he had bragged during the beginning of their relationship, and he apparently no longer enjoyed his food. He complained that at night he slept badly and she quickly imagined him walking back and forth in his apartment, shuffling his feet like an old man in slippers with holes in their soles. One day Nadine, who hardly paid attention to his exterior, noticed that he had gotten much thinner under his light-colored camelhair coat, and he was so pale that he looked sickly.

Yet the more Spencer pursued Nadine, the more he repulsed her. To distract him, she became even more talkative. Yet with each weekly encounter Spencer grew more silent and when he took her out to a movie or dinner, he often just sat next to her, not saying anything and looking morose. To Nadine he sometimes felt like a thing, like a dress one wore but did not need to communicate with. The garment made its statement silently and repeated the same message over and over again.

In the evening, before she boarded her train at Victoria station, he got his good-bye kiss, which he insisted upon. Yet even this token of affection, given lightly on her part and in full view of hundreds of riders getting on or off a train, annoyed Nadine. She only relented because she told herself that such a kiss was but the teddy bear of a small boy who couldn't fall asleep at night without cradling the toy in his arms. Yet apart from this kiss, to which Spencer had looked forward the entire day, there were never any further intimacies. He, of course, suffered under Nadine's remoteness. And sometimes, as they stood near to each other on the busy platform of the station, she could see that he was close to tears. Then, like a reflex of his sadness, vague feelings of pity rose in her. Yet she firmly pushed his hands away when, like a starving man, he tried to touch her shoulders, hips and breasts.

* * *

In Groombridge Nadine found an ally in Julie in whom she confided most of Spencer's behavior. Julie became instantly protective, even slightly possessive when she listened to Nadine's confessions about the Londoner. She had told her several times that her company was enough in exchange for the outings, dinners and movies any beau took her.

"You don't need to feel obligated to a man who wants to spend his time with you", Julie said when she saw that the young girl felt guilty for not measuring out her physical charms more generously.

But it took more than one sermon to give Nadine a little self-confidence. She was not sure of her rights and not for a moment did she consider herself a valuable contribution to mankind. Quite the opposite. Except for moments when she became highly excited by an outstanding film, a book or a painting and forgot about herself, she was usually convinced that her presence on earth was superfluous. She could only see her existence as a complete accident, as nothing but the result of a passionate embrace by her young parents during the wrong time of the month. And she was sure that she would not be missed for an instant, should she fall off the planet's slippery edge. Unable to step outside of herself, she could not even imagine the grief her death would cause her parents. After all, hadn't they told her more than once that she had been a burden for them?

When she felt really miserable, she was convinced that even Christian, who had sworn his eternal love for her, would not wait for her return. After all, it was she who had left him in Germany. He continued to write her tender notes and long mournful letters. Within those smudged pages he would always tell her how much he missed her and that he would love her forever. Some of the pages had watermarks on them. "Those are kisses," he wrote and circled them with a purple pen. But he never spoke about his friends or his leisure activities, and she was afraid that with time he would not be able to resist an attractive female willing to console him. Nadine was particularly thinking of Renate Hansen. She was the singer of the *Limelight Combo* in which Christian had the leading part as a trumpet player. Renate, small, wiry, dark-haired and vivacious, looked more like a pretty Italian than a German. Quite aggressively, she had made it clear from the beginning that she was fond of Christian. She missed no chance to flirt with him and he seemed to be flattered by the girl's consistent attention.

'And she is bigger breasted than I', Nadine thought when she felt lonesome and depressed. 'Who knows, Christian might go for her. So many men have a complex about these two milk-secreting glandular organs. Granted the chest is the seat of affection, but ultimately female breasts are nothing but a source of nourishment. *Ich verstehe wirklich nicht weshalb so viel Theater um dies gemacht wird.* (I really don't understand what the fuss is all about.) If I was informed correctly, men have mammary glands, too. Although theirs exist in a simplified form.'

"I hope you know that by going to England, you will lose your boyfriend," her father had warned her before she took her train from Mannheim to Ostende.

"No matter what he has promised you, he will not wait for you. Not for long in any event," he had added and looked at her sadly. He had also taken a liking to Christian and knew that a breakup between the two young lovers would hurt his daughter.

* * *

Then one day in late autumn, Julie, in whose lap Nadine had thrown a large part of her feelings about Spencer, told her:

"Watch out! Your friend seems serious. He displays all the signs of a man who wants to get married. Don't encourage him if you cannot see yourself as his wife".

Nadine tried to laugh off Julie's warnings but one evening Spencer came to Groombridge to ask her to marry him. She had not wanted him to come to Julie's house and had emphatically tried to discourage him from doing so. But it was no use. On a rainy, dark, cold night in the middle of the week, Spencer had disregarded her request, taken the train to the hamlet and stood in front of Julie's entrance door. Nadine was taken aback and then quickly became upset when she saw that he had lost his accustomed docility. And she felt terrible when he asked her to be his wife.

"If you marry me, I promise you that I'll get your picture on the front page of any magazine you would like," he said and looked at her as eagerly as a young boy who believes that mother is able to make his pain go away.

Spencer had brought his big, black umbrella from London and the limited space under it gave him an excuse to hold Nadine closely. As they walked along the wet village road and passed a few houses that were barely distinguishable in the dark, he inhaled eagerly the scent that rose from the young girl's skin. Some of her hair tickled his cheek and he longed to touch her curls. Pressing her close to his side, he could feel her hipbone as she moved next to him. Her nearness intoxicated him and once or twice he suddenly stopped and attempted to kiss her. But Nadine pulled away from him and preferred to get wet from the rain rather than feel his mouth on her lips. She was repulsed by his arousal and angrily told him:

"If you don't stop behaving like an alley cat, I will leave you standing here. You are quite capable of getting back to the train station by yourself."

„Alright, alright, I get your drift," Spencer said in a vexed voice and moved on reluctantly. But his hand held on to Nadine's wrist as if he were unable to let her go. He soon thought again that he had never been this happy in his life.

It was his little boy's look in a man's face, a man who at thirty-six, was twice as old as the young girl, which pulled at her heartstrings. It made her forget his simple, crude upbringing, which was expressed in every word he spoke and every gesture he made.

But she also was annoyed that he seemed to know her so well and used her vanity to manipulate her. Among her various insecurities and shortcomings, self-admiration was probably the most dominant one. She had often considered her mirror to be her best friend. On the rare afternoons when Judy had left with Lipsey for a dental appointment in Tunbridge Wells and Peter was fast asleep upstairs, Nadine enjoyed taking pictures of herself by aiming a box camera at the mirror. But she was only interested in her face. It didn't matter to her what she looked like from the neck down. As long as she felt halfway comfortable in a swimsuit, was all she cared about the rest of her.

As Nadine kept strolling next to Spencer that night at the village, she finally realized that under his patience and his experience in worldly matters, which had induced a vague sense of security in her that she did not trust, there was a will to which she would have to conform if she did not want to get into trouble. Yet even if she had been in love with the Londoner and would have wanted to marry him, Nadine knew he did not love her as she was but as he wanted her to be. She was sure that he had no idea who she really was. While they moved together under the sturdy umbrella and tried to avoid the big puddles in the road, she felt strongly that he wanted to possess her for what she represented: A young body still covered in certain parts with baby fat and a mind just freshly groomed by an English public school accent Spencer did not have. "*He wants to fiddle with the wrappings but doesn't know about the connection with states of mind*", she had read somewhere. The quotation perfectly applied to her English marriage candidate.

Looking briefly at his nearly forty year old face as they passed a lonely streetlight, she knew that at best she was a timely arrival within his biological framework. He felt ready to get married and she happened to come around his favorite corner at Piccadilly. For him it was the *coup de foudre* to which he wanted to cling for the rest of his life – something that simply was not inherent in thunder and lightening.

Spencer and Nadine must have marched at least three times up and down the main street of Groombridge that was nearly a mile long. The more they walked, the less they talked until none of them spoke any further and both of them became involved in their own thoughts.

Spencer's refusal to see that she was not in love with him greatly disturbed the young girl. And she was upset that his imagination was not able to stretch beyond the few months of their friendship. She considered him dull for not being able to visualize their getting up every morning together for the rest of their lives. It infuriated her that in his limited vision, he just saw her physical attributes. His pertinacious desire to hold her arms and legs and the rest of her, which she just as pigheadedly refused him, disgusted her. And the thought occurred to her over and over again that he wanted her only because of his sexual longing. Little did he understand where she came from or where she was going.

"Man wants what he can't have," Nadine's father had often told her in his concern about her virtue and in his worries that she might no longer fetch the full bridal price. Her father pictured her encased in a marriage bonnet made from stiff, starched and pure white cloth similar to a wimple worn by women in medieval times. He felt that only then would she be safe. Heinrich Tallemann knew that although now more women enrolled at universities and that they were even usually the better students, it was also true that when these highly trained females entered the job market, they were still paid considerably less for the same type of work than their male counterparts. So Nadine's father had a point when pleading for marriage. But from early on in life she had become convinced that there was no safety anywhere.

'I might as well live as a single woman,' Nadine argued with herself. 'It probably will be harder, but at least I can send a lover on his way. Something I couldn't do that easily with a husband. Didn't I see how little my mother was allowed to be herself within the confines of wedlock?'

Finally the evening in Groombridge came to an end. Nadine kissed Spencer good-bye as he climbed up the high steps of the local train that took him back to the city. She told him that she would let him know her decision soon. The answer to his question was a simple "no" on Nadine's part. But seeing how anxious he was, she had not dared to say it to his face. If her silence was a cowardly action on her part, her fear of his potential violence toward her outweighed any other consideration. She knew how brutal man could be. She also knew that in most cases a woman could only fight back to a limited extent because she was physically weaker than man. So the young girl tried to avoid male rage whenever possible. It was sheer survival instinct, not cowardice.

It still rained when the young girl watched with relief the two red lights of the last car moving out of the station. She was grateful when Spencer had insisted that she keep his umbrella for her return to Julie's house. It was typical of him to worry more about her getting wet than himself.

"I can always take a taxi when I get back to London and it hasn't stopped pouring," he had laughed. It was his concern about her well-being, which he expressed in many small ways, that had endeared him to her.

Almost running back to the house, her sense of easement that Spencer was no longer at her side, increased with every step she took. In her mind she saw him now far clearer than when he had still moved next to her. She knew that he could never be her husband, but she had grown used to him and would have liked to keep him as a friend.

Holding the umbrella close over her head, she recalled bit by bit how Spencer's sexual longings had grown consistently over the past few fall and winter months.

"His proposal," she whispered in the dark, "simply shows that he is willing to legitimize his yearnings. If he cannot have me without paying a higher price for me than he has paid for other women in the past, he simply would do so now."

But she knew that there was something terribly amiss in Spencer's logic. In his eagerness for possession he overlooked, or did not want to admit, that she did not feel attracted to him.

"Or, if he realizes that I'm not in love with him," she said to the rain and the silent village road, "he deliberately ignores this fact. I'm no fool. I can see that in this area he's only able to concentrate on his own wishes, not on mine. For all his experience in practical matters and beneath the various, small favors he has bestowed upon me (*bestowed* what a word, she giggled, thrilled with her newly acquired verb), there is this emotional narrow-mindedness and insecurity of his, which frightens me. The only thing of which he seems to be certain is that once we are married, he will be able to change my mind. And meanwhile, he wants me to show a little more affection for him who is lying at my feet. *Aber da kann er lange warten*! (Well, he can wait for that!)"

* * *

"Why don't you like me a little better – like some other women I know?" He had asked her one day as they had lunch in a crowded restaurant in the middle of London. Among the clatter of plates, the pushing of chairs and the conversation of other diners who were so close that they almost rubbed knees with them, she could barely hear him although she understood what he was trying to convey.

"What did you say?" she had asked him loudly. She felt more audacious because so many people surrounded them. And as his face flushed, he had to repeat his question. All of a sudden and quite unusual for him, he seemed to become painfully aware of the bustling crowd around them, even though Nadine could see that no one paid attention to them.

Toward the end of their meal, when he noticed that two young men at the next table had begun to look at Nadine, he became instantly jealous, pulled her arm and said hoarsely: "Let's go. We'll have dessert at another place."

"But I like it here," Nadine, who had also become aware of the strangers, said. She felt flattered that she had caught their attention and, feeling protected by Spencer's presence, would have liked to return their admiring glances. Yet one look at her beau's sore face made her get up from her seat and follow him without a word.

'This is why I can't stand him any longer', she reflected as she reluctantly threaded her way through the busy eating place. 'He spoils any little bit of fun I might have.'

In the evening of that day as they stood in a dark corner at Victoria station and waited for Nadine's train, he reached for her. When she pushed him rudely away, he pretended that it was a game, which she played to entice him. And it needed more than one shove from her before he kept his hands to himself.

'He does not seem to realize that I am completely open with him,' she silently spoke to him as she stared at his face.

'Love is not a game for me! It's the sea into which one is suddenly tossed, thrown roughly overboard like Rabelaisian sheep. And those who cannot swim simply drown sooner than the ones who can. I know that only mermaids and semi-gods with their streamlined bodies and sharply pointed teeth survive the sea. And only for those who are able to exchange their legs for fishtails and their arms for fins, does the sea become a home forever. But I see Spencer at best as a walrus that clumsily climbs over his females and pups alike, ignoring their grunts of protest and pitiful shrieks. His only distinction is his ivory tusks. But I can live quite well without those, thank you very much.'

* * *

The next time Nadine boarded her train for London, she had a carryall slung over her shoulder. As usual, she was late and had been forced to run through the quiet, narrow street of the sleepy hamlet that led to the railway station. She had stuffed a swimsuit into her satchel, as well as shorts, tights, sleeveless shirts and two very thin cotton blouses that became transparent when they got wet. On the bottom of her rucksack was a backless body suit, which a German seamstress had made from black velvet. Between hips and the top of her thighs, the suit was embellished with a voluminous piece of pinkish-orange organdy. It ended in a large, feathery light bow that moved with every step she took and partly revealed her derrière, sharply outlined under the black cloth. The outfit showed her curves in a beguiling manner without exposing them. Back in Mannheim, she had worn black net stockings and high-heeled leather pumps with this carnival inspired fantasy. In the south of Germany where she came from and where Catholicism still reigned, although since World War II more and more people had left the Church, the yearly event of Mardi gras was celebrated with enthusiasm and minus any religious connotation, especially by its youth. Days then had become blurry from lack of sleep. And long nights filled with music and dance dominated. Christian, when he had first seen her new costume, had devoured her with his eyes. Now Spencer was ready to shoot photos of her wearing it. Pictures that, he had boasted, were supposed to turn her into a highly paid top model.

After she got to London, he picked her up at the station and they went to his apartment, where she had not been since the night she had missed her train. This time Spencer's roommate, Ray Sheldon, also a professional photographer whom Spencer had introduced as Ra, was there. Nadine had warned Spencer that she would not enter his abode

Ursula W. Schneider

without his friend's presence. He had rather reluctantly agreed. And after the young girl had put on her first outfit in Spencer's bedroom, she felt quite safe. Back in the small living room both men took considerable pains to show her how to pose.

Ra, stocky, dark-haired and quiet, had started to make a name for himself in the fashion world. Spencer had, on purpose she assumed, not mentioned this to Nadine until she actually met him.

The first few shots went all right. But when Spencer, getting excited by the pretty girl in front of him, insisted that she should bare her bosom a little more, they got into their first fight. Each time he tried to peel her clothes further back and went to the camera to take the shot, she quickly, the moment she saw his back turned, pulled up the strings and straps that held her décolleté. Had they not both been so serious, the scene would have been funny. As it was, it needed Ra's tactful interference to have the two combatants come to an agreement.

"Have a heart Spencer; you can see that she feels uncomfortable this way. And you know it will show if she is tense," Ra said soothingly.

The two men took more shots. Then Ra, studying Nadine whose blouse had once more been buttoned up, added: "Besides, I feel it is sometimes more erotic to show less flesh. Leave something to the imagination."

Nadine fully agreed with Ra and was grateful that he supported her. But Spencer, whose attitude was far less professional than his roommate's, gave him a nasty look. Yet he did not say anything.

After about three hours of different poses and after the young girl had changed her wardrobe more than a dozen times, she had become overheated and bad tempered. Now she was tired of straining her arms and legs under the strong lights, which threatened to melt her make-up and made her hair stick to her forehead. She learned quickly that modeling was a hard job. And monotonous on top of it. The hot, bright lights, Spencer's strained nervousness, the endless clicking of the camera, and her own tension, made her suddenly feel hungry. She always wanted food when she was weary, upset or bored.

"Let's eat something. I'm exhausted," she said to Spencer and smiled.

"In a minute love, just a few more takes," he replied. His voice was muffled under the black cloth he had thrown over the camera and his head. His face, when he reappeared from under his equipment, was red and soaked with perspiration.

She hated it when he used an endearment for her. It was a verbal caress she did not want from him.

"I am getting too stiff," she now complained. Although Spencer had put a large white pad on the floor for her to pose on, it was thin and she felt every bone in her body.

"Don't move! These will be the last few shots," Spencer ordered her and he dived under his black cover again, looking like a headless monster.

The Londoner had taken lots of photos of her before. But they had been snapshots as she stood in front of Buckingham Palace or in the spacious, cobble-stoned courtyard of Windsor. Nadine loved to pose for the camera. The instrument was an objective friend who remained impersonal even when getting very close. It was just the opposite of Spenser who never grew tired of telling her how beautiful she was as his eyes were eating her alive. Snapshots hardly interrupted the flow of life. Modeling under hot lights did. It was a task that quickly eliminated any sense of fun.

* * *

After Spencer had worked so dedicatedly taking Nadine's photos in his small, shared flat, their weekly *tête à têtes* became increasingly tenser. The pleasant *laissez-faire*, a certain light-heartedness and the superficial enjoyment she had experienced in Spencer's presence during their former dates, were gone. Slight misgivings – bubbles that surfaced from below – had become highly visible in their talks and gestures. Their short tempers strained their relationship. To Nadine's displeasure it even happened that their trysts in London sometimes developed into shouting matches.

Without having yet put a ring on Nadine's finger – "I'll get you a pretty one" – Spencer considered himself engaged and started to act like a possessive husband. He no longer just walked next to her on the city's congested streets. But wherever they went, Spencer took hold of her hand or arm and threw intimidating glances at other men who dared to look at Nadine. He considered any male a potential rival. Nadine felt more and more that he treated her like an investment of whose accumulating interest he soon intended to take advantage.

At the slightest pretext his fingers pressed tightly around hers and quickly began to become moist. Nadine found his clammy hand unbearable and after a short while tried to wriggle her fingers out of his. But Spencer seemed to be oblivious to his sweaty palms and did not understand her resistance, which made him hold on even harder. And the young girl was too inhibited to tell him about his perspiring hands. She had to wait until he needed them to buy a newspaper or light a cigarette.

On one of their next rendezvous in London, his jealous behavior turned into an outburst of anger that colored his face a deep red and frightened Nadine. She had been late one more time. As usual he was waiting at the center of Trafalgar Square, next to Nelson's Column and the hundreds of pigeons that considered the impressive statue their permanent home. After she had spotted Spenser among the usual crowd of sightseers, she accelerated her steps and then even broke into a short run. By the time she reached him, she was breathing harder than normal and her face was bathed in a healthy glow.

It was a chilly day and Spencer was wearing the same thick, yellow camelhair coat in which she had met him when he had picked her up at Piccadilly Circus. But now there was an unfamiliar smile on his face, which she could not or did not want to decipher. His hands did not stretch out to greet her as they normally did as soon as he saw her approaching him. This time he just stood immobile like a tower in the cool sunrays and did not take his hands out of his pockets. Only his eyes went quickly from her face to her body and then stared at her barely visible knees and ankles. But he did not say a word.

A little startled by his behavior, but still counting on his usual patience, she quickly apologized. Then she told him laughingly that a distinguished looking man who wore the uniform of the upper class, a double breasted, striped suit, bowler hat, umbrella and a red carnation in his button hole, had tried to proposition her on Bond Street.

"Oh, but he was ancient", she quickly added when she saw that Spencer's face started to show blotches of red. As he took her arm and began to walk quickly across the square teeming with people, she was miserable and blamed herself for having forgotten his new, unaccustomed sensitivity. She felt guilty about being late and never able to bear his silence for long, she started to tell him what she had been doing before she met him. On most days when they got together for lunch, Spencer worked in the morning. Nadine, who arrived around nine o'clock in London, explored the city on her own until she met him between noon and one o'clock in the afternoon.

Now, moving at his side, she attempted to explain that she had grown tired of the hustle and bustle of Oxford Street. Its double-decked buses had lost their charm of newness for her and so had the fast, honking taxies and aggressively driven vans, as well as an unending number of cars.

"Traffic moves on the wrong side of the street in any event. And I hate it when all these vehicles puff their waste into the air. Isn't it already polluted enough?" Nadine looked at Spencer disarmingly.

But he glanced at her with a sullen expression on his face before he opened his mouth:

"Whom are you telling this to? You really talk such gibberish sometimes. What else did you do?"

Nadine blushed. She was hurt by his ill-tempered remark but did not want to show it. For a while she didn't say a word and with her right hand firmly held by Spencer's fist, she just looked at several people whom they were passing beyond the big Square.

Yet unlike the Londoner, she could not remain mute. She had, she told him again – and she looked at him with another timid smile, trying to make him see how innocent and silly it all was – entered the narrow, quiet Bond Street where she squeezed her nose against its sumptuous window displays. But although some of the smaller shops kept their doors invitingly open, she did not enter. They were far too expensive for her tiny budget. Also, she had felt uncomfortable, she said, at the sight of the stores' mostly male clerks who were immaculately dressed and used grandiose gestures even when they spoke just among each other:

"They did not have many customers, so the salesmen had leisure to impress an ingénue like me," Nadine tried a giggle.

"If you had been with me, I would have laughed loudly and called them what they were: monkeys," she kowtowed Spencer who was now listening a little more closely.

"As it was," she added, "I felt scrutinized by the young shopkeepers. They pretended not to see me. But as I passed shop after shop, I could feel the clerks' eyes on my back. My walk made me feel warm and I had taken off my raincoat."

What Nadine didn't tell Spencer was that her back, or rather the elongated part of it, was more emphasized than usual that day because she wore a light gray suit, which clung to her waist, hips and other protruding parts of her anatomy. Her tight skirt did not permit her to take normal, unhindered steps. Instead, the garment forced her to walk rather slowly and more voluptuously. And then there were her shoes whose heels were too high. But the heels, too, although uncomfortable, flattered her legs and increased the sensuous movement of her derrière, "…so near to perfect as to be angelic," Christian had once quoted a favorite writer of his. But beauty, too, has a price to pay. She was now unable to people watch, one of her favorite pastimes, because she had suddenly become an object of stares herself.

This was particularly true of a frail, old man whose wrinkled face she, at one point, noticed behind hers as both of their features were darkly reflected in the glass. At the moment she had been looking into a window where jewelry and watches in great variety – with their price tags turned upside down – were displayed with taste and ingenuity.

"Don't you think the turquoise ring over there is lovely", a voice from the mirror had suddenly said behind her in an irreproachable enunciation. But, when Nadine turned around, her face started to burn as if someone had poured hot water over her head. This man could have been her grandfather. Without saying another word, the old, immaculately dressed stranger also seemed shocked. For an instant he scrutinized Nadine's face. Then realizing his mistake, he slightly tipped his hat with a gloved hand, smiled a little nervously and walked away.

"Afterwards, I jumped on the next bus to meet you", Nadine ended her anecdote and again looked with mixed feelings at Spencer.

He still did not say anything and only once more took in with a proprietary glance her face and legs.

"How pretty she is," he sighed inaudibly. Yet he believed only half of her story.

Meanwhile, they had long left behind the white columns of the National Gallery and the 18th century Church of St. Martin in the Fields. Nadine loved those two buildings that bordered Trafalgar Square. She always admired them anew. Then one day – just off the big Square – she had stumbled upon another construction, which had also become a beloved object of hers. It was the lovely church of Notre-Dame-de-France whose murals Cocteau had painted. Once, on a rainy afternoon, she had taken Spencer there and showed him full of pride her serendipitous discovery. Yet he hardly glanced at the artist's paintings of whom he had, as he grumbled sotto voice, heard before. Then, trying to impress Nadine, he said:

"I don't care for all this modern stuff. Besides, isn't Cocteau this queer who smoked opium most of the time?"

"What does that have to do with his art?" Nadine snapped back at him and looked away to hide her annoyance.

'What an ass he is,' she thought and was hurt by his callous attitude.

Now, while they walked and talked, with Spencer, as usual, mainly listening to the young girl's outpouring, she threw every so often a worried side-glance at his profile. And she was relieved when the red blotches on his cheekbones eventually disappeared and he looked his normal pale self again. But his rude behavior had upset her and nearly destroyed the small amount of trust she had started to place in him.

'Under his agreeable surface sleeps a bully,' she reflected. 'I have to watch him more carefully from now on. And most of all, I must not keep him waiting any more,' she silently decided.

As they had passed the National Gallery, Nadine would have liked to take another look at a Gainsborough, a Cranach or one of the elongated figures of El Greco she knew she would find there. But Spencer pulled her along. One of his acquaintances had recommended a Chinese restaurant at Gerrard Street in Soho and they were heading there.

After they found and entered the place and had sat down at an assigned table, Spencer's mood soon began to change for the better. He seemed to have forgotten his long wait and the sudden pangs of jealousy he had felt toward an invisible competitor. He looked less gloomy. And as soon as they started to eat, Spencer's mental disposition toward Nadine improved drastically. He loved food and it showed on his face. Quite a while ago she had, to her astonishment, discovered that he had developed a sophisticated tongue, far superior to her own. He not only knew the foods from any imaginable country, particularly India, China and Thailand, but also had learned to pronounce their often-impossible names correctly and was able to distinguish minute differences, differences that invariably escaped Nadine. When it came to his taste buds, she had to reluctantly admit, she couldn't challenge him at all.

This afternoon, too, as he inhaled the spicy scent of sweet and sour pork rising from his plate, the expression of his features, from his eyes to his mouth, turned into a beatific, and in the young girl's mind, slightly idiotic grin. While he savored his dish, eating slowly, he didn't stop beaming at her. Holding a hot cup of tea in his sturdy and sometimes surprisingly deft fingers, he spoke about an interesting assignment:

"It promises to be rather lucrative if I pursue it with vigor and a little luck," he began to brag. She did not like it when he talked about himself in glowing colors. Not thinking too highly of him, she expected a more modest behavior on his part. And if he went on speaking in too positive terms about his accomplishments, her smile froze on her face and she stopped listening.

So far nothing had come of Nadine's photographs, which Spencer, as he assured her, had submitted weeks ago to a major fashion magazine. He hadn't made any copies for her so she had no idea what she had looked like during their extensive photo session on that busy afternoon.

When the couple had finished their late lunch, they walked over to Shaftsbury Avenue, which was lined with movie theaters. In the past, some of them had pleasantly surprised Nadine with their elaborate furnishings. The deep, leopard-skin covered seats might not have been in the best of taste, but Nadine didn't know any better and was thrilled with the theater's various trappings. Except for detective stories and horror flicks, which she disdained because they were so predictable, flimsy, and ugly, yet without fail were capable of frightening her, she loved films. And if by chance, (she couldn't rely on Spenser's intuition for the arts because he had almost none), they stumbled upon a film made by a great director, she was in heaven. But, good or bad, she never grew tired of movies and it always was a treat when Spencer took her to a theater. She much preferred it to going to a restaurant, which was the Londoner's favorite pastime. The only thing she disliked about seeing a movie was when Spencer, encouraged by the darkness of the place, tried to become physical. That day, too, Nadine felt the need to brush his hand off her knees. And, forgetting how irritated he had been not too long ago, she said quite loudly:

"Leave my legs alone, or I'll walk out of here."

He became enraged when two people sitting in front of them, turned around and looked at him:

"What are you staring at? Keep your eyes to yourself," he said aggressively to the curious couple. Then he snarled at Nadine:

"Oh, shut up!" But he didn't let his hand stray any longer during the rest of the movie.

When it was time to put Nadine on her train, Spencer scared her once more. He wanted to set a wedding date.

They were standing under a large light near a wooden bench where people sat, talking and waiting for their train. While Spencer spoke to her, Nadine was leaning against the lamppost. In his excitement, he had put both hands on her shoulders and thrust her against the metal pillar whose sharp edge pressed painfully into her back. His face was just a few inches from hers, and he was breathing heavily. Usually, when he had not eaten for a while, his breath became sour smelling, forcing her to turn her head. As she did, she noticed that his cheekbones, even in the inadequate light of the station, seemed very red again.

"Stop it! You are hurting me," Nadine whispered and shoved Spencer away. Hurt by her unexpected, hostile gesture, he let go of her so quickly that she had to take a step forward to keep her balance.

"Aren't you a bit hasty," Nadine said accusingly and tried to look into his eyes. But he was greatly upset by her defensive gesture and mumbling an invective, he walked away a few steps.

The next few minutes before the arrival of the train Spencer, keeping apart from her with his head bent, fell once more into one of his sullen silences. During the previous weeks she had watched how he had become depressed when they had to part, and she had then doubled her effort to overcome his dejection. Tonight, more than ever, she talked as fast as possible and hoped that she would be able to distract him. She felt guilty for not liking him any better and tried to pull him out of the dark-blue hole into which he had fallen again. She did not want him to be depressed on her account and like a reluctant child kept dragging him along on her swiftly conjured images. Smiling and speaking softly, she invited him to float with her on the leaves and small branches that were supposed to gently carry both of them downstream.

But he continued to look at her silently and his arms hung limply at his sides as if her denial to allow them to hold her had made them useless. His arms melted into his crème-colored coat and made him look more than ever like a tower. She hated it when he stared at her without saying a word and when he entered a labyrinth of unpleasant emotions where she refused to follow him. At those moments she was unable to feel any affection for him. His silence always accused her of neglecting his dire bodily needs. But she could not give him what he wanted.

As he stood without moving against the black wall of the train, which was slowly, noisily pulling into the station, his wordless gaze also reduced her to someone with broken limbs. She became a rag doll thrown in a corner, unable to move. She could only watch helplessly as people were flowing by and be grateful that she was not stepped upon. She loathed him then for reducing her to a despicable, hunched-over creature that was unable to act or to please.

Then, when a short, sharp whistle let both of them know that the train was ready to leave the huge, semi-dark, ominous looking station, she was overtaken by a dull pity and wished that she could help him. Although she was tired and wanted nothing more than to be alone, she doubled her efforts to cheer him up. Speaking hastily now and louder, she urged him to fight against the invisible monsters that rose from his soul, similar to the hot steam under the train's engine.

For once, encouraged by her imminent departure, she held his fingers tightly and even patted them soothingly with her other hand. Standing on the lowest step of her car and looking down into his uplifted face, she strained to divert him from his thoughts before they could take an audible shape and drag her down to him. The closer they stood together, the more she was terrified to be bound forever to his side and to a life she did not want. She was not in love with him and was certain that for her their marriage would be banal and meaningless. If not worse.

So as not to have to look at him too long, look at the life he so eagerly offered her, she turned her head sideways and, pushed by unease, began to talk about anything that came to her head. Mostly, it was about minor incidents that had occurred during the week while she had looked after Lipsey and Peter. As she spoke to him in a low, soothing voice, she realized that the two small charges whom she loved were becoming, more and more, a peaceful island onto which she climbed after an exhausting swim.

When the train started to move, Spencer said quickly:

"I'll ring you tomorrow". Standing on the platform, he let his fingertips trail along the sooty window behind which she had taken refuge. His eyes, velvety and sad, focused on her face; they held on to her mouth and neck, separated now from him by the thick, dirty glass. Then, as the train began to increase its speed, his full figure, changing into a tower again, slowly floated out of view.

* * *

With a sigh she leaned back into her seat whose upholstery felt voluptuous to her back.

'Like a lover's hand,' she thought and smiled to herself. Of course, the hand was not Spencer's. It belonged to an unknown man. It was someone whom she had never met and would, she was sure, not ever encounter.

'Perhaps it is someone,' Nadine thought sleepily, 'who might have lived during the age of Beatrice Folco Portinari when one day she had walked across the Arno river and into the wide eyes of a nine year old boy who would render her immortal for the forthcoming centuries.'

When she blinked blindly through the train's window and the fast moving shadows and lights behind it, she saw a handsome stranger who was only real in her soul. In perfect rhythm with the train's movement, his tantalizing image rocked her gently back and forth. It was as if she were once more at the edge of the sea where white-crested breakers pounded the sand and sharp-eyed sea gulls swooped low above the swirling, greenish water. But the face she saw didn't belong to Andrew Gibson, her irresistible Hastings man, who still haunted her daydreams.

The man she saw behind the black window that had turned into a mirror, didn't exist in a concrete form. She couldn't touch or smell him. When she stretched out her arms to hold him, they went right through him. And she clung to nothing but air. But he did live under her closed eyelids. She had often seen him. At night she heard him calling her name. Yet as soon as she drowsily opened her eyes in the morning, vigorously rubbing her eyelids, he disappeared. Ghostlike, he vanished the moment she sat up in her bed and put her feet on the floor, getting ready to take care of Peter and Lipsey's small, hungry stomachs. Her White Knight fled as soon as she put the little boy on his potty and helped his sister tie her shoelaces. The dream man had nothing to do with the two children for whom she was responsible. Only occasionally, when her two adorable burdens happily ran in front of her on a lonely, dusty, parched country road, did she think she detected traces of him in their soft giggles and abrupt, bird-like screams.

While she gazed with half-closed eyes into the train's opaque window, London with its millions of scintillating lights fell away from her like a ball gown a young woman steps out of after a long night.

* * *

The weather started to get colder. Nadine would wrap her short raincoat a little more tightly around her waist as she again rushed for the train that took her on her weekly trip to London. Walking as fast as she could, she thought how stupid it was that no matter how early she got up in the morning to catch her train, in the end she always had to run for it. Now she needed those extra five minutes she had wasted an hour ago when she had lingered in front of the mirror. She had noticed for the first time how uneven the two parts of her face were. Her right zygomatic bone was placed a fraction lower than her left one and seemed to be just a little less prominent. The light, as she had turned her head slightly toward the window, was not reflected as strongly from it, nor was its cavity under the elevated bone as pronounced as on her left side. 'How strange,' she had thought. 'I have to look at Julie's face very closely to see if her face also has two asymmetrical halves.'

At present, those lost moments in front of the mirror, made her breathless with anxiety and in her mind she saw the red lights of the train's last car disappear into the distance, leaving her behind. It was no longer rush hour and there would not be another train for almost two hours.

Her toes and hands felt the approaching winter first. It reminded her of her mother who suffered from arthritis and hated the cold. For an instant she saw Monika Tallemann's green eyes and her hands, which chopped an onion so fast, fingers were barely able to move before the knife came down on one of them. And she remembered that her wrists had gotten broader over the years, especially around their whitish knobs that now seemed always swollen. She became homesick, although she did not long for Germany. At this moment she did not even think of Christian, with whom she was in love and missed more often than she cared to admit. But now she wanted only her mother. Wistfully, she yearned for her love, the oldest love of all, in whose glow she had felt secure as an infant and certainly, she imagined, in the womb. She missed the way Monika smelled. No other person had her scent or her skin; soft, yet firm, keeping her bones and muscles in place. Her perfumed skin, she felt, was like the painstakingly made lid of a jewelry box destined for a queen.

* * *

At 2:00 o'clock in the afternoon that day Nadine was, as usual, supposed to meet Spencer at Trafalgar Square. Over the past months the Square had become so familiar to her that she was beginning to distinguish one or two pigeons when the entire flock would alight and compete for her outstretched hand filled with breadcrumbs. Vividly recalling her last week's lateness, she wanted to surprise her beau by being early for once. She arrived a quarter of an hour before 2:00 o'clock and, not expecting him for a little while, started to walk aimlessly back and forth.

It was a lovely, clear day and in spite of the approaching winter the sun still felt quite warm. There was the usual hustle and bustle of big-city traffic with the honking of taxis, vans and buses and the various cries of street vendors. Among the latter were sellers of eel. Similarly to hotdogs or roasted chestnuts, the snakelike, scale-less, fatty delicacy was sold at small, movable stands and business was good. Every so often, as she went to the edge of the Square, she was startled by the harsh, shrill screech of tires that came to a sudden stop. Even part of the sky was invaded by perpetually blinking, huge, neon cigarette ads. Encircled by this ceaseless commotion, the Square with Nelson in the middle and the pigeons that had taken possession of his 185-foot high statue was like a tiny refuge in a large sea.

Standing at the admiral's stony feet and getting bored, Nadine kept feeding the noisy, fearless birds, most of which seemed to live around Nelson's head and his vast bronze shoulders. Forever hungry, they came fluttering down to her hands and then to her arms, too, as soon as she stretched them toward the birds. Greedily, they picked at the dry crumbs she held out to them. After the fearless pigeons had taken off again, she watched several lawyers and bankers in black bowler hats, carrying umbrellas and attaché cases, as they crossed the Square with long, busy steps that left no doubt of their importance. Their heads were leaning slightly forward and they looked like funny, top-heavy, minuscule vessels bracing a strong wind.

On one side of the Square, in front of the National Gallery, lingered a few young students. Sticking their heads together, they sat with prominently pointed knees at the edge of the pavement and in a childish way poked fun at passers-by. When their occasional laughter and sharp, happy wails reached Nadine's ear, she shook her head in disdain like an old, cranky woman. In her current mood she forgot that less than a year ago, back in Germany, she had been part of just such a group.

* * *

Waiting for Spencer, she remembered how much she had enjoyed shocking the decent burghers of Mannheim with a loud, coarse word thrown at random into their midst.

She saw herself walking through the modern, reconstructed center of town, not far from its enormous, still partly war-damaged, eighteenth century castle, constructed from red sandstone, the common building blocks of the *Rheinebene*. Together with two other girls from their clique, Nadine had shaken her hips provocatively and had held on to her dark skirt under which she wore six nylon petticoats, each one nearly weightless and consisting of a different pastel color. She was dressed and moved as if she were on a dance floor, making a sudden fast turn or swinging around on the arms of a partner. Her skirt and most of her fashionable, top undergarments, pink, bright-yellow and light blue, flew up into the air and revealed more layers of unmentionables and occasionally part of a firm thigh. This was considered an outrageous sight. One could admire tons of well-shaped, fully exposed, slender, young female legs at the beach, but on a busy city street not even a fraction of such feminine charms was allowed to be seen.

It was one thing to reveal part of one's lingerie on the smooth floor of a ballroom or lie half naked at the shore of a lake, but a woman, even a young one, couldn't attempt something similar on the street. Yet Nadine didn't care. Together with her friends she kept dancing through the *Planken*, Mannheim's elegant leisure and shopping center lined with several large department stores. From May till September the owners of small cafés and ice-cream parlors moved chairs, small tables and large umbrellas out on the wide pavements bordering the boulevard. Splashing fountains, hundreds of large, well-tended flowerpots, sparkling glasses, china and white tablecloths made people forget that not too long ago all of this had been nothing but a pile of rubble. Moving along with the other two skirt-swaying, whistling and humming girls, Nadine knew how startled her parents and teachers would be, had they seen her as she, in an outrageous dance step, raised her many skirts up to her knees. But she took a calculated risk. She had such fun shaking her petticoats vigorously with both hands and hoped that she would resemble one of Lautrec's Parisian cancan dancers. Or better still like Frida Kahlo when she executed a tango, defying her deformed body, which she cleverly hid among full, ankle-length skirts. As Nadine lifted her feet and pirouetted, she noticed under half-closed eyelids how disturbing her bare legs were to some of the properly dressed, middle-aged and umbrella carrying people who were ceaselessly moving toward her. While her curls flew and her eyes sparkled mischievously, the teenager deliberately challenged the powerful adult world shouting happily into the indignant faces of Mannheim's good, older citizens.

Nadine had joined her school friends on a drizzly, gray, warm Saturday afternoon when she, for once, did not have to work and had suspended all her homework. Skipping clownishly through the streets of Mannheim, she felt quite safe because she was now marching behind five members of her coterie. Like Nadine, her two female classmates were also, every so often, jumping about on naked feet and shaking their skirts as if they, too, tried to give a performance at the *Moulin Rouge*. Then, half way through the *Planken*, three boys had joined the three girls. Now the game changed. All six youngsters, the boys having rolled up the cuffs of their trousers above their calves, lined up in a row and then moved at the edge of the pavement with one foot on it and the other in the gutter where the dirty, brown rain water had collected in a small stream. Gushing vociferously, the newly created brook carried pages of old newspapers, discarded orange peels, empty soda cans and cigarette butts.

Although the vivacious teenagers occasionally pushed each other, joking continuously, on the whole they walked quite orderly one behind the other and, moving at the edge of the pavement, they stayed out of the way of passers-by. Even if sometimes one of the girls decided to dance around a baby stroller, pushed by a solicitous mother, or approached an elderly burgher who sat by himself under a large, red and white striped *Sonnenschirm* in front of a street café, she, too, kept her distance. But in spite of those precautions, their merriment did not last long.

"Look at those pigs", a male voice had suddenly called out to them. It was an old, short man in a gray suit and tie who had stopped in front of the six students. Stiffly leaning on a walking stick, he stood still and stared at the six youths in undisguised wrath while his lips moved up and down pathetically. A large goiter below his fat chin did not help his appearance.

"You don't need to be jealous, Opa. Come and join us", one of the young men in their midst joyfully called out to the indignant passer-by.

But far from being mollified the irascible stranger screamed: "Go to hell, you disgusting, drunken pigs", and, ungentlemanly, shook his fist at them.

Nadine and her friends shrieked with laughter and waved their hands in a mocking gesture of farewell as they moved in the opposite direction of the furious, decrepit townsman. Giggling and shouting they continued hopping along with one foot in the gutter. And while they splashed with even greater enthusiasm in the drizzle, they made up a song about little pigs and big pigs.

But once more their childish amusement was short-lived. Around the next corner came a policeman. Tall, broad-shouldered and middle-aged, he had a gun strapped to his belt and looked every ounce the fierce symbol of German law and order. He sternly examined the flustered adolescents who had stopped in their tracks and become silent. The officer asked them politely but firmly to get on the pavement with both feet.

"And put on your shoes," he ordered them in a deep voice. They had slung their sneakers and sandals around their necks like the tramp they had admired in an American film.

"Behave yourself like adults", the constable added and tapped his rubber cudgel against his pants. A wide, black leather belt, which clung too tightly to his bulging stomach, held up his trousers. His fat face was full of lines and wrinkles and there was a nasty scar that ran from one corner of his lower lip to his chin. Forgetting that he had once been young himself, he had obviously little tolerance for youthful misbehavior. Nadine and her rambunctious friends did not like him at all. But it was his representation of authority and his uniform, which they hated the most.

Yet, by this time, they were getting tired of their pranks in any event and thought it wiser to obey. In unison they sat down on one of the broad, wooden benches, which the mayor of Mannheim had provided for his constituency and they, still not talking, put on their footwear.During their loud singing and marching, some of Nadine's friends had indeed helped themselves to a can of beer or two and she considered herself lucky that they had not met a person who knew her parents. Mannheim was not large enough for her to easily disappear in a crowd. Even in the most uncommon spots she was likely to run into an acquaintance of her parents. And if she had conducted herself badly, the person who had spotted her usually made it a point to call up either her mother or father. The scene at home, after an improper behavior had been revealed by such gossip, was not pleasant. Her father in particularly, would wail for what seemed like hours and tell her in a whining voice over and over again that she had nothing but "*Flausen im Kopf*" (nonsense in her head) and would never amount to anything.

"When will you grow up? Can't you ever behave decently?" As always, her father's moral sense invariably clashed with her own. She thought him "*altmodisch und spießbürgerlich*" (old fashioned and straight-laced) and Heinrich Tallemann was afraid that with his daughter's taste for the flamboyant, which was for him synonymous with a loose woman, and with her quick tongue and rebellious behavior, she would never find a husband. He strongly felt that an unmarried daughter would reflect badly on his duties as a father. It was the old story of *The Taming of the Shrew* all over again.

Marriage for Heinrich was a state of respectability. Not a religious man, although he had been brought up as a Catholic, he saw a great need to embellish life with an ethical lining. He could not live without it. But for his daughter, as she had grown older, his moral judgments, which she considered far too narrow-minded, had become unbearable. She craved for beauty that was unencumbered by any ethical restrictions. She cried with Dostoevsky, whom she adored: "What to the mind is shameful is beauty and nothing else to the heart."[4]

Then, when one evening Jean Kaiser, her slightly older friend and Christian's rival, talked about the *l'art pour l'art* movement in painting and literature, which proposes that the artist separates his political, religious and moral convictions from his work, she immediately liked it. To her this was art in its purest form and it symbolized in the most vivid and unattached manner the freedom for which she craved. Being young and gullible she still believed that such a freedom existed. She was convinced it was just a matter of finding it.

* * *

"He must be late. It is already a quarter past two o'clock," an unknown male voice suddenly said next to Nadine. Startled, she jumped slightly and blushed a deep red. Thinking about her pranks in Mannheim, she had neither seen nor heard the stranger approach. Only later, in retrospect, did she recall that she had vaguely noticed a man across Trafalgar Square who, like her, impatiently marched up and down the pavement and seemed to be waiting for somebody.

Being invaded by the voice of an outsider, she turned around and immediately looked straight into a mouthful of yellowish-white, healthy, big teeth.

'My goodness these teeth are almost a large as those of a horse,' was Nadine's first reaction to the intruder's physiognomy.

The owner of the teeth was at least a head taller than she. Being used to Spencer's height, who reached barely above her forehead, the stature of the stranger took her by surprise.

'He must be in his early thirties. That makes him Spencer's junior by a decade. Of course, I'm not good at judging ages. He might be far younger or older than this,' did she continue to spin her thoughts.

Then, as she took half a step backwards to emphasize how annoyed she was with the interloper, she noticed blue eyes under rimless eye

---

4　*The Brothers Karamazov*, "The Confession of a passionate Heart – in Verse" glasses and thick, unruly, short hair whose ends stood away from his head in a strangely becoming way.

'He obviously has trouble keeping his hair smooth,' she registered and then deliberately turning her back on the tall man, she faced the Statue again and its ever present, loudly cooing pigeons.

'The nerve he has,' she puffed uncomfortably and wished that Spencer would show up to rescue her. He had never been late before and she began to worry that something might have happened to him.

Although Nadine, with her back turned toward the stranger, could no longer see him, she was uncomfortably conscious that he watched her closely and she pulled her eyebrows together, hoping it would give her a sinister appearance.

"I want to look like Ivan the Terrible," she suddenly whispered, having no idea what the features of this 16th century Russian ruler were like. His name alone upheld the atrocities he had committed. Distracted by the uncommon appellation that had popped up in her mind she started to hypothesize in a disorderly sequence. She wondered why utter cruelty, although it is sometimes collected in one particular face, had no countenance of its own. It existed as an abstract conception. At best it was a mask that was put on an evildoer.

'When one looks at a Nero, Tiberius or a Genghis Khan,' she thought, 'one does not see an individual, but a murderous face where atrocities have been assembled under a stony disguise, acts which are so horrible that no animal is able to commit them. Senseless torture and death caused by a sadomasochistic disposition, a vicious face and a pitiless tongue, seem to cling to a name. And for a long time no child is called by it. I know for a fact that after World War Two no parent in German speaking countries named their son "*Adolf*," she finally finished her reflection.

After last week's episode with the elderly gentleman at Bond Street, Nadine was not inclined to experience another amorous mishap. She started to walk back and forth on the wide Square again. As she did, her eyes squinted against the sun and watched the unknown Englishman through the mist of splashing water jets placed at one end of the plaza. But he had apparently lost his courage to approach her again and pretended that she no longer existed. Instead, he also kept looking at

Nelson and the pigeons, most of which now rested on the admiral's hard, immortal shoulders, soiling them with their excrements.

Nadine decided to move in wider circles so she would avoid getting close to the stranger, who had approached the Statue and calmly stood next to it, ignoring her.

'But he can't fool me,' she thought. Her feet started to ache and she wished again that Spencer would come along.

'Where is he, for God's sake? What's keeping him?' she wondered, trying not to think of any mishap that might have befallen him. And she kept moving around. It was all she could do except leaving the Square. But she didn't want to do that.

Then, as she stopped against a wall at the northeastern corner of the plaza, she noticed a poorly dressed woman leaving through the door of St. Martin's-in-the-Fields. Since she had never been in its interior, she thought this might be a good time to do so. It was getting close to half past two o'clock and there was still no sign of Spencer. The moment she stepped out of the sun and into the twilight of the church, she felt a considerable drop of temperature.

'It is darn cold,' she thought and wished that she had brought a cardigan to wear under her thin coat. She walked on tiptoe toward the front of the church so her high heels would not click against the stone tiles. Near the altar she noticed three elderly ladies. Each one of them had chosen a separate, empty pew and knelt there on footstools. With their heads humbly bent and crouching against the wooden backs of the pews, the three frail women, who had shrunk in their old age, looked like children. Nadine, watching the lonely, pious females, began to become even more conscious of the deep silence around her. Then, looking up, she took measure of the dimly lit arch as sunlight filtered through several, magnificently painted windows.

"Still, this is nothing but a large tomb" she murmured unimpressed.

"But you must admit it is a sumptuous one." The stranger had followed her. Nadine once more leaped a little, yet now she was more embarrassed than intimidated.

"Stop running after me. I am just waiting for a friend of mine", she said coarsely.

"That is quite obvious, isn't it?" the man, ignoring the first part of her impudent address, looked calmly at her. Even in the semi-darkness of the church she could see a distinct sparkle in his eyes, enlarged by his glasses. The tone of his voice and the glint in his eyes exasperated her even more. He seemed in control of a situation in which she felt so ill at ease.

"May I keep you company until he gets here?" he asked formally and in Julie's accent, before he quickly added:

"You might find waiting a little less boring. You see, I know churches quite well. My favorite is the old cathedral at Durham; with its ribbed vaulting, it is most probably the first ever constructed that way. Its pointed arch and concealed flying buttresses are stunning. I wish you could see it."

"Why, did you help build it?" she snapped at him with another impertinent inflection. One of the old women, whose back was pitifully curved under her threadbare coat, raised her head from her prayer book and stared disapprovingly at both of them.

Nadine gave her intruder one more mean look and then took several quick steps forward to get away from him. Yet without wanting to be, she was impressed by how articulated he was.

'And he definitely speaks with an Oxford diction, proof of an upper middle class upbringing', she chuckled inwardly.

"Education is everything," she heard her father's voice rumbling through her mind.

"You can take it anywhere you go. No bomb can destroy it and you cannot lose it on the stock market," he had added. Heinrich Tallemann strongly believing in education had brought her up to also revere it without question.

'Well, it might be fun to get to know English culture a little better,' she mused as she kept walking in front of the stranger.

'Julie is not interested in English art or literature and James has no time to talk to me about it,' she tried to excuse her mellowing attitude.

* * *

At the German gymnasium, which she had attended in Mannheim, Shakespeare and Milton had been touched upon. But she knew only by listening to some of her older friends, mostly to Jean Kaiser, about the great English Romantic poets, such as Byron, Shelley and Keats. The information she had picked up as he raved about their work, and their often-adventuresome lives intrigued her. In particular, the clubfooted, curly-haired Byron appealed to her world of make-believe where she felt at home.

Jean, Christian's slightly older rival, was "into" Byron, as Nadine expressed it, and seeing that he had made a convert of her, spoke to her in vivid colors about him. He couldn't absorb quickly enough the poet's writings and his colorful, short life that vacillated so drastically between devoted love and licentious sensuality, between pretending to be world-weary and true suffering.

"Just imagine, even Goethe was taken by him otherwise he would not have immortalized him in his *Faust II* as Euphorion," he enlightened Nadine who was easily impressed.

Listening to him, she saw Byron, who at the age of twenty-eight had moved to Italy, swimming naked in one of the dirty Venetian canals. It was night and he was holding on to a wooden board that had a burning candle on it. It was his only light on the dark waters when he returned home from a place overflowing with women, song and wine. Before he entered the warm, blackish lagoon that lapped against the foundation of a sixteenth century mansion, he had given his clothes to his manservant and told him to carry them home. Then, after a last look at the palace's brightly lit windows above him, he floated alone in the opaque current of the Adriatic Sea. Occasionally he had to kick hard with his legs, hoping that a late gondolier would see his candle on time and not run him over with his black, coffin-like boat. The thought that a little earlier maids and housewives had emptied their chamber pots into the very inlet where he swam did not cross his mind. Instead, he was haunted by images of England, which he would never see again. He had dared to defy one of society's strongest taboos by having an affair with his unhappily married half sister.

* * *

The stranger at St. Martin's had picked up the almost-imperceptible signs from Nadine, which he quickly interpreted as a more favorable disposition toward him. He was happy that she had started to become more curious about him. Whispering, and moving behind her as they crossed the length and width of the church, he was still a little perturbed by the vexation in her voice. But he brushed his unpleasant considerations aside and kept following the pretty young girl along the passageway under the high arch of the church. Tirelessly, he pointed out every window and every statue they passed. To Nadine's relief his low voice, as it kept up its faultless intonation, sounded more and more agreeable.

By the time they reached the altar again, she not only had an idea about the architectural and artistic history of the church but she also knew that the stranger's name was Dexter Paxton and that he had just visited his parents who lived in Welwyn Garden City in Hertfordshire. He had quickly added, too, that he was on his way back to Eastminster where he lived and taught Latin and Greek.

"Do they still cane boys at public schools?" she had asked him sarcastically when she was able to get a word in herself.

Most of the time he spoke, she had kept her nose straightforward so, even when he caught up with her, he could only see her profile. She felt that there was no need for her to look at him as she walked at his side. But intrigued by his detailed, erudite descriptions, she listened intently to everything he said.

"There is more than one way to educate a child," Dexter adroitly avoided the subject and looked at her smooth cheekbone and her rather long neck only partly visible under the collar of her blouse.

'A Modigliani neck', he thought dreamily and smiled to himself. Then with a start he reprimanded himself:

'Don't be a fool, Dexter! For all you know this girl might be nothing but an attractive scatterbrain. Didn't you meet enough of this sort? You need a scholar, someone who shares your interests.' Yet these reflections did not prevent him from following in the young girl's footsteps. Whether he wanted to admit it or not, his imagination had been caught.

In the momentary silence between them, Nadine saw her new admirer in a long black gown lean toward a boy and painfully pull his ear because his pupil had not prepared his lesson. The youngster felt humiliated in front of his intently watching classmates. Yet in spite of the torment Dexter inflicted upon him, he did not cry out and promised in a high-pitched, trembling voice to do his homework next time.

Suddenly Nadine let out a half subdued shriek. Dexter's eyelids quivered and he looked at her in astonishment.

"It is almost 3:00 o'clock! What on earth am I doing here?" Nadine said breathlessly. And no longer paying attention to Dexter, she rushed toward the exit of the church. As she stepped outside St. Martin's door, she momentarily closed her eyes. The sunlight was too bright after the dark interior of the church. Then she spotted Spencer who stood in the middle of the square looking at his wristwatch.

"I was here a quarter before two o'clock. Where were you?" she cried long before she had reached him.

"I'm sorry I'm late", Spencer mumbled. Yet he was looking not at her but past her and she knew that Dexter had followed her once again. She spun around and, stretching out her arm toward Dexter, she quickly introduced the two men. Then, like a nervous schoolgirl, she started to tell Spencer what her new pursuer had just told her about the interior of the church.

"Dexter knows so much about it," she said, being happy to have learned something new and interesting. In her excited state, she was oblivious of Spencer's jealousy, as he stared at Nadine without saying anything to her or to the stranger. But on his face and neck the first red blotches started to appear.

Then, to release some of the pent-up tension, the two men took Nadine in their midst and the three of them began to slowly walk across the Square. Dexter, being taller than Spencer, needed fewer steps than his rival to keep at her side.

Later Nadine could not recall if it had been the preceptor's long, lei-surely strides or his talk, in which Spencer did not want to participate, that enraged the photographer more. Dexter's clipped speech did not help Spencer's increasing discomfort.

Where the newcomer was easily able to indulge in small talk – "I understand that you are a photographer" – Spencer remained tongue-tied and silently moved along. He wore his thick, yellow wool coat again and the turned up collar made him look as if he had no neck. Next to Dexter, whose large frame did not store an ounce of extra fat, he looked as clumsy as a bear.

During their aimless walk, Spencer had tried several times to get hold of Nadine's hand. But she stubbornly refused to give him this token of their intimacy. She would not have been young and a female, had she not, at least partly, enjoyed the two competitors fighting over her. Having only a limited experience in the matter, she was not worried that the situation might get out of hand if one of the two men should lose his temper. But that's exactly what happened.

Heartlessly, she also forgot that until today it had always been she who was late. Instead, she was upset that Spencer had kept her waiting for so long and blamed him for Dexter's appearance.

'It serves him right,' she thought heatedly as she watched Spencer's face, which had started to become even blotchier.

Her voice and Dexter's mingled quietly during Spencer's ominous silence. From moment to moment he seemed to become more alert to some kind of secret understanding between the stranger and Nadine and it was obvious that he suffered greatly. Anger began to choke him. His face turned into a grimace and began to reflect his fear of losing his lover.

When the three of them reached the southern corner of the Square, Dexter lifted his umbrella to hail a cab.

Looking back, Nadine saw that around Nelson's head, crowned with a pigeon, the first patches of a late afternoon fog had started to assemble. There was only one large, thick cloud in the sky. It seemed fragile in its soft pastel blue.

'How beautiful London is,' she thought and for a moment forgot about the two men at her side.

When a taxi driver pulled up, Dexter smiled and said: "I hope the two of you will join me for a drink."

But Spencer, who had suddenly found his voice again, howled:

"Not on your life, pal", and squeezing past Nadine, he tried to shove Dexter away from the passenger door. She was instantly furious with him. The stranger had made a civil gesture and her friend reacted like a ruffian.

'If Spencer had any manners at all, he would have accepted Dexter's peaceful offer,' she almost cried out aloud. Embarrassed by the photographer's behavior she mercilessly judged him. Then she realized that her friend was beyond any rational analysis and had begun to panic.

From the moment Spencer had given his tall challenger a push, things went very quickly.

Dexter, not anticipating Spencer's physical assault, almost lost his balance and, for a moment, dangled one foot several inches above the ground. But he caught himself and when he stood firmly on the pavement again, he said in a calm voice:

"Sorry Spencer, but this is my cab."

The instructor's face had become very pale; but he remained standing squarely in front of the open taxi door, looking at Spencer and Nadine.

"What's the matter with the bunch of you? I haven't got all day, you know", the taxi driver now cut into the lovers' fervid squabble and stuck a head full of uncombed hair through his front window.

"Whose cab is it anyway?" the young impatient driver wanted to know.

"It's mine", Dexter said and swiftly bending down, he took a seat. Then he looked up at Nadine and asked in his sophisticated, irresistible manner of speaking:

"Won't you come with me? Since your friend doesn't want to participate, I would love your company."

Hearing Dexter's invitation, Spencer stepped forward. The red stains on his face and neck had now become so large that not a single streak of white, except around his eyes, could be seen and Nadine was afraid he might suddenly collapse.

"I'm not her friend, you scum! I am going to marry this girl", he screamed and tried to pull Nadine with him. Had he not reached for her, she might have stayed with him. But his physical possessiveness after his verbal one enraged her once more. Tearing herself hastily away from him, she entered the taxi with a catlike movement and slammed the door shut.

Dexter locked it before Spencer, who instantly pulled hard at the door handle, was able to open it again. Then the driver stepped on the gas and sticking his head out of the window, yelled at the photographer:

"If you hurt my car, I'll get you, you bastard."

For a short while Spencer held on to the side of the taxi and even tried to get his fingers through the small space between the window and doorframe. But Dexter was raising the pane up farther and Spencer, getting quickly out of breath as he ran next to the moving vehicle, could not keep up with them. He had to take his fingers off the closing glass if he did not want to lose them.

"You stupid bitch! You don't know what you are giving up. I would have made you famous!" were the last words Nadine heard from him. As the cab sped away, Spencer's mouth started to look like a small black hole. Now, since she could no longer hear his words, it looked funny. When she turned toward Dexter, she smiled for the first time at him. But her hands, which tightly held her purse, were trembling.

* * *

She never saw Spencer again. And she met Dexter only a few more times. It was difficult for him to take off from Eastminster and for her it soon became too cumbersome to meet him for just an hour or two during a day's trip. When Dexter suggested that she should move to Eastminster and find a job there, she declined. She had grown fond of Julie, Lipsey, Peter and not the least of James, Julie's hard working husband. Also Dexter had barely enlarged her knowledge about the Romantic Period. Apart from Wordsworth and De Quincy, two English Romantics she cared little about, he didn't mention the others. He took pride in his knowledge of the Age of Classicism and would talk at great length about Pope, Dryden, Smollett and Walpole. But Nadine, who at first had listened politely and even eagerly, soon lost interest and started to yawn. She found all four writers a bore. They did not catch her imagination, as Byron had been able to.

Nor could she understand him when he began to rave about Virgil, Ovid or Catullus' delicacies in their use of declensions, the beauty of a noun in the ablative or whether they used even or uneven syllables.

"I hate grammar. I can't even remember which nouns end in *-um* and which in *-ium*," she threw into his face one day when he tried to explain some of these finer points of Latin. When angered, she did not care whom she confronted and tended to display what is considered a typical Teutonic tactlessness.

"But how else can you absorb their gorgeous language," Dexter, who was looking for a new convert in Latin and Greek, patiently asked her.

'Oh, fiddlesticks, (she loved this expression which she had just picked up),' she thought before she retorted dryly: "By reading these dead men in their translation".

"You have no sense for language. Even the best translations lack the spirit of the original composition in which the work was written," Dexter lectured her, thinking 'oh, Lord, the girl is far from being an airhead but why does she now act like one?'

"Not true. Look at Baudelaire. After he translated Poe into French, the French claim that Poe now reads better in their own language than in English," Nadine, raising her voice, which she was apt to do when she became excited about a subject that had caught her interest, retorted.

"Oh, the French are preposterous," Dexter declared not so calmly this time either. Nadine had a quick response on the tip of her tongue. But when she saw how determined he was becoming, she tried to divert him and making a reconciliatory gesture she suggested: "Let's go for a walk."

He had started to make her feel uncomfortable. On his suddenly stern face she seemed to detect the traces of a zealous missionary. And in a flash she saw him standing at the shore of Oahu's Waikiki Beach where he attempted to convince a young Hawaiian beauty that her seductive, grass covered hips would look better in a muumuu. Using both of his arms, which for emphasis he lifted toward Diamond Head, he explained to the brown-skinned and white-teethed girl that if her limbs were properly hidden, she would be more pleasing to an invisible power whose existence no one had ever been able to prove.

That was Nadine's last image of Dexter.

IV

Cornwall

On the day Nadine had arrived in Dover, the tall, ill-humored English customs officer, who had so thoroughly checked her belongings, had told her that within the first two weeks of her arrival in Groombridge she must go to the town's police station to register herself as a foreigner. She had been intimidated by the abrupt behavior of the official and understood only part of what he explained to her. During her new life in England, which exposed her almost every day to a strange, exciting event, she had completely forgotten about the incident at Dover. Yet one sunny morning the British bureaucratic system, being apparently as thorough as the German, caught up with the unsuspecting young girl.

In late June, about eight months after her arrival in Groombridge, the only local policeman knocked at Julie's front door and when Nadine opened it, he asked her if she were Nadine Tallemann. For a moment she stared at the rosy, freshly shaved cheeks of the young officer and the big uniform hat concealing his hairline. She remembered his face from having seen him when she had run to the local store. In the small shop, where his head almost touched the ceiling, he had thoroughly looked her up and down. It had been a half-friendly, half-curious, typical male stare, which had sized her up and made her feel as if she were part of the merchandise in the overstuffed room.

"Of course I am Nadine Tallemann. You know very well who I am," she said without thinking. With the bright June sun outlining his silhouette against the doorframe, the young officer blushed slightly and did not smile. He just stood stiff and straight under the door opening, the unmistaken symbol of British law and order. His wide mouth was tightly shut and his eyes skimmed over the top of her head.

'What an ass you are', Nadine thought and continued to look at him without moving. She was hurt that the officer treated her as if she were a stranger who had committed a crime.

"You must appear in court next Tuesday in Reading", he finally said with a somber voice and handed her an envelope.

"But why?" she cried and without listening to his answer, she ran back into the hallway toward the living room, calling for Julie. The Englishwoman duly appeared and was also told about Nadine's requested appearance at the courthouse of Reading. Then the young constable added in a stilted voice:

"Ms. Tallemann did not register as a working foreigner in Great Britain as she had been told to do when she entered this country."

The policeman had only spoken to Julie, as if Nadine, who stood next to her, no longer existed. Then he tipped two fingers to his temple, turned and walked down the garden path. As soon as he was out of sight, Nadine burst into laughter.

"I'm surprised that he didn't click his heels as well," she said. Now it was Julie's turn to laugh.

"Leave him alone. He is only doing his duty. And in any event, the entire village knows that he's set his cap for you."

"Well, his is a large one, and he certainly has a strange way to portray his sentiments," Nadine said indignantly. She hated uniforms. Uniforms meant accidents, maimed limbs, thoughtless brutality and, worst of all, they signified war for her.

"A funny way of showing his feelings," Julie corrected Nadine. She wanted to distract the young girl whose face had become somber.

"All right, a funny way of showing it," Nadine blushed and repeated Julie's words, feeling sheepish.

Julie went into James's study and called up the county's court clerk. She was hoping that she could straighten out the matter by mail.

"No, it is too late for that. A court date has already been set for this coming Tuesday at 11:00 am; Nadine Tallemann has to appear in person," Julie was told by the filing agent on duty.

"What a nuisance," Julie sighed when she got off the phone. "I believe the best thing might be to drive you there, it is quite a stretch from here. But we must find a babysitter for Lipsey and Peter first."

Nadine was greatly relieved to hear this. She had never been summoned to a court before, much less to an English court where the language would not only be not her mother tongue but also where matters would be expressed in a legal jargon that would be almost impossible for her to understand.

Early Tuesday morning there were only a few clouds in the sky and the air was mild. Lipsey and Peter were sleeping over at one of their little friends' house.

"Let's be grateful for this fine weather," Julie said after Nadine had lightly knocked at her bedroom door and then entered the room where the Englishwoman was about to get dressed. She sat almost naked at her small, stylish dressing table. Bending close to the mirror, she was putting on make-up and removing curlers from her hair.

The windows of the room were wide open and as Nadine glanced below, she saw the gardener, a young village boy, who quietly worked at one end of the rose beds, next to the big lawn. Sitting away from the window, Julie was unperturbed by her exposed body. She behaved as if this were a daily ritual between the two women. Nadine briefly watched, while Julie applied mascara to her eyelashes with a few deft strokes and with a cotton swab took off any excess lipstick. Then she rose from her chair and, dropping her short, transparent nightgown completely, she looked at her breasts. The mirror reflected them white and full and with large reddish-brown nipples. Nadine was amazed that her bosom had kept the roundness of a young girl.

Julie did not seem to mind at all that Nadine saw her in the nude. On the contrary, she knew that although she was in her mid-forties she still had a nearly perfect figure and, being fairly vain, she appreciated the young girl's admiring looks. But Nadine was not comfortable. She mumbled an apology and turned to leave. Yet when she was at the door, Julie walked to her adjoining dressing room, saying:

"Don't be silly. You needn't go. We are both women, aren't we? In boarding school I got used to seeing girls without clothes all the time. There's nothing to it."

Nadine didn't know what to say. Standing still, she moved her head and looked at the back of Julie's thighs. They were long and straight and under their thin, luminous skin she saw the faint play of muscles. Only at one place where the pinkish-white flesh expanded into the buttocks, did Nadine observe two hardly noticeable indentions, harbingers of old age. Her elongated back, round and also fine-skinned (and about twice as large as her bosom) tapered up into a small waist and narrow shoulders. Her back, Nadine felt, was a cello made for a musician to play on or for a gifted artist to paint.

She had seen Julie in white shorts and a bathing suit before and had thought that she knew her figure well. But now, as she lingered for another moment in Julie's room, flushing and staring at her body, she realized that she had never known what Julie actually looked like.

* * *

During several pleasant afternoons, after Lipsey and Peter had been dropped off at the next village for a birthday party, the two women had played tennis together. Or rather Julie, an experienced player, had hit the ball over the net and Nadine, unable to return it, went running after it.

They were playing on the lovely, tree-shaded tennis lawn that was part of a large compound surrounding Julie's house. Nadine, who was a neophyte at tennis, even when played on clay courts, got quickly hot, tired and out of breath. After about twenty minutes, Julie, seeing Nadine's red face where, after each missed stroke, one frown after another occurred in quick sequence, laughed:

"I think we are better off walking or swimming together. You need a more experienced tennis teacher than me."

Nadine was half-happy, half-annoyed at Julie who looked as fresh and unencumbered as at the beginning of their game. Her slender figure was outlined against the symmetrically trimmed shrubbery at the back of the court, where several beds of roses, which gave this English garden its distinctive flavor, were located.

* * *

Looking at the roses in Julie's garden, Nadine suddenly saw another huge collection of carefully cultivated roses among which she had walked one afternoon in Germany, together with Jean. It had been at the *Schloßhotel Kronberg* near Frankfurt. That garden, embedded in the wooded hills of the Taunus, was ten times as large as Julie's and had far more exotic roses. At the turn of the 20th century, *Kronberg* had been one of Victoria's castles, a soon forgotten German empress and the first child of Queen Victoria of England. After her death the royal palace was converted into a luxury hotel. Since then during the month of June, no guest who stayed at this beautiful place, or came to have dinner in one of its splendid rooms, missed admiring the roses the moment the first half-open, delicate buds grew on their long stems. Even just half-grown, the stately flowers already distributed their intoxicating scents throughout the large compound. Especially in the evening after a light rain, sight and odor of the multiple roses were overpowering. Spellbound, Nadine had breathed deeply, as half intoxicated, she and her sweetheart were moving slowly from bush to blooming bush.

But Nadine loved Julie's roses more. Without wanting to, she had looked with critical eyes at German rose gardens and judged their beauty rationally as if she had personally been responsible for their growth. Yet Julie's roses Nadine absorbed unthinkingly with her heart. She looked at them as if they were not real, but as if a great master had painted them. And one day she realized that her love for England had its roots in Julie's garden where Peter and Lipsey chased each other and came running toward her, screaming with joy. Out of breath, their crimson-cheeked faces reflected the luster of the roses.

The Englishwoman's roses were special. Nadine never grew tired of admiring them as they flourished in the half shade of a tall, heavy-leafed silver maple or an oak tree. She relished walking between the border of the flowerbeds and the large lawn whose roots had outlived as many as twenty generations – all those nameless and faceless owners of the four hundred year old house. For the time being, it was Julie and her family who lived within the walls of this timeworn structure. Unperturbed, they used its wooden bathroom floor that was sloping at such a steep angle from one end of the room to its opposite that in the beginning of her stay, Nadine had often nervously wondered why it didn't cave in. But like the curved back of a healthy, hoary woman, room and house continued to steadily carry their burden. Now, only the invisible ghosts of those past, unknown inhabitants hovered about the house and its lovely garden. On certain summer nights without a moon, their shapeless forms seemed to hover through the dreams of their current descendents.

* * *

Julie had put her tennis racquet under her arm and was walking toward the house. As Nadine followed her, lost in reverie, she thought that Julie's roses could only be compared with the gnarled rose trees of Chenonceaux. And immediately, effortlessly, she climbed down into the 16th century and imagined Henry II and Diane de Poitiers strolling among the roses when they were in full bloom. Holding hands, neither one of them were thinking of Catherine de Medici, the sophisticated Italian and Henry II's queen and mother of three sons. Henry and Diane only thought of each other. Caught in a web of dreams, Nadine's mind followed the couple and beyond the rose trees she saw that the letters *H & D* were elaborately inscribed above the high doors of the small, exquisite castle that spanned the river Cher. Then she also remembered that after Henry's untimely death Catherine took Chenonceaux away from Diane. But the "Foreigner", as the French who didn't like Catherine called her, did no harm to the roses. Nor did she remove the initials of her husband and his mistress, who had been eighteen years Henry's senior. "How strange and exciting", Nadine thought, "that four hundred years later the roses still bloom and the initials, *H & D*, still speak of love."

* * *

Just before the two women entered the house, Nadine had almost caught up with Julie, who had turned around to see if the girl was following her. Blinded by an afternoon sun, Nadine was unable to see Julie's face clearly. Yet its wide mouth, for once without lipstick, was appealing and without being able to distinguish the fine net of wrinkles that had begun to form above her upper lip, Julie's face looked younger than usual.

* * *

It was true that Nadine and Julie swam well together. Not just during hot, sunny afternoons when they had taken the children to a big pool not far from Groombridge, but also during their two-week trip to Cornwall where they had shared a large cottage at the sea with a married couple, old friends of Julie and James.

Leaving early in the morning from Groombridge, it had been a day's journey in the family car to get to Cornwall. They had started out their trip with an unaccustomed silence festering between the two women. The young girl had sat with the children in the back of the car and during their long drive spoke in a low voice with Lipsey and Peter. But she never addressed Julie who was in front next to James.

The first rift had occurred between the two women and they were both hurt by it. It had been Nadine's fault. She had capriciously and selfishly wasted a day of the family vacation. Hanna Herbert, a girlfriend of hers, who liked to be called Tim, had gone to France to improve her language skills. In Mannheim, Hanna and Nadine had attended the same gymnasium for several years. Nadine was fond of the blond, vivacious girl who had a weight problem:

"One day I'm going to be slimmer than you," Hanna had challenged her friend several times in her distinct Prussian accent, which Nadine, who was used to a strong southern dialect, enjoyed listening to.

In 1945 Hanna, her parents and a younger sister had escaped from Berlin just before the Russians invaded the city. The family had fled west and south until they reached Mannheim where a business acquaintance of Mr. Herbert helped him find a job.

At school, Hanna didn't have many friends. At the end of World War Two, citizens of Southern Germany were not happy about the influx of East Germans, who invaded their region. In particular, those refugees coming from Berlin were intensely disliked. The good, proud burghers of Mannheim didn't want to be reminded that their city was the province when compared with the capital.

Most fugitives from Berlin had other worries on their mind than such infantile considerations. They needed food and shelter, both of which were hard to find at the end of WWII and its dark aftermath. Former Berlin inhabitants had little time, nor inclination to impress the inhabitants of Mannheim. Yet the moment they opened their mouth and spoke Prussian, the sharp and precisely pronounced German speech they had been taught during their childhood days, their involuntary hosts resented them.

Nadine was very aware of this prejudice and, being curious about the strangers, she made it a point to become friendly with some escapees from Berlin. She got along well with Hanna. She admired her elegantly pronounced syllables and the way she palatalized and labialized her consonants, vowels and semivowels, which were so distinct from her own. The two fifteen-year-old teenagers shared secrets and sometimes they had a crush on the same teacher.

"There is enough of Dr. Teller for both of us," Hanna had whispered as the two of them stared amorously at their French instructor. They were crouching above several individual toilet booths, which belonged to a large bathroom of their school. Helping each other, the two youngsters had climbed to a low row of windows that were installed on the upper part of one bathroom wall. From there, highly uncomfortable in a tight space with their necks bent to fit under the low ceiling, they watched Dr. Teller teach a class. He was in another brick building across a spacious, cobble-stoned courtyard that connected the three reddish-gray constructions of their school.

Neither one of the girls could hear a word their teacher was saying. He was too far away. But that didn't diminish their lovelorn enthusiasm. Glued to small, cobwebbed and dirty glass panes with their legs falling asleep from their cramped positions, they observed his slim, tall figure as he noiselessly moved up and down the classroom of seventeen-year old *Unterprimanerinnen*[5]. Feeling inferior and jealous toward the older students, Hanna and Nadine sighed together with longing when Dr. Teller lifted his hand and combed his fingers through his hair. It was thick and grayish-black and a small strand of it always infringed upon his forehead.

"Isn't he gorgeous," Hanna would whisper as they stared at the slender, middle-aged man.

When school was over, the two girls often waylaid their hapless instructor and flanking him in their middle, they escorted him to a

---

[5]   The second highest level of students at a German gymnasium.

small, glass-roofed booth where the three of them waited for his street-car. Hanna and Nadine would fight over the privilege of walking at his right side, the side of honor. Full of energy, they didn't stop talking until their erudite French idol had gotten on his crowded trolley.

"Did you see how he smiled at me?" Hanna said dreamily.

"He must like fat girls," Nadine giggled and ran away, her book satchel pouncing up and down on her back as her puffing friend pursued her angrily and soon out of breath, failed to catch her.

* * *

A few months after Nadine had gone to England, Hanna had started to write her about the wonders of Paris, urging her friend to pay her a brief visit. Nadine, full of pride and longing showed Hanna's letters to Julie and James and the couple soon agreed to give Nadine a few days off. She left four days before the family was due to go on their summer vacation at one of Cornwall's windblown, rocky shores.

"But be sure you come back on time. Otherwise you'll miss Cornwall," Julie had teased Nadine before she went to France.

* * *

Nadine had a great time in Paris. Hanna, now in her late teens, studied French literature at the Sorbonne and did *au pair* work at the spacious, high-ceilinged home of an architect and his wife near the Eiffel Tower. It was here where Nadine was able to stay for three nights, sharing her friend's small room in the huge, old apartment. This was her first trip to the *City of Light* and she was thrilled with every-thing. There was the inimitable French language, the highly fashion-conscious Parisians, the magnificent squares and the enormous Place de la Concorde where so much blue blood had been spilled during Robespierre's *Reign of Terror*. Like most ingénues, Nadine, guided by Hanna who seemed to know the city far better than the sophisticated *citoyens* themselves, marveled at everything. Talking non-stop with Hanna, she couldn't get enough of the Champs Élysées's vast elegance where, not too long ago, Hitler's army had marched across and where the infuriated inhabitants had watched the hated uniforms of German soldiers and didn't miss a chance to surreptitiously poke fun at the goose steps of their officers.

But even more than the Right Bank, Nadine enjoyed the *Quartier Latin* where she and Hanna could afford to eat in a small, rather dirty restaurant whose food tasted delicious.

"*Mais ici il ne faut jamais aller voir une cuisine*,"[6] Hanna, showing off her French, had smiled as she looked at the crowd swarming across the Boulevard St. Michel.

Arm in arm, the two young girls strolled through the *Jardin de Luxembourg* with its students and its children and their attractive nannies, most of whom wore a white bonnet on their head. Rambling along narrow gravel-walks bordered by shrubberies and flowerbeds, they stumbled across young lovers who were leaning tightly against each other as they dreamt open-eyed on weatherworn benches. Hanna and Nadine watched them with a knowing smile while boy and girl sat, holding sweaty hands, as their tongues explored lips, teeth and ventured into the caves of their mouths. It was clear that the world in front of them had steadfastly disappeared and that they didn't see anyone except their own image in the eyes of each other.

Slowly, the two girls went down Boulevard Raspail and casually dismissed the young Algerians, who often pursued them. They smiled into their dark faces, all of which seemed to possess large, fiery eyes and the most immaculately white teeth that Nadine had yet seen – with the exception of one black countenance…

* * *

After World War II was finally over, Nadine had made friends with an American soldier whose battalion occupied the zone in which she and her parents lived. She had just started to attend school on a regular basis in Ludwigsburg, a pretty South German town. They had lived there for several years before Nadine and her mother's evacuation to a remote mountain village of the Schwäbische Alp during WWII's worst bombing attacks.

---

6   But here, you must never go into a kitchen.

Her new acquaintance was a tall, powerfully built man who was no longer as young as most of his army buddies. When Nadine first saw him, he was chewing gum and wore army boots, which made no sound at all when he marched up and down in front of a large gate. Unlike German footwear, the soles of the American's boots didn't contain nails but were made entirely from rubber. She had never met a man before who wore such shoes and chewed gum, let alone a uniformed member of the army. During the war, she had gotten used to hearing the approach of a German cadet from far away, recognizing him from the sound that the nails of his boots made on the asphalt. It was a hard, crushing sound, multiplied a hundred fold when she watched a parade. The newness of a noiseless boot and moving mandibles fascinated the child. Her mother thought differently.

"Kaugummisoldaten"[7] Monika Tallemann had scornfully called the Americans whose lankiness and laissez-faire behavior she couldn't get used to. In her pride and emaciated state, she even rejected a friendly smile from a member of the occupying army.

Her mother's thinness had been etched into the little girl's memory banks with an accusing cry from Mrs. Reuter, a corpulent family friend:

"Your mother is nothing but skin-and-bones," Mrs. Reuter, who had remained fat even during the worst days of the war, had thrown into Nadine's face as if it had been the child's fault that her mother was starving.

Monika laughed at Mrs. Reuter's clumsy, tactless remarks but she felt that insult was added to injury when American soldiers didn't approach her with harsh words. A victor wasn't supposed to be friendly. He was the enemy. She didn't expect any mercy from a foe of whom she had been in deadly fear for several years.

Nadine was too young and trusting and, like the child she was, she was already forgetting the terror she had lived through in bomb shelters and passenger trains where she and her mother had been shot at by low flying planes. She didn't share Monika's feelings. Instead, she would approach her former adversaries with a smile and a timid, sociable wave of her hand.

---

[7]   chewing gum soldiers

Each day after school, she passed a lovely, white villa. It lay embedded in a deep, only partly visible garden where about two-dozen old oak trees, whose parallel rows were shading the driveway, had survived the bombs. The large house had been the former home of a high-ranking German officer. Now the American army made use of it. Two uniformed sentries had been placed next to its wide, wrought iron entrance gates. One of the guards often was an older, yet still strong looking, tall man whose waist had expanded into a potbelly. His eyelids under his funny round helmet, which seemed so different from the German ones that she was used to, were heavy. He usually looked as if he were half asleep, which gave his countenance a peaceful, gentle expression.

When Nadine first spotted the overweight soldier, he had stood squarely in the sun without moving a leg or an arm. He had taken his rifle off his shoulder and placed it next to him. His feet were enormous and his face and hands with their elongated fingers were of the blackest color.

Nadine had never been close to a black man before. Only once in Treffelshausen, the tiny mountain village in which the child and her mother had found temporary refuge, had a Negro corporal passed her in an open jeep on the other side of the street. It was just after the war and, with sparkling teeth, the American soldier had tossed sweets by the fistful at her and the other children with whom she was playing. Screaming with joy and pushing each other out of the way, the children picked the candies off the dirt-encrusted, dusty village road. Red-cheeked and triumphant, Nadine had raised her hand full of candies into the air and then ran home to show her treasure to her mother. Suddenly, from across the dirt road a peasant woman, who had watched the army officer and the children, shouted:

"Throw them goodies away! They are poisoned! Throw them away! If you eat them, you die!"

Nadine's heart almost stopped, as she looked at the woman whose forehead was hidden under a red kerchief and whose small gray eyes blinked at her like those of a bird of prey. But unlike some of her small friends who obediently dropped their coveted confection, which few children had seen during the war, she held on to hers and sprinted away.

She stormed into the farmhouse where one small corner of it had become their temporary abode in the hamlet to which they had fled at the end of the war. As she pushed the front door open, she yelled breathlessly:

"Mutti, are they really poisoned?"

Monika Tallemann, hearing her child's cry, rushed from the kitchen where she was preparing *Mittagessen*. When she saw her daughter's overheated face, she asked worriedly:

"What poison? Slow down and tell me what this is all about."

Nadine showed her the colorful, round bonbons, each wrapped in their own transparent paper, and told her what had happened. She was greatly relieved when her mother said:

"Oh, these poor old yokels and their tall tales; you can eat those candies, they are not poisoned."

And the small girl screeched with happiness for the second time that day.

* * *

A few weeks after Nadine's first encounter with the American army in Treffelshausen, her mother took her back to Ludwigsburg where she began to go to school at a normal schedule.

One afternoon after her classes she saw the big black soldier leaning sleepily against the gatepost of the mansion. He looked so amiable and lonely that she shyly approached him. The American was bored and homesick; he welcomed the chance to start speaking with Nadine. He thought that the little German girl with her brown curls and the long apron she wore over her dress, looked cute.

'She doesn't seem to be afraid. She can sense it that I am not going to hurt her,' he reflected. There was no evil in his heart. Seeing her, she reminded him of his own daughter when she had been Nadine's age and he just wanted her to be happy.

"Call me Sidney," the soldier told her and pointed with his forefinger to his broad chest.

"*Callmesidney*", Nadine nodded her head and smiled. Then she lifted her hand toward her chin and said: "*Ich heiße Nadine.*"

"Isn't that a pretty name," Sidney replied and flashed a set of perfect teeth at her.

Of course, she didn't comprehend a word he had said but she instantly understood his friendliness and when he held out a piece of chocolate, her eyes lit up and she stretched out an open fist. After she received her unexpected gift, she shook hands with the American and curtsied to him. The black private broke into another broad smile and dazzled her again with the whitest teeth she had ever seen. She had not known that teeth could have such a healthy gleam. Their whiteness seemed to go beyond white until it reached a point where the various shades of silver start on the color scale.

"My, my, aren't we a sweet damsel," Sidney had commented as Nadine acknowledged his compliment with a questioning glance. His voice was dark and kind and she couldn't detect a trace of sarcasm or hostility in it.

"*Ich bin Nadine, Callmesidney,*" she said once more before she bowed her head a little and ran home. Unnoticed by her, the lonely soldier's smile followed her down the road until she turned a corner.

From that day on, Nadine was always on the lookout for her white-toothed friend. When he was not on duty, it was not a good day for her and the small pockets of the apron she wore wouldn't be stuffed with candy and the chewing gum, which she had quickly started to like. In Treffelshausen she had swallowed her first piece of gum as if it had been a sweet. She hadn't known what gum was and no one had told her that she was not supposed to eat it. She had been hungry and the fresh, sugarcoated gum had tasted good.

One afternoon, Sidney had brought a chair to the gate and was sitting in the mild, slightly slanted rays of an autumn sun. Sitting down while on duty was against army regulations. But Sidney's commanding officer was away and he trusted his comrades-in-arms not to tattle on him. Nadine wished her friend a good day and quickly began to tell him in German what school had been like. The soldier listened intently. He was starting to pick-up some German and every so often, he uttered a word, which he had collected at random. It usually didn't fit at all and his awkward pronunciation made Nadine laugh. Familiar German words suddenly had a gurgling sound to it as if a small, rushing spring had opened under her feet. She liked that. But her mother did not and said Americans spoke as if they had a hot potato in their mouths.

"What an atrocious language," Monika Tallemann had remarked several times to her daughter and shaken her head in disgust.

"Especially when you compare English with French. Now there you have a civilized tongue," she added and looked disapprovingly at her small daughter, who so obviously preferred English.

It was easier for Monika to accept the French adversary who lived across the river Rhine than the American foe whose home was across an ocean. One was familiar, the other was not.

Nadine had told her mother about Sidney and while Monika Tallemann didn't forbid her daughter to see the American, she would have preferred her to not become comfortable with him.

On the afternoon when Sidney was sitting in front of the gate, which he was guarding, Nadine pointed at his lap and said: "*Ich bin auch müde.*"[8] Then, without further ado, she climbed onto the soldier's knees.

She couldn't remember when she had sat last on her grandfather's lap and the strong soldier, although younger, reminded her of him. For a while she stopped talking so she could savor more fully the feeling of safety, which Sidney's body gave her. His clean, carefully ironed shirt seemed to smell slightly of the chocolates he had so often supplied her with in his kindness, and the fast beat of her heart, after her audacious climb, started to lessen. The words "safe as in Abraham's lap" that she had heard once or twice from her grandmother, floated through her mind.

"*Du bist wie Abraham, Callmesidney*"[9], she said and smiled at her friend – not knowing that in the United States there were at least two important men called by that name, not just one. The next image, as she felt warm and secure on Sidney's knees and as her eyelids started to close, was Jacob's ladder. But she didn't see any angels ascending skyward.

Nadine knew the sky only as a dangerous space. One day toward the end of World War Two when she was on her way home, a pair of

---

[8]   I'm tired too.

[9]   You are like Abraham, *Callmesidney.*

glittering metal wings, which almost touched the rooftops, had swooped fast and low from the sky. The wings that day had belonged to a small American plane. It was so close to her as she climbed a hilly road that she spotted the barrel of one of its machine guns. It was aiming at her and she was barely able to throw herself flat into the ditch before a row of bullets struck the asphalt. The milk she carried, and for which she had just stood in line for almost an hour in a crowded store, spilled all over her dress and bare knees. With her face in the dirt, her eyes shut tight and her clenched fists clinging to her temples, she lay stiff and terrified as gunfire struck around her. The attack lasted less than a minute. The pilot must have realized that she was nothing but a tiny, harmless, moving spot. Yet during that short time the child knew once again what death was like. Crying hard, she remembered the nights she had spent in shelters and cellars while the buildings above her collapsed with loud crashes, foretelling an imminent and often cruel death.

After the plane had vanished as quickly as it had appeared, Nadine got up from the ground. And although the street around her was pierced with small openings and splattered with pieces of metal where the fusillade had impacted, she seemed unharmed. Still weak and dizzy, she inspected her arms and legs to make sure that she had not been hit. Then she saw that there was a white stream running down the small hill she had just come up, swinging her heavy tin milk can by its handle. Its shiny, rotating movement must have attracted the enemy pilot. Further down the road, the muddied milk formed a small, whitish puddle around a pile of dust and fallen leaves. There would be no milk for the next eight days until they got more ration coupons. And the child began to cry again. She knew her mother would be upset and scold her.

Sitting on Sidney's lap, Nadine didn't join Jacob's angels who climbed up and down the airy ropes of his dream. Instead, she descended the ladder into the ground where she felt far more protected than above it. Effortlessly, with only the flutter of two eyelids, she traversed layers of earth until she met her cousins, the apes and monkeys and Kaa, the python and until she was walking next to Mowgli through his jungle. Soon she reached the place where the beautiful Indian boy buried his face in Baloo's brown fur and slung his arm around Bagheera's strong, silky neck. Here she felt safe. And she dug her nose deeper into the American's big, protective shoulder that felt warm and didn't move.

After some time Nadine started to speak again. But she talked faintly as if she were still half asleep and as if by whispering she could keep Mowgli for a little while longer. Her soldier hadn't stirred at all.

Seeing the child had fallen asleep, he sat still and held her as gently as he could, realizing that she was a rare, small creature. When she finally turned her head, she saw that he had closed his eyes too. From one lid a tear ran down his cheek.

"*Warum weinst du?*[10]" Nadine wanted to know. "*Bist du traurig?*[11]"

"Yes," Sidney said, "and I'm getting awfully stiff." Nadine slid off his lap. Slowly, as if in pain, the soldier started to get up.

"That little thing is one smart cookie. And sweet, too. She'll be a heartbreaker," Sidney mumbled as he watched Nadine skipping down the road. Her satchel was bouncing back and forth on her back in rhythm with her high steps.

* * *

In Paris, the fine-boned bodies and the smallness of the young Algerians and Moroccans who swarmed through the Quartier Latin, had hardly intimidated Hanna or Nadine in spite of their tenacious pursuit. If one of the love stricken young men tried to follow the two girls for more than a few minutes, they turned around and usually Hanna addressed him angrily in German:

"*Verschwinde, Mann! Sonst setzt's was ab!*[12]"

That rude threat, though incomprehensible to the testosterone driven Moroccan, helped. His dazzling smile disappeared and his large glowing eyes suddenly looked distressed. It also didn't hurt that both girls were often taller than their admirers. And Hanna, with her broad hips, large bosom and strong legs, looked like a legendary blond-haired Walküre ready to take a dead warrior to Walhalla, especially when she forgot her upbringing and held both fists at her sides, signaling her

---

[10]   Why do you cry?

[11]   Are you sad?

[12]   Get lost, man! Otherwise you are going to get it!

readiness for action. She looked so much larger than their frail, thin, kinky-haired fans that they went their separate way, leaving the girls alone.

On Nadine's last day in Paris the two friends went to Versailles where they admired Louis XIV in his high heels and white, silk stockings. Shoes and hose showed to their greatest advantage the slender legs of which he was so inordinately proud. Staring at an oversized painting in its huge, sumptuous frame, Hanna remarked:

"Louis had prettier legs than most women I know. And I'm sure his ass was not bad either." Hanna was not inclined toward respect for monarchs. Particularly if they were dead.

Just when the two girls decided to go back to the city, they discovered a small fair and started to walk through it. At one place, they stopped and watched as little, red, blue and green colored cars moved crazily inside a large, low-encased square that was covered by a metal ceiling. The fun seemed to consist of driving each car at top speed into as many other ones during the shortest time possible. A wide, rubber reinforced platform, which ran all around the two-seated vehicles gave the drivers a certain amount of protection on their collision course. High whips at the end of each car scraped along the electrified ceiling. The transmitters looked like thin, erected tails. As they touched the ceiling, they caused a shower of silver-white sparks.

For quite a while, Hanna and Nadine stood spellbound and giggling taking in the colorful scene in front of them where loud music was constantly punctuated by screams and shouts of joy. Talking and laughing and not wanting to leave, they were suddenly approached by two young French men. Half politely, half timidly the strangers invited the two girls to enjoy a ride with them. Neither Nadine nor Hanna had noticed the two cavaliers until they directly stood behind them and started to speak. Both males, still more boys than men, quickly introduced themselves as François and Denis. François was taller than Denis. His waist was flat and almost as slim as a young woman's, whereas Denis had heavier bones with more fat around them. But both young men had intelligent, handsome features and there was a sparkle in François' eyes, which Julie, whom Nadine remembered in moments of a crisis, would have called "naughty".

When their admirers first addressed them, the two girls had blushed in unison. But Hanna, the more aggressive one, had taken a closer look at both boys. When she saw that they were in their early twenties and after she had taken an instant liking to their refined, alert faces, she smiled: "Why not?"

A minute later the four young people were seated in two different cars. A whistle blew, feet stepped on a pedal that supplied them with electricity and off they went. Laughing and screaming, they chased each other across the smooth, square enclosure, spun around their own axis and constantly bumped into several other cars that were in their way. A few times they took so quickly a turn that their vehicles leaned sharply to one side raising two wheels audaciously into the air. Their car momentarily maintained a dangerous balance, with two wheels spinning madly off the ground. There was no time to look at each other. If they didn't want to be thrown overboard, they had to hold on to either a short, heavy bar in the front of the tiny vehicle or the steering wheel itself. In spite of the rubber protection that ran around the little cars, the impact, when they collided with another car, was sometimes so strong that they were lifted out of their seats. For an instant they then stood fully on both feet, even on their toes. A second later they were jolted backwards and dropped hard on their derrières. They screeched and shrieked until they could hardly breathe. And just when they thought that their crazy ride would go on forever, all cars suddenly stopped wherever they happened to be as if some invisible fairy had raised a magic wand. But it was only the operator who had shut off the electricity and unless one paid more money for another ride, one had to make way for the next joy seekers.

François and Denis would have liked to go on but the two girls shook their heads.

"Let's get something to eat then," the young men said and steered Nadine and Hanna toward a beat up *Deux chevaux* on whose back seats one rode as if swinging in a hammock. They left Versailles and drove toward the outskirts of Paris. It was late afternoon and the sun was about to set. A few golden beams hovered across the windows and doors of several tall apartment houses they passed, lined up like soldiers on a drill.

After the excitement of the fair, the four young people started to speak in lower voices. While Hanna struggled along in French, Nadine and François spoke in English since neither mastered the other's native tongue well enough to feel comfortable in it. They moved along what seemed to be an incessant stream of streets packed with six or seven-story high, modern buildings. Then the apartment structures slowly changed into private homes on which the last sunrays continued to paint yellow arabesques. After both young girls had long lost all sense of direction, they suddenly stopped in front of a large, graceful villa and François said:

"My parents had some friends over for lunch today. There is most probably a lot of food left. Would you like to come in?"

Nadine turned around to see what was on Hanna's mind, but her friend was so deeply involved in a conversation with Denis, that she hadn't heard François. Smiling, he repeated his invitation and Hanna said instantly:

"Sure, I'm starving!"

They went inside the house and headed straight for the dining room.

As they entered it, even Hanna, who had been talking almost without interruption, became quiet. It was an astonishingly ornate room. Rectangular, its long dining table was built in the same shape. Two immense crystal candleholders stood close to either end of the table, which was covered by a stiff, white damask cloth. Breadcrumbs and a red wine spot in front of one seat showed that a meal had recently been eaten here. In the middle of the table was a voluminous, intricate flower arrangement that was cleverly composed of several dozens of luscious, slightly fading, yellow roses. Their faint fragrance filled the room and their color corresponded with the tapestry of the Louis Quinze chairs that were grouped around the table. One wall of the oversized room seemed to be made of nothing but windows since it was decorated with heavy folds of turquoise brocade drapes and lace curtains. Elaborate paneling, similar to that which the girls had just seen in Versailles, covered the other walls. Between panels and ceiling ran a broad ribbon of tapestry depicting scenes from Boucher. On the floor was an enormous Oriental carpet whose exquisite colors were fading.

Hanna, who had stopped at the door before she took three steps inside the dining room, then halted again and asked François:

"What does your father do?"

"He is one of Le Figaro's publishers," the young French man replied and went past her into the kitchen to get some food.

"Well, he must be selling a lot of papers," Hanna said as she stared with a big smile at François' disappearing back.

Within a short time a fraction of the table was loaded with camemberts in various degrees of softness, salty brie and the hard, nutty-flavored, squarely cut gruyère. Among the cheeses, François had placed fresh baguettes, a thin Limoges dish, manufactured in the *Comte d'Artois* style, which contained cold salmon and one more plate where a pile of *pâté de foie gras* was heaped on. There were ripe, yellow pears and a bottle of Pinot blanc.

Smiling and talking the four young people sat down to eat.

"And tomorrow I have to go back to England," Nadine said wistfully in the middle of their noisy and enjoyable meal.

"Why can't you stay a day longer?" François wanted to know.

"Because I promised to be back tomorrow; the Johnsons have arranged to leave for Cornwall on the day after I return to London." Nadine said. A little intoxicated, she looked at his eyes and his soft, feathery eyebrows that curved at a high angle toward his temples. As she watched his mouth, whose full lower lip seemed slightly indented in its middle, she thought what a treat it would be to spend more time with him.

"Send Julie a telegram that you were unexpectedly delayed," Hanna, who wanted to prolong their fun too, suggested.

"The post office is closed," Nadine objected.

"You can send it tomorrow morning. Julie expects you only in the afternoon." Hanna gave her friend an encouraging grin. She had an answer for everything.

Nadine felt il-at-ease about the telegram. But after another discussion with Hanna late at night, when the two girls had finally returned to the architect's dwelling, she decided to send the cable early in the morning. The pleasure of being one more day together with François,

Hanna and Denis outweighed her sense of commitment toward the Johnsons.

After she left the post office, Nadine sighed and then suddenly said to her friend who had come with her:

"Oh well, I guess I'll never be a Chimène." Then she laughed a little nervously and lifted her hand with a subconscious impatience toward Hanna, ready to blame her, or anybody else except herself, for her break of promise to be back in England on time for the family's vacation. But Hanna, who sensed that Nadine's conscience plagued her, was quick to divert her:

"So you are into Corneille's *Le Cid* now. How do you like Rodrigue, this wonder of a male creation, which was inspired by the Spanish tradition of *l'honneur castellans*? Yes, and let's not forget Chimène, the flawless woman by whom the hero is smitten, those two honor-driven inamorati who chose duty over love?" Hanna seemed eager to know. She was knee-deep into 17ᵗʰ century French literature and was pleased with Nadine's apparent interest in the golden age of French letters.

"Well to be honest, I am puzzled by Chimène and Rodrigue," Nadine said. "I cannot understand their choice. Why did they renounce their love for the sake of their fathers' quarrel? The two old gentlemen were not such nice guys in the first place. And the young lovers are quite different from their procreators. I don't see the need of their following so closely in their fathers' footsteps."

Nadine looked challengingly at Hanna who revealed her strong, uneven teeth. A self-conscious smile spread all over her face. It was a mixture of newly acquired knowledge and her old, accustomed way of boasting.

The two friends were on their way to meet with François and Denis. Nadine noticed that Hanna had put on her best dress and, as they crossed a busy street, she wondered again about her quick energetic steps and her inward turned toes that were so little in balance with the rest of her heavy figure.

"Have you tried looking at Rodrigue and Chimène as if they were Romeo and Juliet, but with a happy ending?" Hanna asked before, without taking a breath, she added: "As you know, Rodrigue and his lady do not die like the poor young lovers of Verona. Corneille's *amoureux* get married instead. They just had to postpone their wedding for a year. After all, Rodrigue did kill Chimène's father. A year of mourning and atoning sounds appropriate to me."

Hanna was breathing fast now and a few beads of perspiration appeared on her forehead. Her entire face was flushed with pink streaks and her eyes, rather small and set widely apart, were sparkling. It was obvious that she enjoyed their conversation, which she easily dominated.

Nadine did not say anything. She just laughed and stared at Hanna's little nose. She sometimes got thoroughly annoyed with her friend's endless talks, but she also took pleasure in her cleverness and imagination.

"Did you know *Le Cid* is called *"le poème de la gloire amoureuse"*? Hanna tried to impress Nadine again.

"As you can see," she continued, "the emphasis with Corneille is on *"glory"* since he chose a noun for it. Whereas *"love"* he treats as an adjective – *"amoureuse"*, a mere codicil. Love is clearly subjugated to duty in Corneille's world."

Hanna's cheeks and forehead had become inundated in red in her eagerness to show off her refined knowledge of Gallic civilization. The two idealistically inclined girls whole-heartedly, as only youth can, believed in Corneille's baroque beauty. They preferred the mixture of realism and fantasy in his plays to the somber and greater depth of Molière's comedies, or Racine's superb tragedies.

"But Corneille's ideal is directly opposed to mine", Nadine gave the poet a last mumbled thought. "I spell *"Love"* with a capital '*L*'. Duty comes in second place. That's why I was able to send my cable to poor Julie." And for a little while she hung her head guiltily.

* * *

On her last day in Paris, the day she had stolen from Julie and her family's vacation in Cornwall, there was not a cloud above the innumerable chimneys of the city, which huddled in tight clusters on top of often black-slated sloped mansard roofs. Nadine, who had not yet been to Montmartre where Sacré-Coeur sat like a scrumptious wedding cake at its highest point, had cried that the cathedral's vast, white dome must look especially striking in the sun. Everybody agreed and the four young people went off on a brisk walk. Not wanting to slow down, they started to sweat as they run up the multiple, steep, wide, stone steps, closely flanked by crooked, old buildings, which led toward Sacré-Coeur. Then, on top of the stairs, with Paris spread at their feet, they barely reduced their speed as they rushed through the uneven, cobble-stoned roads of Montmartre. Nothing seemed changed about its quaint, crowded cafés, galleries, street sellers, small squares and run-down, colorfully painted houses. Houses and alleys still looked the way Utrillo had cleverly caught the scene on canvass not too long ago.

As they rested outside the big basilica with Paris glistening below them like an enormous jewel François, still out of breath, said:

"The view from up here is fine; but Sacré-Coeur is mainly for tourists. It was not built in the best of taste. Now, Notre Dame and La Sainte Chapelle, they are something else! And there are certain buildings on the Ile St. Louis I like a lot."

François, who was studying architecture, started to sing the praises of Le Vau and Mansart, Versailles's immortal architects. Exhibiting his intellectual acquirements in front of Nadine and Monika's admiring glances, as Denis who had heard it all before wisely remained silent, he also mentioned Le Nôtre who had designed Louis XIV's huge palace gardens with their magnificent display of fountains and sculptures:

"The latter ones often adhere to Greek and Roman ideals by reviving, at least in stone, their gods and goddesses from Diana to Apollo," he lectured in almost flawless English.

The two young girls got more and more enthused.

"Oh, let's go then; we barely saw the park yesterday; moving through the interior of the castle took so much time", Hanna cried and bounced off the low wall on which they had been sitting. The four of them climbed off Montmartre's venerable old back and forming couples they walked through a large part of the city. They talked and laughed and sniffed the air like hungry cats enticed by the odor of a dead fish. Nadine and Hanna wore high heels that ordinarily started to hurt sooner or later. But today, their feet no longer seemed to touch the ground. Reality had disappeared around a corner. It had fallen into the rain gutter over which the four of them had stepped lightly. Instead of deadlines and other duties, they faced a dream landscape, a *cityscape* that tomorrow would be entirely different.

For Nadine, who had to leave the next day, Paris would then cease to exist. But for the moment she wanted to forget who she was and what she was supposed to do. She longed to forget England and Germany and even Christian who had insisted before she left for the British Isles on not bringing any of her more elegant dresses with her. Her face started to burn when she remembered what a fuss he had made over three, hard to come by cocktail garments. They were precious to the young girl because they were the first new clothes, which she had ever owned. As a child and even as a young teenager after the war, new dresses had been impossible to get hold of. It took a long time before department stores were finally able to offer some decent stuff again. Meantime, thanks only to Monika Tallemann's ingenuity discovering an inexpensive seamstress in their neighborhood, Nadine finally became the proud owner of three pretty dresses. There was particularly one red outfit with a deep décolleté, which had caused Christian to stare hard when she first wore it. Nor had he wanted her to take a far more modest, high-necked, yellow dress. She loved its crisp, smooth, black taffeta sash that made her waist look smaller than it was. And mostly perhaps her boyfriend had been against her packing a light-blue, fully lined silk frock. Unlike the other two dresses, this one did not have a flowing skirt. Instead it clung to her like chamois and emphasized every curve of her body. Christian was afraid that another young man might take his place if Nadine looked too attractive. He wanted her to be pretty only for him. At first her vanity had been flattered by his immature, exaggerated attention. He seemed to see things of which she was unaware. But she soon grew tired of his proprietary admiration, which restricted her freedom. Now, as she floated next to François through the streets of Paris, she wished she were wearing her red dress, the daring one, which she had left back in Mannheim.

As she walked for several hours at François' side and intoxicated by his closeness every so often glanced surreptitiously at him, almost overcome by the desire to touch his hand, she no longer wanted to remember her various nightmares, which often depicted her as a little girl when she had succumbed to deadly fears while she clung to her grand-mother. Moving next to the charming young Frenchman, first through city streets and then through Versailles' abundant palace gardens, she did not want to recall how as a child she had hidden her face in Anna Nußbaum's huge, soft bosom so she would not hear the endless roaring of planes over their heads and the detonations of the bombs. Yet it was all in vain. In spite of François' head spinning presence, she suddenly saw herself again as she had screamed during the most terrifying nights in Mannheim when the deadly explosives had hit so close to Anna's apartment building that the eight-story brick construction, in whose deep cellar they had taken refuge, shook in its foundation.

As strong at François's vicinity was, in her current mood, which suddenly encased her, he could not prevent her from seeing again her grandmother's living space, which had only been a block away from Mannheim's large, busy railway station. It was one of the main targets for the slow flying English bombers, which night after night dropped their deadly loads on trains and tracks and the homes of people who lived close by.

Walking through Paris with her French admirer, she saw herself sitting in a constricted, airless shelter into which every so often oxygen from large, heavy bottles had to be released so people would not suf-focate. And she heard again loud wails from the children's mouths that broke forth in perfect timing with each detonation.

As she looked for the last time at François' adorable three-quarter profile, she suddenly recalled a blond, five-year-old girl who had started to scream the moment she came through the heavily bolted door of the shelter. No coaxing and no threats were able to make her stop. Not even after her infuriated mother had grabbed her thin arms, shaking her violently and then – letting go of her – several times slapped her hard across the face. But the mother's abuse did not prevent the child from sobbing loudly. And now, after the parental mistreatment in pub-lic, the little girl was not only scarred but also ashamed of the men and women who were closely grouped around them. Everyone had watched the ugly scene in front of them in dismay; but none had lifted a finger to interfere with the mother's unexpected cruelty. Nobody had gotten up from their seats, often just a rickety, dusty, collapsible beach chair and stopped the mother's unjust punishment. In her distress, the strange, little girl tried to hide her wet face with its red, sore nose, behind her mother's back. Yet she was unable to stop crying loudly. Her fear of death was greater than any pain and humiliation. After an hour of incessant wailing, her voice had become hoarse and it was even more painful to listen to. But the child only ceased to howl when the all-clear alarm was sounded.

While the bombs were falling, Nadine had watched anxiously her grandmother's pinched face.

"Oh, why did I forget to take Hansel," Anna sighed from time to time and hugged her granddaughter closer to her. As they huddled together, both of their faces were blotchy and swollen from distress and grandmother's beautiful white hair looked straggly and greasy in the dim light.

Hansel was grandmother's five-year-old canary, a tiny, fluffy ball of yellow whose long lasting trills in the morning thrilled Nadine's heart. His cage, which each night Anna carefully covered with a soft, white cloth to make him feel more sheltered, hung on the kitchen wall. But sometimes when the full alarm was sounded, grandmother did not have time to take the few steps it needed to reach him, to lift her arm unhooking Hansel's house and carry cage and the frightened bird with her. The enemy planes would arrive so fast that she had only a moment to wake-up Nadine and pull off the old socks the child had worn over her shoes when she went to bed. Under her sheets and blanket, Nadine also always kept on her clothes and during the cold weather even her winter coat. There was no time to get dressed before the bombs fell.

"What is it, Oma?" the just awakened child wanted to know. Then she heard the sirens whistling crazily and instantly fell silent. Toward the end of the war, as soon as the large klaxons blared from rooftops, the planes were overhead. And although Anna and her granddaughter had gone to bed with all their clothes on, they still had to run down four flights of slippery, worn, red sandstone stairs that were barely lit and then cross a pitch-black courtyard to get to the shelter.

Above the elderly woman and the child the dark sky was intersected with long, white beams of light, which guided the German anti-aircraft guns. As they were fired, their dull, heavy thuds, momentarily interrupted the droning of the planes. And sometimes, Anna and Nadine would hear the quick, staccato shots of the small, fast flying *Messerschmidts*, the German fighter planes, whose machine guns were aimed at the cockpit and belly of slower-moving British and American bombers.

Once, as grandmother and grandchild were running at top speed for the shelter, which was still out of reach, Anna started to breathe so heavily that Nadine was sure her heart would break like the one made of glass in the fairy tale. It was then, frightened out of her wits, that the child saw stars falling from the sky. Like Andersen's little match girl, Nadine was convinced that she would go to heaven at any moment. She almost did. She had seen man-made stars. They were guiding devices, which the leading plane of the enemy squadron dropped over their designated targets. Watching those lights fall from the sky "like miniature Christmas trees", as Anna Nußbaum mockingly called them, meant that the bombs were instantly released afterwards.

Some people did not reach the shelter on time and then knocked in vain against its heavy, closed doors. As soon as bombs started to detonate, shelter doors were no longer opened. Savage, pragmatic laws prevailed: Better let two or three people perish than an entire cellar full of them.

During one particular night, which grandmother and grandchild had spent in the shelter, they had sat just below the shelter door at the foot of a short staircase. Toward morning, when it finally seemed safe to open the door again, Anna and Nadine, both stiff from having spent the night on a tiny uncomfortable chair, with the child crouching on Anna's lap, climbed up the stairs leading above ground. As soon as they reached the pavement, the child spotted the body of a young mother outside the door of the air-raid shelter. She had clutched her infant in one arm while, with her other one, she clung to the huge door handle of the bombproof cellar. The thick steel door had never opened to let her inside and to safety.

The mother's body in front of the door had partly slid down toward the ground and her head with her face fully revealed, was twisted at an odd angle. It was only then when the child saw that her mouth was wide open in a horrible, silent scream and she looked into eyes that had no pupils. White and huge the dead eyes seemed to stare at Nadine and she let out a terrified scream. From the murdered woman's body came the faint, persistent cry of a baby. Next to the nursling, an exploding bomb had torn a six-foot deep hole into the asphalt road. It had killed the young adult but not the tiny child that had been protected by her body.

Anna Nußbaum pulled hard at her granddaughter's arm to get her away from the awful scene:

"Don't look, don't look!" she cried, her voice hoarse with grief and fear and helpless anger. But the child had already seen what she was not supposed to see. The dreadful image was imprinted upon her mind and she would carry it with her until she died.

If the shelter was full by the time Anna and Nadine reached it, and they were lucky enough to get inside, they had to stay near its weighty metal door. Usually, just before it was bolted, Nadine watched a pair of strong, medium high, black boots come down the cellar steps. A rifle butt that faced downward and sometimes rattled against the steps accompanied the boots. Army boots and gun were followed by several lightly stepping feet in old, worn shoes, riddled with holes, and dirty slippers. Some of the footwear had only half a sole left, so either several toes or a soiled, torn sock were highly visible. Then came two, well-polished dark leather boots. Their soles, full of large nails, scraped along the wooden staircase. Nadine hated this sound because it scratched her ears.

"Oma, who are these people?" Nadine wanted to know when she had first seen the group of about twelve young men, dressed in coarse, dusty, striped work clothes. Their gaunt faces, shaven heads and large, dark eyes had startled her.

There were not enough chairs in the crowded cellar and the pitiful looking foreigners had to slouch down and settle on the concrete ground. They were only two, at the most three feet away from the child who sat on her grandmother's knees. From the strangers' thin frames exuded an offensive odor of unwashed skin and clothes, clothes that had gotten soaked in perspiration and then dried again while they were worn by steaming bodies.

"Lord, have mercy on us... Be quiet, child! I'll tell you later," Anna Nußbaum lamented in a low voice as her eyes skimmed over the unfortunate forced laborers, Hitler's soldiers brought by the cattle train full from Poland, Hungary, Czechoslovakia, France, Greece and Russia.

The first bombs were starting to fall and as the walls trembled and flakes of paint and mortar trickled on their heads, Nadine held on tight to her grandmother. But a little later between two detonations, she heard a woman, whose hair was covered with a large, paisley-printed babushka say behind her:

"I don't see why we have to share our shelter with these prisoners-of-war. They stink and will give us lice and fleas."

Nadine looked again at the men who huddled together as close as possible for warmth and protection. Most of them were in shirt-sleeves although the weather had turned cold. They sat with their hands clasped around their knees while their chins rested on them and their cast-down eyes sometimes vacantly blinked into the faces of the German civilians. The captives, who performed slave labor in a nearby factory, had dirty, wrinkled faces, which looked far too old for their youthful bodies. Their bald, round heads were so close, each to each that their shoulders were touching. Every so often the dull light of the dank, low-ceilinged room fell on a high cheekbone where its skin stretched too tightly across. Once, a young face, beardless, almost that of a child yet, shyly smiled at the little girl. The handsome, large-eyed boy, whose skull had started to grow the shortest stubs of dark hair, was so young that under different circumstances he and Nadine might have become friends.

"No, they won't infect us," Anna Nußbaum said to her loud voiced neighbor. Then being annoyed at the woman's heartless remark, Anna continued:

"Besides they work for us, don't they? And isn't your son fighting in Russia? If he gets captured, wouldn't you want him to be treated decently?"

"Oh, but that's different," the belligerent neighbor, with her sharp and ugly features, replied. "My son is not an animal; he takes a bath and dresses nicely."

Nadine's grandmother laughed scornfully. "So would these poor men if we gave them a shower and some decent clothes!"

"What do you mean? We are not supposed to get close to them! These *Untermenschen* are our fierce foes and they would cut our throats if they had a chance. Who are you anyway to talk that way? What's wrong with you?" The middle-aged woman spitefully stared at Anna, her suspicion fully aroused.

The two German soldiers who guarded the prisoners had followed the women's argument closely. They were young, too. Bored, both of them were quite willing to engage in a conversation with a couple of elderly German ladies whose language they understood. But before one of the guards could reply, there was another, close detonation. The noise was deafening and the walls of the shelter started to vibrate again. And, as before, from the low ceiling more dust and white flakes rained on everyone's hair and hats. This time not only children screamed but some women started to wail as well. And Nadine watched as several of them anxiously moved closer to the emergency exit where they had been staying next to.

"*Das war ein Volltreffer*,"[13] an old, white-bearded man, who was trying to hide his fear under a technical know-how, announced unsolicitously.

"Right above us, too," he added and nodded his head affirmatively as if someone were ready to dispute him. But everybody was too frightened to pay attention to him. The shelter started to fill with smoke and the children's whimpering became unbearable. The small ones clutched their arms around their mothers' necks and the bigger ones who stood next to them hung on to their skirts and coats, howling and begging to be picked-up. There was fear on everyone's face and except for some of the prisoners-of-war, no one was able to keep their mouths shut. Everybody talked to everybody in an indistinguishable *Kauderwelsch*[14]. The shelter seemed to be filled with one huge, frightened family. In their great fear even the poor captives were no longer looked upon like adversaries. Suddenly, it didn't matter anymore who was friend and

---

[13]   That was a full hit.

[14]   Gibberish

who was foe. They would all die together – after they had been buried alive side by side.

A boy wearing the uniform of the German army rolled a large bottle with oxygen forward and its contents were quickly dispersed within the room.

"Oh, my God – Hansel!" Anna Nußbaum moaned and she rolled her head back and forth while her eyes were closed.

"Perhaps he was able to fly away," Nadine quickly said and patted her grandmother's hand. Then to distract her, the child added:

"Look, grandmother, the bundle our neighbors have taken with them is bigger than the exit escape. How will they get it through?"

"Good Lord, child! I don't know and I don't care," the elderly woman impatiently wailed. Then, as an afterthought, she sighed:

"Why, for goodness sake, do these people try to bring their silver, furs and jewelry when they know they can't get their stuff through the emergency exit? People are so stupid sometimes!"

Anna was afraid and angry enough not to mind whether the whimpering women and men around her heard her or not.

* * *

About fourteen years later on that sunny Tuesday morning in June, the day when Julie took Nadine to the courthouse in Reading, the young girl did not remember the horrors of the war. The Englishwoman's amicable, ceaseless chatter and her walking back and forth in her bedroom without wearing a shred of clothing intrigued her. Then, as Nadine was just beginning to get used to Julie's pale nakedness, she suddenly dove under the window and cried out to the young girl:

"Hurry-up, bring me my dressing gown, please!" The young gardener had come close to the house and Julie was afraid that he might see her in her nudity.

Reading was an old town. For those who wanted to see them, it kept records proving that the Danes had burned the region to the ground. This had happened in 1006. But neither Julie nor Nadine were interested in looking at documents, which proved Reading's ancient roots. They were trying to locate the courthouse and on their search for it they passed a pretty park, which, as they discovered later, happened to contain the attractive remains of a Benedictine abbey founded in 1121 by Henry I. Driving on, the two women threw admiring glances at the perfectly kept lawns of the park and groups of oak trees that stretched some of their long, sturdy branches in an almost straight horizontal line above benches and flower beds. If time had permitted, Nadine and Julie might have become intrigued enough to hunt for the king's tomb. It was, so they were told, a hidden treasure among the ruins of the defunct monastery.

The night before Nadine had to appear in court, Julie's husband had mentioned that in 1892 the University of Reading had been founded by Oxford University. Then James added with a laugh:

"In case the judge decides to put you in jail, you would be in good company. Oscar Wilde has been imprisoned there and even wrote his *Ballad of Reading Gaol* while he was a guest of the town's prison guards."

James never failed to impress Nadine with his encyclopedic knowledge of juicy morsels with which he sprinkled his conversation as a chef does who deftly puts the garnishing touches on a special dish. His astute comments were a welcome change to Julie's quick, strictly practical endeavors to deal with two small children, a husband, a large house and parents who were growing frail and old. And there was also Sally Hibson, her invalid sister with whom she needed to stay in touch.

Afraid to be late for their scheduled appointment, the two women had arrived too early at the nondescript courthouse. They needed to wait for half an hour, sitting on a hard, wooden bench outside their assigned courtroom where another case was still being tried. The bailiff, a small, withered man who in Nadine's eyes seemed strangely over-dressed finally called them inside. Here she had to stand, for what seemed forever, in front of an elderly, severe looking judge, dressed in a long, black robe. His thin, bloodless lips did not smile once as she kept shuffling from one foot to the other. She could not take her eyes off his dense white wig, which reminded her of a carefully groomed, old lion's mane. In a bizarre way, his rimless glasses made him look less human. As he spoke and – uncommon for an educated Englishman who takes pride in not moving any limbs while he talks – underlined his words with impatient gestures of his hand, he bent his head forward so that he could better see the culprit who remained directly below him. As he bent forward and leaned across his narrow, high, dark-stained desk toward Nadine, his thick spectacles slid toward the tip of his nose. This gave him an owl-like appearance. While his eyes and glasses hung above her the odd double vision they produced seemed to penetrate her like two small, malevolent suns. Although it seemed strange his grotesquely enlarged eyes, as she briefly looked at them, were in tune with the lion's image, which the wig projected.

As Nadine had feared, except for her name and the designation of "Dover", which fell several times, she was hardly able to comprehend anything being said. In spite of having to remain standing, she was lulled into an almost hypnotic state of mind by the imposing father figure in front of her whose animal ancestry was so oddly underlined by the clever emblems he wore and so vividly spoke of his refined culture.

Ill at ease and constantly shifting her weight from one leg to the other, the young girl was unable to decide if the judge's glasses and wig contained a human being under its embellishment, which dramatically complemented the wide-sleeved, stately, black gown he wore. His voice, floating past her ears, was stern, yet funnily monotonous. It reminded her of a Sunday preacher who thunders from a pulpit onto the bowed heads of sinners silently sitting under it, ready to do penance.

While under the spell of the judge's voice, she was unable to listen to her own inner one and could not vent the anger and fear she usually felt when she was in the presence of a uniform, representing the power of the state.

As a child, her mother had daily taught her to mistrust any uniform, the symbol of authority and of one man's relentless power – *l'état c'est moi* – over many who were helpless. Nadine's only consolation, as she meekly stood in the courtroom and felt more and more like a criminal, was Julie who had come to fight for her. But the battle ended in defeat: Nadine, or rather Julie because the young girl did not have a penny to spare until she got her allowance, had to pay five pounds for having failed to register as a working alien when she set foot upon Great Britain's soil.

* * *

Their trip to Reading – "almost an entire day wasted," Julie complained to James after their return to Groombridge – had preceded the family's vacation in Cornwall by about two weeks.

After Nadine's delayed return from France, they finally took off for England's romantic southwest coast. Early on a July morning, the family and Nadine had piled into the car that was already crowded with the children's favorite toys, books and clothes, as well as two suitcases filled with adult apparel.

For several hours during their daylong ride, the silence between the two women was almost palpable. James, who was driving during the entire trip, felt uncomfortable in the midst of their unaccustomed taciturnity. At home on winter evenings, when they had sat closely together in front of the fireplace in the living room, sipping hot tea – except for rare cocktail parties, the family didn't drink at all – he was used to his wife's and Nadine's incessant chatter. He then had often wished they would talk a little less so he could read his newspaper in peace.

Now, as they went west through Southern England, he tried to bridge the misgivings Julie and Nadine displayed for each other by pointing out interesting spots during their day's journey.

For hours the five of them were moving straight west and only toward the end of the day, they turned slightly south across a persistently picturesque countryside. This was especially true as they traversed Devonshire with its rolling summer hills and green upland areas, interspersed by trees, hedges and rugged stones. For long stretches of time their car was the only one on the narrow, dusty road, which was bordered by farms and wide stretches of meadows where fat cattle grazed unhurriedly.

They neither passed through Exeter, the county's major town and the most westerly outpost of Roman occupation, nor Plymouth.

"As you know," and James looked through the rear mirror at Nadine on whose lap Peter had fallen asleep while his blond head rested on the girl's shoulder, "it was from Plymouth where many colonists sailed for America. And they say it was quite a sight to see Devonshire bustling with activity during Elizabethan times when its name was synonymous with Walter Raleigh and Francis Drake."

"James sounds just like a history professor again," Nadine mumbled only half awake. But she did not mind. On the contrary, together with the pastoral countryside outside the windows, she greedily swallowed his informative talk. It was a relief from the long hours of driving and most of all James' remarks alleviated the stubborn, silent presence of Julie, which grew heavier and more unbearable by the hour.

As Nadine looked at the portion of James's face that was visible in the small car mirror, she thought for the first time that he was actually quite handsome. During the past months when the two women had been alone in the house in Groombridge, Julie had several times praised her husband's ruddy looks. But the young girl, who knew Julie saw James in a special light, had not been able to agree with her. Of course, she had never said so. For her, James was simply too stout and above all, being in his mid forties, he was far too old to be attractive in her critical, young eyes. Yet now during their quarrel Nadine, who needed an ally, was ready to see James differently. So in no time she began to attach physical attributes to his exterior and an invisible charm to his words – neither one of which he actually possessed.

As they slowly went through Devonshire with James enjoying himself giving Nadine an English history lesson, he, in his tactful and kind-hearted way, neglected to tell her that during the Second World War Plymouth and Exeter had been heavily bombed by the Germans. They had nearly destroyed both cities.

In the late afternoon the family also moved over parts of Dartmoor. Nadine soon became intrigued by this enticing wasteland, which extended in endless rows of low hawthorn shrubs, a few straggly birches and patches of wild grass bushels in front of them. It was a forlorn landscape, which seemed to have eliminated all sounds except their own as they momentarily invaded it. As far as the eye could see, there was nowhere a trace of human habitation.

James, looking once more at the young girl through the rear mirror, did not fail to inform her that it was here where many remains of Bronze Age settlers were found. His face grew several shades redder with excitement when he started to tell her that in 1806 the ill-famous prison at Princetown was built here for French prisoners of war during Napoleon's ruthless hegemony over Europe.

"And did you know..." Nadine saw again James's bluish-green eyes looking at her from the mirror. But this time Julie, who had listened patiently until now, interrupted her husband rather bluntly:

"I wish you were looking more at the road instead of the mirror..." It was a matrimonial advice and the jealous warning from a dominating female to a younger, subordinated one. Julie's voice was strident and made James blush momentarily.

Then, in a somewhat impatient manner that was unusual for him, he retorted:

"I just wanted to let Nadine know that the Dartmoor Prison was not only used as a civilian jail for convicts condemned to hard labor..."

Somewhat defiantly James blinked at his wife who had lapsed into silence again before he continued:

"It had also held many American captives who had been confined here during the war of 1812..."

This was as far as James got before Julie, casting a lizard-eyed look at him and nearly hissing with a voice so flat and sharp that it seemed to scrape the bottom of a pan, uttered once more:

"It is almost 5:00 o'clock in the afternoon. Don't you think it is time to stop for tea somewhere? The children shouldn't have to wait this long..."

Thus, Nadine did not discover until much later that many of those American detainees at Dartmoor had been severely mistreated. Reading on her own about Dartmoor, she also discovered that after the war of 1812, an Anglo-American commission had conducted an investigation. And she read that this delegation apparently made belated amends to the family members of the prisoners who had died there.

"Well, that's a relief", she sighed as she put down her book.

It was the syllable "*moor*" in *Dartmoor* that had caught Nadine's ear each time she heard the word. It instantly brought forth the well-known image of the *Hound of the Baskervilles*. And she easily envisioned huge beasts as night after night they had howled at the invisible end of this landscape. In its complete isolation, gnarled trees, disorderly growing hedges and grass and even the luminous sky above looked threatening. There was no easy escape from this part of England.

Then she heard James' voice again. This time he was softly pleading with his wife:

"Julie, don't be angry with me but I do want to remind our *wißbegieriges deutsches Mädchen*[15] that it was Dartmoor, which Dickens describes in his first pages of *Great Expectations*. It had been in these moors where young Pip and the escaped, hunted convict, his legs still shackled by a heavy chain, stealthily moved among forgotten and eerie headstones, which were only half visible in a night fog.

"The fog", James chuckled, "is an important ingredient. It is impossible to imagine any of Dickens Gothic novels without it".

This time Julie did not interrupt her husband who had briefly smiled at her and then concentrated on his driving. She couldn't help being proud of his German knowledge.

But "*moor*", the German word for "swamp", also reminded Nadine of *Moorleichen*, those almost perfectly preserved dead bodies from the Bronze Age in the northwestern parts of Europe. One day, Nadine's father had mentioned those mummy-like men and women to her. Looking up from the newspaper he was reading, he remarked that anthropologists had discovered altogether over seven hundred *Moorleichen*.

"And look, they are all dressed in their period costumes", he had grinned and waved his newspaper at her.

On the photos he showed her, the two mummies didn't look at all as if they had slowly and dreadfully perished in a black bog. Instead, they rather resembled living persons who were taking a brief nap on some grassy and apparently quite solid hill. It was a nap that had started in 3500 B.C. And one corpse, the most famous one from Jütland with his leather leggings and little hat, which framed a completely modern and rather intelligent face, looked as if he might wake up at any moment.

* * *

It was long after suppertime before the Johnsons and Nadine reached St. Ives, one of Cornwall's three pretty costal towns where they

---

[15]   inquisitive German girl

would stay. At the outer periphery of St. Ives, James and Julie had rented a large cottage. They were sharing it together with Helen and Bruce McDonald, a married couple and their two freckle-faced, fair-skinned, young children, whom the Johnsons had known for some time.

Old, demure and weather-beaten, the house sat on the rim of a high plateau whose cliffs steeply, quite forbiddingly rose out of the sea. The side of the building, where the volcanic cones faced the tumultuous ocean below, sharply broke off like a damaged tooth. The ancient house and its site looked unexpectedly dramatic and even a little frightening especially during their first night. When Nadine went to bed, a strong wind kept whistling and howling around their abode as if a hundred drowned sailors were complaining about their harsh fate. Yet the next morning everything was calm and sunny. Julie and James's friends, who had arrived two days before them, were quick to point out a precipitous, rocky path that safely led from their doorsteps to the beach.

* * *

Just before they got to St. Ives, the endless rocking motion of the car had made Nadine drowsy. Half asleep, she remembered a night in Groombridge about a week before her departure to Paris.

She had just fallen into a slumber when she heard faint crying. Reluctantly opening her eyes, she saw Peter standing next to her bed. In his long nightgown, he looked adorable and even smaller than during the day. While his pudgy fist angrily wiped tears from his eyes, he kept saying:

"I hate him! I am going to chop off his head and put it in the dustbin…" Remaining in front of her, little and utterly vulnerable, he was shaking with indignation and fear.

"Who is it, darling?" Nadine attempted to get to the bottom of Peter's nightmare. She sat up and lifted the little boy on her bed. As she propped up her pillowcase against the headboard to be more comfortable, she tried to calm him down with tender words. Talking in a very low voice, she stroked his head and face, which were embedded in her shoulder.

"The man who had wanted to blow up the big house said that he would blow me up too."

"You mean the big building in London, the one they call the Parliament?" Nadine asked.

"Yes him! He has such a nasty face. And I am going to..."

"Yes, I know, chop of his head..." Nadine laughed softly and reassuringly patted Peter's moist cheek before she added:

"But you don't have to. This man is dead. He was executed four hundred years ago. It was Guy Fawkes, a Catholic soldier who had fought in Flanders." She had just read about this hero/terrorist and was happy to pass on her knowledge to the frightened child:

"I can tell you", she said, squeezing his moist, pudgy fingers, "that he was the only person caught red-handed as he walked into the cellar under the House of Lords where he and several other conspirators had managed to store thirty-six barrels of gunpowder. Together, they were plotting to blow up the Parliament and King James I."

Nadine was whispering now, afraid to wake up Peter's parents.

"But why did they want to do that?" The little boy asked, as he, too, lowered his voice. He had stopped shivering and was beginning to forget his bad dream as he listened to Nadine. He loved it when she told stories. But he still held on tightly to her.

"Because people," the young girl continued to spin her tale, "were often ignorant, poor and cruel and it took a long time for them to learn what religious tolerance was. Even today many churchgoers are not much more broad-minded against those who do not practice their own beliefs. But in the 16th century after England had become Protestant, thanks to Henry VIII, English Catholics were no longer allowed to adhere to their rituals and credences. They were savagely punished if the law thought that they had strayed from their narrowly defined limits. The gunpowder plot was a protest against inhuman, pitiless prohibitions. It was an audacious objection by a handful of Catholics against an overpowering majority of Protestants. Catholics had been severely suffering under the terrible decrees, which had been imposed upon their faith."

Comforting the child, Nadine had murmured all of this fast and hot-tongued while she hugged him closely to her so he would not think that she was mad at him, her little English boy, whom she loved as if he had been her own. She knew that, according to Julie's rules, she was overstepping her limits by telling a frightening story to a small child. But she was also aware that Peter did not understand half of what she said. Yet if his mother had heard her, she would have reprimanded Nadine touching upon a controversial subject with Peter who was still so young. But she couldn't help it. She enjoyed the moment too much: It was a fine, warm summer night, the house was still and safe and she loved the trust the little boy had put in her. And having come to her room to be comforted, not to his mother's, filled her with pride and confidence.

Yet while she mumbled to Peter who was more and more snuggling up to her, and while she forgot that he was only three years old, she also thought bitterly how often religion, one of mankind's most prized possessions, had done more harm than good.

Softly rocking Peter, who was falling asleep again, back and forth, she saw an enormous, white egg rise through the semi darkness of her room. Getting tired, she smiled to herself as she remembered how cleverly Swift had solved the deadly dilemma of Catholics versus Protestants by having the first ones open their hardboiled eggs on top and the latter on the bottom, or vice versa. And she almost burst out laughing when she considered the satirist's perfect symbol for religious conflicts.

As she sat in the dark and gently held the sleeping child, she wondered why the English, whom she had come to love indiscriminately, continued to celebrate November 5, Guy Fawkes Day, by burning effigies of the conspirators when it actually signified religious intolerance.

"Tomorrow I must talk to Julie about this," she murmured and yawned. Once more, she pressed Peter close to her and hoped that some of her thoughts would rub off on him while he slept next to her. Naively she believed that it might be possible for her good feelings to be absorbed by his skin and his pores. She wanted him to grow up a tolerant man. And at night, when it was the children's bedtime, she started to read small, carefully chosen sections of *Gulliver's Travels* to them. She did not ask Julie's permission to do so. Being afraid that Lipsey and Peter's mother wouldn't like the idea, she had once more sworn the kids to secrecy, as she did the first time when Peter had missed a steppingstone in their neighbor's enchanted park and fallen into the lake. She knew from her own damaging experience as a little girl that children kept secrets when asked to do so. Kids were so innocent and usually did what adults wanted them to do. Grownups were the role models children needed, yet a small child was unable to distinguish between the demands of a good person versus a bad one.

* * *

The sun was slowly setting as the Johnsons and Nadine were still driving through one of the beautiful river valleys of Cornwall. Field upon field of carefully cultivated vegetables interrupted large, often sloping meadows with big, slowly grazing cows. But, as before, they did not see any people. Only their farms and white cottages, often sitting neatly on a small hill, were visible from the road. For the last time on their journey Nadine attentively listened as James populated the landscape with old tales about the Cornish.

"Their language is related to the Welsh and Breton tongues," he started to lecture. Then, quickly looking at Julie for her approval, James filled the countryside with sword and knife swinging pirates. Nadine had little trouble seeing these feisty, lawless sailors with their inevitable black patches over one eye as they got ready to anchor their ship and penetrate the rocky costal barriers of Cornwall. Julie, who had heard James's stories several times before, seemed tired, bored and irritated. But Nadine was all ears. So were Lipsey and Peter.

"By the way," James was saying, "Cornwall had resisted for a long time both Saxon invasion and the Norman ways of life. Also, several centuries later, the Cornish people realized that their part of the country was far from London and the all-powerful Henry VIII. When he ordered Cornwall's men and their women folk to accept the Reformation and the laws of the English church that he had created, ten thousand of them took up arms, ready to defend the Roman church."

James smiled when he saw Nadine's flushed face and her eyes, which met his with youthful enthusiasm each time he looked at her through the rear mirror of the car.

"I want you to know," he continued for Julie's sake in a soft voice, "that for these fiercely independent 16th century Cornishmen and women, King Arthur was still alive. They never grew tired of telling their children about his many good and often heroic deeds. And as soon as their offspring were big enough, their parents took them to Tintagel, now unfortunately in a thousand ruins, where King Arthur was supposed to have been born."

* * *

During their stay at St. Ives, Nadine had looked forward with a daily growing impatience to see Tintagel. But when Julie, the children and she finally got there, she was quite disappointed. Almost nothing, except a heap of stones way below them, had remained of what must have been once an impressive castle. To get to the poor debris of Tintagel, they all had to climb down a steep, winding and barely visible path, filled with rubble on which it was easy to slip and fall. As they carefully descended one behind the other, with Peter following Nadine's heels, the wind from the sea pulled at their hair. To Nadine's childish delight the strong breeze kept blowing up her multicolored petticoats and made her feel like a three-master with reefed sails in all its beauty.

When the four of them reached the bottom of the hill, the children and young girl immediately started to climb like sure-footed mountain goats among the broken, dusty remnants of Tintagel's Norman church. Julie did not join them. She had sat down on a rock and stayed, looking at the sea. From afar she resembled a long-limbed mermaid who had crept up to the shore to sing one of her strange, immortal songs.

As the three of them scampered about, Nadine became more and more sad that almost no traces of the former British and Saxon strongholds were still visible. There was but one small consolation: Tintagel Head! It was a promontory that boldly stuck out its tongue into the sea and had become almost separated from the mainland.

"It's like a child trying to tear its hand out of its mother's firm grip," she whispered as she gazed at the vast ocean in front of her.

* * *

On the night of their arrival at St. Ives, Nadine had been so tired that she went to her room as soon as she had bathed Lipsey and Peter and put them to bed, reading to them only half of their usual nightly story. The next morning she got up early and was in the kitchen preparing breakfast long before Julie appeared. When she finally came downstairs, she was still exhausted from yesterday's long car ride and not in a good mood.

"Why did you disappear so quickly last night?" she asked aggressively. And she crossly stared at Nadine so that her forehead wrinkled and her eyes lit up with sparks. Then she added:

"There were lots of things to unpack and get ready for today. I was counting on you and you let me down. You better get the children's clothes in order before they wake up."

Nadine, who had felt fine a moment ago and had greeted Julie as if they were still on good terms, fell silent again. And once more she did not speak to the Englishwoman for the rest of the day unless she had to.

But inwardly she was raging and kept thinking: 'This is too much! I believe it's time for a change. Julie is taking me for granted. I have become less than her mirror on the wall, which she consults several times a day. I don't like this one bit.'

Nadine had become emotionally attached to Julie and needed her attention. Insecure, she quickly felt rejected by the whole world when Julie did not speak to her.

Except for the children, Julie was the only person in England, to whom Nadine felt close and trusted completely. And she knew if Julie continued to treat her like a stranger, she would become one. She would go away. She would go back to Paris, where Hanna kept urging her by phone calls and letters to join her.

"We would have so much fun together. Denis turned out to be the nicest guy and François keeps asking about you," Hanna wrote.

Compared with François' handsome face, which when she heard his name, floated above her like a bewitching full moon, England, and even Cornwall, seemed colorless.

The days went by slowly. If the afternoons were sunny and not too windy, Nadine would put on a pair of shorts and take Lipsey and her brother to the beach. Together they marched around or climbed over the gray-black rocks of all sizes, which covered the shore in spectacular profusion. They watched the bottoms of some boulders as one minute they heavily sat in soft sand and the next they seemed to float in the fast swirling white foam of the breakers. The sides of the rocks facing the sea had become smooth and slimy and were different from their other parts, which were dry, looked at the land and were more protected from the constant salt spray. Resembling a guardian deity, the big, coarse rocks were able to see in two directions at once.

The children squeaked with joy when the sea tickled their toes and licked their feet like the rough tongue of an affectionate cat. Even when the sun shone brightly, there was always a breeze and no one ever felt hot. The sea was too rough to swim in for Peter and Lipsey. There was a strong undertow and the danger of being thrown against a half submerged boulder was always present. But the two siblings were quite happy to build sand castles and run back and forth at the edge of the water with their buckets and brightly colored beach shovels, which they dragged behind them. As Nadine watched their small, skinny bodies – with the five-year-old girl already showing traces of her mother's long thighs – her stomach contracted and turning into the wind, she whispered to herself:

"I can't leave the children. They need me. I have become their big sister. They would miss me terribly if I were no longer close to them."

As she looked lovingly at their games among sand, sun and water, she forgot that she had to get up before anyone else in the morning for Peter and his sister's sake. Glancing fondly at them, she no longer recalled that they made a big fuss, howling and throwing a spoon across the table when she wanted them to eat their spinach, a vegetable they hated. And watching them against the sea's breakers, she did not remember that brother and sister quarreled and screamed at each other over a new toy. Or when during the middle of a seemingly endless day, as she tried to be alone for a few minutes, the two of them stormed into her room demanding her full attention.

Playing with them now in the wet sand that stuck to their legs and arms and got into their swimsuits, she was no longer annoyed when she had to talk to them in their idiom. Once more, wiping off the saltwater from their faces and drying their fine hair, she patiently explained things to their inquisitive minds. And she didn't mind that she had to repeat the same answer half a dozen times before both children were satisfied or had become distracted by something else.

"Why are there holes in the street?" Lipsey had wanted to know during one of their daily walks back in Groombridge. And Peter, who didn't like to fall behind his big sister, was suddenly in great need to inquire: "Why do cows eat grass? It doesn't taste good."

On their first day at the beach, both children demanded to be told who had made the sea so salty.

"I don't like it," Peter had cried after he had stumbled and gotten a mouthful of seawater.

Nadine laughed as she carefully rubbed his small, sweet face saying "I know, I know. It tastes awful. But it won't hurt you."

During their afternoons at the seashore, Nadine would have loved to take a swim but she did not dare to do so while she was in charge of Lipsey and Peter. Julie had left her with the kids and had gone shopping with Helen, her housemate.

Before the three of them had descended to the beach, Nadine had spread a lot of suntan lotion on the children's bodies. But when she saw that after an hour of playing at the shore their noses and shoulders were still starting to get red, she took them back up the rocky hill and into the house where she gave them their tea a little earlier than usual. Yet it was no easy task to get them off the beach. There were always wild cries of protests first.

"We want to stay a little longer. We have just come down here. It's not nice to make us go inside," both children hurdled at her before she was able to drag them along. Usually she had to bribe them first:

"I'll read you a story that you don't know yet." Or: "Mummy promised to let you have some ice cream if you don't make a racket coming with me."

When the Johnsons and Nadine had stayed for about ten days at St. Ives, the young girl started to feel less and less happy and spot-bound.

Julie, noticing that the young girl was becoming moody and depressed, finally mellowed and asked her to come for an afternoon swim with her. James had volunteered to take the children for a long walk at the foot of the rocky hill that embraced their section of the beach in a dramatic half circle. Like a natural fortress the rocks reached several hundred feet into the air. At night, when Nadine took a last look out of her room's window, the moon shed a pale light across their craggy points and added an inexplicable eeriness to the seascape. High rocks, moon and the sea then always made her think of drowned sailors and mermaids. She would see their long, straight hair flowing in the wind, partly concealing their faces like a silk curtain.

Helen had taken her husband and children to visit a friend of hers in Bodmin, the county town. Nadine did not like Helen. She was jealous that Julie spent so much time with her.

"Why does she have such a lovely name when no ship will ever sail for her sake," Nadine disapprovingly murmured after Julie had introduced her to the middle-aged, plain looking woman, giving no credit to Leda's beautiful twin daughter. Her nose was her most awkward feature. It was curved, too prominent and ended in a bulbous tip. And to make matters worse, this olfactory organ didn't seem to be formed from skin and cartilage like other noses. Instead, it protruded from poor Helen's face like a small, thick piece of dried-up wood.

That afternoon at the beach as the two women stretched out on their towels, Nadine was glad to have Julie to herself. In a happy mood they talked for a while and enjoyed the sun on their backs, which due to a strong breeze, didn't feel hot on their bodies. After about an hour, Nadine became restless and wanted to take a swim.

"I think I would like to test the water," she said, getting up from the sand. "Are you coming with me?" She asked and smiled at Julie.

"OK, I will," Julie said. "I know how much you enjoy a swim. But let's be careful. This rocky shore is treacherous," she added as she lazily followed Nadine.

The two of them waded slowly across a long stretch of wet sand to reach the sea. The water, as it eventually came up to their thighs and waists, was cold and when they finally were immersed in it, it soon proved almost impossible to swim away from the shore. The sea, like a huge puppy at play, would always toss them back to the beach.

The two women, in addition to getting used to the chilly sea, had needed time to pick their way cautiously among rocks and breakers. Waist-deep in water, they lifted their arms, using both of them for balance, and they were often forced to bend forward and hold on to half hidden, slippery rocks.

As they proceeded inch by inch into deeper water, they began to laugh and shout like children while the sea roared below them and its breakers furiously smashed into boulders, which kept blocking their way. They had to be careful not to lose ground under their feet as they swayed like seaweed to and fro in the high waves. The surf hissed at their thighs and waists. Without interruption the wild water foamed around them and Nadine would stare at it; she was fascinated by its fast swirling eddies at the foot of big bulky rocks whose upper parts glistened in the sun. And even after the sea had almost reached their shoulders, both women were constantly at risk of being thrown hard against a sharp obstacle by the churning waters.

At times, the sea's frenzied roar was so loud that Nadine couldn't hear a word Julie, who was right behind her, said. Julie soon gave up the idea of a swim and returned to the dry, warm sand. But Nadine, being farther out in the sea, was suddenly caught by a riptide, which quickly pulled her toward the open ocean. Here, the water was much calmer. When she got used to the sea's coldness, it started to feel quite pleasant on her skin.

Glad to have escaped the rocks and mad breakers, Nadine, who had no fear of water whether it was a river, lake or the sea, enjoyed her swim. Whenever she wanted a change from moving fast, she lay on her back like a sea otter, ready to groom its thick pelt. Languidly, she blinked at the sky, the other ocean whose black depth no one had yet been able to measure. And she watched without worrying as the shore slowly receded. For quite a while she let herself be carried by the surface of the sea, remaining completely immobile or just paddling leisurely with her feet. She loved to float on top of the water. It made her feel as if she were suspended between two oceans with nothing but a blanket of air between them.

Her trust in water was complete. Taught by her father, an excellent swimmer, she did not tire easily. Also, while immersed in water, she had never been in a dangerous situation before. Her fears stemmed from land-bound monsters, the ones that had mimicked her father, claiming that they were her best friends while they betrayed her, misused her, and robbed her of treasures the child didn't know it possessed. And, of course, she had been terrified of the bombs, which had daily been falling out of the sky, had landed in her backyard or on the little, steep street connecting her house with a small dairy store. Beast-like men had injured her, had tried to kill her. The thought that sharks or other threatening sea fiends from below could try to do the same by mistaking her for food, never crossed her mind.

After a while, as every pore of her body absorbed the salty liquid in which she drifted as aimlessly as a loose cork in a wine bottle, she became oblivious to her surrounding. Her thoughts turned into a shamble of unfocused patterns. Various configurations seemed to retreat to unexplored recesses of her mind and, in the momentary void that was created, odd, dreamlike, sensory figures crisscrossed each other in quick succession. Amorphous shapes only half visualized reduced her to a being that was no longer able to reflect rationally. Instead, she started to rely solely on her instincts. Yet although her sensations were keen, they were utterly chaotic and seemed to have descended to an almost infantile level.

As she was carried on the surface of the sea and squinted against the sun, she felt as if she were lying in a huge cradle rocked by oversized arms. Resting on her back, her ears were totally under water. Even her chin, forehead and eyes were quite often inundated as a sudden, small wave swapped over her head. Only her nose stuck out of the transparent, silver-edged element that kept her in a lover's embrace. Her hair, usually curly, had become long and straight and weaved around her head like a dark veil, which sometimes annoyingly invaded her eyes.

Normally when she swam, she felt ugly. She then identified with the ancient Greeks who had equated ugliness and old age with sin. But on this day, while she was carried by the sea as if she had been one of its creatures, it would not have surprised her if her skin, muscles and the tendons of her legs had suddenly grown together and formed a fish tail.

Of course, it would not be an ordinary tail but a thick caudal fin that was studded with three wide diamond clasps. Those were the jewels, which she had been supposed to receive on three consecutive birthdays while she was slowly maturing from child to young adult.

As she was dreaming and the water no longer seemed cold to her she had, without realizing it, drifted quite far out into the ocean.

At first she did not hear Julie who called out to her from the shore. The Englishwoman's mouth seemed to open and close in rapid movements but, as if Nadine had become deaf, its sounds did not reach her. Julie waved her arms wildly around their axis and Nadine had to laugh at the funny, windmill shaped figure she cut. Then she realized that Julie was beckoning her back to the shore, screaming something the wind and distance snatched away before it could reach her.

Nadine took a quick look around her but she saw nothing except the empty ocean on three sides of her – sides without angles that enclosed her in an unsteadily moving, shimmering semicircle – while, closest to her, the beach formed a solid line on the forth side. As she looked at the shore, the high volcanic hills rose behind the sand and its treacherous rocks. Seen from far, it all seemed utterly picturesque. It had lost its former weirdness.

As if alive, the hills wound themselves in a half-moon shape along the sea and the madly waving Julie, running along the shore, was tiny and appeared to be out of place with her odd, frantic movements.

"Tonight, I should take a closer look at those rocks," Nadine mumbled to herself.

"It must be fun to walk along its top," she mused and smiled to herself.

Then, just before she rolled over on her back again, she saw it.

At first it seemed to be nothing but a thin, vertical line that swam rapidly toward her. But as she watched, the line turned a little to the right and metamorphosed into a black triangle scintillating in the sun. Nadine's heart stopped. She thought that she was having a nightmare. James had warned her and his wife about whirlpools and undertows near the shore, and he had cautioned them to slowly pick their way among the multiple rocks and boulders. But no one had said a word about sharks in this part of the sea. It had not even occurred to Nadine to ask if there were any.

Anger mixed with intense fear, which seemed to burn the back of her head and freeze her neck where her bristles used to be, rose in her. Terror and rage and the large amount of adrenaline that her system suddenly produced, made her swim as fast as she could toward the shore. But she knew that she would never be able to out-swim this ancient predator. Each second she turned her head a little the fin was closer and stood out more threateningly against the horizon which it split into two halves.

"When I will no longer see it, his jaw is going to snap shut, with my shoulder blade, or one of my thighs between it," she said aloud in a shaky voice.

As soon as she saw that image, she panicked. Her breath was coming so hard that her chest started to ache and her heart began to beat in her throat, cutting off part of the air her lungs urgently needed.

The shore was just as far as before and Julie's flailing arms had not become any bigger.

When Nadine realized that she could not escape and that injury or death was imminent, she did something totally insane. It was a bold, forbidding movement she had once watched a man do in a documentary about sharks.

Lifting neck and head out of the water, she looked one more time at the triangle to be sure where it was. Then she took a deep breath and under water blindly steered toward the big, threatening fish.

As she got close to the black, solid and terrifying cloud that was now almost on top of her, there was no longer a thought in her head. Her mind had snapped. It had shut like an oyster and she swam as if she had been a puppet whose strings were pulled forward by that horrible shape she could not escape. Then, when fish and human were almost mouth-to-mouth, teeth to horrible teeth that were still hidden under the shark's jaw, she opened her mouth and screamed as loud as her lungs would allow her. For an instant she saw the long, yellow teeth of a horse that had bitten her as a child. But she knew that they were nothing compared with the invisible, pointed and razor sharp ones, which faced her. Those teeth were capable of growing again and again like Jason's dragon teeth.

Then, as her head seemed to explode from lack of air, she made a fist and aimed it at the heavy beast. Shooting her arm forward, she screeched again and pointed it at the jaw of this dreadful immortal, which had hunted the depths for millions of years.

By accident she had stumbled into the shark's range of smell and vibration. Thoughtlessly, stupidly, she had invaded his territory, a place, which was no longer hers. While swimming too far off shore, she had become nothing but a few elongated, fat upholstered pieces of flesh destined to fill a stomach larger than hers. Yet fortunate for her the shark seemed to be more curious than hungry. It appeared that he was pursuing her as if she were one of the seals he had killed and eaten not too long ago. Without malice the large, sleek fish would follow his prey. He only obeyed his instinct. He had to eat if he wanted to survive. No thought of revenge or hate ever entered his brain. He was incapable of the smallest idea of evil, cruelty or insult. Those were human commodities; they did not belong to the spheres of sharks. Even innocent, little Peter was capable of hurting the girl's feelings a hundred times more than this superbly designed eating and breeding machine.

Nadine had been taught these facts. Yet in her dread of a horrible death, she was no longer able to think in rational terms. At this moment the shark symbolized nothing less than the very gates of hell, which were opening in front of her to swallow her alive. She only knew that within seconds she would burn in boiling oil until her flesh fell piece by piece from her bones.

She never touched the shark. When she thought the two of them were about to collide and as part of his big body seemed to push against her hip so that she felt as if his rough skin were ripping her swimsuit apart and tearing her skin open, his huge form, magnified when seen under water, silently glided past her. Then, miraculously, he kept sliding farther away from her and with a few effortless strokes of his tailfin swam back into the deep sea from where he had ghostlike appeared.

Starting to suffocate in earnest, Nadine shot up into the air, filled her lungs with it and then dove once more. For the third time, she yelled at the retreating shark with all her strength. When she realized that his ominous shadow continued to distance itself from her, she felt a great sense of relief. Her chest no longer seemed to be clenched in a vise whose screws had kept turning. After she surfaced this time, the shark's fin had started to become quite small. With her remaining strength Nadine turned around and resumed her swim toward the beach.

It took her a long time to do so. She was exhausted and the riptide near the shore kept throwing her back into deep water. At one point, when she thought that she would not make it, she calmly said to herself – there was no strength left in her to become excited or upset:

"Perhaps I should have let the shark have his dinner. It takes longer to drown."

But Julie, who nervously paced back and forth on the deserted beach, kept urging her on:

"You've almost made it! Just a few more strokes! Don't give up now," she tirelessly called out to her.

When Nadine was finally able to drag herself into shallow water, she collapsed in the sand at Julie's feet. Still breathing hard so that she felt as if she had a hundred leaking lungs, Julie, who had bent over her, anxiously asked:

"For God's sake how did you escape him? He was not supposed to be there. Sharks, although they like cold water, are a rarity on the coast of Cornwall."

"I screamed at him, like my father used to scream at me," Nadine whispered and faintly smiled at her friend.

"You must be mad," Julie said, but her mouth, the only thing Nadine was aware of as she looked up, relaxed into a relieved laughter.

"It worked, didn't it?" Nadine replied a little more spiritedly. She finally started to feel safe as she sat up and stared at Julie's calves and knees, which protruded in front of her.

"Yes, apparently, but how did you do it?"

"I told you, I just yelled at him. I had once seen a scientific film, which concentrated on a deep-sea diver and his encounters with sharks, including the Great White one. He claimed that a shark's hearing mechanism is so sensitive to sound waves under water that one can frighten him away with shrieks. I tried it. There was nothing else I could do. I am not Maldoror."

"Who?" Julie asked.

"Lautréamont's Maldoror – the young man with thin lips and a knife, an ominous anti-hero who mated with a female shark."

Wide-eyed, Nadine raised her head and blinked at her friend's face. She suddenly felt very cold. Julie, who spoke French far better than Nadine, thought:

'The girl is insane. The shock was too much for her'.

Nadine, in spite of her teeth that began to chatter, wanted to shout with laughter as she thought of Julie's French magazines, which she received once a month and where she zealously followed the latest news about Parisian fashion without ever encountering the name of Count Isidore Ducasse, Lautréamont's proper name, who was born in Montevideo, Uruguay. And she remembered that the poet, who had created a character called Maldoror, a figure of unrelenting evil, was already thirteen before his father sent him to high school in France. She admired the writer of *Les Chants de Maldoror* because she had understood that he forced his readers to stop taking their world for granted. Isidore Ducasse had succeeded, where others had failed, in making his followers see reality for what it is: A chimerical nightmare...

Then she whispered:

"Oh, but I don't give a damn," and she buried her face in her sandy, saltwater-covered forearms because she was ashamed that Julie might see the tears streaming down her face.

"She couldn't care less about the Surrealists who discovered Lautréamont and soon claimed him as one of the *poètes maudits*[16]. And she doesn't give a hoot that those people placed him next to Baudelaire and Rimbaud, whom she never read either. To be honest if I hadn't stumbled upon Isidore among my father's books where his *Chants de Maldoror* was just a slim volume gathering dust in a forgotten corner, I wouldn't know anything either about this gifted Surrealist. I recall reading that he, among others, inspired Salvador Dali, Max Ernst, Joan Miro and Modigliani. Jean, too, told me once that the latter painter used to walk around Montparnasse mumbling to himself as he quoted

---

[16]   accursed poets

from *Maldoror*. And André Breton, the founder of Surrealism, has integrated Isidore into his *Anthology of Black Humour*. So he must count for something. But even Breton recognized Lautréamont's significance only in 1940, long after November 24, 1870, the day he died. I still cannot believe it that he was just twenty-four then."

Nadine sat on the sand weeping. Now that the danger of a loss of limb, or worse, was behind her, she started to shake and break down helplessly. And then she saw what she had not seen in the water: A large eye that had looked at her. It was the shark's enormous round eye, black as a deep hole in the ground, which her mind had absorbed as it had no other eye before.

* * *

The following day after lunch Julie and Nadine sunbathed again on the beach while the children took their nap. It was hazy and for a long time the sun hid its face behind a fine mist. But the air was warm and pleasant. The only sound came from the crashing, breathing, receding and forward slashing breakers. Otherwise it was utterly calm and peaceful. The world seemed empty of any threats or worries. Nadine and Julie spoke softly in the light of the serene, early afternoon. It was the hour of the faun.

After their quarrel and after Nadine's terrifying adventure at sea – she would never swim again without fear as she had prior to her encounter with the shark – they were closer than before. Every so often, they talked to each other and then just lay sleepily on the sand with their eyes closed. Once in a while, one of them would voluptuously stretch a leg or a hip as the sun began to caress their bodies. There was no question about going into the water.

Lying on the beach, they carried each other's face as clearly behind their closed lids as if their eyes had been open. When they spoke without stirring a hand or a foot, they seemed to float up and down on the sound of their voices like two butterflies chasing each other. It was not long before the two women, who had turned over on their stomachs, soundly fell asleep.

An hour later, when they woke up, their backs and thighs were a fiery red. They rushed home to get out of the sun and put more oil on themselves. But by evening the redness of their skin had increased, as had their discomfort. Nadine was not as badly off. Hers was the younger skin; it had more resilience and was of a slightly darker pigment. But the extremely fair-skinned Julie was in such agony that at 4:00 o'clock in the morning James had to call a doctor to come to the cottage and look at his wife.

There was not much the physician, an elderly man who was taciturn, grumpy and resentful from having been wakened in the very early morning hours, could do, except give Julie a painkiller and prescribe more ointments. Her thin, whitish, almost transparent skin had second, if not third-degree burns. On one or two places at the inside of her thighs large, horrid-looking bubbles had formed. Together with Lipsey and Peter, Nadine went back to the beach the next day, covered with a short-sleeved T-shirt. But it took several days of bed rest before Julie could walk without pain again.

For the rest of their stay at St. Ives Julie only went for night walks at the beach. Sometimes she would then sit on one of the large rocks that divided the land from the ocean and at high tide became partly immersed in water. Immobile, the soles of her bare feet clung to its steep, rough, moist surface. As the wind gently lifted her hair and brought with it the salty perfume of the water, she kept looking at the sea. Unable to express what she felt as she remained like this at the edge of a world, which had swallowed and born hundreds of other worlds before her and would do so long after she had gone, she was humming to herself in a low voice. It was an old nursery rhyme from her childhood, which she had not remembered until now. As the cupped hands of sand and water held her, she looked young and vulnerable. And there was suddenly a great resemblance between her and her small daughter.

V

Harrogate

Between Christmas and New Years, the Johnsons went to see Julie's parents in Harrogate. For days the children, who knew their grandparents' place from previous visits, were highly excited and Nadine had to spend twice the time in the evening for their bedtime stories. Peter and Lipsey's eyes were large with expectation and as they lay in their bright blue colored beds their smalls hands crumpled sheets, blankets and pillowcases between their hot fingers, interrupting the young girl's reading several times with:

"Will we take the pretty train again? Who is going to sleep in the green bedroom? Is Beatrice making her plum pudding for us like last holiday? How many presents will we get?"

Nadine could not answer these questions. But they made her look forward to this trip with the same joy as the children did. Her eyes were almost as lustrous as theirs as she became more and more enticed by this pending journey, which promised to be fun. At night it also took her longer to fall asleep. Her eyes lingered among the somber branches outside her window. She watched as clusters of dark green holly trees wafted slowly back and forth. The evening air that came into her room from the open window was soft, humid and cold.

Finally the morning of their departure arrived. Contrary to Nadine's rushed, last minute arrivals at the little station of Groombridge on her days off, the family was early and had to wait for the train taking them to London. Peter had brought his own small, sturdy leather suitcase. While he marched up and down next to the tracks, he carried it proudly. His short legs tried to imitate his father's long strides. He looked so funny and sweet in his self-absorbed endeavor that Nadine had to smile. At the same time, she kept a sharp eye on him since she could never be sure what he might do next. It made her nervous that the child was so close to the tracks where they expected any moment the massive, black, soot-covered locomotive to appear. But she did not want to spoil his sense of excitement and bravura. After she had watched him for some time, she noticed that one of her eyelids, mostly the left one, started to break into an involuntary flutter. It embarrassed her and she tried not to look at anybody while the twitching lasted.

Then the train came. They boarded, found their compartment and, putting their luggage away, watched as the village slowly receded behind them. They were at last on their way north.

When the family arrived in London, their first stop, they took a taxi from Victoria Station and crossed the city until they reached Paddington Station from where the *Queen of Scots* would take them to Yorkshire. London was at its usual bustling best and they had trouble storing their entire luggage in a cab. The driver was rude and barely assisted James with the bulky, heavy suitcases, which Julie and Nadine had carefully packed the night before. As they overtook one red, dou-ble-decked, slowly moving bus after another, Nadine buttoned and unbuttoned Peter's gray, woolen winter coat about three times.

"I'm too hot," he would complain, prompting Nadine to open the two top buttons of his coat.

"Watch it that he doesn't catch a cold," Julie warned with motherly concern when she saw that Peter stuck his head through the open car window. So Nadine pulled the small, angrily protesting boy away and closed up his coat again.

She had no time to help Lipsey with her garment, which was of the same cut and color as her brother's and matched their smart hats. And just when Nadine thought that they would never get to Paddington, the taxi driver pulled up at the curb of the station and the family disembarked.

They had no trouble finding their Pullman train and quickly located their assigned seats. Nadine sat down opposite James and Julie and took a deep breath and when she heard that the train would take them straight to Harrogate without their having to make another cum-bersome transfer, she was glad.

"Keep still," she told Peter two minutes later in a high-pitched, impatient voice as she squeezed his hand. The little boy had not stopped skipping up and down on his feet since they left the house in Groombridge. Even sitting in their first train and then the taxi, he could not hold his legs in one place.

Having taken their seats, with the two children closest to the window of the *Queen of Scots* Nadine looked more tired than Julie. During their entire train ride Julie only occasionally reached across the sturdy, steel-bordered table that was placed between them and patted her son's small, pudgy fingers. Otherwise she left her children in the young girl's care. She had confidence in her and preferred to pay more attention to James whose presence she clearly and in Nadine's critical eyes even somewhat braggingly enjoyed.

Julie had dressed with greater care than usual. Instead of wearing a blouse, cardigan and skirt, her standard uniform in Groombridge, she had put on a simple suit that subtly fitted her figure. She even wore patent leather shoes with a heel. They were so different from the flat, long-soled footgear in which Nadine was used to seeing her that she kept glancing at Julie's legs. The heels made her pretty ankles appear even slimmer and stretched her calves in a more becoming way.

"How lovely she looks today," Nadine mumbled with a twinge of envy. Yet she was also aware of a sisterly pride as if Julie's attractiveness were a reflection on herself as well.

During their journey north, Nadine noticed again that whenever she was in Julie and James's company, Julie seemed inspired to be more affectionate with her husband than when she was not there. There was a strong competitive spirit in Julie, which almost imperceptibly mingled with exhibitionism. It was as if the older woman had a constant need to prove to the younger one that she was still sexually desirable to the man she had married. But Julie, in spite of her easily provoked, yet nearly always half-suppressed jealousy, was also very fond of Nadine. Every so often during James's late nights at the London office, when she got lonely waiting for him at the house, she would call Nadine to the bathroom to scrub her back. It was all quite innocent. The young girl enjoyed running a soapy sponge along Julie's spine and between her well-rounded shoulders. The muscles of her back were clearly defined and would move in a vivid dance under a smooth skin. But more than touching Julie, Nadine savored being so near to the woman whom she admired and felt close to, often closer than to her mother and siblings.

The two of them would talk and laugh together and confide in each other as if they had known each other all their lives.

"Sometimes I think I know you better than my sister with whom I grew up," Julie once said and then had broken into a short, embarrassed laugh, which indicated her deep feelings. She didn't get along well with her slightly younger sibling.

"Even when we were still in our late teens, we competed too closely with each other," she tried to explain.

"We should have left some space between us and shared our men friends instead of possessively guarding them from each other," Julie sighed as her face darkened and showed sadness and regret.

Then she told Nadine that after her sister had married she had come with her husband to Nairobi to visit her and James there. But one day while staying at their home in East Africa, tragedy struck: Sally, Julie's sister, fell ill with polio.

"After being terribly sick for weeks and months and hovering at the brink of death, the disease left her a cripple. Now her husband pushes her in a wheelchair. She will never have any children." Julie gave Nadine a despairing look.

"It is not your fault," Nadine said quickly, her cheeks flushing and ready to fight Julie's ghosts of the past.

"I know! But why did it have to happen while she was visiting me halfway around the world?" Julie cried, as her face grew even more somber.

"I have no idea. Perhaps East Africa was the place where the germs were more common than anywhere else. I really don't know. But I do know that it wasn't your fault," Nadine kept repeating herself. She was taken aback by Julie's strong feelings of guilt. She had not seen this side of her before and, not knowing how to handle it, she felt helpless, aggressive and angry.

During their train ride to Yorkshire on that cold winter morning, Nadine remembered the keen closeness she had experienced when Julie had spoken to her from her heart during the stillness of the night. She always relished the brief times when she had Julie to herself. She knew that she filled an important gap in the Englishwoman's life at those moments. It gave her a feeling of joy and power when she didn't have to share Julie with the rest of her family. Sensitive and inclined toward possessiveness and jealousy, Nadine had discovered a long time ago that when James was at home, her importance, and even that of the children, diminished in Julie's eyes. When James was at work, Julie and Nadine were a unity, with enough room for the kids in their intimate circle. But as soon as his tall and somewhat stout figure moved about the house and garden, this union was divided into two camps: Julie and James were on one side, Nadine and the children on the other. There was an invisible line between the two parties that was not easily crossed. As ludicrous as it seemed, this division made Nadine feel as if she were stranded at the border between two countries where traffic had come to a full halt and people, forced to open their luggage, were inspected by taciturn, sour-faced, pistol-wearing custom officers.

Since Nadine had come to live with the Johnsons, her closeness to the family allowed Julie, relieved from much of the burden of her offspring, to feel as if she and James were just lovers again. When James was in the house, Julie invariably looked more appealing and her beautiful skin seemed even softer and whiter than it already was. It was as if something within her, yet completely out of her control, responded favorably to her husband's proximity. In his presence she, in Nadine's effusive glances, often seemed to be a ballerina whose long, utterly graceful arms and hands extended toward him, inviting him to a *pas de deux*. Somehow the miracle of an almost perfect marriage seemed to happen right under Nadine's watchful eyes.

Coming from an upper middleclass family Julie had been brought up to marry and have children. Nothing else. It was by sheer accident that World War Two made her an officer in her Majesty's Navy. A soldier's career, with commanding powers, had not been a goal she had envisioned. And if, at the beginning of their marriage, Julie had some difficulty getting used to cadets no longer snapping to attention when she passed, she overcame her initial apprehensions with little effort. Within a year or two she had adapted herself to looking after a husband and raising her children. She then could no longer imagine what her life would have been like without James, especially not after Lipsey and Peter had been born. Once she was married, her tours of duty to Hong Kong in a heavily armed war vessel slowly receded into the background. And over the years her service in the British Navy had become an anecdote she enjoyed referring to when she was among friends. But Nadine, captivated by photos from Julie's past, thought that she had looked elegant in her navy blue hat and uniform with its brass-buttoned jacket, which seductively underlined her slender waist. And she regretted not having known her then.

Julie's practical intelligence and her general calm moods were based on a strong will. And her tolerant attitude toward matrimony didn't hurt the good relationship between husband and wife. Her parents' time-tested marriage, which had served her as a model during her childhood, helped also. And then there was James and Julie's harmonious relationship when it came to their, Nadine suspected, rather infrequent, love making. But between husband and wife their sexual cravings and satisfaction seemed to be almost mutual. It was not as if one of them, lets say James, wanted to sleep with Julie and she, for one reason or another was unreceptive. The young, curious girl, who kept observing the couple closely, never noticed James' hunger for his wife's body, which she, because she didn't feel the same biological urges, refused him. Nadine was sure he didn't have to plead with Julie, to wheedle his way into her good graces so that he could satisfy his testosterone driven impulses. And Julie, if not enticed by his physique, didn't need to feel guilty for having tried to escape her husband's amorous approaches, nor for ardently wishing that she were somewhere else, or with someone else, while he relentlessly, helplessly, ludicrously hovered around her, caught in his own spermatozoal net, as his senses took over and indiscriminately coveted every part of her body.

Julie did not seem to dislike the idea of their lovemaking. Their marriage was one of those rare ones where apparently both partners desired each other more or less equally. Usually, Julie seemed to want James as much as he did her.

But perhaps more importantly than sex was the fact that within the context of matrimony the two of them had become friends. They were not just lovers. The couple shared common ideas and beliefs and in spite of having become so intimate, so familiar with each other, they still were able to keep a certain amount of esteem for each other.

Married for several years when Nadine met the couple, they had managed to become emotionally very close to each other. At night, while sharing the same bed in the dark, the two of them would talk with low voices into each other's ears. Like brother and sister they held hands before they fell asleep. Slowly, voluptuously, they sank into a velvety darkness that welcomed them.

During the night, if Julie became half awake as James turned on his side, she moved closer to his large body until her knees lightly touched the small of his back. Sighing contentedly, she would put one of her arms around his shoulder. Barely conscious of a few incoherent images and reassured by the familiar scent of James's skin, she continued to slumber. Inhaling his odor, she softly glided back into the bottomless depth of dreams, whispering to herself:

"I have to watch that he doesn't put on any more weight." And even sleep could not erase the smile on her wide, half open mouth.

Day by day each of them had slowly learned to trust the other. By trial and error, heartache, tears, and boiling rages husband and wife had learned the art to give up parts of themselves and to open their hearts to each other as if they were the thin pages of a book, they were reading together.

Of course, they have had their fights. This was especially so early on during wedlock and after the charm of their honeymoon had worn off. They had broken a vase or two and a few dishes during some of their shouting matches. Once Julie, with a red, bloated face, crying hard and half-choking from anger and pain, had taken their infant daughter and run home to her parents in England while James remained in Kenya. Night after night, he had sat alone in their large house at the outskirts of Nairobi, listening to the incessant rain pounding on the corrugated iron rooftop until he went almost mad. He longed for Julie and his small child.

Then, when he could no longer stand his loneliness, James had followed his wife and daughter to England. There, they had glued the broken pieces together and seemed to be the stronger for it. Peter was the result of their newly formed bond. When Nadine came to live with the Johnsons, husband and wife knew each other's bodies to such an extent that James was quite content to use Julie's dirty bubble baths during their perpetual shortage of water. And most of their emotions had become such familiar landscapes to them that they sometimes seemed to be able to read each other's thoughts.

"I'm so glad I no longer have to hunt for the right man," Julie had said once before Nadine left the house for a date. The young girl, in the last year of her teens, was still at the stage where chasing men and being pursued by them was considered fun. She did not understand what Julie meant. As she closed the old, weighty door of the hallway behind her and rushed for her train, she shrugged her shoulders and whispered:

"Well, one day when I'm her ripe old age, I will find out what she means."

Strong-faced, red-skinned and determined, James had stepped further outside of himself during their marriage than Julie. He had wanted to know more keenly who he was. At night, when he sat alone in his train bringing him back from London, he had more thoroughly looked at the life he was leading than his wife whose blond hair and slender figure he, after several years of marriage, wanted as much as ever. Julie came from a fine family and her parents had provided her with more money than he would ever have been able to amass in the diplomatic service. Eventually, as James slowly placed one small mosaic next to another during their married life, he came to the conclusion that although Julie's life was in many ways not right for him, he could, at least up to a point, adapt to it. Partly he did so for Lipsey and Peter's sake whom he loved dearly. And one day his male ego, whose superiority over the female had been reinforced throughout centuries that were dominated by patriarchy, understood that Julie, fine-boned, far smaller than him and more adept in solving daily chores, proved to be the stronger of the two.

* * *

The *Queen of Scots* had not yet pulled out of Paddington station when Peter reported loudly:

"My body hurts. I have to make *pipi*." Nadine blushed and hoped no one else on the train, which was getting more crowded by the minute, had heard the little boy's announcement.

"Make sure you cover the toilet seat with lots of paper before he sits down," Julie, without lowering her voice, advised Nadine unperturbed.

"But I thought we could not use the bathroom while the train is still at the station," Nadine timidly objected and looked at James who did not lift his head from the newspaper he was reading.

"Oh, don't be so fastidious. Peter is only three years old. Nobody will mind. Besides, we didn't bring his potty, did we?" Julie laughed and brushed Nadine's bashful deliberations aside.

She smiled as she watched the young girl and Peter walk away in search of the facilities. Julie had grown very fond of Nadine. But she never spoke of her feelings to her. With her Victorian upbringing, such a display didn't seem appropriate and she hoped that it was enough for Nadine to know that she liked her. But it was not. She needed to hear affectionate expressions.

Julie frequently used terms of endearments for her children and on weekends her shouts of "darling" vibrated through the house when she couldn't find James. Those were the times when Nadine suddenly found herself left out, standing alone in a vast, unknown, bare field. She then often felt as if moments ago she had been dropped from a considerable height. And just before she fell, with her stomach rising to her throat, she had a glimpse of the gulf that existed between her and the English family she had come to love. Experiencing rejection, she once more imagined the body of water as it stretched between Dover and Calais. And she saw herself as a child again, sitting in a German shelter terrified of the English bombers above her, which had flown across the sea. They came at night. And they never failed to bring destruction and death with them. During those imagined instants in the midst of an idyllic English landscape, which her mind easily produced, innocent Julie and her family became the enemy again.

"I wish that just once Julie would call me, too, with a *Kosenamen*,[17]" Nadine murmured. But the Englishwoman never did. No magic wand was raised to release the ban.

* * *

Hand-in-hand the pretty girl and little boy moved along the thickly carpeted corridor, which divided the open compartments of the *Queen of Scots* on their left and right. Both of their eyes were flashing with excitement as they looked around them with great curiosity.

The standard brass lamps on most of the small tables between their upholstered seats were switched on. Their soft lights added comfort and elegance on a dark, misty winter day. The glimmering bulbs were focal points in the midst of the constant bustle as passengers were still arriving. On white, starched tablecloths, cutlery sparkled among immaculately clean crystal. And each expansive seat with its elaborate headrest in front of a table looked inviting. It was the most luxurious train Nadine had ever seen, but at the moment she had no time for its unaccustomed beauty. Peter was yanking her hand and as they marched on with the boy often in front of her, she watched his knee socks slide down. From frequent washings their rubber-reinforced edge had become lose and it hardly helped to pull them up several times. Yet this did not prevent Nadine from interrupting once in a while their march and, kneeling on the floor, keep jerking at the sliding socks anyway. She did this without thinking, obeying a strong impulse to create order. As she struggled with Peter's socks, she tried to ignore his restlessly shuffling feet.

"Hold still," she commanded the little boy brusquely. Then feeling that she had been too harsh with him, she arched her neck upward and brushed with her cheek against the child's soft face.

"Silly boy", she said tenderly, got off her knees and continued to look for the bathroom. As they passed from one car to the next, Nadine prayed the toilet door would not be locked until the train started to move. Fortunately, they finally found a lavatory door that opened eas-

---

[17] pet name

ily enough and, to Nadine's relief, the rather spacious cabinet was also clean.

Peter took his time and exhibited a scatological delight in listening to and watching his urine as it noisily ran down the white toilet bowl onto the tracks. He wanted to flush the water several times. And he, who hated to have his hands washed, let the soap run twice across his chubby fingers. Nadine had a hard time getting rid of the bubbles and drying his hands. While she attended to the small boy, she nervously watched the vague silhouettes of passengers as they scurried past the milky glass of the window outside the train, less than a foot away from them. And she hoped nobody would pay attention to the splashing water, which was highly audible.

Afterwards, for the rest of their six-hour trip, when it was perfectly all right to use any bathroom on the train, Peter did not have to go. But Lipsey made up for it.

Young, noiselessly moving and well-trained stewards served lunch at the proper time. Busily walking back and forth and keeping their trays in perfect balance on the jostling train, the waiters smiled a lot and bowed gracefully from a slender waist, but they would talk little.

After their leisurely-taken meal, the children, at the impatient insistence of their mother, took a five-minute nap. Then, quickly sitting up again, they once more glued their noses to the window. But they were unable to catch more than a glimpse of the landscape outside the moving train.

Inundated in thick fog, field upon field was revealed specter-like. In a swift semicircle the countryside silently approached the train, only to spin out of sight just as fast as it had appeared. Like kids at play, a few cottages sprang forward among trees and bushes and then hastily receded into the background again. Uninterrupted, only occasionally slowing down, the train carried its human freight through strange, hardly recognizable territory. Without resting once, the wheels sang their monotonous song. Nadine started to feel very sleepy. Yet there was no chance to lean her head back and close her eyes. The children demanded her attention.

After the first three hours, Peter and Lipsey got thoroughly bored. Fidgeting on their seats, they stood up on them and where the table was not in their way, hopped onto the floor. Red-faced and sweaty, they reached for each other, giggling, pushing and whining like a bunch of puppies until Julie told them sharply: "Stop that"!

Nadine, seeing brother and sister near tears, began to read to them some of their favorite stories. But that did not prevent either Peter or Lipsey from asking every ten minutes:

"Aren't we there yet?"

* * *

They arrived in the late afternoon with an almost two hour delay. A few times the train had been forced to slow from its accustomed speed because of the constant fog, which had invaded the countryside. The children were cranky, especially Peter who still needed to sleep an hour in the afternoon. Having missed his nap, he whimpered and demanded to be carried by Nadine.

A beige, spotlessly clean Rolls Royce picked the family up from the station at Harrogate. Rudolph Hibson, Julie's father, was driving. He greeted his daughter and grandchildren warmly, shook hands with James and gave Nadine an appreciative look. There was a twinkle in his eye and she liked the dimple on one of his rosy cheeks. She knew right away that she would have no trouble getting along with him.

But she was not so sure about Mrs. Hibson. She was waiting for them at 14 Beech Hollow, her lovely home, and instantly made a great fuss about Lipsey and Peter. By contrast, she paid almost no attention to their father and at first did not seem to even notice Nadine. Only Julie got a quick hug.

During the confusion of their arrival at the house, Nadine had ample time to observe Julie's mother. Melanie Hibson was small, fine-boned, and very thin. She was dressed in a fashionable suit, more stylish, and far more expensive, than Julie's. A perfectly cut diamond, or so Nadine believed, replaced the last button of her high-collared silk blouse. It was plain that she never wore the tweed skirts and simple wool sweaters her daughter felt comfortable in when at home. Mrs. Hibson, as Nadine would always refer to her, obviously took great pains with her clothes and her speech was, if possible, even more clipped than

Julie's. But she rolled her "r" in a noticeable manner, adding a Yorkshire flavor to her carefully chosen words. Her mouth was minute and she enhanced her wrinkled, bloodless lips with dark rouge, which in the young girl's eyes, was not becoming at all. The faint, almost imperceptible odor of a costly perfume met Nadine's nose as Melanie Hibson at last came toward her and shook hands.

"How pleasant it is to finally meet you. Julie did not stop speaking about you," she said as her eyes shrank into slits among layers of crowfeet.

Nadine discovered the rumbling "r" once more in the spacious kitchen where Beatrice, the seventy-nine year old, fat cook, was preparing tea. As soon as the young girl took a close look at her, she thought that she had never seen so many vertical and horizontal wrinkles in one face. Most of them were around her eyes and mouth, yet some also descended to her double chin. But Beatrice wore her withered skin as if the countless gashes time had carved into her flesh were battle scars. There was nothing shy about the debilitated cook. Nor did Nadine detect a trace of boastfulness. This was a woman who had grown old by serving others. Rickety and worn, she sluggishly shuffled on flattened feet through her domain, with the kitchen and pantry being at the heart of it, as she went about her work during many hours of the day. The cook had started to move her lips in an incessant, indistinguishable babble, as if trying to express any and every thought, which fleetingly ran through her brain. And her head was trembling when she bent over a pile of vegetables or a big slice of beefsteak, but she was still fast with her hands. Every morning she would get up at dawn. And in the evening, she went to bed "with the chickens", as Melanie Hibson called it. Beatrice had been with the family for over fifty years and was in calm control of the house and its inhabitants.

"I don't know what we would do without her," Mrs. Hibson said at least twice a day during her daughter's visit. It was mostly this forcefully stated admission of her dependence upon the cook, which made her likeable in Nadine's eyes.

In their mutual treatment of each other the distinction between servant and mistress had almost disappeared. Over many years an almost sister-like companionship had been established among the two elderly women who had weathered most of life's hardships together. Their relationship limped a little since one "*sister*" was not only older but also infinitely poorer than the other. Yet money was not the bond that bound the two women together. Their friendship had gone far beyond any material considerations.

Fascinated as the young are by the old, Nadine frequently watched the two women. One of them was gaunt, wiry and always impeccably dressed and the other was tall, was never seen wearing anything but an old house frock and painfully moved about in a heavy, slow gait. The cook was in perpetual anguish over the big staircase of the house, which she had to climb twice a day. And although she would have loved to take a nap in the afternoon, the stairs prevented her from doing so. After lunch, she dozed at the big, shiny kitchen table. She would put her head, where patches of her scalp were visible under white-yellowish, greasy looking hair on her plump forearms, sigh deeply and close her eyes. And almost immediately rhythmic snoring assailed the room.

"Don't disturb her," Julie, who hardly ever entered Beatrice's sphere, told Nadine on the second day of their arrival.

"And for the next hour keep the children out of the kitchen as well," she added with one of her pleasant smiles.

As usual, the young girl saw more than there was. Parading in front of her eyes was most of *Un coeur simple*. But it was Beatrice, the Yorkshire cook, instead of her French precursor, who played the main part of the courageous, unselfish servant. Nadine had no trouble replacing Flaubert's Pont-l'Évêque and the small town of Trouville, where the action takes place, with Harrogate. A country maid's portrait by the great 19th century French realist, a passionate believer in *L'art objectif*, (Flaubert almost literally dissected his characters which he based on extensive if not excessive research and documentation) immortalizing a simple woman who sacrifices her life to the family she works for greatly helped Nadine's quick fondness for the old Yorkshire woman.

As soon as Beatrice had Nadine to herself in the kitchen, she wanted to know all about her. The old cook was quite curious about the young German girl. The only Germans she had ever seen from afar had been prisoners-of-war:

" Do you enjoy your stay in England?" She tactfully asked as she sat at the heavy, square table that stood in the middle of the room, deftly unsheathing a pile of peas.

"Oh, yes I do! I have come to love England and its people," Nadine answered enthusiastically. She knew, of course, what her newly found friend wanted to hear. But she also meant what she had said. She didn't need to lie.

The cook uttered in a loud, high-pitched voice:

"Speak up, girl. I cannot hear you. My ears are no longer what they used to be."

Taken for a moment aback by the woman's raised voice, Nadine reassured her again how fond she had become of the Johnsons, especially the children. And she added how much she enjoyed seeing the coastal cities of England.

"Brighton and Cornwall are beautiful", she murmured before she giggled:

"And then there is London!" The young girl had spoken from the heart. Beatrice understood her admiring honesty and, having a warm nature, as well as an inquisitive one, she decided that she liked Nadine.

But as far as no longer being able to hear well, the cook had exaggerated matters. She was more than half deaf and had to heavily rely on reading lips and people shouting at her. Twice the size of Melanie Hibson, Beatrice also liked to sit a lot, which was bad for her health. She often complained about a constant pain in her legs:

"It's arthritis. And I can tell rain is coming three days ahead of time," she screamed.

In Nadine's eyes the cook's forecast did not seem such a difficult task since it rained almost every day during her visit to England's north. Except one day after Boxing Day when it had started to snow, the weather was awful. But this time, instead of saying what was on her mind, she only reassuringly patted Beatrice's hand, the back of which was so profusely covered with liver spots that the whiteness of her skin almost disappeared.

The large home of Julie's parents was situated at the outskirts of Harrogate. With its two pointed gables, which divided the façade of the three-story high villa into two equal halves, it stood serene, and somewhat portly, in a quiet street with lots of old, carefully kept shrubbery and tall, slender pines. In front of the mansion ran a large, cobble-stoned circle and within its enormous elliptic shape were six semi-round lawns, bordered by dozens of sturdy looking rose trees. Symmetrically shaped pathways led to the center of the orbit where further clusters of roses had grown to a substantial size. Even now in December and in spite of their dead leaves and nearly naked, pruned branches, the plants looked appealing. Within well-spaced intervals, the driveway of the house was lined with big stone vases. These, too, were filled with rose bushes.

Nadine never counted the windows of the villa. Many of them were large and thanks to a daily caretaker they were so clean that they could have served anyone as a mirror. Yet it was the seven bedrooms of the house, all located on the second floor, which were the part of the mansion that impressed Nadine the most. Each one of the rooms was spacious and named after the color in which they were decorated. And to the young girl's pleasant surprise they all contained a working fireplace.

When she first stepped into the house, she took a deep breath and then almost whistled like a street urchin when she saw the voluminous, high-ceilinged, timber embellished hallway. The semi-dark vestibule reminded her of a small church except that it did not have any pews and instead of the stone slabs commonly found in places of worship, worn Persian rugs covered most of an oak floor.

During the first two days of the young girl's visit in Harrogate whenever she walked up on the wide staircase of the hall, she expected to hear the sounds of cymbals and trumpets. But the steps were forever kept in soft somberness, especially now in December. Beautifully wrought brass lamps had been installed too sparingly.

"It looks as if someone wants to save electricity," Nadine said under her breath, as she tried not to stumble in the twilight. Beatrice's fear of the dark staircase suddenly made a lot of sense to her.

When she had first climbed the stairs, she was not surprised to find a spacious, stained glass window on the landing between the ground and second floor. No church would have looked down upon its lovely design and workmanship. Below the window three tall, delicate Chinese vases stood like pregnant princesses against the wall. To add a masculine touch, two fox heads, which Julie's father had shot in his younger days, hung on either side of the walls next to the window.

On the first floor of the house was the morning room whose focal point was a huge fireplace. It was here where the family would spend the day when at home. A spacious sofa and several heavy, black leather chairs were picturesquely grouped around the hearth. Luxuriant, dark-brown velvet curtains embellished four high windows. There were several mahogany bookshelves, most of them climbing the walls from floor to ceiling and about half a dozen highly polished, beech-wooded secretaries of various shapes and sizes had been distributed throughout the room. Their tables were loaded with writing utensils, letters, news-papers, magazines and more books.

Next to the morning room was a formal drawing room. Julie had told the young girl that during her and her sister's childhood, cocktail parties for well over a hundred guests had been given there on a regular basis.

"But only in the summer," she had laughed.

"In the winter even with several fireplaces going full blast, as well as electric heaters, we would have frozen. The room was simply too big to be comfortable."

Along three of the salon's walls hung several French Impressionists, and one or two older masters. Among them Nadine even discovered a small portrait by Rembrandt. The fourth wall contained the same large windows as the other big rooms. But here the most elaborate, green brocade curtains, which were held by thick, golden tassels, had been installed. The sumptuous fabric was so well maintained that it looked new. In front of the windows resided the largest, round, white leather pillows, which Nadine had ever seen. Overwhelmed by this unaccus-tomed collection of furniture and art, she went from item to item. But in the end it was the pictures on the wall that interested her the most. Whenever she had a few instants during the day to herself, she would slip into the vast, unheated room where, shivering with cold, she would put her nose closely to the wooden and gilded frames of the paintings as if by sniffing them her sense of sight would be heightened. The size of the room and its costly collection always made her feel as if she were in a museum where benches were offered to the viewers who got tired from gorging themselves with visual delights.

While Nadine, Julie and her family stayed in Yorkshire, the big drawing room, blazing with fireplaces, but still cold, was used only once. It was in the afternoon on Christmas Day when Queen Elizabeth II gave her annual speech for the festive season. James stood at attention. Straight as a rod, tall, red-faced and fleshy, he remained upright in a rigid position during the regent's entire thirty-minute talk. Nadine, quickly getting bored, stared at his hands that were pressed motionless against the seams of his pants just a little above and sideways to his knees. Everybody else was also on his or her feet while the young monarch spoke. Nadine, who didn't care for her high pitched, squeaky, monotonous sounding voice, kept looking at James. She was fascinated by the display of concentration on his facial features as he focused his eyes on the radio, which suddenly seemed to have become a substitute for the Holy Grail. For a while she was not so sure if she should laugh or cry at so much blatantly displayed patriotism. During the queen's long speech every muscle around his eyes and mouth and their nerve endings beneath them seemed to remember that he was the only son of an English general.

Lipsey and Peter were exquisitely dressed for the occasion and both of them wore black patent leather shoes with white stockings. But Elizabeth's public address was an ordeal for them. They were so irritated by the invisible queen's laborious, wearying communication, which forced them into silence, that their only relief was a constant hop from one foot to the other. And every few moments they would tug at Nadine's skirt wanting to know when this strange young woman, who was hidden in a brown wooden box and often sounded more like a bird than a human, would finally stop talking.

"Soon, soon", Nadine, who refused to fall under the queen's feckless charm, which apparently held the other adults captive, whispered, putting her index finger on her lips. But the queen's shy, girlish voice kept on in an everlasting, tedious singsong rhythm, which bored the young girl to no end.

"Even standing up, I could fall asleep," she sighed and then tried to hide her yawn by holding her hand in front of her mouth.

Listlessly, Elizabeth II read her speech, which, Nadine repeatedly thought, would have benefited a great deal by being shorter. It also did not help that the tone of her voice clearly indicated that she wished she were doing something else. Except in the beginning, the queen's heart seemed to have quickly escaped to better places. It certainly was not in her flat, nasal utterances.

"She has a cold, poor woman," Julie said rather loudly, bending her face toward Nadine. And she wrinkled her forehead in disapproval as she looked at the young girl who could not stop yawning. That afternoon Julie was not happy with her German au pair. She blamed her for the fidgetiness of her two offspring and she didn't at all like the way Nadine's eyes had mockingly and repeatedly wandered to her husband's face and figure during the monarch's endless speech.

Opposite the enormous, cold living room was the smaller and considerably warmer dining room. Here the Christmas meal was served in its full splendor of crystal, china, silver and the decorated holly branches, which had been placed next to each plate. Their spiny-margined leaves scratched a diner's wrist each time he or she came too close to them. Two seascapes by Turner hung on the room's walls. Individual lights had been fastened above their frames to enhance the painting's allure.

The kitchen and scullery next to the dining room with their huge, often somewhat bulging stone tiles were as large as a small house. Beatrice did not stop lamenting about the floor's iciness:

"My poor feet, I can't keep them warm any longer," she would moan several times a day.

On Christmas Day after the queen's speech, which had been followed by their big meal, Rudolph Hibson and his son-in-law walked back and forth in the scullery. Laughing and joking, they dried the dishes, pots, and pans Nadine had just thoroughly scrubbed and rinsed. Beatrice was exhausted after having cooked their big dinner.

"Besides, the cook never washes dishes," James laughed. After several glasses of port, both men were in high spirits having, as they did, the pretty young girl to themselves. Good-naturedly, they teased her about her accent and kept imitating certain words, which she pronounced in a droll manner. Halfway through their work, Nadine turned matters around by addressing James in German. On a few occasions, he had impressed her by quoting passages from Gottfried Keller, Novalis and Goethe. But now he was scrambling for common words. It was the young girl's turn to laugh:

"They don't seem to teach you simple things in Cambridge, like keeping up a humble conversation," she challenged him.

"Anybody with a halfway working memory can quote from *Gretchen am Spinnrad*," she added with a mischievous smile.

On the third floor of the big house were the maid's quarters. For the past few years only the cook had been occupying those plainly furnished rooms. But for some reason one of the largest bathtubs in the house was located here. On most evenings Nadine gave the children their bath in it, not only because of its ample size but also she saw that brother and sister loved climbing up the wide wooden staircase to the third floor. Being quick on their small, short legs, they always tried to outrace the young girl. Gasping, after she had given them a head start, she scampered after them and cried:

"Wait until I get hold of you two rascals! I'm going to eat you alive."

Her mock threat evoked happy squeals and breathless giggles from Lipsey and Peter as they scrambled in front of her. Nadine was still faster than the two small kids. When she caught up with them, she lifted first Peter and then his sister off the ground, put her head on their chests and blew against them a mouthful of hot breath. Her puffing lips would tickle them and both children exploded in laughter. At the same time, they struggled hard to squeeze out of Nadine's arms. The three of them never tired of this little game that would rarely vary.

Later at night, before Nadine reached her and the children's bedroom she needed to cross another large, carpeted hall on the second floor. The entire foyer looked larger than it was because it contained nothing but an old, intricately carved oak chest of drawers. It was placed against one long wall and flanked by two overgrown, potted, healthy looking gum trees.

Nadine's bedroom was about five times the size of the one she occupied in Groombridge and was done in blue. It too was high ceilinged, like the rest of the mansion. A fluffy blue rug spread from wall to wall and was a novelty for Nadine who was not used to fully carpeted rooms. Blue, full length silk and lace curtains, a little faded and torn in some places, but without their defects being easily detectible, were fastened at three windows. The twin beds, looking rather small in the big room, were covered with thick, soft, blue bedspreads. The only items that were not blue were the dressing table and the fireplace. Above it, several empty, expensive vases of different sizes were displayed on the mantle piece. There was also a sumptuous, white washbasin. The items on her vanity table, the mirrors and small jewelry cases in which she took a childish delight, as well as various delicate jars for crèmes and make-up removers and not just one, but three different-sized bottles of eau de cologne, were all made of blue and silver. So was a large comb and brush.

Adjoining her bedroom was a spacious dressing room and a bathroom, which she shared with Lipsey, whose bedroom was done in lilac and contained a four-poster bed. Of course, the little girl loved it and kept pestering her mother about it:

"Why can't I have a bed like this in Groombridge? I want to sleep there under a silk covered sky, too. I love looking up to it while I fall asleep."

The master bedroom, kept in perfect order by an elderly maid who came every day for a few hours, was decorated in purple and even larger than the rest of the other bedrooms. The over-sized bed was round and placed on a wooden platform, which contained concealed drawers. Lined up rather stiffly on the wide satin bedcover were about two-dozen different sized purple pillows. And at any time of the day, several diamond rings, pearl necklaces and heavy gold bracelets were spread in colorful confusion all over Melanie Hibson's dressing table. Only her most valuable jewels, which she wore for special occasions, were kept in a safe.

Four long rows of shoes and several minks in different colors were assembled in her dressing room. She didn't need to share it with her husband because he had his own. Among her elaborate coats, but set somewhat apart as if to indicate its superiority, was the softest of soft furs: a long, black sable.

Sometimes when Nadine remained for a few minutes alone upstairs, she would pay the sable a quick visit. In the silence around her, she breathed in deeply the air, which was saturated with Guerlain's *Mitsouko*. It was, as she soon discovered, Melanie's favorite perfume. Slyly, noiselessly opening the door of the dressing room, she would straight away walk toward the coat and caress its smooth, perfect texture. Closing her eyes, she put her face into its fragrant, black softness as if it were a living being she longed to be close to.

* * *

Just before the holidays, it began to snow. Then the nights became cold and the snow turned to ice. Snow and ice were piled high on the ground and it became more difficult to walk or drive.

Julie and her mother visited a lot of old friends in town, leaving Nadine behind in the big house to look after the children. But just before the young girl, who, as always, wanted to be close to Julie, started to feel neglected, both women kind-heartedly announced that they would like for her to have contact with people her own age, too. Julie and Melanie urged her to go to one of the dances, which were popular around Christmas time not only in Harrogate but also all over England:

"Both of us are sure that you would enjoy meeting young people. You must be tired of us old folks," Julie said tongue-in-cheek as she winked at Nadine.

In Germany the young girl had known Christmas as a rather solemn festivity that was celebrated at home among close family members and at church. In the south, where Catholicism was dominant, the attendance at a midnight mass on December 24, especially among the elderly, was *de rigeur*. But to her pleasant surprise, she quickly learned that Christmas in England was a gay and social occurrence. It was then when business acquaintances and good friends, family and strangers seemed to gather everywhere in festively decorated public and private places, where music, wine and good food inundated large and small rooms, and often overflowed into hallways.

The day before the holidays, Nadine was on her way to one of the better hotels in town. It was a cold and snowy evening with patches of fog, which was partly hiding streets, trees, buildings and people alike. She wore ugly but warm winter boots and carried her high-heeled, open-toed shoes in a bag. After a few minutes of vigorous walking, her skin was aglow from the cold. Melanie Hibson had given her the name of the hotel and told her that some of the most eligible bachelors of Harrogate assembled at the place during special events.

At first Nadine had not wanted to go. The house at 14 Beech Hollow felt so pleasant and warm with its soft lights and its enormous, wooden logs crackling in the various fireplaces of the big house. Everything was quiet and cheerful after she had tucked in the children and gone back to her room. She did not look forward to a long walk in a strange, dark, cloud-shrouded city. The weather was certainly not inviting. Not a single bird was still awake. Outside her windows the starless night seemed to have solidified into a black, threatening mass.

Earlier during the day she had taken the children for their daily exercise to a park close by. At one point, they had watched a squirrel whose tail had been half cut off. As the three of them looked on in horror and disgust the dead end of the squirrel's tail was hanging down at a weird angle. Scampering along a low hanging, bare branch that jutted straight out into the air, the little rodent helplessly dragged along the injured part of its tail. The hurt mammal looked so different from its companions, who were bushy-tailed and victoriously scurrying along in search for food, that it hardly resembled a squirrel.

In the early evening, after Nadine had given Lipsey and Peter their tea, she did not feel like dressing up. Only after Julie had knocked twice at her door and urged her to try her luck – "come on, you can't meet anyone by staying home and there are good people out there, I know..." – did she finally put on one of the two cocktail dresses, which she had in defiance of Christian's wishes, asked her mother to send her from Germany. But she did not bother with any make-up:

"I don't care what I look like among people who do not know me," she whispered to her mirror. Yet even while she said this, she knew that she lied to herself. She did want to look pretty among strangers. But she was not motivated to beautify herself because she had little hope of meeting someone she might like. Similar to a sleepy sloth, she preferred to cling to a tree branch and was content to observe under semi-closed eyes the foliage around her. But Julie chased her out of the house:

"You always tell me how much fun you had with Hanna in Paris. English men are not worse than French boys. You need young people to keep you company," Julie laughed as she accompanied Nadine to the front door of the mansion.

Having refused a ride in Rudolph Hibson's Rolls Royce, which he had kindly offered, she needed to walk about forty-five minutes through Harrogate's poorly lit, cold streets, before she finally found the hotel, which Julie and her mother had recommended. Even from the exterior it looked lovely, as it lay only half visible under tall shrubbery, covered by snow and a thick mist. She hesitatingly crossed its doorstep and took a quick look at its warm, tastefully furnished lobby. Then she almost turned around to go back home. She had expected rather modest accommodations. Instead, chandeliers, sparkling lights and thick rugs greeted her. Against the walls stood heavy, dark cupboards loaded with flowers and faint laughter appeared to come from every corner. The low humming of male and female voices was interrupted by music, which wafted through two large, constantly opening and closing doors. Not only were the young girls who rushed to and from, impeccably dressed and attractive, but handsome men also accompanied many of them. Everyone Nadine observed was in evening attire.

Standing intimidated next to a low Queen Ann's table and its two matching chairs, she was convinced Melanie Hibson had given her the wrong address. She suddenly felt very shabby and was embarrassed that she had come. As she timidly looked about her, she was driven by one idea:

"Why did I come in the first place when I was so much better off at home, "...wo die Räume stiller, der Kaffee besser und keine Unterhaltung nötig ist."[18]

But before she could turn around and leave, a friendly middle-aged woman approached her. It was the manager of the hotel who gave her a quick, professional smile asking if she had come to dance.

---

[18]   "...where the rooms are more restful, the coffee better and no conversation is needed." From a poem by Gottfried Benn.

"Only if there are any single men available," Nadine said clumsily, her voice edged with anger.

The smile on the woman's face deepened and her green eyes, which had momentarily blinked, again sparkled at Nadine. She was dressed in a graceful, long, brown velvet skirt. Experienced, she quickly saw how shy the young girl, who spoke with an accent, was. Being in a pleasant mood and having an indulgent disposition, she said:

"Oh, there are plenty of nice bachelors here. Come with me. I'll introduce you to my younger sister who is also here by herself. The two of you will enjoy meeting each other. And we do have several agreeable young men in the house."

Like a good fairy, the manager introduced Nadine to her sister. Janet was short, even stocky. Her shoulder-length, dark hair was cut in bangs over her eyes, almost concealing them. With her black curls she looked rather French than English. As she spoke, her deep blue eyes moved back and forth from Nadine's face to other people close to them. It was as if Janet, driven by nervous restlessness, needed to size up, sort out and judge her environment minute by minute. Yet the young girl could not have been more friendly and openhearted; with a lively gesture she immediately offered Nadine a chair, which stood next to her. And before long, she told Nadine almost everything about her studies at the University of Leeds:

"I'm a psychology major and like college life a lot. The workload is all right and it's not the worst place to catch a husband," Janet beamed at Nadine as she dabbed powder on her nose and protruding, pointed chin.

The two young girls were sitting in a large ladies lounge where several mirrors reflected the mellow light of the room a hundred fold. Nadine soon started to feel more comfortable. While she was busily putting on mascara and lipstick, she chatted all the time with Janet. And after about twenty minutes, both of them felt as if they had known each other their entire lives.

When the two new friends finally walked out of the cloakroom and entered the ballroom through its heavy, swinging doors, Nadine no longer felt alone. Nor did she think that she looked ugly.

She had feared that the room from where the music came would be one of the large, cold, high ceilinged dance halls upon which she had stumbled in Brighton and then again in London, where the atmosphere lacked even an ounce of social intimacy. Those ballrooms had usually been just half filled by groups of young men and women, who had forlornly collected in a corner or two of the immense place. All evening the dancers would stand or move to the sound of a live band in crammed quarters at the edge of the floor, hardly ever venturing forth, leaving the center of the hall, where the largest chandeliers reigned in solitary, unchallenged splendor, vacant. It was as if the middle of the big place had been a threatening spot, a swampy region that swarmed with semi-aquatic pit vipers, which had to be avoided at all cost.

But Nadine was used to the minute, crowded dancing floors in Germany's jazz- and nightclubs. Here she had soon discovered the glitter of perfect skin and the sensuous, synchronized movements of two young people in love. In small German clubs, where candles and a single fresh rose on tiny tables rendered most of its guests beautiful, she had listened to the whispered, amorous nonsense from a mouth she desired. As she clung to Christian, she had absorbed his scent, a mixture of aftershave lotion and perspiration, which together with his low laughter and muscle-reinforced arms, held her captive. Yet these marvels of life, which had made her young head spin and caused a distinct, short-lived feeling of happiness, had died in London under a thousand empty lights, which were more appropriate for operating rooms in hospitals than a ballroom. And Spencer had never been able to replace Christian.

* * *

Nadine gave a sigh of relief when she saw that the size of the Harrogate's hotel ballroom was quite comfortable and its maple floor seemed to be excellent for dancing. She also liked the small, black lacquered tables, its chairs and couches, all in good taste, which here and there bordered the edge of the dance floor.

Janet and Nadine remained standing near the entrance, next to two potted palm trees. From there they had a good view of the scene in front of them. Looking at the various dancers with bright eyes, the two girls continued to banter with each other. To relieve their tension, they broke into laughter after almost every sentence they uttered. By now Nadine felt almost totally relaxed in Janet's company. Then a medium-sized man approached the young girls and destroyed their intimacy by asking Nadine for a dance.

Blond-haired with a strongly receding hairline, the stranger had seductive, brown eyes. Walking toward the two young women he seemed to discreetly weigh every inch of their bodies before his choice fell upon Nadine. And, as soon as she was close enough, he also, with much less subtlety began to scrutinize her face. From the instant he confronted both of them, Nadine was struck by his assurance. He had the suave manners of a worldly, somewhat older man who knew what he liked and how to get what he wanted.

Nadine was not at all at ease under his intense looks, which had so soon disregarded her new friend. With an ironic smile she shook her curls, turned her head and asked sarcastically:

"When did you buy your last slave girl?"

"Oh, what nationality are you?" he laughed ignoring her question. He had a pleasant voice where once more the Yorkshire "r" took up a distinct and quite audible space. As soon as he spoke, he made her see the loosely piled-up stone walls that cross the sloping northern English landscape with such sweeping and stunning lines.

"You are not Turkish, are you?" The Yorkshire man now wanted to know. Nadine was amused. She enjoyed having people guess her nationality. And, although since coming to England she had been mistaken for a Frenchwoman, an Italian, or a Russian, no one had yet thought she might be from Turkey.

"Why, don't you like Turks?" She asked without a muscle moving in her face.

"Well, if you do want to know, I enjoyed visiting Ankara and Istanbul. And, as far as the old Ottoman Empire is concerned, I wish I had been able to climb Mt. Ararat, which now, as you must be aware, the Armenians have started to claim as their own," the Harrogate man suavely responded as he once more avoided her provocative remark. Then he quickly added:

"By the way, I am Arnold Illingrose. What's your name?"

The corners of the man's lips had curled upward and the skin around the edges of his eyes produced wrinkles, which Nadine noticed for the first time.

'I don't believe it! It is someone older again,' she thought and was not pleased.

"I don't understand why I seem to attract father figures. I am no longer a baby," she sighed as she averted her eyes from the man's slightly graying temples.

But, of course, in many ways she still was. Physically she had blossomed and sprouted. As she had grown into an appealing adolescent, she had produced enough twigs and branches and the requisite abundance of foliage to compete with fully-grown trees. Yet inside, under her rough bark and below the bird nests and the crawling insects, there still was the small child that had been bruised and harmed. The child in her had not ceased to be dominant. She still relied a great deal on her healthy instincts. And her strongest mental abilities were not the logic and the argumentative ability which she occasionally admired in others. Instead, she mainly thought in associations, and as if carried by air, her element, she let herself drift upon images that covered a vast area. Often she saw herself as a water lily with wide, long stemmed leaves floating on a summer pond, yet spot-bound. And she was always startled when the face of her maternal grandmother, whom she had loved, would suddenly appear.

Although Nadine had an astute mind, mathematics and science were not her strong point. She was the type whose feelings ran deep and under her easy smile and luminous skin she was quickly hurt. Although incapable of bearing a grudge, she hardly ever forgot an incident during which she had suffered.

"You have the mind of an elephant," Monika Tallemann would say to her daughter when Nadine referred in startling details to an incident from her childhood, which her mother had long forgotten.

Arnold Illingrose gently led her across the hotel's dance floor. But as soon as both of them began to sway to the music, she started to withdraw into herself. While the arms of the stranger held her, she thought that she had not yet found a goal worth fighting for. In her life the illusive ends of each rainbow continued to look alike. None was for her. It was still a man's world. And that environment, although technologically more advanced than other parts of the globe where women had fewer opportunities to fight for themselves, still left her less space than if she had been born a boy. She did not know who she was or what she wanted to achieve. She only was certain what she didn't want: To be nothing but a wife and mother. She had been brought up to consider those functions to be her biological obligations and she was willing enough to fulfill them. But only if men – still the only slightly disputed masters of the better things in life – would allow her to expand her mind as well. She did not want to be at a man's beck and call – ever. Somewhat like Virginia Woolf before her, she longed for a room of her own where she could remain undisturbed – away from reality and its constant, dire needs. Her fear of being dominated was great. She was in terror of an image, which showed her being pushed toward a stone mound where she was kept against her will until her limbs had almost penetrated the hard surface and where, unable to move, her arms and legs would turn so stiff that they appeared to have become one with the wall. She did not like to be simply the reflection of a male introspective self-consciousness and his ego. She wanted to use her own ingenuity – however inadequate it might be. She knew that there grew many things in her inner worlds of which few men knew they existed. And none she thus far met had been capable of bringing them forth. Not even Christian. She alone could do it. But she needed luck, some outside support and, most of all, lots of hard, lonesome work.

As soon as Nadine mentioned her family name, it put an end to Arnold's guessing game, which he had relished with a boyish joy.

"Why Mt. Ararat?" Nadine asked.

"Well, don't you believe in Noah's ark?" Arnold answered with another question and revealed a row of impeccable white teeth, which showed a large gap in the middle of his upper mandible.

'He will be able to spit like a llama. I better watch myself,' Nadine thought half seriously. Then she said:

"Of course, I do relish fairy tales and myths. I always thought they were good for the soul. Most of our culture grew out of them."

Nadine returned Arnold's smile under which she opposed him in an almost palpable way. But this time he just looked at her again. He apparently liked her reply and even more her exuberance. After their first two dances it became clear that he enjoyed speaking with her also off the dance floor.

Her new admirer walked her home that night.

"I would have driven you, but with the petrol rationing, I couldn't get enough fuel for my car," Arnold explained while they leisurely moved through Harrogate's cold, snow covered, sparsely lighted streets. Some spots, often in the middle of a road, which they needed to cross, were so icy that both of them had to slither across them while they laughed and held on to each other. Neither one of them was afraid to fall and break a bone.

'It's hard to tell if he lies or not,' Nadine reflected under yet another one of her deceptively bright smiles. Lately, everybody to whom she talked, seemed to own a car but could not drive it because there was not enough gas. It was the time of the Suez Canal crisis, which had begun on October 29, 1956 when Israel, whose ships were denied passage through the Canal during the past six years, was invading Egyptian territory. Great Britain and France had quickly sent its troops to retake the Canal. Then fortunately, in early November, a United Nation's emergency force intervened and replaced the British and French soldiers. But the Canal remained closed for another six months. It took that long to repair the damages caused by Israel's army and to raise the ships sunk during the war. In the meantime, Europe had almost no fuel to drive its vehicles.

Talking most of the time, the Harrogate man moved smoothly next to the young girl on the quiet, deserted roads with their rows of large, dark homes surrounded by wide lawns. It was late. Only here and there a light still burned in an upper room. The man was barely taller than the German, but wide-shouldered. His breath was visible in the freezing night and his words, as he exhaled, seemed to turn into faint, white strips of gauze. After a while, as she kept marching at his side she, in spite of the thick, fur-collared winter coat he wore, became aware how strongly his muscles were flexed. He was about the same age as Spencer. This meant that he was in his late thirties and, as before, too old in her eyes. Yet earlier during the evening she had also noticed that there was not a trace of a paunch to be seen anywhere.

"Thank heaven for that!" Nadine almost said aloud, as she recalled Spencer's heavy waistline. But she was not attracted by the Harrogate man's looks. His well-kept figure was not tall enough for her and his shoulders were too broad for his short-legged figure. Yet although she didn't realize it at first, it wasn't just his exterior to which she wasn't drawn. Beneath his sophisticated surface, there was also something odd about his behavior, which culminated in an overly solicitous, almost patriarchal decorum. Under Spencer's tutelage she had grown weary of being patronized and had become determined to fight it or any other sign of gender domination from then on. She was no longer quite as amicable, nor as passive or sweet, as she had been before she met Spencer. She had become more mature and in certain places her skin was hardening; it was turning less vulnerable from the fustigations she had taken.

Since Nadine quickly knew that she didn't care enough for Arnold Illingrose, she had tried several times during the evening to meet other people at the hotel. But Arnold had kept his swift, brown eyes on her. The moment she reappeared at the edge of the dance floor after her prolonged escapes to the ladies room, he had stood next to her making sure that she wouldn't speak to other available men. Some of these had looked at her with appreciation and she was certain that on one or two occasions only their good upbringing had kept them from uttering a wolf's whistle. Vain and insecure, she was soon registering these signs of admiration and at first had been frustrated by Arnold's consistent scrutiny. But after a while she just shrugged her shoulders and let him be. His undivided attention eventually began to amuse her and at the end of the night when she grew tired she was even quite flattered that he wanted to take her home.

Without knowing it at the time, she had already submitted to a will stronger than her own. Her hardened patches of skin would be of little help to her with Arnold. She was drawn toward him by his forceful-ness, which like an iron-tipped arrowhead, was directed straight at her. Against his experience and his primitive desire, her only weapon was withdrawal, by changing herself into a mercury-like substance, able to disintegrate into tiny silver balls and roll away at a touch. And if pursued too strongly, she hoped that her substitution would have a poisonous effect on the hunter. Yet this metamorphosis was hard to accomplish and she was often too lazy or too weary to execute it.

* * *

After breakfast the next day, the children got off their highchairs at the dining room table and started to play for a while in one of the corners of the morning room. James had piled up several logs of wood in the large fireplace where they sizzled and gave off an exquisitely pungent odor. Julie and Melanie Hibson were in a peaceful mood. Both of them wanted to know if Nadine's evening had gone well. Julie, familiar with the young girl's previous escapades, was especially consumed by curiosity. At one point she intensely looked at Nadine, which made her blush and feel uncomfortable. She knew that Julie wished her well and wanted her to meet a nice, young man. But with her mixed feelings about Arnold, Nadine wasn't at all sure if he would qualify in her eyes.

When she mentioned Arnold's name, Julie's mother raised her eyebrows. Nadine watched in amazement as they almost disappeared among the scantily growing blondish curls, which she had pulled far into her forehead. Her thin lips barely parted when she pronounced:

"You couldn't have done much better than that. Like quite a few less successful men and women here, the Illingroses are into steel. Arnold is their only offspring. There is breeding and money in this family."

Nadine's face flushed again when she heard the unexpected praise from this elderly, sophisticated woman. She didn't dare to say that she didn't find Arnold attractive. Nor did she mention that good looks and kindheartedness were more important for her than money or name.

When she left the room to get Lipsey and Peter ready for their walk, Christian came to her mind. She compared Arnold's attributes with those of her German beau and she immediately decided that the Harrogate man couldn't hold a candle to Christian.

"Arnold is just a bore compared to Christian," she angrily whispered. But even while she murmured those words, she knew that there was more to him than she liked to admit. The Yorkshire man possessed great advantages over Christian, such as a thorough formal education, based on a fortune amassed by his wealthy parents, who were also responsible for his utterly polished expressions, none of which had missed their effect on the young girl. There was a purposeful, carefully cultivated elegance about him that was absent in the considerably younger Christian, a graphic design student, who was far from being poor, but was without ambition except for his trumpet and the pursuit of love, if not simply sex.

Later during the day when Peter took his nap, Nadine went into the kitchen and told Beatrice about her conquest. The old cook knew the family well too.

"Better watch out, girl. The mother wants her son to marry money."

Under her thousand wrinkles the obese woman looked at Nadine with compassion. She had rapidly become quite devoted to the young German.

"But I am only here for a few days. Then we will go back to London and I'll never see him again." Nadine, who knew Beatrice liked her and returned her affection, tried to reason.

"I'm not so sure. If he wants you, he'll come and get you. London is not far for him." The cook adjusted her glasses and scrutinized Nadine's face whose cheeks had become a fiery red again. She felt more pain than joy. Knowing that she was overpowered, she used what she considered her most important weapon: beauty. For her the world and everything in it was justified by it. Nothing else was of equal importance.

"I wish he were more beautiful..." Nadine blurted out before she realized what she was trying to say. By now, her face had turned even redder and her whole body felt hot and uncomfortable. She didn't understand why she was so affected by this man whom she hardly knew.

"Handsome! Girl! A man is handsome. A female is beautiful. If you keep confusing the two, you are going to get into trouble. And money will make him handsome enough for you." Beatrice nodded her white-haired head. It was shaking again like a forgotten apple that had been left hanging in a cold wind. The cook had become silent and was drifting off into her own world. Absentmindedly, she continued to peel her potatoes.

Nadine slowly turned and left the kitchen. Going upstairs, to look after Lipsey while her little brother took his afternoon nap, she was disappointed that even Beatrice did not seem to understand her disdain for money. The young girl was at an age when matters of money or a patrician background made little sense. It was beauty and love she was after. She was surprised that her elders, people so much wiser than she, and upon whose good judgment she depended, did not appear to understand this. Why did they think that money – the most boring of all subjects – was so important? Confused, Nadine shook her head as she was bending down to tie Lipsey's shoelaces.

"Well, my life will be different from others," she whispered. Like most young adults she mistook her youthful ignorance for superior intelligence. Experience, incorporated in some of its most brutal forms such as exploding bombs that daily fell from the sky, or machine guns from small, low flying, strafing planes and even in the deceptive, hateful shape of a child molester, had confronted her as a child. But she had survived those threats and now, as a young adult, the world stretched in front of her like an unknown, seemingly peaceful ocean.

"In any case, since Arnold's mother is keen for her son to marry a rich woman, I don't need to worry," she mumbled, attempting to console herself. But when Arnold took her home one evening to meet his mother, Nadine quickly became nervous.

As she sat next to Arnold in his two-seater, she was unusually quiet. He wore short, soft, beige, finely-stitched driving gloves, which left his knuckles bare and had a half-circle shaped hole on the back of his hand that could be widened by leaving a button unclosed. She had never seen anyone wearing such a highly stylized glove before and found it enthralling. Knowing the streets of Harrogate well, he was leaning back on his leather seat as they crossed the town at a high speed. Swiftly, they passed several small gray churches and parks whose trees outlined the sky with their bare branches, which the city displayed in ceaseless abundance. Nadine tried to picture what Mrs. Illingrose would be like. But the images her mind conjured in limited variety, vanished before she could solidify them. She did not move on her deep seat as she looked out of the car's window. Her shoulders were stooped forward and her hands rested in her lap. Rationally, she understood that there was no reason for her uneasiness. But on an emotional level she wanted to make a good impression on this woman for whom, as she saw well, she would at best be just another lady friend of Arnold's. From his boastful hints, she had learned that over the years Isolde Illingrose had seen quite a few of them. Yet apparently, so her admirer claimed, none of the young women had so far met with his mother's approval.

The closer Arnold and Nadine got to his parent's house, the more she became aware that in spite of her efforts every ounce of competitiveness she possessed rushed to the surface. The instant she got hold of Mrs. Illingrose, although, as they were driving onto Arnold's large property it was only her back, which she saw first, she knew that she would need large amounts of an adrenaline-inspired fighting spirit to greet this woman.

It was in the early evening hours. A weak sun was setting and, as if a door had been opened to welcome the dusk, it almost immediately grew colder. Isolde Illingrose was returning from having taken a cross-country ride. It was, as Arnold told Nadine in a drawling voice, a daily exercise in which his mother engaged. In the quickly diminishing blue light, the young girl watched as Isolde unhurriedly walked across the cobble-stoned courtyard and past several parts of the sprawling house. Holding the bridle with her gloved hand, she led her large, steaming, long-maned steed back to the stable. Like the experienced horsewoman she apparently was, she firmly guided the black horse which, chewing on its steel bit and dancing on his hooves, kept its head bent in an utterly graceful posture.

When the woman heard a car approaching, she turned half around. Recognizing her son's vehicle, she lifted her riding crop and tipped it toward his car. But the moment she realized (her eyesight was no longer what it used to be) that Arnold had a woman with him, her smile disappeared from her face and she turned her back again. Walking along in front of her son's car, she seemed to wonder about the stranger who sat next to him.

Isolde had one of those girlish figures, at the moment accentuated by tightly fitting, flattering riding breeches, which seem to stay young forever. Nadine, looking through the car's front window, stared at her round elongated back, which seductively undulated next to the equine's huge black one while woman and animal continued to walk as if they were the only figures on the stage in front of her.

Arnold finally stopped the car and the two of them got out of the vehicle. Slowly, they approached Mrs. Illingrose, who had removed her black riding hat and finally fully turned around to face her son's new friend. With a small nose and large, blue eyes, her face was surrounded by blond hair that was lovely to look at even after a sweaty ride. In dismay, Nadine felt the hair on her lower neck starting to bristle as Arnold and she stood in front of the Yorkshire woman. Her son's average looks had not prepared her for the mother's distinct attractiveness. In Arnold's features she only vaguely recognized his mother's luminous smile and her large eyes.

Isolde Illingrose was the northern European type of beauty. Usually in such heavy-blooded women, a particular coldness of spirit and an aristocratic aloofness that often become emphasized at a certain age, do not allow for any soft edges or dreamy looks. Arnold's mother reminded Nadine of a longhaired mermaid frozen in ice and snow. As the *Seejungfrau*[19] remained immobile, another nude female figure appeared before her eyes. It was one of those unfortunate women the Vikings used to chain alive on the bow of their ships during one of their treacherous night attacks while they were raiding a sleeping, defenseless village. The captured and shackled woman, her mouth torn apart from horrible shrieks, had slowly died while she stared in agony at the white foaming sea below her. As the Vikings' wooden ships were sailing back to their home shores, sleet and a howling wind were lashing without mercy the exposed body of the captive. Sluggishly, the storm had been turning the glacial skin of the woman blue and tough as stone. Under the gloating eyes of the victors, young, female flesh was changing into a lifeless, rock-hard statue.

Seeing the tortured woman in front of her, Nadine was sure that her spirit had roamed the arctic, rough seas for a long time. Having become invisible, she had bewailed her cruel fate until the day when she had descended upon a woman such as Isolde Illingrose.

---

[19] siren

Nadine was kept spellbound at the sight of the Yorkshire woman and couldn't utter a word when Arnold introduced her to his mother. To the young girl's imagination, she seemed the living proof of beauty and cruelty. It would not have taken much for the young girl to make a curtsy in front of the Harrogate woman as one bows to a queen or a powerful witch. Nadine felt extremely ill at ease in Isolde's vicinity and she wanted to be anywhere else except where she was. In her heated fantasy, Arnold's mother suddenly outranked Elizabeth II's lean figure, always dressed in a style far too conservative and matronly for her youth. And the young queen's dark-haired prettiness drastically diminished in front of this older woman's haughty looks.

Arnold Illingrose had finally become aware of the girl's uneasiness. For a moment he felt half-amused, half-sorry for her. Then, mumbling an excuse to his mother, he pulled Nadine away from her mesmerizing sight. As they walked to the house, he pressed her close to him and whispered:

"It's only mother. You don't need to be afraid of her. Her horse bites occasionally. But she doesn't. Although I must admit she has big teeth."

He laughed silently and for a moment Nadine thought him handsome because he sympathized with her anguish. She started to relax a little but still wished she hadn't come. She only breathed normally again when she could no longer see Isolde.

Arnold still lived with his parents. He occupied a smaller wing of the immense Tudor house that had been built in the 16th century. Before he and Nadine went to his quarters of the mansion, he took her through a triple-ceilinged living room where his parents entertained their guests. The room was so large and so dimly illuminated that, standing at the entrance of the room, she could barely make out a bulky billiard table at the other end of it.

"What's the matter with these huge, dark rooms? Is it so hard to put up a few more lights?" Nadine mumbled as she slowly walked behind Arnold through the enormous, closed-in space. Once more, she felt as if she were in church or a country chapel. In her mind, she prepared herself to stumble upon the forgotten relics of a saint and all sorts of lesser spirits that seemed to hover above her along the almost indistinguishable ceiling. As she looked about her, a shadowy outline appeared to be descending into a dark corner of the room. Or was it just the strange flicker of a light that played on the somber walls and furniture?

An orbit of about a dozen lamps each had been inserted into three intricately wrought cast iron wreaths, which were suspended from the ceiling on several long, heavy chains. The huge, ugly, strange contraptions, which looked as if they had come from a forgotten, medieval castle, or right out of one of Poe's fantastic, classic tales, were the room's only source of light. Nadine, whose perceptions were still running away with her, would not have been surprised if one of those black, intricately shaped circles had suddenly been pulled upward on their awkward, clanking links. Lifting her head, she kept looking at a steel wreath that hung ominously above her. And as she did, she thought that the huge, circular iron braid, studded with lights and fixed way above the ground, started to move in circular rotations. Then, in a red flash, she saw human figures set on fire as they were tossing grotesquely from the chandelier. With their limbs helplessly flailing in all directions and seeming to hear their ghastly screams, she became petrified. The horrors of *The Masque of the Red Death* had become real for her. Stifling a howl, she thought that she could smell burning flesh. The terrifying image lasted less than a minute but for that time it left her breathless.

When she returned to normalcy again, she was grateful that Arnold apparently hadn't noticed anything. Then she whispered in her typical illogical way:

"After all, although Poe is a true-blooded American, his education has started in England and Scotland. And who knows, perhaps even in a room like this."

In spite of the complex iron wreathwork, there were no other lights in the room so that its four corners were kept in almost complete darkness. Especially on this bleak evening. Penetrating farther into the room, Nadine noticed just one big window. But it was so forbiddingly curtained that she was not sure what lurked there. She did not care to find out and was afraid that at best she would have met with clouds of dust. To her it looked as if this endless, inhospitable room, stuffed with Chippendale chairs, Victorian desks and Venetian mirrors, would be somber even during a more pleasant day. The longer she remained in the room, the more it seemed nothing but a testimony to a past whose roots probably meant a lot to Arnold's family, yet made little sense to a guest who came for the first time to the house.

Arnold and Nadine continued to slowly cross the room from one end to the other; but until they almost directly stood in front of a piece of furniture, it was too dark for the young girl to see what it was. Walking behind the Harrogate man with her head raised once more toward the ceiling, she almost fell over a Chippendale sofa or love seat of which at least three stood around the room. But although she ran her shin quite painfully against the leg of the sofa, she was grateful that it was only a piece of furniture. It could have been something else, the coffin of a child perhaps. Or the casket in which the heir of the *House of Usher* had mistakenly entombed his living sister. By now, as she continued to be enclosed in semi-darkness, she expected anything out of the ordinary. And Poe was still very much on her mind.

Mostly grouped around chairs, loveseats and low bookcases were a great number of small, sturdy tables. Nadine couldn't identify their styles but they seemed to be made from mahogany. Their surfaces were so highly polished that they could have served as mirrors, if there had been more light. When the couple eventually reached the middle of the room, Nadine located a huge fireplace where a large amount of ashes from half-burned logs covered the floor. Sniffing the air suspiciously, she sighed with relief when she didn't discover a shrieking, squirming female whose feet were roasted on hot cinders.

For quite a while the young girl had not been sure if there were other people at the far end of the room. Arnold's father perhaps or some of his aunts and uncles. Without being able to see anyone, she thought that she felt the presence of others. She slowly followed Arnold's lead. Now, after her painful bungle with the sofa, she kept her eyes mostly on his back. Being in a nervous, highly excitable mood, she expected at any moment for someone to step out of the shadows of the huge, inhospitable room or, like a black-winged angel, to descend from the dark, frightening ceiling.

She knew it was utterly crazy but she could have sworn that she smelled burned bodies. Of course, they were mostly Poe's murdered men and women, but she also imagined to see a great number of recent victims from World War Two, including the most innocent of all sufferers: small children. For some inexplicable reason, a few of them seemed to have left traces of their tortured deaths in this very room and with every hesitating step she took, she felt like an intruder, or an enemy, rather than a guest.

The strong sensation of not being welcome was reinforced by nearly life-sized oil paintings, which were suspended on the wall.

"Those are relatives of mine. They are mostly deceased," Arnold explained off-handedly as they walked in front of them. But Nadine was not convinced. She rather felt that each of the gloomy figures was alive and ready to step out of their luxuriant frames and pounce on her. She was sure that their eyes, especially those of several stern-looking ladies who were laboriously dressed in a fashion of forgotten decades, were following her every step. One woman frightened her particularly because she strongly resembled Isolde Illingrose.

"No wonder English people believe in ghosts," Nadine mumbled.

"What did you say?" Arnold asked her. He had finally stopped in front of the billiard table at the other end of the room.

"You must not be intimidated by all this junk," he said kindly when he saw that Nadine's face had lost most of its color. She suddenly looked white and cold. Her high cheekbones, which Arnold particularly liked, seemed to have lost their translucent glimmer.

'What is wrong with the girl?' He wondered. Then he said in a loud, steady voice:

"If it were up to me, I would throw out most of this stuff, paint the room white and put in lots of lights. But my parents enjoy this semi-darkness in which they sometimes sit and read. They also like to give parties here after the servants have dusted and scrubbed down the place, put up candles and lit a large fire. Many of my parent's friends think that this room is quite romantic."

Arnold smiled at Nadine once more.

"Well, I don't. It's utterly creepy," Nadine replied before she could check herself and she felt ashamed of her old childhood fears. They were getting the better of her.

"That's true," Arnold cried. He had no idea what was going on in her mind. Thinking that she was joking, he tried to hug her closely. But she escaped him with a quick turn of her shoulder and arm.

"Do you know how to play billiards?" Arnold grumpily asked her, not being thrilled by her rejection. Then, with his anger quickly rising, he thought:

"Who does she think she is, the little German tease?"

Earlier in the evening Nadine had annoyed him when, in the midst of his friends, she had blatantly disregarded his verbal approaches claiming her as his own.

"No", Nadine said. "And I am not interested in learning the game either," she quickly added as she anticipated Arnold's next question.

"You should. It is a lot of fun." Arnold could not help lecturing. Then he started to roll one of the balls across the smooth, blatantly green surface of the table that had a large, shaded light above its middle. Nadine could see how much he wanted to play and normally would have tried to please him. But all at once she felt very tired and wanted to leave this room that had such a weird impact on her.

"Another time perhaps. I think I should be going home," she said and stared sullenly at her watch. Arnold looked at her soft profile and her straight nose with its slightly upward turned tip and he wanted again to press her close to him. He felt an urgent need to inhale her odor and nuzzle his head against her ear and clavicle. It was the spot where his horse put her moist, velvet nostrils after he had fed her a carrot.

* * *

Before Nadine and Arnold had come to his home, they had been out to a pub in the countryside, called *The Squinting Cat*, where Nadine had met several of Arnold's male acquaintances. After a couple of drinks, some of the men had started to play a game of darts. As they threw the tiny, multi-colored arrows halfway across the room, they were laughing and shouting. The pink flesh of their faces got quickly rosy and their light eyes sparkled.

'I don't know where the myth of the cold, well-mannered Englishman comes from,' Nadine thought as she watched the rambunctious men. They were showing off like little boys in front of a girl they liked. When one or two of them realized that Nadine seemed to be interested in their romp, they invited her to join them. She had become bored with Arnold's sweetly whispered nonsense as he leaned close to her and, with a quick nod, she slid off her bar stool.

Although her tight dress did not give her enough freedom, it wasn't difficult to pick-up the game in which Arnold chose not to participate. But from his seat at the bar he kept a close watch on her.

At one point, as she raised her right arm too far, the sleeve of her garment split open at the shoulder and revealed her armpit. The ripping noise of the material and the sight of her shaved skin evoked peals of laughter from the men around her in which she joined. After two beers she was rather intoxicated and only saw the funny side of life.

She had a low tolerance for alcohol. But the occasional glass of wine or beer in which she indulged, helped her to unwind and lose some of her inhibitions. Alcohol reinforced her natural inclination toward liking and trusting people. She thought that Arnold's friends, who obviously enjoyed the way she spoke and moved, were rather nice and said so. Each time she threw a dart in the smoke filled, low-ceilinged tavern, where a gentle, flattering light hung over every table, the men's eyes followed the undulations of her hips and bosom. For the moment her world was tinted in a pleasant purple, and contrary to her usual frame of mind, she did not care about the raw sexuality, which seemed to chase her like hounds a fox. Within the room's softly glittering gleam she even enjoyed being the focus of attention. Young and with a newly realized streak of exhibitionism, she started to like being fawned upon by the men's hot glances and felt sorry when Arnold soon walked toward her and taking her by the hand said it was time to leave. For once she had been sure of herself. She had felt graceful and was not intimidated by the wanton looks that followed every move of her waist and firm, round buttocks. Ale, laughter, cigarette smoke and the muted lights that smoothed over most sharp edges in the faces of Nadine's male entourage had instilled a false sense of security within her.

In the car, before they started on their way to his parent's home, Arnold was keenly aware of Nadine's light-hearted mood and although he was annoyed by the desiring glances of his friends, their openly displayed promiscuousness apparently had also excited him. He repeatedly tried to kiss her. But after one or two successful attempts she pushed him away. Pointing to the foggy windows, she giggled:

"Even your car can't take all this passion." Not amused by the young girl's comment and beginning to think that one of his friends had seriously caught her attention, Arnold mumbled a brief, hostile objection. He was pulling his eyebrows together so that a sharp wrinkle appeared between his eyes, which gave him an unexpected, unpleasant if not threatening expression. But this time he kept his temper and reluctantly started the engine.

On the way from the *Squinting Cat* to his house, Nadine continued to be in high spirits. Yet she firmly removed Arnold's hand when it strayed to her knee and tried to climb higher along her thigh. And after he had ventured once more below her waist – a self-imposed borderline she did not want to cross – she used her claws. At least that was what her father called her long, strong fingernails she was in the habit of painstakingly varnishing in silver or pale red. She did not scratch him. Instead, she dug her nails in his flesh, deliberately increasing pressure, until he withdrew his arm. There were four, deep, small red imprints on the back of his hand when he let her go.

"Battle scars," Arnold laughed. But he was angry with her.

'She's a wildcat who needs taming,' he thought as he slowly put both of his hands on the steering wheel. Yet it did not take long before his left arm strayed again. After Arnold's third amorous endeavor, Nadine not only applied her hand but her tongue as well:

"You are driving too fast. You better keep your mind on the road," she told him without looking at his face. Naively, she thought that she could control his sexual arousal by turning a cold profile toward him and by not mentioning any of her anatomical parts. Sitting low and comfortable in Arnold's red Jaguar, she did not want his audacious caresses. Had it been Christian, she most probably would have responded to his carnal attempts. In her current mood, while she still rode on the last waves of the alcohol she had consumed, she would have liked to feel Christian's arms around her. By contrast, the Harrogate man did not have enough sensuous appeal for her. And emotionally she was unable to trust him. He was too fast and forceful and seemed too shallow under his patrician make-up. She was afraid that if they ever were making love, he would consume her completely and leave only a shell of bones and skin. She felt almost certain that her awakening mind, which was still half buried in her, would be devoured by his ego until she had become his mirror image, which breathed and spoke and laughed like him. And when there would be nothing left of her and she was flattened out like a cat a truck had run over, he would discard her. He would throw her on a dung heap to be eaten by flies and worms, and then he would go on to his next conquest as if she had never existed.

Staring out of the car window, she tried to enjoy their drive through the wintry Yorkshire landscape, all new and exciting for her, where the sun was about to set. In a haze, the sun's blood was melting within an uneven, white horizontal line. Then, still looking at the earth-wide circle of sun and horizon, she suddenly felt imprisoned like a hamster running in a rotating cylinder. Her humor had drastically changed. She had become quite depressed as she sat next to the impassioned Yorkshire man who was panting and pouting into her ear.

After she had met Arnold's mother and walked through his parents' dramatically staged living room, Nadine had withdrawn even more into herself. Like a frightened turtle she had hissed and pulled her head and limbs within her shell. She had become sober and silent. And she avoided looking at Arnold as she stared into space.

"Mother sometimes has this effect on people," Arnold, who had enjoyed Nadine's frivolous playfulness, sighed. During the past few years he had dated mostly women his own age, and he had forgotten how inexperienced and difficult young girls could be. But also how irresistible they sometimes were.

'I'll never understand women,' he thought as he gently took hold of Nadine's hand. And he wished he were with Kathy Woodbridge, his girlfriend of half a decade. She not only willingly submitted to his sexual needs, but also had no trouble initiating his lust.

* * *

Night had fully descended. Arnold and Nadine had finally left his parent's living room with its ludicrously exaggerated, sinister air and were heading toward an area of the rambling building, which he occupied by himself. Once more leading the way, he said:

"I know you would rather go home, but first I want you to listen to something. I think you'll like it." He turned and flashed his teeth at her.

"Can't we do this another time? I am getting tired and have to get up early tomorrow morning," Nadine timidly objected.

In front of her rose Lipsey's face with her fine, almost luminescent skin and the two blue veins at her temples that became starkly visible when she got excited. Nadine saw her little, pink mouth and her gray eyes. Large and luminous, they were surrounded by straight black lashes that added unusual depth to them. Like any proud mother, Nadine felt that this child, whom she considered her own, just as much as her small brother, was special. Had Arnold asked her, she would have predicted a bright future for the little girl she loved. As she kept moving at the Harrogate man's side through the old mansion, she would have been far happier to be with Lipsey and Peter than an impetuous lover whom she did not know how to handle.

Arnold was still holding her hand. Together they continued to walk toward the part of the house he claimed as his own. Once inside, here, too, the dimensions of the building were extensive and confusing. They first crossed a wide hall with black, bulky wooden beams along the ceiling and more gold-framed pictures on the walls. But this time Arnold's grim-looking ancestors had been replaced by a row of small German expressionists. Their familiar aspects were a relief for Nadine and she wouldn't have minded lingering for a closer look at the paintings. Yet Arnold, who knew every brushstroke and had told many times the story about each purchase of the exquisite artwork, pulled her along as if she had been a truculent child.

"Not today," he murmured as he went ahead of her and she followed him with her eyes at the back of his head where his hair, which was missing on his forehead, curled in abundance.

They took a narrow corridor that led them first up a few steps and then past several firmly shut doors. The closed doors instantly incited Nadine's curiosity and like one of Bluebeard's wives, she would have loved to discover what was behind them. But again Arnold didn't stop and before long they went down a short, wide-open staircase and came to another small hall that suddenly expanded into a large, door-less sitting room.

Nadine had lost all sense of direction and if Arnold had told her that this vast, bewildering structure had played a part in *The House of Usher*, she would have believed him, although by now she was perfectly aware that things were happening more in her mind than anywhere else.

Both hall and room had dark, ample wooden beams that ran along white ceilings. The oak was blackened from age and the recessed, alabaster height of the place formed a strong contrast to the dry, worm-eaten wood. The stone floors, wherever thick, lovely patterned rugs did not happen to cover them, reverberated from the sound of Nadine's high-heeled shoes. The big, silent house had many secrets and in spite of her fear, the aspect of discovering some of them intrigued Nadine.

Without thinking, Arnold immediately went to the fireplace, which took up part of one wall. He opened the large brass screen and lit a match. Within minutes the carefully piled-up wood started to crackle and exude a pleasant odor. Then large flames began their fiery, silent dance and the room soon lost some of its damp chilliness. Nadine, who was cold to the point of being somewhat shivery, started to relax a little as she stood close to the fire. But then she noticed that the room had no windows. That disturbed her again. For a moment one of her eyes started to twitch and she searched for the mullioned windows, which she had noticed in front of the house as they came up the long driveway that had led them through the middle of a park.

"I wonder if the Illingroses still have to pay taxes on windows, as it had been the case in 18th and 19th century England," she murmured to the fireplace. But instead of asking Arnold, she tried to remember parts of one of Elizabeth Gaskell's fine novels in which taxed windows were a common occurrence. Seeing one or two of the writer's well-drawn characters in front of her, she soon lost interest in finding out if those taxes were still current in present-day England.

Three walls of Arnold's drawing room were covered with books and there was a large, brown leather couch placed in front of the hearth. Here and there several unpretentious, comfortable looking chairs were disbursed. Arnold invited her to sit down on one of them that stood next to a small table with a record player on it. As he carefully put on a large, black, phonographic disk, he said:

"I want you to listen to this with both ears and tell me what it says. The songs are in German." Nadine ignored his slightly condescending tone and became curious. Expectantly, she leaned back in her chair and prepared herself to hear Schubertian and Schumann's melodies.

The moment Arnold had mentioned German songs, she thought of the *Lieder* she had become familiar with while she was still in school. And she saw herself as a half-grown child again when she was taught some of the rudimentary ideas about classical music.

In Mannheim, at the age of eleven, she had started to attend a gymnasium for girls. From the beginning German *Lieder* had been part of the school's weekly curriculum. In a class of about seventeen students, Mr. Heidlauf, their music teacher, had spoken enthusiastically about romantic songs, using classic libretti, with many of them being poems by Goethe, as he accompanied himself at the piano. Peter Heidlauf, a married man with three small children of his own, was a popular instructor. Easy going, he was a short, rotund, middle-aged man with a vigorous voice, which was lively and easily reached clear, high notes. Yet his voice was somewhat reserved, too, and abundantly possessed the voluptuous, velvety modulations of a gifted tenor. The instant he started to sing, his small pupils forgot how absurd he looked with his stocky, fat legs that barely seemed to support his big stomach. Instead, their eyes clung to his mouth and throat from where the loveliest, softest yet powerful sounds poured forth in a steady stream. Now, in the middle of Arnold's unfamiliar room, Nadine saw Peter Heidlauf opening his mouth fully. While his upper lip was raised at a funny angle, he revealed two rows of long, yellow teeth.

"Here comes our little horse again," she had impishly whispered to the girl sitting next to her in the music room. The two classmates broke into a giggle and then quickly put their hands over the mouths. They did not know if Mr. Heidlauf had heard them and didn't want to offend him. As he began to interpret "*Die schöne Müllerin*", Nadine and the rest of the poorly dressed, thin and hungry girls watched spellbound. Yet in spite of their fascination with the new worlds he opened up to them, they couldn't help noticing that often in the middle of a song both sides of his small nose blew out like the velvet nostrils of a horse. The poor man suffered from asthma and easily got out of breath.

When Peter Heidlauf sang, Nadine was able to ignore that her stomach was grumbling from hunger. And during one of his recitals, she forgot that she dreamed almost every night of bread, marmalade, butter and cheese – food her growing body craved but did not get. She was fortunate to be fed a large potato or two, the daily ration her father was in pain to provide for his family. Several of her classmates did not even have that. Their only food was the *Hooverspeise* at school, the hot oatmeal at noon, which a magnanimous American president had provided for starving children in the western part of Germany. Dominated by Berlin, the eastern section of the country, which was nothing but a pile of rubble occupied by the Russians, didn't know such a charitable act. Germans, elderly adults and children alike, daily died from starvation. And hardly anyone cared. On the contrary, all over the world many people thought that starvation and death were a just punishment for the "NAZIS". Yet it wasn't the "NAZIS" who were dying. The actual evildoers, men in high command, and there had been plenty of horrible ones, had either committed suicide, were executed or imprisoned or had, at the last minute, fled the country. As always, it was mostly the children and the old ones who died.

It was a year after World War Two and except for farmers in the remote countryside almost nobody in Germany had anything to eat, or to dress with, or to live in. The few homes left standing after the devastating daily bombings of cities were occupied by American officers and their families who had followed them overseas.

The Tallemanns, too, had been forced out of their apartment. One early morning a young American sergeant in full dress uniform had appeared at the front door of their home and ordered the family to leave within the next two hours. He allowed them to take only their personal stuff, such as clothes and shoes. While they franticly gathered their belongings, Nadine noticed that a neighbor's pretty teenage daughter was chatting with the soldier, trying to distract him from his task. The Tallemanns, realizing what the girl attempted, took advantage of the sergeant's momentary diversion, ran behind the house and threw some bedding into another neighbor's garden. But the American suddenly came around the corner of the building again from where he, as he had followed the blond young girl's inviting smiles, had vanished. When he saw Monika Tallemann standing at the fence of her property, dropping a blanket, he raised his pistol and fired into the air. Monika shrieked and stumbled toward her daughter whom she gathered into her arms. She thought that their last hour had come and despairingly looked at her husband. But fortunately the soldier had only fired a warning shot. After a strong reprimand of which mother and daughter didn't understand a word, but clearly its barked meaning, he let them go.

For a couple of nights, the Tallemanns were able to sleep on the floor at a friend's house across the street until Nadine's parents, trying their utmost, had found a temporary abode. It was a large villa at a different end of town, which they had to share with several families.

* * *

For close to two years after the war, almost every city dweller, no matter where in Germany, was starving. Being constantly hungry, people tried to eat anything from tree bark to insects and from dandelion leaves to snails. During the short summer, entire families marched to the outskirts of town to collect herbs and mushrooms. And on sunny fall days children and women hunted the forests for beechnuts, while some men tried to snare a hare or even a deer. For the Germans history was turned back to well over ten thousand years, long before the invention of agriculture and cattle-breeding, to the millions of years lasting period while the slowly emerging human race barely subsisted as hunters and gatherers.

Since no fat of any kind, nor cream, butter, oil or margarine, were available, Nadine and her family could only boil their potatoes in water. One day, Nadine's mother tried frying their small ration of potatoes in castor oil. She had found a small bottle of it while cleaning out a forgotten medicine cabinet. The castor oil was a noble attempt on Monika's part to feed husband and child. But her brave act had disastrous results. As she fried the potato pancakes, the penetrating smell of the hot oil filled the entire house with a nauseating vapor. Before long, members of the other families living in the villa invaded the kitchen and asked Monika such embarrassing questions as:

"Are you alright? We thought the house was burning down. Do you need any help? What, for heaven's sake, are you cooking?" the other tenants were eager to know as they watched Monika bending red-faced over the stove.

On the day following their odd-tasting meal, first Nadine and then her parents, occupied the bathroom for lengthy periods of time. Unfortunately, in this the large and once beautiful home, which had belonged to a wealthy coffee manufacturer, there were only two lavatories. Like most of the other rooms, its door could not be locked and it had to be shared with the rest of the mansion's inhabitants. While Nadine was occupying the bathroom, she kept staring at the door handle, afraid that someone else with urgent needs would turn it at any moment. Being very embarrassed by the awful smell and sound that issued from her intestines and wanting desperately to be somewhere else, her cramps came and went almost without interruption. Crying and remaining in a hunched-over position for a quarter of an hour at a time, she thought her abdomen would never stop aching, as its contents painfully forced their way from her in a thin, stinking, brown flow. Several times, the moment she left the bathroom, she had to run back for another humiliating and distressing session. Then finally, twenty-four hours later, her colic subsided.

On a normal night, it would take the Tallemanns a long time to fall asleep. Their stomachs were growling and the house they shared with so many people was noisy until late at night. Somewhere close by a baby kept crying or a mother was scolding a cranky child. Before they went to bed, Heinrich Tallemann told his daughter to drink as much water as possible to eliminate some of her hunger pangs. But then she had to get up more than once during the night. And she often barely made it to the bathroom. One time, on her way back to her room and still sleepy, she fell over an open box and hurt her foot. Her subdued scream woke up her mother who called out:

"*Bist du das, Nadine? Was ist los? Warum machst du so viel Krach?*[20]"

Back in bed, softly sobbing, she shivered and as she nursed her aching toes, she tried to ignore her intestines, which did not stop craving food. Sometimes she watched the dawn rising before she was able to fall asleep again. When she got up to get ready for school, she had a headache and was drowsy. In class, her teachers often had to call her twice before she heard them.

At school, noontime was the big event. Shortly after eleven o'clock in the morning, the children, even the older girls on the upper floors, started to smell the porridge that was cooked in the basement. And, as if a gentle breeze had been blowing, the pupils on every floor took deep, audible breaths and began to fidget on their benches. With the scent of food in the air, they no longer were able to concentrate on their lessons. Their stomachs told them in no uncertain terms that soon, together with a thick piece of white bread or even a sweetened bun, the cooked oats would be distributed on the first floor of the school.

White bread was still a novelty for Nadine. She didn't know that it had almost no nutritional value and she loved its softness and taste. During the war, she had only been familiar with brown and black bread, the hard, healthy *Kommisbrot*, with which the German soldiers on the battlefields were provided.

Sitting on the staircase in the hallway together with the other children, she hardly chewed her piece of white bread and would swallow half a slice in one bite. And she was always surprised anew that the soft bread had no odor. While she devoured her hot oats within a couple of minutes, she forgot all table manners. Coming to the end of her meal, she clenched her spoon between her fist and scratched hard and noisily along the bottom of her bowl. Then, when she saw that there were still traces of porridge left at the sides of the deep dish, which even her spoon couldn't catch, she took her index finger to wipe everything clean. Still hungry and wearing a thin mustache of oats on her upper lip, she looked around in the futile hope that one of her classmates

---

[20] Is that you, Nadine? What's the matter? Why are you making so much noise?

didn't want their food. But she was nearly always out of luck. Like starving dogs, the little girls ate as fast as they could, fearful that someone else might snatch up their portion.

Students and teachers alike referred to the school lunch as the *"Hooverspeise"*, paying homage to this American president who had not only preceded Harry S. Truman, the current president of the United States, but also Franklin D. Roosevelt. More than one instructor told Nadine and her classmates that Mr. Hoover had taken pity on thousands of severely undernourished German children. But it was not clear to her what Herbert Hoover, who had been the American president such a long time ago, namely from 1929 to 1933, had to do with alleviating her present plight in 1947. Nor did she understand the implementation of the far-reaching *Marshall Plan*, a European Recovery Program and brainchild of George Catlett Marshal, the US Secretary of State[21], for which he received the well-deserved 1953 Nobel Peace Prize.

Lunch often was the only meal of the day for a great number of German school kids, especially in winter, when they suffered the most. As soon as frost fell on the leaf-covered ground of the woods, Nadine, together with hundreds of other children with whom she had competed for access to mushrooms, berries and nuts severely missed this additional source of food. In the fall, when the weather was still nice, she had felt at ease as she, together with other famished families, was able to stuff her mouth with tiny, sweet, wild strawberries and handfuls of blue, delicious *Heidelbeeren*[22]. She wasn't concerned that she took away the food, which was usually reserved for the wild pigs and the deer that lived among the fir trees and the thick undergrowth. Except for domesticated dogs and cats, she was always too hungry to nourish any feelings of pity toward animals.

Nor, as soon as the cold weather set in, were there any snails to harvest. She never forgot when she had first collected a few dozen of them.

On an afternoon in June her parents took her into the suburbs of Mannheim where the fields of farmers and their orchards started.

---

[21]   1947-1949

[22]   Bilberries

Fortunate owners of gardens and old, well-kept farms were the only citizens who did not crave food twenty-four hours a day.

Along the banks of the Rhine and Neckar lay plot after plot of carefully cultivated land where sturdy, annual corn stood as tall as a man's shoulder. But the big, cylindrical husks, growing in abundance between hard, sharp-edged green leaves and stalks, were hardly the edible ones which are planted for human consumption. This type of maize was only fit to be fed to pigs and chicken. Even for the strongest human teeth and no matter how great the hunger, that type of corn was usually too difficult to chew and didn't taste good. So this Garden of Eden was off limits to emaciated city dwellers and their weakened off-spring. Yet as soon as the colder fall days arrived and the potatoes were ready to be harvested, things changed. To the dismay of many farmers, and however ingeniously they tried to protect their goods, potato fields were regularly raided.

During the first two hours after midnight when thin-faced, bony city people were less at risk of meeting armed peasants and their vora-cious canines, one could spot everywhere their fast moving, dim forms, mere shadows from an underworld. Men and women hovered at the edge of sizeable patches, filled with symmetrical rows of tiny, low shrubs indicating the hidden tubers in the ground. Silently, the starving peo-ple dug into the earth, filling their small bags with the precious plants and left as quickly as they had come. In spite of the late hour and the almost impenetrable darkness, they were still afraid to be caught by a sly, outraged peasant on the hunt. Yet sometimes even under a moonlit sky, the hungry thieves risked a stab from a long knife or a bite from a large hound. Nadine learned early that hunger was a fierce taskmaster, and one that hardly knew any morals.

Coal was stolen too. Each time a freight train, whose open cars were filled with coal, slowly pulled in or out of a *Güterbahnhof*[3], children and adults would risk their lives as they emerged from behind banks where they had hidden, and ran across busy tracks before they climbed aboard the slowly moving, heavy train for a bucket full of warmth and fuel to boil potatoes.

---

[23]   Yard

By the first days of winter the forests had long been depleted of their fallen, dead branches, bare bushes and old trees. It all had been used as firewood. And many a deer died a slow and cruel death in a primitive trap. Hunger and cold made everyone a prowler. People killed for a loaf of bread or a bucket full of coal. Again and again Nadine was taught that most ethical considerations came only after a good dinner. And she saw that ravenous people were not the same as those whose stomachs did not growl.

During that afternoon in early June while the sun's rays were pleasantly warm, the Tallemanns walked wearily and bad-tempered from starvation along large rows of strawberries. The wide, open, carefully cultivated field belonged to a peasant close by. Yet this time the farmer welcomed hungry city dwellers. He knew that they would rid his fields of noxious creatures. And the fruit was still too small, hard and green to be eaten. But among its soft leaves lived many snails. It was these the Tallemann family was after. As soon as the slimy animals were touched, they retracted into their light brown, spirally coiled shells. When the snails were no longer visible, Nadine pretended that she was picking up a tiny, hard apple, which she quickly transferred into a washable, small-mashed shopping net. As long as her fingers did not come in contact with the slithery bodies of the mollusks, she could imagine that they were something else. It was the only way she was able to keep her nausea under control.

The sun was about to set when their nets were nearly full. Slowly, the tired family returned home. Back in their apartment, Monika Tallemann dropped the snails into a large pot and put a heavy lid on it.

"This will do until tomorrow morning when I am going to boil them," she said before she turned away from the stove.

The following day Nadine entered the kitchen first. She often did this in search of a morsel of food to appease her stomach. She hardly had taken a step into the room where the sunlight had started to filter in before she stopped short and at the top of her lungs called for her mother.

"Quick, quick, Mutti, come here and look at this!" As soon as Monika heard her daughter cry out, she stormed into the kitchen with her nightgown billowing behind her. In spite of her eyes still being half-closed from sleep, she had an anxious and questioning look on her face. Then the strange sight arrested her, too. Yet, quickly recovering from her morning fright, she scolded Nadine:

"You don't have to scream like this just because of a few snails."

Nadine glared in disbelief at her mother and then, trembling with disgust, took a few steps backwards.

'But doesn't mother realize how ghastly the kitchen looks', she thought as she peered in horror at several dozen of the sluggishly moving Gastropodia that seemed to be everywhere.

In spite of having put a sturdy cover on the cauldron, the imprisoned snails had managed to shift it to the side and made their escape. They had climbed down the stove, crossed part of the kitchen floor, ascended the table and chairs and most of them had crawled up the walls where they hung in large clusters. Some of the poor prisoners had even managed to get to the ceiling. It took half an hour to collect them again. Nadine felt that it was one of the worst tasks she had ever been ordered to do. Back in the pot, Monika mercilessly poured scalding hot water over the snails. They died the same horrid death as lobsters. Only the mollusks didn't scream.

When the meal was ready, Nadine was encouraged by her parents to try a snail, which they ate with obvious relish. Delicately holding a snail house between their fingers, they attempted to get to its content with a small fork. But Nadine still saw the small creatures crawling up the kitchen wall in search of liberty and strawberries. Staring at her parents, her stomach issued signals of distress and she could not bring herself to taste one of the delicacies.

Only years later, when she visited Hanna in Paris, and the two girls had spent their last penny in a large-windowed restaurant on the upper floor located at the Champs Élysées, did she finally try snails. By then they were disguised under the pretentious sounding name of *escargots*. The tiny fractions of meat she had difficulty digging out of its shell, even with the help of a small silver fork, were heavily drenched in garlic and butter. She would never have believed that each pleasantly tasting morsel was a snail, had she not held on to its carapace with a pair of fragile, tiny tongs.

* * *

From the age of eleven – after passing an entry examination she had first taken at ten and failed – mainly due to having missed school for over two years while she and her mother had been evacuated to small villages – Nadine had attended a German gymnasium strictly for girls in Mannheim. Mannheim, together with Ludwigshafen, her urban twin just across the Rhine, were industrial cities that had been heavily bombed during WWII. Most buildings of both towns were destroyed. They had either completely collapsed looking like huge burial mounds, or the interiors of a home, after having belonged for generations to the same family, had burned out. Only their ghostlike, window-less exterior walls remained. Without eyes, former houses were haunting skeletons where once life had flourished. Life had fled from the suburbs too. Throughout empty streets that suddenly led nowhere, every so often a half destroyed family home emerged from the debris like a rotten tooth in bleeding, foul-smelling gums.

At the gymnasium, classes were conducted in a partly destroyed building her school had to share with another institute of learning. Her own lyceum, the *Liselotteschule*, to which she had been assigned, had been totally erased by bombs. It took many years, various loans from banks, few were willing to lend, and a great deal of effort to rebuild it. Meanwhile, Nadine and several hundred small and big girls went to a different *Realgymnasium*, the *Elisabethschule*, which was located much farther away from their homes.

In the early morning on their way to school, Nadine and her friends took a crowded streetcar, which frequently had to stop to let passengers get off and on. While moving at a moderate speed through the center of the city, the conductor used his bell almost uninterruptedly. Often overworked and weak from hunger, he stepped angrily on the metal buzzer located under his foot. As his old, partly torn leather shoe danced up and down, he would mumble obscenities under his breath.

The conductor of a streetcar was always a man. After the war women were suddenly considered incapable of performing this type of work. While German soldiers had been fighting Hitler's horrible battles and no able-bodied men were allowed to remain private citizens, women had been trained to drive trains, streetcars and buses. Young girls, mothers of two and three children, who had become heads of households, middle-aged spouses, even some grandmothers were sorely needed to work at factory's assembly lines and in various mines. Bright female adults also took over surgeons' work at hospitals and more women began to teach at universities and secured their own law offices. In spite of having to take care of their children and homes, they soon mastered their jobs and performed them well. But at the end of World War Two, the women had to hand over their work to their returning husbands, brothers and fathers. Women, no longer in urgent demand, lost their status as skilled laborers and professionals and became simple housewives and mothers again. It was ironic that Hitler, who had reinforced the three K's of *Küche, Kirche and Kinder*, which confined women to a narrow and often stifling world, had unwittingly given them more freedom than the newly established, post-war democracy under Adenauer.

Awed by the power the conductor displayed, Nadine sometimes squeezed into a tight spot next to him and watched him as he worked behind the heavy engine that was concealed under a wide, painted steel box. Always standing, he would stare straight through the large window of the streetcar as he skillfully maneuvered the large steering handle that controlled the speed of the tram. Watching the traffic in front of him, he held on to a heavy, black handlebar, which he used in abrupt, staccato movements clockwise half around a circle and then back again, increasing or decreasing speed as needed. During rush hour, he would operate the brass bell almost constantly with his foot so that it looked as if he were beating time to a strident melody. Nadine was utterly enticed by his performance.

The streetcar, following its tracks through town, always hugged the middle of the road and several times there was a last minute obstacle the conductor had to warn to get out of his way. It usually was a bicyclist in a hurry, or one of those small, three-wheeled trucks, often for some reason painted in green, that looked like an oversized tricycle with a roof. Like sheep herded by a black and white-coated Border collie, people and vehicles fled in front of the tramway.

Most of the time, Nadine was only able to see half of the secretly admired, middle-aged driver's face. But he never paid the slightest attention to the child standing next to him. This was partly so because he was occupied by observing the road for a constant flow of cars, trucks and American army jeeps and partly because he did not have the slightest interest in schoolgirls. In his eyes Nadine was simply a brat. And he had enough of those at home, enough worry to fill their ever hungry, ever growing stomachs with food so hard to come by.

Inside the tram were the slowly moving, red-eyed laborers who came home from night shifts at an assembly plant, some of which had begun to operate again. And Nadine could always count on tired-looking businessmen, carrying shabby looking leather cases as they rushed to a meeting. Next to them stood housewives with large, empty shopping bags and school children, who never took off their worn, oversized satchels, were squeezed in between.

While the conductor drove, he was not supposed to look at his passengers who stood in thick rows left and right and behind him. Occasionally a man or a woman was pushed into his unprotected back, which most of the time resulted in an outburst of rage on the driver's part. A big sign in the window told passengers that they were not supposed to speak with the conductor, nor he to them, so that he would not be distracted from his nerve racking, but monotonous task. Yet the driver himself often broke the rule of silence. Particularly, when he got excited about someone who decided to make a fast dash to the other side of the street right before the onslaught of his heavy vehicle, he began to scream:

"Did you see that stupid woman? She had to cross the rails just in front of me! Would you believe it? Like a chicken without a head!"

With flashing eyes he would turn half around and look for a sympathetic face among the crowd. But mostly he just met with eyes that were indifferent and absent-minded. The German people he transported in his car had survived Hitler's atrocities and the bombings of the Allies. But there was not a single family that was not haunted by the constant specter of the dead, killed by bombs, machineguns or grenades, or a loved-one who was slowly perishing as a prisoner of war in various countries where the daily death rates were high. Especially the Russian death camps, under Stalin's gruesome rule, put terror into everyone's heart. These fears were greater than the one of being injured or killed in a traffic accident.

Eventually, the driver would calm down, only to erupt again after a short while.

If it was summer, he tried to stick his head out of the window and howl an insult at a reckless walker in front of the streetcar. Guilt ridden, the verbally abused person pretended not to hear him. But if an absent-minded pedestrian had actually not heard the fast approaching tram and was startled out of his thoughts he, too, often became angry and screamed back at the driver, sometimes raising a middle finger as he hustled out of the way. The driver then turned crimson with rage – like a caged animal that attempts to assault an offender by pushing a paw through the bars of his jail. In the winter when windows and doors were shut to keep out rain and snow, the conductor had to be content to use his brakes heavily and suddenly. Yet even then he caused havoc: as the streetcar came to a jerky and unscheduled stop, it invariably jostled several riders against each other.

Those people who were standing up and a moment ago had silently suffered when the reeking breath of strangers was blown into their faces, or an underarm odor became offensive, were now glad there was not enough space to fall. There was always the fear of being trampled upon if one stumbled. Human lives were not held in high esteem. It didn't take much to get killed. And it was certainly less painful to be thrown against someone's shoulder or chest than on the floor.

Nadine, based on her daily observations, was convinced that sadistic instincts surfaced quicker in tram drivers, including her favorite one, than in other citizens. Those men would invariably smile when their passengers cried out in fear or pain. Yet fortunately, a serious streetcar accident was rare. And for the conductor, the screeches and loud protests of passengers who tumbled against each other broke the wearisome sameness of going back and forth on a never changing route. These men worked long, backbreaking hours, didn't have enough to eat and often had to get up before dawn.

For the little girl a conductor had unlimited prestige and supremacy, and she had been taught to adhere to and applaud authority. She had learned early to fear the system in which she had been raised as a small child. But she knew no other.

When Nadine was not occupied approving of the man in charge of a streetcar, she sometimes put her head so close to one of her girlfriends that wisps of her fine hair tickled the girl's cheek. In spite of the little food the children had to eat, they were bursting with energy. Keeping close together with their vilified, brown leather school satchels strapped to their backs and their legs spread apart to support the constant rocking motion of the tram, the ten to fifteen-year-old girls talked non-stop about the school's events, their homework and their teachers. And sotto voce they enjoyed criticizing their immediate surroundings.

"Look, did you notice this lady's purple lipstick?" Nadine sometimes suddenly interrupted one of her friends to whom she stood closest. And she would rudely point to a woman who sat almost at the other end of the car.

She was early interested in make-up. Long before she realized that its main purpose was to attract the opposite sex, she delighted in discovering what various shades of black and red could do to a face. Beauty had great appeal to her, and she never grew tired of admiring its infinite expressions, even if they only appeared in the limited colors of a lipstick or mascara.

She clearly remembered the day when a seventeen-year-old girl at the *Liselotteschule* had first applied orange-colored rouge to her mouth. She had so long and eventually in a loud voice coming straight from her heart, admired the older girl that she, in order to get rid of Nadine, used some of her stridently colored lipstick on her as well.

"Open you mouth," the tall student one day ordered Nadine who stood with a fast beating heart in front of her.

"If you keep your lips pinched together, I cannot work on them," she said and quickly bending over Nadine's face the worshipped pupil began to apply the *batôn de rouge*.

It was a happy and unforgettable moment in the teenager's life. Her vividly orange glowing lips made her feel beautiful and she hated it when she had to remove the shiny, blatant color before she attended her next lesson. For two years, until the make-up artist took her *Abitur* and left the school, Nadine followed her around in undiminished pursuit and admiration and in the hope of another beauty session. But the older girl never weakened again.

Nadine's classroom was located below the one she had just climbed to admire the pretty teenager who was two, possibly three years her senior. Every step she descended, made her feel more miserable because her lips had been returned to their natural state, a state of boredom. But it was beauty she craved. Beauty was the Promised Garden. Ugliness was its sinful intruder. Instinctively, she adhered to the classic Greek ideal. Without knowing what it was, she had apparently lived from early on by its long lasting rules, so opposed to Christian doctrines with its teaching of mercy toward the weak, the old and the ordinary to which she was daily exposed. Yet as young as she was, Nadine felt that beauty was not just the high-spirited, obvious, shallow thing of which Hellenists were often accused.

The teenager never forgot when during a brief visit of Hans, her only male cousin and a medical student at a university in Sweden had quoted one of Cocteau's famous aphorisms for her: "La beauté est née invisible"[24]. Nine years her senior, he had towered over her at the kitchen table in Stuttgart where they remained standing, deeply involved in a rare conversation. Hans was a tall, dark-haired and swift-tongued young man, still steeped in idealism, who loved to show off his eruditeness:

"While we are at the subject, let me also tell you about Baudelaire," he had grinned at her, as his garlic-flavored breath brushed against her cheek: "You'll learn later who he was. But for now I'll just tell you that he is a poet who claimed, and quite successfully so, that he took Parisian dirt and turned it into gold."

"And since I seem to have caught your attention," he again self-importantly smiled at her, basking in her admiration: "Proust, as you'll also discover when you are grown up and have studied French, did the same in his long novel *A la Recherche du Temps perdu.*"

The teenager could not believe her ears and clung to every word that dropped from her cousin's strongly scented mouth. And long after Hans had left again for Malmö, she was delighted to learn on her own that a gifted writer could take an ordinary item, one seen a hundred

---

[24]   Beauty is born invisible.

times, and render it unusual, adding a somber sparkle to it as he looked at it from an unusual angle, suddenly making a new world, raw and beautiful, visible. In due time she discovered, too, that a good artist was able to paint a nobody and all at once he became the most interesting, fascinating person anyone could have ever contemplated. But it also made sense to her that not everybody could see beauty. Some needed a lot of help to do so. She understood that not everyone was able to savor the harmony of a contemporary symphony or an opera. And she wasn't surprised to read that when Bizet's *Carmen* was first performed, spectators were shocked. They had not liked at all the fiery work, which became such a favorite.

* * *

It was right after the war when Nadine first became conscious of her strong penchant toward aesthetics. At that time she and her parents had moved to the outskirts of Mannheim. Their immediate neighbor was a young woman who was renting a shabby apartment on the third floor adjacent to their new home. Nadine had first heard about Adelheid König when a neighbor across the street had said to her mother:

"Of course her hair is clean and shiny. She washes it once a day. Can you imagine that? All that waste of hot water and shampoo! And she is even rinsing the skin of her scalp with chamomile tea. I can't believe this woman! What is she trying to prove?"

The meddlesome neighbor's indignation was somewhat understandable. A daily shower was unheard of in those days when a weekly bath was still difficult to manage for most German families. To scrub oneself thoroughly, from head to toe every Saturday, was considered adequate to get rid of dirt and bodily odor. Anyone who could afford a bath more often quickly became a subject of suspicion.

A *Kriegerwitwe*[25] at twenty-three and childless, the pretty woman, whose married name was König, was shunned by all her neighbors. She was worse off than a prostitute who, at least, has a girlfriend or two with whom she can communicate. But Mrs. König was without any female support. And some of the men, hard-working fathers and

---

[25] War-widow

several husbands still sickly in mind and body from the horrors of war and its aftermath spent as prisoners-of-war, openly called Adelheid a slut. Yet nobody had told Nadine why Mrs. König was treated as a *persona non grata* so she could not understand the social stigma that was attached to the tall, voluptuously curved woman and was puzzled by it. And soon the mystery that surrounded their blond neighbor began to intrigue her more and more.

She started to watch Mrs. König as she went past her parent's house. Her beauty was even more visible on a warm, sunny day when she did not wear a coat and partly revealed her long-legged figure. Apparently enjoying her brisk walk, the widow's hips undulated provocatively in tight fitting and brightly colored clothes. Or sometimes, when she was in a different mood, she would wear a short-sleeved, low cut dress, which showed her arms and full bosom to their greatest advantage. Delicately, she balanced on open-toed high heels and, to Nadine's delight, revealed blood-red toenails. Varnished finger and toenails were physical details to which Nadine was not accustomed. In war-torn Germany cosmetics had quickly become a luxury. Hitler had reinforced the natural look in women and – with much more serious consequences since he didn't have good taste – in the arts as well. Abstract paintings or attempts at surrealism, symbolism and cubism were considered decadent. And if the artist had been a Jew, his work, however valuable and coveted by connoisseurs around the world, would be banned or even destroyed.

Drawn by a cloud of perfume, which surrounded the intriguing Mrs. König like an invisible veil, Nadine's thin neck followed the widow's bewitching shape until she went around a corner. The young woman's face, silver-skinned like the full moon, was always immaculately made-up. Her pouting lips looked luscious in a raspberry red. To render her mouth even more irresistible, she defined its contours in a darker carmine. Nadine, unused to such aesthetic refinements, considered her neighbor more beautiful than any other female she had known so far. She would have loved to talk to her. But her parents, especially her father, didn't allow her to do so:

"You know what this woman does. I want you to stay away from her!" Heinrich Tallemann looked crossly at his half-grown, immature daughter.

Nadine had no idea what the widow was doing that forced her to live like an outcast. Nor did she care to ask her father, who had made it clear that he didn't want to discuss Mrs. König. But, of course, Heinrich's reluctance to speak about their attractive neighbor made her even more irresistible in the teenager's eyes. The more Nadine saw her, the more she was drawn to this lovely, bewildering woman. It was not so much her actual "flesh and bones" that appealed to the schoolgirl, but her role as an embodiment of beauty. For Nadine their neighbor was a vision that could not be touched but only admired and longed for from a distance as a universal concept, an *idée-force*. She didn't realize until much later that she had seen her ideal self in the attractive stranger. If someone had explained to her that it was her own sexual awakening that made Mrs. König so appealing to her, she would have been aghast. As it was, she felt like a lost pup that selects at random a trustworthy, inspiring figure. Without thinking she followed the confusing and sensual shadow that the beautiful woman was casting.

Nadine tried to keep her fascination with the young widow hidden from her father. She knew if it would come to a confrontation between them, he would pitilessly destroy her reveries. He had done so several times in the past. Of course, she realized that he had her best interest at heart when he wanted her to be as objective as possible. As he tore into a thousand shreds the dreams she revealed to him, she understood that her father hoped by performing his destructive act she would be able to see things as they were and not as she wanted them to be. It was also clear to her that his reluctance to let her spin her dreams grew out of fear for her survival in a brutal world. But she still bitterly resented that her father defeated that which she desired the most: those ideas that existed only in amorphous shapes and barely outlined silhouettes within her. His sermons prevented those visions from ripening and taking form. In his paternal eagerness to make her perfect, he cut too deeply. He tore out roots where perhaps he should have just trimmed the plant, and instead of trying to drown it in a constant deluge, it would have been better to water it gently. She did not know what it was that lived in her. But, in spite of being ridiculed when she tried to express her feelings, she slowly came to believe that the multiple, invisible apparitions, which she carried in her head were the best she had to offer to the world around her.

The teenager was gradually becoming aware that even those who were so much older and wiser than she also lived in their own subjective worlds. Almost every adult she met lately seemed to look at others through their own color-driven, idiosyncratic glasses. But parents and teachers would not admit to the dreams they cherished. They were hiding their reveries and wishful thinking under practical advice and preached reality instead.

"What hypocrites grown-ups are," Nadine thought more and more often. And sometimes, in the middle of a sentence, she would walk away from a neighbor or instructor who was still talking to her. Those men and women were offended by her behavior and saw her as a rebel who caused her parents a lot of trouble.

"Such a shame. After all, she's a pretty little thing and bright, too. But self-possessed and obstinate as a mule," were some of the less derogatory remarks she overheard friends of her parents making on her behalf. Yet what hurt her far more than those unfriendly, narrow-minded comments was the mental disposition of Monika and Heinrich. As far as she could see, neither one of them came openly to her defense. For whatever reason, Nadine suspected it was mostly from sheer physical exhaustion caused by hunger, which made everyone listless and highly nervous, that her parents didn't seem to feel the need to protect her from severe criticism. And the teenager, overly sensitive, took Monika and Heinrich's attitude as a sign that they didn't love her.

Her father periodically made hazardous trips on overcrowded trains to small mountain villages. There, he would barter for food their last possessions, such as a set of heavy silver spoons, which Monika had saved from her wedding and while the war lasted had put in a storage place where, she hoped, bombs would not destroy them. During one such prolonged absence of Heinrich, Nadine went through his desk, hunting for adoption papers.

"I cannot possibly be their child," she kept whispering to herself.

"My parents don't care about me. Otherwise they would stand up for me. But it is quite clear that I am not their daughter. That's why I mean so little to them." As she rummaged from drawer to drawer, spreading most of their contents kept in different labeled folders in front of her, her tears were dripping on the invoices, letters, photos, old Christmas cards and bank statements at which she was looking. Then, unable to find any pertinent documents and suddenly afraid that she might be caught, she put the moistened papers away again. Since she was not adopted, she never could discover any proof, in spite of repeated searches. But for a long time she suffered intensely, imagining over awful, lonely hours that the Tallemanns were not her biological parents.

Like everyone else in their neighborhood, Nadine noticed the comings and goings of three American soldiers who frequently visited Mrs. König. Two of them were young and tall. The third was long past his prime, much shorter, stocky and balding. But he had a friendly, good-hearted smile that made him likeable. All three of the unfamiliar and strangely dressed men paid court to the young woman at any time of the day. Those foreign looking admirers of hers, whose shoes were polished to perfection and whose clothes were freshly laundered, scandalized the neighborhood, especially because they came, riding fast, in open jeeps or green American army cars as big as boats. And as if their vehicles had not been offensive enough, the three men had a most annoying habit: Afraid that their cars might be side-swiped, they would park them halfway up on the pavements where they surpassed in their splendor and newness the few small, damaged, old German cars that were meticulously positioned next to the curb. The good burghers of Mannheim had never seen a vehicle stationed halfway on the street and halfway off it, taking away space on the *trottoir* where people felt safe from traffic. The strangers' actions disturbed their German sense of order and evoked a thick-blooded contempt, if not envy.

The three Americans indulged in an even worse habit: Each time they opened their mouths they spoke loudly and in complete disregard of their surroundings, using an uncivilized, ugly tongue. Everybody gossiped about the way those men kept rolling their words in their throats, especially their "r's", as if they were biting into a hot potato. And although the men seemed to attempt to speak the King's English, they obviously were unable to do so. Not even Nadine's professor at the gymnasium, who before the war had studied in Oxford, and later in

Cambridge, was able to make sense of the language the three soldiers spoke.

Nadine's mother, who was used to the elegant sounds of French and Italian, called Mrs. König's three military men disdainfully, *Kaugummisoldaten,*[26] although when they came to visit the pretty woman, they mostly wore civilian clothes.

"Chewing gum makes them look like cows in the field," Monika Tallemann poked fun at them with little respect for their sex. And if occasionally one of the three visitors did wear his army outfit, she would criticize his boots as well because they had rubber soles:

"One cannot even hear these oafs," she once complained, after the tallest and lankiest of Adelheid König's admirers, merely a boy, had silently overtaken her as he had come up behind her on the pavement. With a shriek Monika had jumped into the air and she refused to be pacified even when the young American turned around and smiled at her apologetically, spilling forth a deluge of words she couldn't understand.

"And he was mumbling as if he were trying to swallow a piece of raw meat stuck in his throat," Monika angrily commented, ashamed of her betrayal of fear.

Nadine's parents and the rest of their neighborhood in Feudenheim, one of Mannheim's suburbs, ostracized Adelheid König because her three visitors belonged to the enemy's army. During the first few years after the Second World War, no decent German woman wanted to be seen dead next to an American soldier. Or so Nadine was made to believe by proud, older Germans, who had suffered a great deal from their foes and were not inclined to be amicable toward them. Mothers and fathers who had lost their sons, and jobless widows, mourning their killed husbands, were unwilling to offer a conciliatory hand to their victors. And those young German women who, often driven by hunger and a feminine need to be clean or to wear once again decent clothes, succumbed to the lures of unaccustomed luxuries, which American army men offered them, were instantly cast out.

"They have nothing but straw in their heads, these bitches," was one of the less offensive remark their elders made. And their eyes, as they

---

[26] Chewing gum soldiers

stared after such a scarlet woman, were full of hatred and resentfulness. It would not have taken much for them to vent their rage by thrashing some of the hapless creatures. Often only their fear of retaliation held them back. The American soldiers, whom the German women dated, were usually strong, young and quite obviously not afraid to get into a skirmish.

But to Nadine the enticing widow next door did not look like a harlot nor did Adelheid seem to notice that people whispered behind her back. For the teenager her beauty put the woman above any current and commonly accepted moral concepts. This was partly so because each time she passed Nadine, of whose admiring glances she was well aware, she seemed to sense an ally in her and gracefully nodding her head, she broke into a dazzling smile. And the teenager was flattered that a mature woman wanted to be her friend.

At night – especially during the summer when windows on their first floor apartment were wide open and a stray cat in search of water occasionally squeezed through iron bars, invading their bathtub, where her small, dirty footprints angered Monika – Nadine sometimes heard the widow's soft laughter. Listening to the merrymaking next door, she knew that Adelheid König entertained one or sometimes two of her admirers. And the girl's imagination ran wild trying to figure out what went on.

One day after school, Nadine became aware that she had not seen the widow for several days. She asked her mother what happened and was told that the young woman had become ill.

"Tonight, before your father comes home, I want you to take some potato soup to her," Monika Tallemann said.

Her mother, especially after a fight with her father, often deliberately ignored her husband's higher ethical beliefs or even delighted in breaking them. After years of fierce marital battles Monika's anger, as she challenged her husband, usually was not a conscious one. He had simply become a symbol of male supremacy, which she provoked. Her aggression had become part of the constant and irresistible expression of her need to assert herself. That compulsion was greater than the desire to preserve her marriage. Only her child, grown in her and part of herself for many months, was as important to her as her own goals and desires.

On a cold and sunny day, shortly after the first two years of the war, Monika had been left standing alone in a desolate railway station whose departing train was bound for Russia. After the last car had disappeared from view and she had dried her tears, she had slowly walked back to an empty bed. She was twenty-two years old and knew that from then on she would have to fend for herself and her baby. Reluctantly and with little self-confidence, she had been forced to take on a large amount of responsibility. But to her surprise, together with various liabilities had also come a type of freedom she had never tasted before. In spite of daily bombings and a steadily reduced supply of food, and regardless of having to cope with lack of water and electricity after a night spent in the shelter and with no hope of getting a new pair of shoes for her daughter, she had started to accept and eventually appreciate her latest life as a "*straw widow*", the name given to women whose husbands were absent. Without wanting to, she had become one of millions of young married women whose partners were fighting the war. These women and a few frail old men were supposed to keep life going "*on the home front*", including long hours of factory work and hospital duties, as well as frequently fairly important administrative jobs. And, of course, there were the children to care for.

After the end of the war Heinrich Tallemann had miraculously returned to Germany from Russia. In that huge, war-torn, freezing country he had survived four horrible years of combat and had even managed to make a last minute escape from Russian imprisonment, where he surely would have died. He returned to Stuttgart, thin as a rake, sick with dysentery, and suffering from post-dramatic stress disorder, nobody knew anything about, but alive. And the moment he crossed the threshold of his home, he was ready to become head of his small household again. But his wife was not about to give up her hard-won privileges. She had earned those rights as a woman multitasking inside and outside her home and prepared to defend them with all her might.

Emaciated to the point where her breasts were considerably reduced and one could count the four bones in the middle above her bosom,

Monika was weak from lack of food and her nerves were in shreds. But, if challenged by her haggard looking husband, she gathered her last remnants of strength and fiercely fought him in awful verbal confrontations.

Nadine dreaded those terrible scenes as much as she did the air raids under which she had suffered so relentlessly. The girl was usually caught in the midst of the prolonged quarrels of her parents. Frightened, she watched as their wasted arms, whose skeletal appearance made them seem longer than they were, stabbing the air in vicious attacks. There was no escape for her. The marital battles of her parents were fought just above her head and because she was forced to stand between them, Nadine, too, invariably was abused. Each scream struck her like a blow to the head. In their blind, loud-voiced anger, Monika and Heinrich often forgot that their daughter, although quite tall now, stood next to them.

Innocently, Nadine suffered. She only knew that she was hungry and begged her mother and father for food. But she didn't realize that she was often the cause of their mutual abuse. As if she were kept in a transparent bubble that floated as high as her parents' shoulders, she didn't see how hard it was for them to provide the necessities of life for her and themselves.

Food, clean water, heat in the winter and adequate clothing were almost impossible to get hold of during the postwar years. Nadine didn't realize that her father during his hazardous country trips would rather starve than eat a small part of cheese or a slice of bread over which he had haggled with a greedy farmer before he could share these vital goods with his family.

To get hold of their food, he was forced to go to distant mountain villages south of Mannheim, where he was sometimes able to trade half a pound of butter for a prettily framed *nature morte* or a small, valuable rug. Almost any household item that the family had been able to save from the bombs, Heinrich would take to small, forgotten hamlets. He was skillful in handling some of the most stubborn peasants who did not want money, since it was worthless before the *Währungsreform*[27], but merchandise for the surplus food they stored in

[27]   Currency reform

often abundant quantities. The interior of farmers' homes started to look like overstuffed, small mansions, so filled were they with expensive furnishings. Monika, always quick with her tongue, would say that now even a peasant's _Kuhstall_[28] was lined with oriental rugs.

For transportation around town Heinrich Tallemann had a bicycle. But it wasn't very helpful for the long distances he had to cover on weekends. The German army had long confiscated his car and it would have been almost useless anyway because roads were still so cratered from the bombings that one could hardly use them. Just a few trains had started to operate again. They mostly carried freight, coal and wood, or were so crowded that he had to ride on the rooftop or between the cars. Not only were train trips dangerous, but also they were often checked by German police for people like Heinrich who carried illegal food.

Bartering with farmers meant dealing in the black market. And the government was not kindly disposed toward such action. When German citizens were caught with provisions whose whereabouts they couldn't explain, their hard-won bread, eggs, sausages or meat were claimed. And its owners had to pay a fine. But even with an empty stomach and at the risk of losing his valuable sustenance, Heinrich would not touch the cheese or butter he had traded until he got back home to share his provisions with his wife and child. His will power, determination and his moral convictions were unusually strong.

During the years the war was raging and her father was fighting in Russia, Nadine had been very close to her mother. In Stuttgart night after night, Monika Tallemann had dragged her child from bomb shelter to bomb shelter. It took many days of terror before they finally fled to a small village in southern Germany.

As a small child, Nadine was hardly afraid of her mother whom she knew and loved. Yet it was different with her father who had returned from the war a stranger, a tall, thin, impatient man. Unable to show the deep affection he felt for his offspring, he was ready to punish the child for small misdeeds. She soon learned to fear him. So it was natural for her to take her mother's side when her parents quarreled. But in spite of the strong aversion she harbored toward her father, she soon understood that he often fought more fairly than her mother.

---

[28] Cow stable

"Well, he is far bigger and stronger than I. He can afford to be more magnanimous," Monika angrily blurted out after Nadine had confided her discovery to her. She was stung by her daughter's observation.

"Why don't you run to him and sit on his lap if you like him so much," Monika had nastily added, knowing quite well how afraid her daughter was of her father.

As the years passed, Nadine began fearing Heinrich more and more because she couldn't get close to him and therefore was unable to trust him. She couldn't get used to the sudden bursts of temper to which he was prone at any hour of the day. He was far less able to control his emotions than Monika, who usually managed to remain calm, at least on the surface.

Where Nadine ran with flushed cheeks toward her mother and, pulling at the sleeve of her blouse, eagerly told her about a new friend, she, by contrast, became silent and hung her head when she stood in front of her father. She was uncomfortable and even scared to be near him.

"Look at me when I speak to you," he would sternly say, demanding her full attention. As she unwillingly stared at him, trying not to blink her eyes, which often filled with unwanted tears, she withdrew even more into herself and answered his questions only with an almost inaudible "yes" or "no", and she never volunteered any information.

In the evening, when it was time to go to bed, she did not want to kiss him on his cheek, as he required. Since her father, who was very fond of her, but could not show his love and yet insisted that she kiss him, this normally tender ritual soon became revolting and ugly for her. She began to dread bedtime, too.

The interminable struggle for power between her parents almost daily swept Nadine into a corner, discarded and ignored. Helplessly, she suffered through their bad moods and their unending fights. Sometimes she felt that the war, which had long ended on an exterior level, had been metamorphosed into a personal one that raged between her parents.

There were many nights, outwardly peaceful, when Nadine's sleep was interrupted by a nightmare. Waking up with a scream, it took her a while to realize that her bad dream was not real. Afterwards, as she calmed down, she silently cried into her pillow. She didn't call for her mother who hadn't heard her howl. Sleeping in her husband's bed again, she had gradually become less available to her daughter than she had been during the war when he was in Russia. Having more limited access to Monika, the woman, whom she now had to share with her returned husband, didn't make Nadine like Heinrich any better.

Any escape from home was a relief for the girl. She was only too willing to run next door and pay the pretty widow, who was surrounded by such luscious secrets, a visit.

Slowly walking across the street, she carried the large bowl Monika had filled with thick hot soup. Not to spill her offering, she was forced to move in slow motion. Though wanting to run, she forced herself to climb the three flights of stairs that led to the apartment of Mrs. König with faltering steps. But when Adelheid König opened her door, the teenager almost dropped her food. Facing her stood a sloppily dressed, large-hipped and barefoot woman who seemed to have shrunk to medium height. Her hair was hidden under an ugly, red kerchief and her face was a wall from which its expensive paper had been pulled off. Her lips were thinner and so pale that they almost melted into the rest of her white skin. Her eyes, so large and luminous before, now appeared much smaller, almost pig-like.

"How do you feel, Mrs. König," Nadine stammered, hoping that it would be someone else. But it was she, all right. The girl was only a little relieved when the widow gave her the accustomed smile although even that had lost a lot of its luster. Her friendly remark:

"I am much better, thank you. How nice of you to come and pay me a visit," was hardly heard by Nadine, who still stood, thunderstruck and staring, at the poor young woman. Finally, gathering her wits and removing her eyes from her neighbor's face, Nadine stammered:

"Mother wants you to have this soup." And as her face became red and hot, she added with a stutter:

"I must be going back. I have a lot of homework." Adelheid König did not try to detain Nadine. She had seen the shock on the face of the young teenager. It made her sad and keenly conscious of her sloppy sight. And most of all, in spite of her twenty-three years, she suddenly felt quite old.

When Nadine ran down the stairs again she had just come up, she was crying. In front of her was nothing but Mrs. König's ravaged beauty.

Yet hardly a week later in the early evening she heard once more the young woman's pleasant laughter and when she saw her the next day, she was as lovely as ever.

"You see, the soup helped her," Monika Tallemann said and looked briefly into her daughter's flushed face. Nadine, who was upset that her mother still treated her like a child, remained silent. She knew it was neither food nor kindness, but make-up that had transformed the widow back into her seductive self again.

Nadine never forgot the lesson their captivating neighbor taught her. Morals or any ethical considerations had nothing to do with it. The teenager couldn't care less that for several years after the war, the German population condemned the occupying army as the enemy. She would always remember her kind black soldier whom she had encountered on a cold spring day as a first grader on her way home from school. She then still lived near Stuttgart, in Ludwigsburg, the small, pretty 17th century town, which had solely been created to serve an extensive baroque castle and a big-bodied king. And soon afterwards she experienced more of the pleasant human side of some American officers and their wives. They, too, had been nice to her. One couple in particular had invited her to step across the threshold of its sequestered German home that was now the domicile of this former enemy. Once inside, her hosts had made her feel welcome and even more important: They fed her.

Nadine had become friends with the wife of the childless couple. The petite and fragile American was endowed with the smallest waist Nadine had ever seen in a grown-up. Nor did she have the slightest trace of a stomach. When she sat down, her skirt barely covered her round knees, so that she showed them and a fraction of her slender thighs each time she crossed her legs. With not a single hair on them, they looked nude in their nylon stockings. Those sheers were one of the most craved raiments by German women of all ages who had no access to them. The skin of the young American was light and covered with freckles. One afternoon, as she leafed through a thick, glossy catalogue the likes of which Nadine had never seen, the little girl noticed that she needed glasses. Even those were unusual with their big, polished, purple frames that sat at the tip of her nose and covered almost half of her face. Not as beautiful as Mrs. König, Mrs. Fairbanks, the wife of an older, dark-haired, trim and ambitious looking colonel from Texas, whom Nadine met only once, was more refined.

But perhaps more than anything else what surprised Nadine most about the officer's wife, was her almost immediate offer to address her by her first name:

"Call me Cathy," Mrs. Fairbanks had laughed after the child's second visit. Nadine was flabbergasted. Never in her life had she been allowed to call an adult by her or his first name. Not even her parents or grandparents. Everyone had a title, which a youngster was asked to use. Even a longtime neighbor was always a "Mr." or a "Mrs.", never just a "Hans" or a "Brigitte" for a child or a teenager.

One afternoon the hospitable, brown-haired Texan, who was dressed with unaccustomed elegance, had given Nadine a ride in her car. The large vehicle was sky-blue on the outside and inside it had soft seats that were as white as snow. And the dashboard sparkled with silver, especially the well-functioning radio. Nadine had not been in such a huge, well-upholstered automobile before and as she stretched out her legs, which were still a little too short to reach the floor, she felt like Cinderella being taken to the ball.

Fascinated, she stared at Cathy Fairbanks's medium-heeled, right shoe whose toe lightly leaned on the gas pedal and every so often daintily stepped on the brake, but nothing else. Unlike German cars, this American vehicle didn't have a clutch and the gears shifted automatically. Also, the steering wheel seemed to obey the slightest touch of Cathy's fingers, whose polished nails she wore quite long and pink with a clearly defined moon. Those, too, were utterly enticing in Nadine's eyes.

"Great," the child said, having just picked up the new word and she almost touched the young stranger's hands. Mrs. Fairbanks glanced at her, revealed flawless, white teeth and drove on. Later, on the way home, she had to back the car up. And Nadine, who like a hawk, watched every movement of hers, took note that she didn't need to cling to the steering wheel with all her strength, as drivers of German vehicles were often forced to do. Instead, just a light twist from the woman's frail wrist turned the big automobile easily, soundlessly around.

Everything the young Texan did seemed effortless, as if done by magic. Back at the house, the spellbound child would follow her around like a playful kitten. She was amazed and thrilled with the new, different culture that almost daily unfolded under her eyes.

On another afternoon after she finished her homework, Nadine had once more rung the doorbell and Cathy Fairbanks, walking courteously in front of her, led her to the empty living room. Here she bade her – more with a gesture and a smile than with words – to take a seat. Afterwards, the friendly hostess went into the kitchen and the child heard the sound of a metal spoon being rapidly turned in a glass full of liquid. When Cathy returned, she held a tall glass filled with a thick, red juice and small ice cubes, which she slowly set down in front of Nadine. The small girl politely bowed her head and grinned, revealing a gaping hole where she had lost another front tooth, and took a big sip of the juice. But she quickly put the container back on the low, glass-topped coffee table and made a wry face.

"*Dieses Zeug schmeckt aber komisch,*[29]," she thought and was disappointed that the cold tomato juice was salty instead of sweet – as she had anticipated. Even ten years later when the German *Wirtschaftswunder*[30] was finally able to start offering tomato juice to its citizens, she never took a liking to it. Her first encounter with it had ruined her taste for it.

The pretty Texan was sitting close to an end table of the sofa, not far from Nadine, and spoke into a phone. Without understanding a word, the child watched in fascination as the tip of her red tongue darted in and out between her teeth and lips. Germans did not speak like that and Nadine wasn't sure if she liked the unaccustomed movements of tongue and lips.

"*Mutti glaubt sicher, daß dies eine schreckliche Angewohnheit sei*[31]," she reflected as she kept closely observing Mrs. Fairbanks. Then, when

---

[29]　This stuff tastes weird.

[30]　Economic miracle

[31]　I'm sure mother thinks that this is a terrible habit.

she realized that it was a lengthy conversation between the American and an invisible friend at the other end of the wire she, wanting to please her charming hostess, took another small sip of tomato juice, trying hard not to grimace, got up, curtsied and left. Cathy, still talking into the phone, smiled and, as the ends of her fingers flashed salmon-colored, she waved good-bye before Nadine let herself out of the door.

German ethics were still tinted with barbaric leftovers from Hitler's horrible world. For years Nadine would identify Wagner's music with the one the *Führer* had admired. And she didn't read even the best novellas by Gerhard Hauptmann because the writer had sympathized with certain ideas of the Nazis. Unlike other German artists, scientists and authors such as Emile Nolde, Albert Einstein, Thomas Mann, Hermann Broch and Georg Kaiser, Hauptmann, bowing to the regime, had not been forced into emigration. Like tomato juice, Gerhard Hauptmann, in spite of his considerable talent, did not rank among her favorites.

Trying to escape the German way of life as much as she could, the child passionately embraced the new life that had come across the Atlantic Ocean.

The young Texan woman and the ostracized German widow gave Nadine her first instruction in aesthetics. War-torn Germany had instilled fear, hunger and ugliness in her. Like most other German children, Nadine was starved for light, warmth, a full stomach and refinement. The unaccustomed American culture seemed to fulfill those requirements, at least on a superficial level.

Only as a young adult would she be able to distinguish subtleties and separate "*Kitsch*" from art, and material longings from ideals, things she discovered in the new world. It took many years before she was able to overcome the horrors of the war and appreciate the great German intellectual accomplishments and the unique role, which the country in which she was born had played in the Western world during the past.

During part of her childhood and most of her adolescence she had started to observe the new world, the American one, and the few contacts she had made with it were favorable. Viewed from her limited angle and against the bleakness of Germany, Americans seemed to be friendlier, taller, cleaner and richer than her own people. As she grew older, she continued to reject most of the old world and to accept the new one. Its unabashed adherence to materialism appealed to her, to the child she was. How could she understand its drawbacks?

A few years later in the early afternoons, after school was finally over, Nadine and her classmates, now quite a bit older, often got thoroughly bored on their long ride home as the streetcar went through Mannheim's busy streets and made its way to the suburbs of the city. Jammed against unsuspecting passengers, they tried to vent their frustrations by playing tricks.

One day in March when the sky had lost most of its grayness and the first yellow crocuses could be seen under neglected shrubbery, one of the girls whose father was a pharmacist, got hold of a small amount of sneezing powder. In great secrecy the little box was handed around among the classmates. Being careful, the girls managed to open the lid of the container unseen and to blow most of its content into the air toward adult riders. Its effect was immediate, quite dramatic and funny. The passengers who stood closest to the girls started to sneeze violently, fumbling for a handkerchief. The girls giggled so hard they almost couldn't breathe. They thought the sneezing grown-ups were the most hilarious sight they had ever seen. Men and women alike pressed various colored cloths against their noses. And as tears streamed from their eyes, they tried to suppress the awful trickle in their nostrils. But even while Nadine and her friends were gasping for air, they carefully watched the faces of the adults who surrounded them. As soon as they caught a suspicious look, eying them from above, the kids pretended to be sneezing hard themselves. They were afraid that a tall, angry man might drag one of them by the ear to the exit of the car and dispose of his victim like a sack full of flour as soon as the tram slowed down. Nadine had seen it done to other children who had played their jokes too close to home. On the street, a child could usually outrun an adult after it had indulged in a prank, like ringing a few door bells or climbing in and out of a cellar window left open and, in the worst case, painting graffiti on a white wall. But in a crowded streetcar there was no escape. Yet this additional risk, rather than intimidating most of the restless pupils, increased their idea of fun and adventure.

During the war the kids had learned to look at almost every grown-up as a thoughtless tyrant whose rules they were forced to accept as law although they hardly made sense to them. Rebellion was in their blood and tasted delicious. The redder the noses of the sneezing adults around them got, as the streetcar rattled on, and the more their eyes watered, the happier the mischievous girls were.

Once, as a little girl, Nadine had loved adults, indiscriminately. But then, when she was five years old, a man had abused her. One afternoon, he had forced his thick, meaty and badly tasting tongue into her mouth and throat. Slimy, and smelling of cigarettes, he had rubbed his organ against her milk teeth and filled her orifice with his swollen, malodorous flesh to such an unbearable extent that she started to choke.

Fred Brandt, the molester, lived on the first floor of the same clean, modern, four-story building in which the Tallemanns were renting an apartment on the second floor. When his wife or his three small daughters, with whom Nadine played nearly every day, were not home and he spotted her, he tried to lure her into his living room. Sitting down on the couch or on one of the black leather chairs of the big room, where usually a glass and half an open bottle of wine stood on his desk, he took her on his lap. Whispering, he put his mouth close to her ear and told her what a pretty little thing she was. If she wanted to get off his knees, he held her harder and closer to him. And always after a little while, his big hands touched and squeezed her stomach and thighs. Even if he couldn't get his fingers under her short skirt, which she kept self-consciously pulling down, he soon began a strange rocking motion that lifted her up and down on his legs. Sometimes, she felt as if she were riding a horse. While he moved her, he continued to mumble endearments and tried to kiss her neck, arms and, if he could, her tummy. But now his tender words were mixed with invectives such as "my beautiful clever bitch" that frightened Nadine, and she struggled harder to get away from the excited man. But he wouldn't let her go. As if enticed by his own ugly words, his mouth got dry and he began to heave and breathe hard. In a strange way it seemed as if he were sprinting uphill although he never got off his chair.

The child knew he couldn't run at all, but only limp because he had lost a leg. While sleigh riding as a youngster, he had been badly injured by the engine of an onrushing train. Although he had been able to throw himself between the rails just before the train thundered over him, a hanging wire, or something, had caught his left leg, jerked it onto one gleaming steel rail, where it was cut off by the wheels of the train. His amputated leg, severed mid-thigh, could not be retrieved and he had been fitted with an artificial limb, which he had to strap on each morning when he got up.

"I never felt a thing until every single car had thundered over me," he had told the little girl several times. "And I was lucky someone quickly found me before I bled to death," he sometimes added.

Because of his awful, life-changing accident, Brandt had not been enlisted in the army during the war. Instead, he stayed home and managed his medium-sized shoe factory at the outskirts of Ludwigsburg, near a large garrison. He mostly handled his manufacturing plant with the help of Hitler's slave laborers from the East, the Poles, the Russians, the Yugoslavs, the Czechoslovakians and orthodox Jews, all prisoners who were sent to Germany under the most horrid conditions, taken there by an unending stream of cattle cars. On the train the captives were left without food or water for days on end. Sometimes there were so many men and women, almost all civilians, cramped into one dark space that none of them could sit, much less lie down. They held on to each other when sleep overcame them. The air stank with sweat, urine and feces. And wails of the sick, wounded and dying penetrated the walls. Just the able-bodied and the young survived. But at the end of the war, Brandt, the one-legged monster, had not only outlasted the worst air raids but was quickly becoming a wealthy man.

The pedophile who mistreated her was her father's best friend and her most bitter enemy.

The small child never spoke to her father about Brandt. He was a shrewd man who had told her that his holding her was their secret, a secret, which she must never divulge to anyone, least of all to her parents.

"In any event," he smiled nastily, "if you tell them, they won't believe you. They know you make up stories all the time. Do you think that they would have faith in you rather than me, your father's loyal friend? They know you are a compulsive little liar and they would give you a good spanking."

The pedophile looked at her with his dark-bluish eyes that seemed on fire under their coppery eyebrows. His hair was crinkly, with a reddish tint and there was a lot of it. He was vain about his coif, which a barber kept in shape, and several times a day he would comb it with his fingers. Nadine thought that he was the most repulsive man she had ever known, so she was surprised when one day a woman who lived on their street, called him handsome.

"In spite of his limp and artificial leg, I find Fred Brandt quite attractive," the neighbor had shamefacedly laughed. Speaking to a friend of hers, she was trying to giggle like the young girl she no longer was. But instead of laughter, she emitted a row of yelps, which sounded more doglike than coming from a human being. Both women were standing in a long line in front of a bakery where, not far behind them, the little girl was waiting too. Worn down by the daily tedium of limited food supply, the two gossipy females confided in each other. Later Nadine discovered that her overpowering adversary was also popular among the waitresses of a small restaurant he frequented not far from his factory. He was a womanizer and his wife, a simple soul and a former salesgirl, who had turned into a good housekeeper and solicitous mother, had reason to be jealous.

Nadine was afraid of Brandt and did what he wanted. She had once come upon him when he had taken a switch to his eldest daughter's bare bottom, and she knew that he could, without fear of reprimand, do the same to her.

She kept her awful secret. She did not then know her encounter with Brandt had ended the possibility of any pleasure she might later, as an adult, have in intercourse. Her father had often called her a fabulist whom no one could rely on. She was sure that Heinrich would rather believe his friend, with whom he played skat[32] once a week, than his tale-telling daughter.

---

[32]   A three-hand card game popular in Germany.

After she grew up and the time had come to make love, she couldn't enjoy it. The sexual act was dirty. It smelled of cigarette butts, ashtrays and sour wine. The first time she submitted to it was out of sheer curiosity and afterwards, when she saw that the boy, Jean Kaiser, was in love with her, she tried to please him. But sex even with him, whose gentle, unselfish understanding she gratefully acknowledged, was something to be gotten over with as quickly as possible. The only relief came through awkward, agitated, vehement dreams where rage and pain were strangely mixed with orgasm.

"I was born to be a nun," Nadine tried to reason with herself, although after World War Two religion, in spite of her two pious grandmothers, had completely lost its meaning for her. If someone had asked her, but no one did, she would have said that she was a firm, but non-militant atheist. An almighty father figure as a god, as a benign superhuman being, was not for her. She had never found any evidence that such a magical creation was able to live up to reality. She was sure, a conviction daily reinforced by the horrors of war surrounding her that an all-powerful god would never have agreed to the murder of children, young boys, mothers in their prime and starving, toothless old men. There simply was no god. At best he was a human invention, created out of necessity.

As a little girl, before she had become the blemished plaything of a child molester, Nadine had eagerly run into the outstretched arms of an adult male relative to greet him. Now she slowly walked toward the same man and hesitatingly, as she scrutinized him, shook his hand. And she would only fleetingly kiss an aunt or a niece on the cheek, never an uncle or a male cousin. If she was held closely, she struggled and started to scream. Monika Tallemann, upset about the odd, changed behavior of her daughter, wanted to know what had happened. But Nadine, still under the spell of the ominous factory owner, was convinced that her mother would not believe her either if she were to tell her about the pedophile.

* * *

The building of Nadine's school in Mannheim contained six floors. But for years she and her classmates couldn't use all of them. The girls, big and small, could only walk in certain hallways because some corridors had been blown away by bombs and, for a long time, were blocked off. Also, more than half of the gymnasium's broken windows had been permanently nailed shut with thin, ugly, light-depriving wooden boards. As a result, even on a sunny day the old edifice with its large sculpture-adorned portal was immersed in semidarkness. In the winter, the lack of light caused serious psychological problems to students and teachers alike. Most of them felt that they still lived in a bomb shelter. And from November till the first days of April the cold weather didn't help the depression and hunger, which were the constant phenomena in almost every household.

At different sections of the large, venerable school were three stone staircases with low, wide steps gathered by black iron wrought railings that led in graceful sweeps from floor to floor. But only one was useable. The other two flights of stairs ended abruptly in the air and left a deep, charcoal, dangerous hole just below the last, half demolished step. Long, thin, twisted bands of steel dangled like petrified intestines above an abyss. At the end of every class, with the roaring onslaught of many girls rushing up and down, the steps of the only *escalier* left undamaged visibly shook and trembled. Nadine was sure that even the useable staircase was perilous and, unless fortified, would collapse one day in an avalanche of dust, debris, terrified screams with indistinguishable limbs and bodies flying through the air. There were no safety regulations. And even if there had been certain rules, which the city of Mannheim was trying to impose again, there was hardly anyone to enforce them. Everywhere the German government, a mortally wounded centipede, still lay in shambles.

The *Elisabeth* School had almost no heat in the winter. Everybody wore gloves in the classrooms and the long underwear and bloomers of teachers, whose desks stood on a platform, were often visible when they sat down or got up. It was a sight Nadine and her friends daily watched for. Their repressed giggles at the appearance of a teacher's clean but badly worn undergarments, whose torn parts had been carefully mended, provided much needed comic relief from a tedious lesson.

Being able to poke fun at an instructor was a diversion from their fears of being called upon when they were sloppily prepared for class.

All year round the students, hungry, tired, cold in the winter and always badly dressed, did at best just half of their homework. Pulling the leg of a superior, who had unlimited authority over the better part of their pupil's day, filled the children with a lush, though short-lived, sense of power. Although the students could express their temporary dominance only in a subversive form, the teachers – the hostile tribe that lived on the other side of a rock-clustered hill – immediately felt the kids' control. Nearly none of Nadine's instructors liked to see a smile on the faces of their students that was not evoked by one of them. The professors, keenly lacking a sense of humor, instinctively mistrusted impulsive smiles. They knew only too well that the children's *schaden-frohe*[33] smirks were mostly bought at their expense.

The students, girls from the age of ten through eighteen, were forbidden to giggle or laugh while sitting in overcrowded classrooms. Screams and other expressions of joy and irrepressible energy during recess were not allowed either. Whenever there had been too much noise in the courtyard during the *große Pause*[34]* at eleven o'clock, each class, after they had returned to their rooms, was reprimanded separately. After a high-pitched, impatient lecture by a frustrated teacher, the label "geese", for the bird with the supposedly smallest brain in the animal kingdom, was applied to the pupils several times during the rest of the day to make it stick. Some of the smaller girls broke into tears upon hearing this insult over and over again, although eventually its very repetitiveness decreased the intended, mental pain. Nadine, who knew better, smiled inwardly. She did not feel insulted when she was compared to a goose. For her the white-feathered, handsome bird was a magnificent creature.

* * *

While she and her mother had been evacuated to a tiny mountain village during the war, Nadine had gotten to know and like geese and thought them to be enticing animals, demanding her respect. Ganders in particular were something to be reckoned with, as she had discovered

---

[33] gloating
[34] *Big break

on a still cool spring morning after she was, for no apparent reason, confronted by one of them. It was shortly after her arrival in Treffelshausen when a loudly screeching gander had come running toward her on a narrow dirt path, which was surrounded by high hedges that afforded no escape. The big bird was thrusting his head and neck forward and hissed like a snake. While his wide, blatantly white wings beat the air furiously, whirling up large clouds of dust from the dry ground, he seemed twice as large and thoroughly frightened her. The gander, storming toward the little girl, looked almost as tall as she did. She did not wait to find out what it was he had on his supposedly limited mind. Turning around, pinkish-brown cotton skirt flipping high, a red flag signaling distress, she ran away as fast as her still short legs would permit. Madly squawking, the furious bird wouldn't give up that easily, but continued to pursue her for a few yards. Yet finally he called it quits. When she risked a peek behind her, she saw him slowly fold his wings one after the other. Then, his small head now proudly raised up, he shuffled back to his waiting flock. Behind him, uninterruptedly squeaking, the rest of the geese had waddled about in a semicircle on their flat, webbed feet, watching the gander. It looked as if the flock had cheered him on in the pursuit of his foe. Nadine quickly developed a sense of almost awe for the huge, lovely birds. None of her teachers' scolding could take that experience away from her. In her memory, her *recapitulation of consciousness*, the gander continued to exist as an aristocrat, angry and aggressive and stunningly beautiful.

* * *

For quite a while after the war there had been a great lack of pedagogues all over Germany. The best of them had been killed or, being utterly abandoned, had starved to death as prisoners of war in one of the dreadful Russian camps. Those instructors who were available were often past retirement age or had severe health problems.

Nadine remembered well, a certain Christel Stein, a math teacher of hers. The woman was still fairly young and rather attractive with her shoulder-length, straight, blond-grayish hair, which she wore nearly every day in a different style. Dr. Stein had a lovely whitish skin. But her most notable feature was her lips, too full and thick to remain within the strict confines of classical beauty, yet quite sensual. Whenever she was not writing on the blackboard or pointing a bony finger at a child, she would put both hands around her cheeks, absentmindedly holding them there as if her face had been a fragile, transparent, handle-less porcelain cup. Then, still subconsciously, she started to stroke her pale, sunken zygomatic bones with the tips of her fingers. She bit down her nails as far as she could, almost cutting into the flesh, and rendering her hands with their stunted, naked, reddish fingertips close to being no longer, or not yet, human.

"Look, Stein is straightening out her tablecloth again," Nadine's seatmate whispered. And as soon as the preceptor's back was turned, the girl imitated in a nasty, exaggerated way the teacher's lethargic gestures. But the worst were Mrs. Stein's eyes. Their color was hidden within an ambiguous, indefinable opacity. One of Nadine's classmates, who could not stand her, said they were red like the devil's. Dr. Stein suffered from a nervous disease, which forced her to blink without interruption and for that reason most students hated to be called upon by her. Hearing their names, they had to stand up and face the instructor while answering her question. Nadine called it *looking at the head of Medusa* because invariably after a prolonged stare at the unfortunate teacher's incessantly opening and closing eyes, the students started to blink as well. At the end of one of Dr. Stein's classes, Nadine was usually so irritated that she did not want to talk with anyone, not even with a close friend. She couldn't make up her mind if she detested or pitied this afflicted pedagogue, who had never been unkind to her. Not knowing what to do, she vacillated between admiration and contempt within short intervals. But the effort to understand the young woman's ailment drained her emotionally.

And then there was Ms. Löwenhaupt, their Latin teacher. She had never been married, was ancient and fat and had a plain, rather stern face in which her serious eyes almost disappeared under gray, bushy eyebrows. Her white hair was pulled back from her high, balding forehead and twisted into a sparse bun at the nape of her neck. She was overweight, except for her neck which was scrawny and quite long, as though she were a hungry ostrich tripling back and forth on her enormous feet, searching the grass-covered ground for food. Anybody could tell that, even in her youth, the lusterless Ms. Löwenhaupt had not been pleasant to look at. Now in her old age, she was downright unsightly. Plagued by rheumatism and diabetes, she should have long been retired and resting at home. But since almost none of the younger teachers had returned from the war, Ms. Löwenhaupt went on teaching.

Sometimes Latin was scheduled to be the first lesson of the day and most students hated to see Ms. Löwenhaupt so early in the morning. They tried not to look at her but kept their heads bent over their books. Yet as soon as they lifted their eyes, they saw her face, where large patches of skin had turned an almost blackish-brown and was as scarred with wrinkles as if someone had crumbled a newspaper into a ball so it was no longer readable. Awful, old-fashioned clothes from which an indeterminate, unhealthy odor exuded, underlined her grotesque appearance. Nadine avoided at all cost getting too close to her. The smell of her terrible skin, which died faster than it was able to renew itself, nauseated her. Tiny particles of the old woman's membrane were retained in the folds of clothes and her unmentionables where they mingled with perspiration and dirt from infrequent baths. Deodorants did not exist. And Ms. Löwenhaupt was not the type to use perfume.

Until the day this teacher spoke to Nadine after class she thought – with the cruelty of which a child is quite capable – that she was unbearably disgusting.

"Here comes the ape," Nadine hissed when her ailing instructor slowly entered their classroom, heavily leaning on a cane. She dragged her feet along the floor, unable to lift them without causing considerable pain to her ankles and knees.

Unhappy with Nadine's performance, Ms. Löwenhaupt had asked her in a strained, dull voice to come and see her after school. Nadine dreaded the interview. Half angry, half intimidated, she braced herself for the expected dressing-down to which she had closed both ears long before she confronted the awkward teacher.

After Nadine had knocked and entered Ms. Löwenhaupt's tiny, overcrowded office, she remained as close as possible to the door from where she faced her instructor. Sitting at her desk, Ms. Löwenhaupt's eyes shifted from Nadine's figure past her to the wall and then back again to her table where she kept glancing at a stack of tests, which she was grading. The beginning of her lecture was, as Nadine had anticipated, a reprimand. At a safe distance from her teacher and appreciating that Ms. Löwenhaupt didn't force her to come closer, Nadine had taken a deep breath. Afterwards she just stood there with her arms listlessly dangling at her side. But she tried to look as much as possible into Ms. Löwenhaupt's eyes. Nadine's father always insisted upon eye contact:

"It is impolite not to pay attention to your superiors. You do that simply by looking straight into their faces," Heinrich Tallemann had lectured her. Nadine hated the direct eye approach. Not focusing on the facial features of an adult permitted her to escape into her own world where she felt far more at ease and safer.

Unable to move, Nadine watched the teacher's thin, wasted lips from where words, with little meaning and occasionally mixed with spittle, rolled forth like small stones.

"She's simply abominable! What a stupid, beastly woman," Nadine kept thinking.

But then something happened and the slimy pebbles escaping from the spinster's uncouth mouth turned into scintillating, weightless bubbles that floated upward under Nadine's astonished eyes. She was no longer conscious of Ms. Löwenhaupt's bad body odor or her offending ugliness. It must have happened the moment after her instructor had finished speaking what her conscience had dictated and then asked Nadine a few quick questions about herself, her family and her home.

"Tell me where do you and your parents live? What does your father do? Do you have brothers or sisters?" She had wanted to know as she indulgently and somewhat timidly smiled at her.

Within minutes Ms. Löwenhaupt had changed from a fearful figure of authority to a friendly person who seemed to like Nadine and who, so the girl sensed, needed more help that she herself did. That was a revelation – if not an illumination! For the first time in her young life Nadine had gotten a glimpse of the human being who existed under a teacher's mask.

She never forgot it and from that day on Latin was no longer the big nuisance it had been for the past two years. When her classmates noticed Nadine's changed behavior toward their elderly, utterly homely instructor and teased her about it, she snapped at them:

"Leave her alone! She isn't such a bad sport after all."

* * *

Carefully and slowly, as if he were performing a ritual, Arnold Illingrose put a disk on his record player. He was standing in a corner of his wide, windowless living room and wordlessly watched the needle descend on the big, flat, rippled platter. The music that started to pour forth belonged neither to the romantic nor the classical period, although as Arnold and Nadine began to listen, there appeared to be some traces of romanticism hidden among the stridently streamlined notes. Or rather there was a suffused longing for it. The modern melodies that began to fill the room sometimes with unbearable anguish and sometimes softer than silk were completely unfamiliar to her. At first, not having ever heard anything like it, she thought the harsh, discordant notes were distasteful. And for a few minutes, as she listened to the text of the song, the appalling sounds seemed to increase in ever more unbearable, unending crescendos.

The first *Lied* began with a high-pitched voice, which apparently came from a lofty wall or a tower because it commanded the listener to look down – somewhere below:

"Seht dort hinab!"...Someone demanded. Then the voice explained that there was moonlight on top of tombs:

"Im Mondschein auf den Gräbern..." And the invisible singer added that a savage, ghost-like figure – "hockt eine wild-gespentische Gestalt..." – crouched on one of the graves.

"It is an ape", the song continued, reinforcing the shock the listener had already received, and was still suffering from:

"Ein Aff' ist's..." Immediately afterwards Arnold and Nadine were confronted with a frightening question:

"Are you able to hear its howling?" "Hört ihr, wie sein Heulen...?"

To heighten the dramatic effect, the text continued in the present tense and the couple was told that the ape screams into the sweet scent of life:

"Hinausgellt in den süßen Duft des Lebens..."

By this time Nadine no longer leaned back on her chair but sat curled up in a fetal position. She kept her head as close as possible to the record player. She had forgotten where she was or how she had come into this room, which enclosed her like a dream – or rather like a terrifying, yet strangely compelling nightmare. Each time Arnold tried to interrupt her intense concentration and asked her for a quick translation, she waved her hand in annoyance and told him:

"Later, later...", afraid to miss a word.

"This is as good as any Poe," Nadine whispered as she absorbed the great, forceful beauty of the chant that unfolded in front of her.

"Or better, perhaps, as if one were able to compare Poe with Gustav Mahler", she thought. It was *Das Lied von der Erde*[35], a Chinese poem for which, in 1908, Mahler had composed the music that now held, as Arnold knew it would, the young girl imprisoned in her seat, with her senses blurred, yet in acute attention, spinning uncontrollably in all directions. Nadine did not pay any attention to the Yorkshire man. Instead, as he watched her with an ironic, if not sarcastic smile, she closed her eyes and greedily swallowed every word and note. She might not have possessed the best ear for music, her mother who did, had called her more than once tone-deaf, but her *Sprachgefühl* was highly sensitized and never led her wrong.

The young girl did not see her admirer's impertinently curved lips. He no longer existed for her. She was transfixed by the performance, the well pronounced German text and odd, enticing sounds and kept closing and opening her eyes in disbelief. Remaining motionless in her chair, she completely forgot that she was supposed to translate the text for her host. When the long cycle of six songs had come to the end, Nadine wanted to hear them again.

---

[35] Song of the Earth

"I thought you wanted to go home," Arnold teased her and lightly, patronizingly patted her on the shoulder.

"I know, I know. It's most probably getting late and I mustn't keep you. But just once more," Nadine, blind to Arnold, the room they were in, or the seat that held her, begged, her voice as small as a child's. Then, as she again listened intently, she almost unconsciously began to translate the German text into English as well as she could. But before they were half way through the songs for the second time, she suddenly got up and said:

"That's enough. I can't bear it any longer. This is pure madness yet unbelievably beautiful. Please take me home."

The frightening feeling of not getting enough air, which Nadine had experienced when she had first entered the room, had come back to her. She thought that she would choke if she would stay a moment longer. Arnold looked at her face where her protruding cheekbones had turned from a fiery pink into a sickly white. And he also saw that her eyes were glazed over with a feverish glint. Emphasized by dark lashes, her irises looked huge in the semi dark room.

"The little wretch is drunk with Mahler," Arnold thought and was annoyed. He couldn't bear that the young German preferred anyone to him. "Even if it is Mahler," he snickered sotto voce.

As Nadine stared at him, he knew that she didn't see him but looked right through him into a landscape with which he was unfamiliar and was not sure if he wanted to get to know.

"Well, if you like Mahler this much, we have to listen to *Salomé* by Strauß, not Johann but Richard, tomorrow. And you won't need to translate. Are you familiar with Oscar Wilde's plays?" The Harrogate man made an effort to sound civil.

When Nadine shook her head in denial, he went to an adjoining room where most of his bookshelves were located and soon returned with a slim volume.

"Read it. You'll enjoy him, I think. Strauß took his *Salomé* straight from Wilde. A German liking an Englishman! Now that's something, you'll not find every day," Arnold announced before he got her thick, blue winter coat. But Nadine did not hear him.

As they walked back through the house, it was as quiet as a church-yard. And the young girl would not have been surprised if a hairy foot or hand of Mahler's Chinese ape had suddenly appeared as they turned a corner.

VI

The Montcalm Hotel

Nadine, not yet twenty years old, was killed on a cool, foggy spring night while crossing London in her bare feet. Carrying a pair of red, open-toed shoes whose heels were so high that they soon became uncomfortable during her long, late walk, she was run over by a taxi as she stepped off the pavement without looking. The bearded, swarthy-skinned, young driver, an illegal immigrant from Pakistan, was sobbing loudly when the police questioned him:

"I couldn't see girl. Look at her darkish coat! You are not able to see nothing in black night. What was her doing? No shoes! She walk onto my road with eyes closed."

Nadine had been struck from the side.

"At most" said the paramedics, whose ambulance had arrived fairly quickly on the scene, "she would have seen a flashing light seconds before the fatal impact."

It was 3:00 o'clock in the morning and the driver, after a night's work, had wanted to go home to his wife and small child. Later, when the police, the London Bobbies whom Nadine had liked, pushed the cabdriver hard, he admitted that he had been going too fast. And the young girl had been too tired and emotionally upset to notice him coming.

* * *

She had spent the evening with Arnold Illingrose who had come down to London from Harrogate to take her out to dinner. Afterwards they went to *Annabel's*, a trendy nightclub to which he and his parents, as he had quickly, vainly assured her, belonged. Beatrice, Melanie Hibson's old cook, had been right. When Arnold didn't prefer fox hunting or taking one of his hawks out on horseback to exercise the raptor on a hilly, almost treeless, lonely stretch of the Yorkshire landscape, where a huge field was often semi encircled by loosely-piled stone hedges, he didn't think it was a big deal to jump on a Pullman train and travel the six hours it took to get from Harrogate to London. Once in the city, he stayed with friends of his or his parents, bought clothes and went to a show or a club.

The Yorkshire man only shopped in London, "because it is the best place for a man to do so; women might go to Paris, but men stay right here", he had laughed when Nadine asked him why he did.

"My shoes are by Lobb and I buy most of my suits from Savile Row, whereas my shirts come from Turnbull and Asser. But I also like to shop around Mayfair. And, of course, Harrod's, which even the Queen frequents, is one of my favorites. I leave Selfridges to the common man," he had boasted in his dark, rather pleasant but occasionally, for Nadine's taste, too loud a voice. Yet his hard-to-bear sense of superiority was lost on her. Except for Harrod's, whose palatial emporium covered an entire Knightsbridge block and the less impressive Selfridges on Oxford Street, she didn't know what Arnold was talking about when he mentioned the shoe, suit and shirt establishments. She had never heard of these shops before. Certainly not from James Johnson. As an employee of the Foreign Office, where prestige took preference over monetary matters, the hardworking man couldn't afford such expensive items. When she was unable to admire the Yorkshire man's expensive habits, with which most English women of his class would have been as little impressed as Nadine was, he was quick to show his disappointment in the young German girl:

"Don't you know anything?" He chided her as she tried to gracefully glide onto the uncomfortable backseat of a London cab. Seeing that he was quite serious, she forced a giggle from her dry throat:

"No, I don't."

They silently rode to Café Royal. Arnold wanted to watch the young girl's eyes as they reflected this dining facility with its gilded mirrors, red velvet curtains and elaborate decoration that recalled the turn of the century when the better restaurants tried to furbish their interior in an ultra baroque style.

Not having seen Nadine for a while he was enthralled anew by her luminous skin, and the way her upper lip curved and slightly protruded over her lower one that was perhaps not quite big enough, but full and soft, and as he fondly recalled, slightly tasting of raspberry, his favorite fruit.

"But it might be just her lipstick. Women use so many tricks. I don't need to get too excited. There is plenty of time for that later tonight," he admonished himself as he glanced again and again at the young girl sitting next to him.

Nadine did not utter a word. Nor did she look at him. The longer the ride took, the less comfortable she felt in the car's dark interior with Arnold sitting too close, afraid of his touch. Not for a moment could she escape the scent of his skin and the eau de cologne he had lavishly splashed on his face.

"*Ich kann ihn wirklich nicht riechen*," she thought unhappily and recalled the old German saying that not liking the scent of a human being meant that one did not want to have anything to do with him or her. "Odor", her father had once told her, "is our most primitive sense and because of that it probably connects us the closest to our animal instincts. We should trust it," he had smiled at her when he saw her surprised expression.

Arnold and his date finally arrived in front of the Café Royal.

"I hope you'll appreciate that such literary gourmets as Oscar Wilde and George Bernhard Shaw have dined here", Arnold now teased Nadine, winking at her. But she still didn't want to talk to him. She might not have known the names of London's best men's stores, but that didn't prevent her from realizing what a showoff he was. Being annoyed with him she didn't tell him either that meanwhile she had read each single play of Oscar Wilde, including his *Salomé*, to whom Arnold had introduced her. She had forgotten to bring the slender volume, which he had lent her in Harrogate and felt guilty about it.

"I didn't know that he could be so foppish. I pictured him coming from old money, which doesn't need to brag," she thought and kept walking in front of him, as they crossed the restaurant's short hallway. In her high heels she was the same height as he. "Good," she thought once more, "at least he's unable to tower over me when he stands next to me."

Once seated, Arnold, again with the awkward flair of the *nouveau riches*, which embarrassed Nadine, recommended the *Turbot Calèche*. It was a favorite dish among the eatery's customers. But the young girl, perhaps simply out of protest against the Yorkshire man's pretentious display, didn't particularly enjoy it. And said so. Yet she loved the dessert: a scrumptious apple pie made from scratch, including the fresh picked fruit. She also took a close look at the wine list and asked her date rather innocently:

"Are you sure the restaurant doesn't boast a little here? I've never in my life seen such a long enumeration of red and white wines. And I've grown up in wine country."

"Why do you think, like so many Continentals, that the English do not know their wines? They do, you know! At least the more sophisticated ones. You don't need to be arrogant about it," the Yorkshire man half seriously reprimanded her. Once more Nadine didn't reply. Yet she was blushing and bent her head low over the endless wine card.

After dinner the two of them took another cab to an elegant, old London theater where they watched *A Hatful of Rain*, an exceptionally well-performed comedy. Then Arnold accompanied the young girl to *Annabel's*. To her surprise the establishment not only featured a small dance floor but also card games, roulette tables and oval-shaped dice pools. London, as she quickly discovered, was not a bit squeamish about gambling. *Annabel's* was an odd mixture between a frightfully respectable Gentlemen's club, such as she had seen in movies, and a more modern version of a dance club. It was dark, private and understated. They could have eaten here, too, because the food supposedly was very good. So was the staff. But ordinary Londoners had little chance of being admitted to this place. One needed to be a member and to become one, one had to be either important or know an important person. The Illingroses belonged to the latter category. They knew, as Arnold self-importantly announced while they waited for the hatcheck girl to take their coats, a member of the Churchill family.

At about two o'clock in the morning Arnold had brought Nadine to the Montcalm Hotel where he was staying. Smaller than Claridges or the Connaught and perhaps a trifle less luxurious than the Dorchester, she had instantly liked the recently restored, sophisticated façade of the

Montcalm – at least as far as she could see it in the vague glimmer of a few street lights.

But while the couple still lingered in the hotel lobby whose subtle elegance was underlined by superb lighting and large, exquisite, fresh flower arrangements that seemed to fill every corner of the hall with their costly fragrance, she staunchly refused to go upstairs to Arnold's room.

"Oh, do come. Don't be such a prude," he had whispered, conscious of the sleepy hotel clerk who was bored reading his newspaper and kept watching the couple with furtive glances. Contemptuously turning his back to the curious employee and knowing Nadine's foible for beauty, Arnold said softly:

"You'll like my room. It's very prettily done. And I ordered champagne and strawberries for us." "But I don't want to go upstairs with you," Nadine, who knew that he wanted more than champagne, said stubbornly. She deliberately looked past Arnold where the elaborate entrance door through which they had just entered still seemed to vibrate.

"Why do I feel as if I were a prisoner of his sexual drives?" Nadine, as she kept watching the large brass-enhanced glass door, asked herself. "I'm perfectly free to turn my head and walk through that door," she thought. "But then why don't I? I haven't the slightest inclination to sleep with him. Yet why can't I simply tell him that and then leave?"

But she couldn't. Even while she was still questioning herself, she knew that she was unable to pull away from this man whose presence kept her glued to the spot. Tired from the long evening's excitement and still intoxicated from the heavy red wine that had been served at dinner in glasses so thin she was afraid she would break hers if she didn't hold its fragile roundness in the palm of both of her hands, the glass was certainly big enough for that, her willpower had slackened and her thoughts were no longer as cohesive as she now needed them. Constantly forming sentences in her mind she briefly (there was no time to be more thorough) reflected upon them with fearful curiosity. But instead of making sense, the words changed into a sequence of images that swiftly flowed past her. Try as she might, she couldn't put order into those confusing impressions, which her imagination restlessly formed in her head. And she couldn't catch the phrases that she needed to assert herself so she would be able to show Arnold that she was in control of her world. Finally, still making an effort to hide her dizziness, she realized that there was nothing she could do but let herself drift on the current of the night, and watch herself being carried by the velvet light of the big hall that was reflected in wall mirrors. At most she was conscious that she deeply inhaled the perfume of the flowers. At short intervals, while she slept with open eyes, she no longer heard Arnold's voice that was tender with honeyed words and lustful passion and even a little breathless, as if he had been running for some time.

"You are being silly. Let's take the elevator. I'm not going to hurt you. You don't have to do anything you don't feel like." Arnold pleaded again with her as he tried to catch her eye. But through her drowsiness Nadine could sense his impatience and anger, both of which were intensified by fatigue. The exertion he made to keep his emotions under control was visible in the fast movement of his eyes, and the sharp wrinkle that had suddenly formed between his brows. With each breath he took he tried hard to infect the young girl with his excited nervousness. Nadine felt as if invisible strands of a spider's net were spun from him to her. His nearly imperceptible vibrations made her even afraid to be kissed by him. And the idea of his touch became revolting. She could sense that beneath the smooth surface of his face, still smelling of eau de cologne, every ounce of gentleness and good behavior, which civilization and the best public schools England were able to impose upon his upbringing, had disappeared. Underneath his silk suit and his diamond cufflinks, whose brilliance had fascinated her during dinner, there was nothing but raw sexual thrust in his arousal and the relentless wish to exercise his male power over her, the physically weaker female he desired.

"I'm tired and want to go home," she said with her voice trembling. She was afraid of the beast within him.

"I had a great time and enjoyed seeing you again but now I would like to leave," she added and this time she looked at him with large eyes. Her face was pale from lack of sleep and the shadows below her cheekbones had vanished, making her features look mask-like. Her feet were hurting terribly. The high-heeled shoes, in which she had walked and danced most of the evening, had began to more and more hurt the arches of her feet. She longed to take them off. But not while she was still with the Harrogate man. Her heels made her look as tall as he and she strongly felt that any sign of being shorter or weaker than him, would not be good for her while he was in his present predatory mood. It was clear that he wanted her, wanted to throw her down – on a bed, on the floor, anywhere – and show her in a simple, crude form that he was the more powerful of the two. She knew that he didn't love her and she couldn't help feeling degraded by this blunt push of unadulterated testosterone, which had built up in him during the evening and was purely physical. His drive had little to do with her as an individual, but only with her assets as a young, attractive girl. At this moment she could have been any female who had appeared on his horizon at the wrong time and wrong place. His emotions, she knew, were not involved, only his sexuality.

As far as she was concerned, she did not desire him at all. Being considerably older than her, he was too much of a father figure who willfully exercised his authority and without taking her own hesitation into account. There was little he said or did that made her willing to submit to him. Being with him now and in the past was as if her inside, she wasn't sure which part of it, it could have been some obscure corner of her brain or her heart muscle or some hidden alleyways of her womb, had turned into some type of a big eye, or the reflector a lighthouse uses, or the searchlight, which German antiaircraft guns had aimed at the night sky during the war that watched him with almost total detachment.

"Cool like ice! You are an iceberg that looks like a volcano," the Yorkshireman had once accused her. His remark had taken her by surprise, an unpleasant surprise. She had seen herself as a warmhearted creature, ready to play and always curious about life and men.

She liked to hear him speak and move and watch his hands with their immaculately kept, short nails that were shining as if he put varnish on them, which he, with one of those little laughs she was never quite sure what to make of, assured her that he did not. She, of course, did not believe him. She visualized him sitting regularly in a secluded corner of a beauty salon where a young manicurist attentively bent over his long digits, polishing them to perfection. But Nadine enjoyed listening to his low, guttural laugh that sometimes would burst forth unexpectedly, would come from deep within him where, next to a fur-covered brute, he stored his golden apples and pears, the sparkling jewels he possessed, yet was hardly aware of. And she had come to recognize those times when she was able to tiptoe past the hairy monster, pluck its fruits and give them to him so he could enjoy them as well. At other times her wishful thinking went as far as picturing him as a child again, an adorable boy, white-skinned, rough-kneed and fluffy-haired, who was unaware of the growing ape within. She also saw him as an utterly likeable youngster who, smiling and handsome, kept running through a summer meadow where he picked flowers at random until he had collected a sizable nosegay that he proudly took home to show his mother. That was all she wanted. She didn't want the grown man, the spoiled heir to a sizeable fortune, the male, unbearably conceited of his money and sexual conquests.

Yet in his urgent need to possess her, Arnold had chased the child and boy away and only left a panting, teeth-baring, fore and hind-legged creature that made her feel extremely uneasy.

She did not like to be held by him and to feel his body, all muscle and heat, pushing against hers. Nor did she crave his mouth. His lips were too thin and their most obvious taste was those of cigarettes, a sensation that was putrid to her. Even less did she care about his tongue, which boldly explored the cave of her mouth and intertwined in a dance with her own, a suffocating dance that aroused him quickly to a high pitch, but not her. Sometimes he held her so tightly that she could barely breathe. At those moments she felt like a rider who had been thrown off its horse, but was caught with one foot still in the stirrup and was being painfully, dangerously dragged along while the full-blooded steed continued to gallop forward as if she were still sitting in the saddle. Slowly, she had even grown tired of listening to the sweet nonsense he poured into her ear with his impeccable English public school accent, unabashedly in front of people, or when they were alone, at all times and wherever they went. His tender, ingratiating words would have pleased her if he had been the right man. But

Arnold was not. And his softly whispered sentences became the symbol of a faulty, constantly running water faucet, which he apparently couldn't turn off. No, she certainly did not want to sleep with him. She was not curious to discover what he looked like without his clothes and she was not attracted to any parts of his body. Not even to his chest, which aside from the flat, muscular stomach he liked to display, was his best feature and part of which he had revealed one day when wearing a sport shirt. Slightly below his throat his skin was covered with coarse blond hair, the kind of hair, she immediately knew, she didn't want to touch.

"Well, ok, you little wench, suit yourself," Arnold suddenly said, annoyed at the prolonged silence into which she had, as several times before, escaped. His eyes, as they still stood in the hotel lobby, were blackened with anger. For the last time they blazed at her before he turned around and walked with dragging, tired steps toward the elevator door.

"I hope you enjoy your way back to the station," he said offensively, his voice brimming with hate, contempt and disappointment. And without looking at her while he stepped inside the small lift whose doors slowly closed behind him.

Nadine blushed and nodding at the clerk, she hastily left the hotel. The uncongenial Harrogateman knew that she had no money left to pay for a cab. Earlier at the club when he had put his arm around her bare shoulders, she had called a prettily legged, short-skirted flower girl to their table and had bought a yellow rose. It was outrageously expensive, but Nadine had laughed:

"Well, here goes my taxi money. But I must have the rose. It goes perfectly with my dress, don't you think?" She smiled at Arnold and, invisibly under the table, tapped her foot to the music that came in muted sounds from the dance floor. She had been sipping another glass of red wine and was in a high-spirited mood. Her beau looked at her black outfit, which clung to her waist and hips in seductive curves. Then he grinned:

"If you had bought a red rose, I would have paid for it." For a moment she stared at his smiling mouth, unable to utter a word. As before, she was stung by his cold, worldly manner with which he always seemed to be able to outmaneuver her.

"What a hypocrite you are!" She suddenly threw her words into his face as if it had been a glass of cold water.

"You know that you don't love me. And most of the time you don't even like me. How can you talk about red roses?"

For a moment Arnold's face became a shade darker and his eyes flashed. Over the years, helped by a long chain of genes, he had learned to keep his emotions under control. But Nadine had a way of saying things so bluntly that they sometimes still caught him unaware. Lacking sophistication, she had a sharp eye and when angry her normal inhibitions vanished and she did not hesitate to let him know what she thought of him. Quite a while ago he had, to his surprise, understood that she did not think very highly of him. Her abrasive attitude not only stung his vanity but had also puzzled him. Women usually liked him, or at least his money, and Cathy Woodbridge, his girlfriend, was truly fond of him. She was there when he needed her. Solicitous about his well being she tried hard to please him and often hovered about him like a mother hen. Most of the time, he cared little about Cathy's protective manner. But when Nadine snapped at him with her sharp white teeth, he always longed for his calm, mature, gentle lover.

"You are like a rude puppy," he had told Nadine once.

"And you think you are clever in your wolfish way," she retorted without fail. "You don't impress me one bit!" She had added, staring at his face, which flushed darkly.

Arnold had shrugged his shoulders and laughed but he knew that she spoke the truth. His money and his name meant little to her. In the beginning of their relationship, he had thought that she was just playing a clever game. But then he understood that her disregard for wealth was genuine. He was amazed by that and had said on one occasion:

"You are still too young to know what power means. As you grow older, you'll learn its value."

Yet an instant later she made him sound like a pompous ass. Giggling, she bent forward so the scent of her fresh, healthy, strikingly white skin filled his nostrils and, for an instant, made him quiver with longing. He started to look like a rabbit in heat. Nadine, with the thoughtless cruelty of a young girl, and not being in love with him began to laugh even more. Then she spoke in such a low voice that he could hardly hear her:

"How little you know me. I, too, want power. I wouldn't be human if I didn't desire it. But the power I want uses money only as a means to achieve its goal. Wealth by itself, without an underlying motif, as, I'm afraid is the case with you, has no value for me. And the thing I covet the most, cannot be bought. It is given. It is similar to Calvin's belief in God's grace, which cannot be earned but has to be granted. I thought you knew something about religion," she added rather ceremoniously.

In her usual manner, Nadine had jumped from one image to the next. Her lack of logic and structure instantly infuriated him.

'The girl makes no sense. When will she learn to think in an orderly manner so one can discuss things properly with her," he thought angrily.

At the end of her retort, Nadine had been referring to their first conversation in the ballroom of the Harrogate hotel when Arnold had seemed to show interest in Mount Ararat and the remains of Noah's Arc, which are supposedly buried inside craggy mountainsides.

"Sometimes you are too clever for your own good," Arnold said calmly and like a beaten opponent he moved slightly away from her. The soft light of the clubrooms added depth to his three quarter profile, and made the slight curve of his nose and his thin nostril, the one she could see, look more attractive. But an instant later he was his old, undesired, feisty self again:

"Let's pin the rose on your dress. That's what you bought it for, isn't it?" He smiled pleasantly at her as he tried to find the right spot for the silky, yellow, subtly scented blossom.

"Arnold has a way of bringing me down to earth," Nadine thought and never told him what kind of power she had in mind. Raising her chin, she let him fasten the magnificent, still half-closed flower to her neck. She wore a tight, short black dress, which – while closing in front as high as her chin – exposed her shoulders, part of her distinct clavicles and her back almost as low as her waist.

"That collar makes you look like a priest," Arnold, who liked the dress a lot, had joked when he first saw her in it. And he lost no opportunity to put his hand on her exposed shoulder blades and, with his perfectly filed fingertips, kept stroking her back as if it had been the sensitive fur of a cat.

"What a fine body you have," he said admiringly. Then nibbling at her earlobe, he let his tongue slide around a large faux pearl earring she had clipped on.

"Oh, stop it, *c'est vraiment assez*," she said and raising her long neck to its full length, she pushed his head playfully away. She was smiling and found his tender demonstrations, although they were in public, not unpleasant. She tolerated his open fondling partly from a sense of sheer vanity that would overcome her when she least expected it. She considered this boastful impulse to be the sudden reversal of her inhibitions. But the moment she became conscious of it, she was deeply ashamed of it, because she perceived it as if she were waving a large, red flag, calling out to strangers who passed her at random:

"Look at me! I do exist. I am not invisible. I am not a substance you can only perceive with your olfactory sense as if I were a nosegay. I'm more than that. You just can't see it. It is not that I'm invisible but that you are blind!"

During certain evenings back in Harrogate, after she had put Lipsey and Peter to bed, Nadine would excuse herself from the two couples sitting together in Melanie Hibson's room by saying that she wanted to read in her room. But occasionally, after looking at a few pages she would put her book down to indulge in lengthy monologues with herself:

"I'm far from having discovered who I am," she would sometimes start out, "but I think I know what I want. I would like to achieve something, either in the sciences or the arts, yes – I think especially in the arts, because it is something that gives people joy. I want them to look at a picture of mine or read a book I will write, something based on ideas floating through my mind and which I'll somehow be able to pour into a concrete form so that they express an image in a way never seen before. I know that there is nothing new under the sun. My father has told me this many times. But that's not important. What is important is a certain specific angle from which we see something familiar and yet so different, possibly so distorted that we don't recognize the familiarity of it and it then becomes something new. I'm thinking of Kafka's *Metamorphoses*, for example, where a young man wakes up one morning only to find himself transformed into a big bug of some kind, and from that day on he sees himself, symbolically, of course, as a small creature helplessly scuttling between the legs of humans feeling that he is despised by everyone. Especially his own father. What a change of perspective! Imagine seeing the height of a human reduced to a tiny, defenseless animal and then think that this giant insect, or whatever else it was, fears man as an all-powerful giant! Well, I guess Swift tried to do something of the sort when he had Gulliver enter the country of the Brobdingnagians. But Kafka adds a great deal more psychological insight into the human soul than Swift was able to do.

"The most important thing though, is that the painting we look at, the book we read, or the piece of music to which we listen, gives us not just wonder but mostly joy. The world is filled with such misery that everyone needs more happiness. Not fun, which is too superficial and short-lived, but joy that goes to the root of things. I have watched people who are deeply religious occasionally achieve such joy. I want to experience it through beauty, or possibly through love, but not religion. I would like to create something that fills people with wonder and joy. That's the power I want to attain, a kind of power which is quite differ-ent from the one Arnold Illingrose is currently so fond of."

Nadine, sitting late at night next to the Yorkshire man in his London club, accepted his public amorous tokens partly because she felt safe being at his side in the open, where he had to maintain a certain image, mostly the one his peers expected from him. She was well aware when he caressed her in front of everyone he had to control himself. There was comfort in the curious glances of some of the guests who were close to them and every so often stared at them with, what seemed to her, mocking expectancy. As the night progressed and more alcohol was consumed, an almost palpable pleasure in voyeurism exuded from various club members and appeared to surround Arnold and Nadine in a nearly visible form.

She continued to stay close to him on their thickly upholstered bench and breathed in the air that had become visible from cigarette smoke, when Arnold's reference to her intellect struck her to be of the same paternal advice that her father had given her a few years ago.

It was already late in the day and being in a hurry as usual, Heinrich Tallemann, for some reason, was holding the front door of their home open for her. They must have returned together from somewhere and were briefly conversing about Christian whom she was going to leave behind as she prepared herself to go to England. Her father had been talking most of the time when he suddenly said:

"Remember, if a girl is pretty and intelligent, let her hide the latter. Men do not like clever women. They annoy them. Men usually prefer a woman whom they can impress and do not feel threatened by. They want a submissive female who allows them being their protector."

It was the same age-old idea of men controlling women and, to make matters worse, being hypocritical about it. The first time her father had uttered this wisdom of his, which seemed to have little evolved since the Paleolithic age, he had shocked his daughter. But she had learned, painfully and slowly, not to refute him directly. In a cowardly way, for which she hated herself, she only complained behind his back. Besides, she was grateful that, although they both knew whom he meant, her father had at least made an attempt to create an aesthetic distance between the two of them by not addressing her directly.

Heinrich had never told his daughter that she was comely and intelligent because he was convinced that such outspoken praise would spoil her. He did not believe in flattering a child – only in criticizing it. Yet a few years later he was unpleasantly surprised that, more than half-grown, Nadine had so little self-confidence.

She knew, of course, that she was neither ugly nor stupid. Except for her parents, the two people who had the most control over her life, friends, classmates, acquaintances, even a couple of teachers and Dr. Ritter, her dentist, whom, of all people, she had a crush on, had assured her that she was attractive and astute.

She was, therefore, all the more outraged to discover that she was not supposed to use her wit in the unequal battle between men and women. What else did she have since she was physically weaker than most men? She had not learned to use her body and sensed that she would never fully master the art of seduction. Fred Brandt, who had groped her on multiple occasions, had trampled upon her when she was young and defenseless, had spoiled sexual encounters for her. Eve and her apple were out of reach and no serpent had power over her. Fred Brandt's big, clumsy foot, the artificial limb he had to strap on each morning when he got up, had stepped on her and had pitilessly pushed her protective angel aside. She had become deaf to the reptile's brilliant, incessant whispers. She could only admire the writhing, enticing body of Salomé as she danced in front of Herod Antipas, the weak, fat, decadent son of Herod the Great. She knew that she would never dance like the sensuous princess. Yet she could try to speak like her to John the Baptist. Like Wilde's Salomé, she could attempt to bend over the head of the bearded saint, the symbol of the unreachable. Barely able to see the man whose threatening body had been imprisoned in a barred hole, dug straight down into the earth, she watched herself taking in his scent. From behind bars as thick as her wrist, his odor floated up to her and, after his first words, Nadine turned Salomé, understood that during the months without light, which the man had spent in his ghastly jail, his spirit had turned his body into a single organ. His tongue sang. Wilde, adhering to tradition, also had his Baptist reject Salomé, the most seductive woman of the Jewish kingdom. John did not reach out to her – she who wanted him, as she had never desired a man before. Only with the Baptist had her flesh not triumphed. When he refused her, as if she had been vermin, she castrated him by having his head cut off. Afterwards she kissed his dead lips, "Oh, Jocaan..." Wilde's seductress sang softly as tears dropped out of her eyes and fell hard on the chopped-off, now gruesome head partly covered by her long, glistening hair. That was before the historical Salomé married Aristobul of Chalkis from Lebanon, her second husband, the one who had come after Philippus.

* * *

When Arnold had come down to London to meet with Nadine, he had arrived early enough to have a late lunch with her. He took her to Carrier's, half hidden in the middle of the Camden Passage antiques market. By now the young girl knew a little about Arnold's expensive taste, and she had anticipated a posh place, some type of Victorian setting of distinguished elegance. Instead, they entered a building, which resembled a French provincial house, where only a few bare wooden tables and chairs fill the dining room. Most of the windows and large parts of one wall were covered with brightly colored fabrics, which Nadine didn't like at all. But for once, following the maître d' who walked ramrod straight in front of her, she wisely kept her mouth shut. Somewhat uncomfortable, she was quickly caught by the professional attention with which the waiters surrounded her and the Harrogateman the moment they reached their seats. The attention of the three silent young men in black evening attire, who seemed to be watching Arnold's raised fingertips and rushed to their table before he could wriggle one of them, was in Nadine's eyes quite pretentious. But when, under the supervision of an older, pot-bellied and dignified waiter, they served the food, it was superb.

Nadine didn't have any breakfast and hardly chewed her portion of a rack of lamb, which was prettily decorated with crushed green peppercorns and lemon-flavored breadcrumbs. Arnold, as his face unfolded into one of his superior *savoir-faire* smiles, had, as always, recommended the dish. After she had cut her meat into tiny pieces, she swirled them in her mouth and more with her tongue than with her teeth, she sucked the tender morsels dry before she finally swallowed them. It took her forever to get to the bottom of her plate, which had been hot when one of the waiters had set it down in front of her.

"Aren't you hungry?" Arnold, whose dish had been emptied long before she let hers be taken away, wanted to know.

"I am not sure," she said in her funny accent and smiled at him, revealing a row of almost even teeth, which looked whiter than normal under a heavy layer of rose-colored lipstick she had carefully put on.

"The food is so good I want to prolong the pleasure," she said again and was surprised at herself. Although she had starved as a child, food had never become an important part of her life. Except for Brussels sprouts and beets, which her father loved and she did not like at all, she indiscriminately ate everything. But she would only put food in her mouth to appease her stomach. Yet their meal at Carrier's was different. Here, each dish had been turned into art and she understood for the first time why many people, especially the middle-aged and elderly, took such voracious joy in it, apparently not caring about their expanded waistlines.

Their lunch for two was a ritual and – helped by a glass of a heavy, aromatic red wine – Arnold looked at it as an alluring, extended foreplay. Whereas for Nadine, who long ago had made up her mind not to sleep with him, their two meals, followed by a dance at his club, were the main acts she attempted to prolong.

"Remember no matter where Arnold takes you, and I am sure he will try to show you some of the better places in London, you do not need to make love to him just because he paid for lunch or dinner. He can well afford it," Julie had said after Nadine had told her that Arnold would come down from Harrogate to spend an afternoon and evening with her in the big city.

"He is much older than you and has experience with women. But do try and stay in the driver's seat. He can't very well force you to do something you don't want to do."

Julie fondly looked at Nadine, reinforcing the sister-like kinship they felt for each other. Julie knew that Nadine trusted her. She even sensed that if Nadine's own mother had cautioned her this way, the young girl would most probably not have listened to her. But, as it was, Nadine felt closer to Julie than to her mother. Nadine wasn't sure if this were so only because Julie was younger than Monika Tallemann and had not yet lost sight of the girl's generation. After all the months Julie and Nadine had spent together, the young girl was convinced that Julie understood her better than her mother.

But even Julie's well-meant advice had not prepared Nadine for Arnold's boorish and calculatedly punishing behavior when he had taken her to the Montcalm Hotel. As they stood in its elaborate, flower-filled hall, she had tried to make him understand her refusal to go to bed with him.

"Look, when I was little, there was a man...," she started to say in a barely audible voice. Yet before she could continue, the image of the one-footed Fred Brandt stood in front of her with his thick hair and the wide smile she hated. Limping, he approached her. His face, bent toward her in a falsely solicitous manner, seemed to grow larger with each slow and dragging step he took. She hated the sound of his creaking shoe and the way he set his wooden foot with an audible click on the floor. By the time he reached her, he had lost his human form and appeared to be a hard-edged, rough boulder that blocked her way. His smile had become bigger too, as he inevitably closed in on her, and she saw the tip of his fleshy tongue, which, in an abominable moment, would penetrate her. Snakelike, his horrible organ would explore her while he held her so she could neither scream nor escape.

"Well, yes and what happened?" Arnold looked at her with his face suddenly wide open like an exotic night blooming plant and his slightly blue lids, which had half covered his eyes like those of a sleepy cat, were no longer drooping. If a moment ago, he was frustrated and tired, he was now all at once awake with curiosity. Nadine searched in his face and his voice for a sign of sympathy, a token of understanding of that which she was about to say. When she saw nothing but lurid inquisitiveness and not a spark of pity on his intelligent features, she mumbled:

"Oh, it was just one of those things. I imagine they happen to a lot of children...but we don't hear about them until it is far too late."

"Come on, don't be such a nuisance. I was looking forward to hearing a sensuously tearful story. You must have been a pretty child. How can you lead me on this way?" Arnold's voice was hoarse with disappointment as he poured his poison into the girl's heart.

Watching his face, which once more looked tired and much older, Nadine saw again how much he had counted on making love to her. If, at that instant, he had taken her by the hand and led her gently away, she would have slept with him. Not out of love but out of disdain and pity and the desire to get away from his endless, consistent begging. Yet the moment passed and a few minutes later Nadine walked through London's deserted streets. After she had gone several blocks and reached the outskirts of one of London's many parks, she took off her shoes. Her feet were stabbing her like knives.

"There must be some truth to Andersen's nameless mermaid," she whispered to herself. And she remembered the fairytale teller's dazzling image of a glittering, diamond studded fishtail metamorphosing into legs that could walk but where each step would be filled with pain.

It was the prize a mermaid had to pay for wanting to move like a human.

For a moment Nadine was sure that she could smell the Thames and she remembered the day Spencer had taken her to the Tower built in the eleventh century to guard the access from the river. Once more, as Spencer held her hand, she looked at the Crown Jewels with its thousands of costly stones, which were displayed in one part of the Tower. As she bent toward the treasure, two of the largest diamonds suddenly grew even bigger until they seemed to be almost the size of a bird, of Hansel, grandmother's beloved canary. Then, already from afar, she heard a crash and simultaneously with the horrid noise she felt as if someone had thrown a hard ball at her head. For a split second she saw herself as a child standing in front of Mrs. Smith's house in Ludwigsburg where her husband had tried out a new golf club. As he funnily contorted his body and hit the small white ball with a wide swing, he, not seeing the little girl in time, struck her in the temple. Not knowing what was happening, she had instantly dropped to the grass. Then the world turned black and the stunning stones, which she had seen an instant ago in the Tower, exploded into a brilliant blaze that rendered her blind.